The Angel's Cup

Patricia Little

Writers Club Press

San Jose   New York   Lincoln   Shanghai

Down With Love-pg 2, words and music by E. Y. Harburg and Harold Arlen, ©1937

Moonglow-pg 28, words and music by Will Hudson, Eddie Delange & Irving Mills © 1934

I Got a Right To Sing the Blues- pg 72, words and music by Ted Koehler & Harold Arlen, © 1932

The Angel's Cup

Published by Writers Club Press
an imprint of iUniverse.com, Inc.

For information address:
iUniverse.com, Inc.
620 North 48th Street
Suite 201
Lincoln, NE 68504-3467
www.iuniverse.com

ISBN: 0-595-09389-2

Printed in the United States of America

*D*edicated, with love, to Margaret
and Harry, who always believed in angels.

Millions of spiritual creatures walk the earth;
Unseen, both when we wake and when we sleep.

—John Milton

Twice or thrice had I loved thee
Before I knew thy face or name.
So in a voice, so in a shapeless flame,
Angels affect us oft, and worshipped be.

—John Donne

In heaven an angel is
Nobody in particular.

—George Bernard Shaw

Author's Note

*T*he inspiration for this story was a barely remembered visit to Hearst Castle years ago. That wisp of memory developed into a tapestry of wholly fictional characters and events. There was never a mysterious death at the castle in 1937, nor are any of my main characters meant to resemble actual persons living or working at Hearst Castle, past or present.

William Randolph Hearst, Marion Davies, and Julia Morgan are, of course, real historical figures. I've tried to represent them, and some of the celebrities and staff present with them at the castle, as accurately as possible, while creating a fictional story set in the extraordinary world they created.

Some events described are factual. Hearst did come close to bankruptcy in the late 1930's, and many items from his art collection were sold at Gimble's department store in New York.

Prologue

❖

Anna's Diary—January 15, 1937

It happened today. My hands still shake as I write this entry. I must write it down now, before someone comes.

I woke to a glorious sunrise this morning; a clear, sunny day made to tempt the angels down out of Heaven. I hadn't the slightest premonition anything was wrong. Just another ordinary day, I thought, and smiled to myself, for no day could ever be ordinary here at the castle. La Cuesta Encantada, as Mr. Hearst has so fittingly named this place. The Enchanted Hill. I remember thinking how lucky I've been these past months to work here in the midst of unbelievable luxury, when so many are still without jobs.

I went about my duties, daydreaming a little about Cary Grant whom I'd just seen the night before, both on the movie screen and sitting several rows in front of me in Mr. Hearst's private theater. Still, he couldn't hold a candle to

Mr. Winter, the most interesting of all Mr. Hearst's guests. With his fair, hand-some face and quick smile, I thought Mr. Winter the most wonderful man I'd ever met.

How could I have been so horribly wrong?

The morning passed in a familiar round of cleaning up after Mr. Hearst's guests, making sure that my corner of the castle sparkled. Since every room in the two guest houses is occupied this week, I had to hurry through my chores to finish by suppertime. By early afternoon I was a little ahead of schedule.

I slowed my pace as I finished dusting the main sitting room of "A" House, and paused afterward to look out windows to the broad expanse of hillside rolling down to the Pacific. It looked different from up here, as though the vast ocean was meant to be seen from this one spot in all the world. I ran my fin-gers over the satiny smooth surface of a table that I had been told was over 400 years old. Next I started cleaning the guest bath, though it didn't have a proper bathtub at all, but one of those French cascades, where water showers down from above.

It was there that Mr. Winter found me on hands and knees, scouring the marble floor. I hardly recognized him. His lovely face was white and stretched in an ugly grimace. I had thought he was only a few years older than I was, but the hard expression around his eyes made him seem suddenly ancient.

"Where is it?" He spat the words in my face and jerked me to my feet with shaking hands, his grip like iron. The scrub brush flew from my fingers and hit the wall, soapy water dripping down the tile surface. Water splashed on the front of his immaculate gray coat. I watched the stain spread, unable to meet his eyes.

"Somehow you knew what it was, didn't you?" He spoke to me as though I were hard of hearing, or dim-witted. As indeed, I must have seemed when I finally looked at him in astonishment, for his words made no sense to me. The affable, gentle Mr. Winter that I knew had disappeared, replaced by this vio-lent stranger. He shook me again and I felt his fingers digging into my arms. I couldn't have spoken a word to save my life, for I thought he had suddenly gone crazy.

"*Damn it, girl! You've stolen it from my room! Do you realize what you've done?*"

When I heard him say stolen, I almost fainted away. My hands went numb and I felt disoriented, as though the solid floor was tilting. I didn't know what had been stolen from him, but if he accused me my future would be bleak. Mr. Hearst hated dishonesty; he'd never tolerate a thief working in his home. To be sent away from the castle! Perhaps even sent to prison! I had little hope Mr. Hearst would take my side when his own guest accused me.

Mr. Winter must have seen my fear then, and judged me guilty. I could see it in the grim set of his mouth.

I found my voice at last, words tumbling out of my mouth faster and faster. "I didn't take anything from you. I did up your room this morning after you went out, but I took nothing, I swear. I'd never steal from anyone, Mr. Winter. I swear it!" Still he stared at me, implacable, his face inches from mine. I shrank before those cold, blue eyes. The silence stretched between us. I couldn't bear it.

"You've got to believe me!" I whispered.

"You're wrong. I don't." He pushed me away with an oath and left me there, huddled against the cold tile wall.

I sit in my own little room as I write this, filled with despair. I dread a knock on my door. Will it be the housekeeper who throws me out? Or perhaps the police will come from San Luis Obispo. Who will believe me?

Chapter 1

❖

*T*he breeze from the open window whipped through Maggy's hair as she left Morrow Bay behind and drove north on Highway 1. The cool air against her scalp felt wonderful. Even though she'd been traveling since early that morning, she wasn't tired. It had been a long time since she'd felt this good.

Maggy looked at the Pacific Ocean sparkling with whitecaps on her left and the California hills off to her right. Bright sunlight played over dry grasses that covered the rounded mounds and hollows, as though they wore a shaggy, palomino-colored coat. This was a welcome contrast to the green mountains of her Oregon home. Maggy was glad to be away from that home for awhile, away from familiar surroundings. So many little things triggered thoughts of Anna, and the heartache that followed. When she could push those memories away, they'd be replaced by images of

Jason, unwelcome reminders that either had her fuming impotently, or feeling sorry for herself.

The thought of Jason was enough to make her rifle through her oversized handbag for a sure-fire remedy. She found one of her favorite tapes and put it in the cassette player of her rental car. This was the music Anna had adored, and Maggy had grown up to the songs of Tommy Dorsey and Jerome Kern instead of the Rolling Stones. She loved singing along as she drove to work, belting out a gorgeous song with a sweet saxophone backup. She'd never win any music awards, but it sure beat listening to the latest mayhem on the news, or worse, thinking of Jason. Maggy tapped her toe to the music and sang at the top of her voice.

Down with love, with flowers and rice and shoes
Down with love, the root of all midnight blues
Down with things that give you that well-known pain,
Take that moon and wrap it in cellophane.
Down with eyes, romantic and stupid,
Down with sighs, down with cupid,
Brother let's stuff that dove,
Down with love!

After her musical attitude adjustment, Maggy turned off the highway and drove through rolling foothills to the little town of Cambria. There was one main street, lined with a profusion of art galleries, shops and gardens thick with late blooming flowers. After consulting her map, she decided to keep driving two miles up the coast to the Beach House Inn. She wasn't going to let her notoriously bad sense of direction get her lost again. Her grin broadened as she realized it wouldn't matter if she got lost, since she had all the time in the world. No appointments to keep. No deadlines, or bills to worry about, or clients to interview.

She found the inn easily, nestled on a point of land that extended out to the sea on Moonstone Beach Drive. It was a sprawling, single-story house with weathered cedar siding and an exquisite garden. Vivid purple lupine bloomed alongside California poppies and a dozen plants that she couldn't identify. The riotous combination of colors was breathtaking. She turned off the engine of her rental car and sat for a moment, listening to the rhythmic sound of the surf and gulls calling overhead.

As she pulled her suitcase from the car, a gray-haired man came down the path to help her. He looked just as weathered and neatly kept as the house and grounds he was tending. "You must be Maggy Lane," he said. "I'm John Clark. Welcome to the Beach House Inn." He smiled and held out a callused hand to her. "You're our last guest to arrive this evening."

He took her suitcase and preceded her up the path to the entrance. A bell tinkled as he opened the door. "This is my wife Nancy," he introduced the diminutive woman standing behind the counter, whose brown hair was dusted with gray and fell in soft waves around her face. A kind face, Maggy thought.

"Your room is the furthest back from the beach." Nancy said as she checked Maggy in and gave her the key. "But I think it has the best view in the house. Breakfast is served between 7:00 and 9:00 in the dining room, and dinner is at eight. Will you be joining us tonight, dear?"

"Yes, that sounds lovely," Maggy replied.

"Wonderful. That will make four guests for dinner this evening. There's Harry—he's doing work up at the castle again, and Mr. and Mrs. Sorenson from Canada. I'm sure you'll enjoy meeting them. I'll just show you the dining room now before you go to your room."

Nancy led Maggy through a spacious living room replete with over-stuffed chairs and sofas. A wall of windows presented a breathtaking view of the ocean. A brick fireplace with a wide stone hearth, unlit now, would provide warmth on cool evenings. The dining area opened off the living room and offered further unbroken views of the beach, illuminated by afternoon sun slanting in through the windows.

"Our little town is sometimes overlooked, what with such a famous castle up on the hill." Nancy's smile warmed her face. "But if you take the time to explore, you won't be disappointed." She chattered on about the town of Cambria, which she clearly loved. The town had become a haven for artists and writers, and now even had a local theater group. "My John has always been a quiet one, but once Mrs. McCutcheon convinced him to join in the local stage productions—well! Now he's an actor, of all things! You live with a man for thirty years and he can still surprise you." Nancy laughed and shook her head, but also seemed proud of her husband.

Maggy had rarely felt so comfortable with someone she'd just met. As she closed the door to her room she realized that Nancy reminded her a little bit of her grandmother. Nancy was much younger, probably only in her fifties, but she seemed to have the same warmth and easy ways that Anna had.

Sudden tears welled up in her eyes. Damn. Even after so much time had passed. Anna was gone, and there was nothing Maggy could do to change it. She knew from bitter experience that tears would only make it worse.

Maggy sighed and ran her fingers through her snarled, wind-knotted hair. One look in the mirror convinced her that she should take a shower before dinner and change out of her jeans and T-shirt. She opened her suitcase and hesitated. Lying on top of her neatly folded clothes was the first volume of Anna's diary. Reluctantly, she picked it up and ran her hands over the gray cover.

She still hadn't read the diary. After the trauma of Anna's death, Maggy couldn't bring herself to face it. Each attempt had reminded her that Anna was gone forever. Then would come images of the horrible day when she found her grandmother lying on the floor of her bedroom, dead for hours, her house a shambles. Maggy took a deep breath and stretched her tight shoulders, driving the memory away as she always did. No, she hadn't been able to read Anna's diary. She'd barely been able to talk about Anna's death to anyone, even her best friend, Carol.

But Maggy had seen enough to convince her that the diary was valuable. Anna had written it when she was very young, working as a housemaid at Hearst Castle. It was a historical document that revealed life at the famous castle in its heyday. She had an appointment next week with an expert from the castle, a Mr. Logan. Regardless of what he thought, she wouldn't make her final decision about donating Anna's diary until she had read every page. She would start reading it in earnest tonight after dinner.

Maggy thought of Carol's parting words to her yesterday. "You won't last 24 hours before you break down and call to see how things are going here without you." She had to laugh as she dialed Carol's home number. Unlike Maggy, Carol was committed to spending only forty hours a week at work, so she could have time with her family.

"Maggy! I knew it! Couldn't help worrying about us, could you?"

"I'm not worried in the least. I just called to tell you how lovely my room is. I'm lying on the bed right now, looking out at a panoramic view of Moonstone Beach. Sand dunes and crashing waves as far as the eye can see."

"Stop! I'm green—deeply, violently green with envy." Maggy heard Carol's two children shrieking in the background.

Maggy laughed. "Well, you're still in Oregon. Everything's green there. By the way, is it still raining?"

"No, only a little heavy mist. Just enough to frizz up your hair."

"On you it looks good," Maggy said, thinking of Carol's dark, bouncy curls. Not like her own blonde mop that turned into a hairball when it got damp.

"Thanks. I take it you found the place ok, then?"

"If you mean did I get lost, the answer is no."

"I find that hard to believe."

"Carol, you know very well I can get anywhere with a map."

"But usually not on the first try. I still think you have a perfect sense of direction —just completely backwards. I won't remind you that you were lost the first day I met you, looking for the student union building and tearing off in the opposite direction."

"Thanks so much for not reminding me," Maggy said.

"You know I'm right, you're always 180 degrees off kilter. So you have to know the right direction, in order to always go exactly the wrong way."

"Give it a rest, Carol. I didn't call so you could browbeat me."

"Now, now, it's one of the odd little things that's so endearing about you."

"Very funny. And as usual, you're exaggerating."

"So," Carol deftly changed the subject, "tell me you're not the least bit curious about the Morrison file Jim is handling for you while you're gone?"

"Oh no, what happened? That's one of our best accounts. We're in trouble if we lose it."

"Relax, everything's fine. Just proving a point. In spite of what you think, we can get along just fine without you."

Nonetheless, she persuaded Carol to fill her in on the day's various business crises. Their small research firm seemed to have survived one day without Maggy at the helm.

Finally, Carol had had enough. "This is so typical of you. Here you are on vacation and what do you talk about? You really don't need to worry about the business anymore, you know. We're on solid ground now. I want you to forget about us and concentrate on having fun. OK?"

"OK! I surrender!"

"Is the Beach House Inn as wonderful as the brochures promised?"

"Even better, if you can believe it. It's almost like staying at a friend's summer cottage where the friend does all the cooking. The Clark's are great, and I'll be meeting the other guests at dinner tonight."

"Good. So I don't have to worry about you reading a book the whole time and not meeting anybody. And while I'm on the subject, are there any likely-looking men around?"

Maggy rolled her eyes. She knew Carol wouldn't rest until she had Maggy's love life settled to her own satisfaction. "You know I'm not interested in meeting anyone. I wish you'd quit hounding me about it."

"Every guy isn't like Jason, you know."

"You mean every guy isn't a two-timing liar."

That made Carol pause for a minute. "Well, yeah. Exactly that."

"I know," Maggy said, her voice lowered. "The thing is that I believed him completely. I don't know if I can trust my own judgment anymore."

Carol's voice softened to match Maggy's tone. "Don't blame yourself, honey. You're the brightest, most sensible person I know. And tall, blonde and gorgeous to boot. You're bound to meet someone who has the sense to realize how wonderful you are. But not if you shut yourself away and give up on men altogether."

"Hey, I'm only thirty, hardly an old crone! I've got plenty of time. Besides, I need to be on my own for awhile. Believe me, you'll be the first to know when I'm ready to do battle again."

"As though you would ever do battle with a man. If you were half as assertive in love as you are in business, you'd do much better."

"Enough advice, you nag. I don't know why I put up with you."

"Because I tell you the truth, of course."

"The truth according to Carol. And I've always hated it!" Maggy laughed. "Especially on those rare occasions when you happen to be right."

With a start, she realized she was almost late for dinner. Unheard of! Maggy was always on time for everything, no matter what. She quickly said her good-byes and raced to get ready.

She paused with her hairbrush in mid-air, took a deep breath and reminded herself for the hundredth time that she wasn't at work. She was a world away from work, at the Beach House Inn on a lovely California beach. The sky wasn't going to fall if she was a few minutes late for dinner. She'd try being the kind of person who could saunter in after everyone else and just not worry about it.

With that thought, Maggy decided to take a little time on her appearance tonight. She brushed her hair until it gleamed as it swung smoothly to her chin, without the slightest hint of frizz. Was she gorgeous? At least

Carol thought so. And her grandmother had never been shy with compliments. Hardly unbiased sources though. This whole thing with Jason had made her feel unappealing, like she didn't measure up in some way. Maggy put down the hairbrush with a little shrug. She'd get over it. In fact, she was ninety percent over it already.

She smoothed jasmine scented lotion on her arms and shoulders and chose a soft peach dress that hugged her figure and brought out the green in her eyes. Casual, but elegant—the perfect dress for an independent woman, entirely capable of being happy on her own. Now she was ready.

Maggy turned the corner in the hallway and abruptly slammed into someone hurrying in the opposite direction. Her jaw collided with a shoulder hard enough to make her lose her balance for a moment.

"Oh! Excuse me!" She looked up at a pair of the bluest eyes she'd ever seen, and a face that seemed to be laughing at her embarrassment.

"I don't know why I should excuse you, since I'm the one who came barreling around the corner without looking." His voice was deep and slightly amused.

What an annoying person. With a start she realized her hand was still pressed against his chest where she had caught herself from falling. She stepped back quickly.

"I wasn't admitting guilt, you know. Just being polite."

He continued to look at her intently, almost as though he knew her. His slow grin was as unsettling as his voice. "You must be Maggy."

"How did you know that?"

"I make it my business to know everything that happens around here. Besides, John and Nancy always tell us who's coming to dinner. I'm Harry, by the way. And dinner is in that direction."

True to form, she had turned the wrong way again. This did little to improve her sudden irritation. And to crash into him right after her conversation with Carol was really too much.

She took a closer look at Harry as they walked down the hallway. He'd managed to bring out her argumentative side in less than thirty seconds.

He was tall and broad-shouldered, with sandy blonde hair that looked tousled as though he'd just stepped out of the shower. She felt a sudden urge to reach up and comb it into place, and was appalled at the thought leaping into her mind unbidden. How irritating! She wouldn't be thinking such idiotic thoughts if Carol hadn't gotten her started.

Maggy noticed for the first time that he wore glasses, which didn't give him a scholarly appearance at all. He looked as though he was just about to tell you a wonderful secret.

Well, thank heavens for those glasses. He'd be entirely too good-looking without them. Maggy noticed that he was looking at her intently, with a quizzical expression on his face. She had an uncomfortable feeling that he knew exactly what she was thinking.

"Nancy said you work at the Castle," she said. "What do you do there?"

"You could call me the repair man. I come down every chance I get to do restoration work. There are so many treasures in the estate, I could spend a lifetime at it."

"You're an art historian, then?"

"Among other things."

Before she could ask him what other things he meant, they arrived at the dining room, where Nancy and John Clark had already started dinner. The aroma of roasted chicken and garlic reminded Maggy that she hadn't eaten since she'd had a bag of peanuts on the plane from Portland that morning.

Nancy stood up as they walked into the room. "Maggy, you sit here where you can see the view as the sun sets. It's really quite spectacular tonight. Harry's seen it dozens of times, so he can sit next to me."

Maggy was momentarily distracted from the wealth of food spread out on the table. The view of Moonstone Beach was truly magnificent, tinged with long shadows and golden light from the setting sun. Tiny lights had come on in the garden that would soon dominate the view as the daylight faded.

Nancy introduced the Sorensons, a young couple celebrating their first anniversary, and obviously still very taken with each other. "Nancy was just telling us that you're the resident expert on the castle," Emily Sorenson said.

"I've spent enough time there to qualify," Harry answered.

"Don't be so modest, Harry." Nancy chided him. "He was the curator until three years ago. Now the estate won't let anyone else work on those old pots that he finds so fascinating. When they can get him away from the University, that is. He's very much in demand."

Harry laughed. "Nancy, the only thing in demand here is your cooking." He looked around the table for confirmation. Everyone stopped eating long enough to compliment their hostess.

"There you go again, always changing the subject." Nancy said. "Most men love to talk about themselves, but not Harry."

"You're a professor, too?" Maggy asked him.

"Yes, but I'm not teaching this year."

"I don't know how you find time to teach, anyway, what with your work here at the Castle and then running off on your adventures at the drop of a hat," Nancy said.

"Leave the boy alone, dear," John said. "Maggy, will you be taking a tour of the castle while you're here?"

"First thing tomorrow I'm taking the one that includes the gardens and the first two floors, and I think the large guest house."

"Perfect," said Nancy. "Then you must have Harry go along with you. The tour guides are good, but Harry brings the place to life."

"Oh no, you don't need to—" Maggy said quickly.

"It's no problem." Harry seemed to enjoy disagreeing with her. "It will be a welcome break for me. Nancy has been telling you all about me. It's only fair that we hear your story as well."

"I'm just on vacation here. Long overdue, in fact."

"What keeps you so busy that you've missed having a vacation?"

"My business—well, my partner and I have a small business, a data research company. This is the first time I could leave and still have a business to come back to. A milestone, I guess!"

"How interesting," Emily said. "What type of research do you do?"

"Most of it is pretty dry; market statistics for small companies that don't have their own research departments, a lot of demographics. We're entirely online now, so we don't even leave the office very often."

"Isn't the internet hurting your business?" Emily asked. "I mean, can't anybody just look up what they want to know on the web?"

"We worried about that for awhile," Maggy said. "Instead of killing our business, we've used the internet to market our services. It can be a real time sink for people who are too busy to weed through the junk. We've even hired a research assistant, which is how I'm able to get away for a week. And we do the occasional odd job: background research for film companies, or for novelists. Sometimes we locate missing people. In seven years, we've located four missing heirs, and several lost classmates for reunions."

"So you're really a detective," said Harry.

"Well, yes," Maggy said, secretly pleased. She'd often thought of herself as a sort of Sherlock Holmes, ferreting out answers to sometimes obscure questions. "But it's not as glamorous as the detectives on TV. The real secret of our success is that we're both stubborn. You can find out almost anything if you don't take no for an answer; you just find a new way to keep looking."

"A woman who won't take no for an answer?" Harry leaned back in his chair, his arms folded, eyes watchful. "That sounds dangerous."

Maggy felt her face grow warm under his amused scrutiny. God, she was blushing like a teenager. She tried to think of something mildly articulate to say, but found her mind wasn't cooperating.

"Only to those who try to keep secrets," she said. Why was this man throwing her off-balance this way? Was he flirting with her? Is that what was setting her on edge? But that shouldn't be difficult to handle. She was hardly a tongue-tied college girl anymore. Despite his careless good looks, he wasn't half as charming as he seemed to think.

She realized Nancy had been talking about tomorrow's trip to the castle. "The road up to the castle is closed to the public. You meet at the Visitor Center and drive up by bus with your tour group."

"I start working long before then," Harry said. "I'll catch up with you when you get to the Roman Pool, Maggy. I look forward to showing it to you." For once he seemed to be serious, without that habitual look of amusement in his eyes. "Now, if you'll excuse me, I have work to finish this evening."

After Harry left, the Sorensons quickly followed. Maggy returned to her room and toyed with various excuses to get out of her meeting with Harry as she finished unpacking her suitcase. No, she was being silly. Most people would jump at a chance to get a private tour from an expert on the castle. She'd go, and that would be that.

Maggy looked around her room with satisfaction. It was a charming combination of Victorian coziness and modern comfort with a canopy bed, vaulted ceilings and an airy skylight that had brought in sunlight earlier that day. A large picture window looked out at Moonstone Beach, now hidden in darkness. A small fireplace was tucked in the corner. She clicked on the gas flames and took her time getting ready for bed, then flipped through the unfamiliar local channels on the television hidden away in an armoire, but nothing held her interest.

Unable to put it off any longer, she picked up the first volume of Anna's diary. It had been a year since her grandmother's death, and almost eight months since she'd found the diary tucked away in Anna's dresser. It was strange to see the faded handwriting that looked similar to her grandmother's familiar scrawl, but more carefully formed. A young woman's handwriting. The Anna she had never met.

Anna's Diary—July 14, 1936

   Mr. Soto just came by the house to tell me the news. I've been hired to work at the Castle! I can't believe my good fortune. Though I should have had more faith, especially since father lit a candle for me at church this week. I went for the interview on the very day I turned eighteen. Undoubtedly, that brought me luck. Mr. Soto finished his regular delivery of groceries at the castle and brought back a letter for me. In it Mrs. Redelsperger, who is the head house-keeper and ever so proper, explains my wages will be a full dollar a day plus room and board. I'll be able to give most of my pay to father.

   It's as though a huge weight has been lifted from us. Father tried not to show it when I told him, but I could see the relief he felt. I'll miss him terribly when I move to the castle, the first time I've ever lived away from home. But Mrs. Sully has promised to look in on him, and I'll visit him each week on my free day. He assures me that he'll be just fine without me, with his books to keep him company. I have to admit, I can hardly wait for tomorrow to get here. I didn't let myself hope for fear of being disappointed, but when I first saw The Enchanted Hill two days ago, I fell under it's sorcerer's spell. To live and work surrounded by such beauty!

July 20, 1936

   I sit in my own little room at the castle. It is as modestly furnished as my room at home but much larger. It suits me quite well. I've made a friend in Emma, one of the housemaids. She has copper hair the color of a shiny new penny, a dusting of freckles that she hates, and a smile for everyone. I spent my first day trailing along behind her as she made her rounds of the rooms assigned to her. Emma and I are work in "A" House. It's proper name is La Casa del Mar, or House of the Sea. Imagine a guest cottage that has twenty rooms!

   I've worked here for five days, changing beds, scrubbing floors and windows, dusting and polishing objects that are so beautiful I was afraid to touch them at first. Five marvelous days of good hard work to make me strong, and sights that will astound father when I tell him. Only this morning we welcomed the film actor, David Niven, to the castle. I'll be cleaning his very rooms! At the same time, I caught my first glimpse of Mr. Hearst and Miss Davies. I know father doesn't approve of them, but Miss Davies came and said hello to me with great kindness. She's far more beautiful in life than the image I've seen at the movie house. No black and white picture could begin to capture her colorful presence, with her flaxen hair and remarkable sapphire eyes. It's incredible that she lives openly with Mr. Hearst as his mistress. She is quite plainly devoted to him though he must be thirty years her senior. Mrs. Hearst lives in New York and rarely ever comes here. When she does, Emma assures me that Miss Davies is hustled off to another mansion somewhere. Still, Marion Davies is the true mistress of the castle.

It's good that I work so hard at my duties, or I'd grow terribly fat with the rich food we are served. We often have the same dishes that the guests are served in the refectory, food like I've never tasted before. Succulent beef, or pheasant that is raised here on the ranch, or lobster from Maine, even shrimp from New Orleans!

Of course, I haven't seen the refectory when guests are dining there. But this afternoon I walked through it when it was entirely empty, my footsteps echoing on the stone floor. When I entered the dining hall, with its huge gothic fireplace and ancient tapestries on the walls, it was almost as if I had stepped through time itself to a medieval lord's palace. Sunlight filtering through the windows high above illuminated a glittering array of silver and colorful silk banners flying over the long convent table in the center of the room. Here one is reminded that the ordinary world has been left far behind.

If I ever forget that fundamental truth, I'll undoubtedly be reminded of it countless times in the course of my workday. Yesterday, for instance, as I crossed the terrace to "A" house with fresh bed linens and supplies, I stopped dead in my tracks when I saw Miss Davies petting a small elephant! This creature was as tall as a pony. I learned that the baby elephant is called Marianne, named for Miss Davies' first talking picture. I was warned to treat Marianne with caution, since she has a particularly nasty disposition.

Last night as I lay in my bed, I heard the strangest cries from below. They were most unsettling. I couldn't guess what horrible creature could make such a mournful, desolate noise. Today Emma told me it was the peacocks, the gorgeous birds that I've seen parading with their fine, iridescent feathers unfurled. They are cursed with that dark, ugly voice. This disturbed me a great deal more than it warranted, for it got me thinking about my strange life here. I've been quick to succumb to the wealth and beauty I see every day, everywhere I look. I've taken it all at face value, without looking deeper. I find myself touching things as I pass, a polished table, the cool marble of a sculpture. I especially love the polished wrought iron faces on the doors to La Casa del Sol, each face with a distinct personality. So much of what I see calls out to be touched, savored. I must take a step back, curb my enthusiasm. This is not my world, and I'd best remember that.

Maggy closed the diary and put it on the nightstand next to her bed, a thoughtful expression on her face. She could almost see Anna standing in front of her, not the young girl who had written these words in her strong handwriting, but her own grandmother, her hair streaked with white. God, she missed her!

* * *

"Damn!"

Harry threw down his pencil in disgust. It was no use. He'd fully intended to sketch out a plan for restoration of an Attic kantharos from the fifth century BC. He stared at the photographs of the Greek portrait cup, but couldn't summon his usual enthusiasm. This, and a few similar projects, were the ostensible reasons for his trip to the castle. A thin smile barely curled his lips. At least that's what he'd told the Clarks. But he had a far more compelling motivation this time.

Maggy Lane.

Since Steve had passed on her letter to Harry three weeks ago, he'd barely thought of anything else. Steve Liggett had taken over Harry's position as curator of the museum after Harry had made him promise to send him any unusual queries or documents about the castle in the late thirties. After so many years, so many dead ends and disappointments, could Maggy Lane's appearance at the castle be as innocent as it seemed?

Now that he'd met her, he was no nearer to a solution. But what had he expected? That she'd give herself away immediately? She seemed transparent, her lovely face as revealing of her thoughts as a child's. He smiled again briefly, this time with genuine warmth. Obviously, not a child. He thought of the blush that had stolen up her cheeks when he teased her. A beautiful woman. Maybe shy, even self-conscious. His eyes clouded for a moment as he was struck by a sudden memory. There was something about her. He'd sensed it the moment she raised those wide green eyes to his. Some elusive quality that reminded him of Marie. He couldn't say what it was. There was certainly no physical resemblance. Maggy was tall and willowy, where Marie had been—

What was wrong with him? He hadn't thought of Marie in ages. Now that he pictured her face again he felt the old pain, and with it the familiar sense of helpless rage washed over him. Damn! Marie was just as dead now as she had been the last time he held her in his arms. This woman was nothing like her. Why had he even thought it?

Maggy was one of two things. A woman as free of ulterior motives as she seemed. Or a very talented actress.

He stood up and looked out the window to the small garden, the scent of lavender reminiscent of the vast gardens at the castle. He barely saw the dark plane of the ocean beyond the road.

Who was she? And how much did she know?

Until he knew the truth about Maggy Lane, he'd have to do a little acting himself. He smiled again in the dim light. Whatever he found out about her, it should prove to be more than interesting.

Chapter 2

*M*aggy woke early the next morning with a delicious feeling of anticipation. She told herself this was due to her interest in the castle and the way her grandmother had described it to her so many times over the years. Having an insider like Harry reveal some of the castle's secrets would add something to the experience, even if he did set her on edge. The thought of seeing him again certainly wasn't giving her this subtle charge of expectation.

She opened the curtains to a shining expanse of blue, a crystal blue sky with faint clouds in the distance and long, lazy waves rolling gently onto the beach. A day to make the angels fly down out of heaven! She smiled at the memory of her grandmother's well-worn expression. When Maggy was seven years old Anna had told her about guardian angels. It had been one of those rare, sunny days in Portland. They had been drinking lemonade on the back porch after working in the yard for hours, with the scent of cut grass filling the air. Anna had told her that every person on earth, no matter how poor, or even mean-spirited, had a guardian angel watching over, ready to offer comfort and peace. Maggy asked if Anna had ever seen an angel herself. Her grandmother had told her a wonderful tale of the day she saw an angel, sparkling with light and love. That afternoon had been special, one of many afternoons shared with Anna.

A frown shadowed her face as she followed her memories to their inevitable conclusion. That was the year her parents were killed in a car accident. She'd begged Anna to talk to the angels, to make them give back her parents. She still remembered the stricken look on Anna's face when Maggy screamed at her. "Why won't they bring back mommy and daddy? They can, but they won't! They're mean! I hate them—I hate angels. I hate you!" Anna had taken Maggy into her arms and held her until the torrent passed.

After that, it was easier for Maggy to let the angels fade away along with other childhood fairytales. Like Santa Claus or the tooth fairy, which she also outgrew that year.

But who needed angels on a day like this? She looked up the beach to the rocky shoreline covered with lupine and poppies that glowed like jewels in the morning sunlight. She felt her heart lift at the sight.

Maggy hummed a tune as she dressed in jeans and her favorite T-shirt, a rendition of an Indian stick figure playing the flute and dancing with animal fetishes. Not that she believed in good luck charms, of course. She slipped on the silver and turquoise bracelet and earrings that had been a gift from Carol, and then ran a comb quickly through her hair.

After a hasty breakfast and a few minutes getting directions from Nancy, Maggy was on the road heading north. The bus was already boarding when Maggy found the visitor center. Today it didn't bother her in the least, as it normally would have. Instead of rushing to catch the bus, she took a minute to quickly jot down a reminder about where her car was parked. This would undoubtedly save her the aggravation of losing her car when she got back. She smiled to herself at the new sense of freedom she felt.

The bus was crowded with an assortment of tourists, cameras slung around necks, many of them chattering happily as they drove up the hillside covered with grass and occasional, majestic live oak trees. Beneath the jangle of excited voices, Maggy could hear the loudspeaker playing an old tune from the thirties, and then an announcer welcomed them as though he was an old-time radio host. She peered up ahead and saw the twin towers of the castle shining like an alabaster crown perched on the hilltop amidst dense, green vegetation. Off to the left she saw the striking black and white flash of zebras, remnants of Hearst's private zoo. She thought of the ill-tempered elephant, Marianne, and the crying peacocks. She imagined ostriches, giraffes and kangaroos wandering around the estate at will. They passed a sign reading "Animals Have the Right of Way at All Times," and then empty zoo enclosures that had once held lions, tigers and bears safely away from unwary guests. Maggy felt a little bit like Dorothy entering the land of Oz.

* * *

"Please gather round me," a tall, thin woman called out to the group after they disembarked. Maggy was surprised to see well-manicured shrubs and hedges that were really citrus trees laden with ripe tangerines and lemons. Tiled steps led upward, but little was visible from this vantage point except a broad expanse of cement wall.

"I'm Lois, and I'll be your tour guide today. I have just a few rules to tell you about." There was a collective groan from the little crowd, but Lois continued, undaunted. "You will feel a strong urge to touch some of the beautiful things you will see. Please resist it! Acid and oils from the hands of a million visitors each year will destroy the fine artwork you see. Don't wander away from the group, and walk only on the gray carpeting we've placed for public use. And please deposit your chewing gum in this receptacle before we start the tour."

Maggy felt like a child on a school outing as the group climbed up the stairs, laughing and complaining alternately. They entered a courtyard enclosed on three sides by a single story Spanish-style building, red tiles adorning the low roof. Bougainvillea and climbing ivy draped the walls. The heavy, wooden doors in the center were covered by elaborate wrought iron grills.

"Welcome to Casa del Sol, or House of the Sun, named for its sunset view to the west. This was the last guest cottage to be built and was originally known as "C" House. "A" House became Casa del Mar, for its ocean view. "B" House is Casa del Monte, House of the Mountain. Casa del Sol looks rather small from here, but its three stories are built downward from where you stand, right into the hillside. It has eighteen rooms and is 6,500 square feet."

"The ironwork on the doors was made by Ed Trinkeller for Mr. Hearst in 1924. If you look closely you will see that each portrait head is different, made to resemble some of his fellow artisans. His work appears throughout the castle."

With a start of recognition, Maggy thought of the wrought iron faces Anna had mentioned in her diary. Sure enough, among the sculpted flowers and dragons the grillwork formed many faces in profile, each one with its own unique character.

As they trailed through the various rooms, Lois explained that most of the ceilings in the guest cottages were copies designed by architect Julia Morgan and made by her artisans at the castle to match the genuine antique ceilings of la Casa Grande. Everywhere Maggy looked was a feast for the eyes, rich with silk hangings, Persian pottery, paintings, silver, or magnificently carved and gilded window moldings that framed spectacular views of gardens and ocean vistas.

Lois took them back outside along the Esplanade that wound through the gardens toward the main house, past a marble sarcophagus from the third-century. Maggy smiled to herself. The long-dead Roman who had commissioned that work saw himself as Apollo accompanied by the nine muses.

She was unprepared for the entrance to la Casa Grande. It had been hidden from view at the lower level of the cottages. The size of it! Even though she had caught quick glimpses of it through the trees, its massive reality was daunting.

"The twin bell towers rise 137 feet above the courtyard. They were inspired by the Cathedral of Santa Maria La Mayor in Ronda, Spain. The main house is 73,500 square feet. Julia Morgan designed the facade to contain reliefs and sculptures dating from the 13th to the 16th century."

"We won't enter through the main doors, to protect the Roman tile mosaic in the vestibule. It was discovered in Pompeii, and is extremely fragile." She led them around the side of the north tower to enter through a rear door.

"The Assembly Room," Lois announced. "Sometimes called the Great Hall. This was where Hearst's guests would gather for drinks before dinner. He would often come down from his rooms on the third floor in an elevator, and come in through this hidden door."

Maggy looked at the door as it closed behind the last person in the group. After it clicked shut, it seemed to disappear from sight. It was designed to match the carved wooden choir stalls that lined the entire room.

"Mr. Hearst liked to surprise his guests," Lois said. "This was one of his little jokes."

Maggy's senses were getting numb from the overload they were receiving. And they were only in the first room of the castle! The dates and descriptions that Lois called out washed over her, quickly forgotten. They passed a sixteen-foot high French Renaissance fireplace and entered the Refectory, through another unobtrusive doorway.

Now this room Maggy recognized. She'd read about it last night in Anna's diary. Maggy imagined her grandmother tiptoeing through this cavernous room all alone. The light from the high windows played on the colorful silk banners overhead and the tapestries lining the walls. One huge table stretched the length of the room. It looked to Maggy like the whole room belonged in Windsor castle. Except for the ketchup and mustard bottles on the table, right next to the silver and china place settings.

"Another one of Mr. Hearst's little jokes," Lois commented.

The rest of the tour passed in a blur. The Morning Room, the Billiard Room, the Main Library, the Gothic Suite. This tour only covered a portion of the estate, but it was too much to take in. The layout of the castle added to her disorientation. Instead of a grand staircase that led visually to the higher floors, every one of the six staircases was hidden away in a tower, invisible from any of the rooms.

Maggy finally caught her breath in the private theater, where the group stopped to see a short home movie showing Hearst and his guests cavorting at the entrance to the castle in the early thirties. How eerie to see her grandmother's employer on the screen, along with Marion Davies and Charlie Chaplin. Hearst was a formidable figure, towering over both of his companions.

Finally they walked out into bright daylight for the last part of the tour, the part Maggy had been waiting for. Anna had mentioned the two great swimming pools to her so many times she could visualize them in elaborate detail.

Tennis courts were separated from the west wing of the castle by a terrace leading to the Esplanade with its giant palms and profusion of plants. The huge North Terrace was below to their left. Maggy was eager to continue around the courts to the chamber she knew was beneath them. Despite her impatience, she trailed behind the group, listening to their voices echo in the large chamber ahead. As she entered the Roman Pool, she was struck by the impression that the she had entered an undersea realm. Blue light was everywhere. Every surface of walls, ceiling and floor was covered by small, turquoise and gold tiles set in intricate designs. The play of sunlight filtering in from floor to ceiling windows reflected in the blue depths of the water to enhance the surreal effect. Seeming to float around the edges of the pool were life-sized, white marble sculptures draped in flowing Roman tunics.

Someone placed a hand firmly on Maggy's shoulders. She gasped and whirled around.

"Harry! You startled me!"

"You were a million miles away. You didn't even hear me say hello."

She was acutely aware of his hand on her shoulder and her racing heartbeat. His eyes held hers for a moment, with a strange expression. Almost as though he'd been the one caught off guard. He seemed to be searching for something, some response from her. Slowly, his hand dropped away from her shoulder.

"This room can have quite an impact." Harry's voice had a slight echoing quality. "Let's wait until the others have gone. I told Lois I'd take you the rest of the way." He waved to the tour guide up ahead who gave a jaunty salute in return.

As the voices of the group diminished in the distance, the impression of an eerie, undersea palace was heightened. Maggy looked at Harry, and almost thought she had imagined the mystifying look that had passed between them. She shivered involuntarily.

"Are you cold? This room is usually cooler than the rest of the castle."

"No, I'm fine. It's just this pool—it's magnificent! I've never seen anything like it. There's a magical quality to it, especially now that the rest have gone."

"I know what you mean. I have to agree with Cary Grant, who said this is the most romantic spot on earth. At least when it's quiet like this." He smiled down at her, his blue eyes intensified by the colors all around them.

"In Hearst's time the pool was heated. The entire chamber would be filled with steam rising from the water. The mosaic tiles you see are Venetian glass, with 22-carat gold leaf inlay. When you look closely at the designs, you can see why it took three years to complete."

Maggy was fascinated by an exquisite rendering of a mermaid and a school of colorful fish. "There's a whimsical feel to the design as well. The artists must have loved making this room."

"Julia Morgan was the architect who designed all this. When she saw the first section, she told the tile-setter it was too perfect. She was trying to reproduce the look of a Roman bath, so she wanted it to look perfect, but old at the same time. He finally thought of banging his fist randomly on the tile before it set, so the surface would be uneven in places. If you look closely you can see those depressions throughout the whole chamber."

"Yes, I see what you mean. It's hard to imagine such painstaking hand work, on a scale like this."

"Miss Morgan was an exacting taskmaster. She designed everything you see at the castle, down to the finest detail. She worked on it with Mr. Hearst for almost three decades."

"I know. I remember my grandmother speaking of her. She was a tiny woman, always dressed in a tailored business suit, and soft-spoken like Mr. Hearst. But Anna said her word was law to the construction crew. Julia Morgan must have been formidable to have broken into a man's profession in those days."

"Who was your grandmother?"

"Anna Lane, though her maiden name was Cummins. She worked here as a housemaid."

"I can see that you might have a few stories to tell me about the castle that I haven't heard about," Harry said.

"I don't know that my recollections are historically accurate. Anna would tell me bedtime stories about a magical castle with it's fantastic zoo and glamorous visitors. I always thought she tailored the stories for my benefit. But I know she loved her time here." Maggy hesitated. "I have several volumes of her diary from that time. I've been thinking I might donate them to the State."

Harry stopped walking. "Of course! You're Ms. Lane! I believe we have an appointment next week to discuss those diaries."

"Oh. I guess Nancy didn't introduce us by our last names. You must be Mr. —," she had forgotten the name.

"Logan. During my stint as curator I interviewed some of the staff who worked at the castle in it's heyday. But most of them were in their eighties, and memories of sixty years ago aren't always reliable. A diary is quite a valuable find."

"I haven't made a firm decision yet, though. I've never read the diaries straight through." She saw his look of astonishment. "My grandmother and I were very close, but she never shared her diaries with me when she was alive. I found them after she died."

"But you didn't read them?"

"I couldn't. Anna's death was…" Maggy struggled to speak past the tightening in her throat. "She must have come home that day and surprised a burglar robbing her house. There was no sign that he touched her, but she died from a heart attack. She was seventy-eight. The police thought the thief was so scared he ran off without taking anything."

"Did they find him?" Harry asked.

"No, they never did. I couldn't believe she was gone. I just couldn't believe it. When I found the diaries I tried to read them, but I couldn't do it. I read the first one last night."

As soon as she finished speaking, Maggy wondered why in the world she had told him all that. She never talked about Anna's death. Carol was the only one she had confided in. And here she was, spilling her heart out to a stranger. She looked at him closely as they resumed walking away from the pool. She couldn't say why exactly, but it felt right to tell him. Now he seemed to be choosing his words carefully.

"I'm sorry," he said. "That must have been hard to live through. I know how painful reminders of the past can be."

Maggy raised her eyes to his. She caught a glimpse of desolation in his expression, a shadow that was quickly hidden away. In that instant, she knew he'd suffered a great loss as well.

"Of course, the diaries are yours. It's your decision."

Maggy blinked in the sudden brightness as they walked outside. Maybe she'd have to revise her opinion of Harry. He might be irritating at times, with his penchant for teasing, but she suspected there was another side to him. One that he didn't reveal easily.

They had only gone a few paces when she noticed a tingling sensation in her hands. She rubbed them together and shivered as a chill passed over her. What was wrong with her? The sensation seemed to increase as she drew in each breath, almost as if the air was charged with electricity. In the next moment Maggy heard a woman's voice singing the beginning notes of a familiar song from the thirties. The richness of the voice and music gave the words a strange poignancy.

It must have been Moonglow
Way up in the blue,
It must have been Moonglow
That led me straight to you.
We seemed to float right through the air,
Heavenly songs seemed to come from everywhere.

Maggy heard the voice floating in the air all around them, it's timbre and depth lovely beyond anything she'd ever experienced. She could even feel it physically, the resonance vibrating deep in her chest. She stopped and grabbed Harry's arm without thought.

"That voice; how beautiful!" Her face was alight with pleasure.

Harry looked uncertain. "I don't hear anything. What—"

Maggy shook his arm impatiently. "Shhh. Oh, it's the most lovely singing, and piano, and I think a saxophone. But the voice—how marvelous." She closed her eyes so she could fully absorb the music, unlike anything she had ever heard before. She swayed gently, unconscious of her movement, as the music seemed to reverberate through her entire body, filling her with a strange mixture of almost giddy pleasure and a melancholy yearning for—for what? She didn't know. Just as suddenly as it had come, the music stopped. She felt herself sag with disappointment.

Her eyes flew open. She had literally forgotten where she was. Harry was standing in front of her with a bewildered expression on his face. She let go of his arm and stepped away from him self-consciously.

"Are you all right?" He asked, putting his arm around her shoulder as though he thought she might faint. "What happened?"

"Didn't you hear that?"

"No, I didn't hear anything."

"But you must have. It was so loud, so immense and beautiful—"

"Maggy, I didn't hear anything. Not a single note, no voice, no music. Nothing."

"But, it was…" her voice trailed off as she looked at her surroundings, then back at Harry. The concern in his eyes only made her feel worse. "It was real. She was singing Moonglow, of all things! I don't understand this at all. How could you be standing right beside me and not hear it?"

"I don't know what to say. From your description of whatever it was you heard, I don't see how I could've missed it." He hesitated and then looked directly into her eyes. "Are you sure you didn't imagine it?"

Even as a denial came to her lips, she realized the immediacy of the mysterious music was fading. She remembered the strange, tingling sensation she had experienced. Maggy was suddenly aware of Harry's arm around her shoulder, and his face inches from her own. She could feel his breath on her cheek. She felt the first pinprick of doubt.

"I don't think so. I've never been prone to hallucinations, you know. Imagining voices, or in this case a whole orchestra—it's too bizarre."

"You did say you've been working for years without a break. You're sure nothing like this has ever happened to you before?"

"Never! I'm really very practical and down-to-earth." She disengaged herself from his solicitous embrace. "I'm quite sane, if that's what you're asking."

"I'm sorry, I didn't mean to imply—" He stopped speaking abruptly. "I just want to make sure you're okay."

"I'm fine, really. Let's just forget about it." Maggy wasn't so sure she could forget it that easily, but she didn't want to spoil this visit. She'd worry about it later.

She smiled at Harry. "I still want to see the Neptune Pool. It was my grandmother's favorite spot here. She described it to me so many times, I'm dying to see if it will live up to my expectations."

"I'll be happy to take you there. But first I want to show you something." He took her hand and led her back toward the main building. They entered a side door with a circular staircase tower rising upward before them. Instead of going up, Harry led her down the steep stairs fashioned of gray slabs of rock.

"Are you taking me to the dungeon?" Maggy held on to the iron railing to keep her balance.

"Almost. These rocks are actually concrete made to look like stone. And I'm taking you to the basement vaults, where I do most of my work."

The enclosed staircase opened out to a landing where a larger staircase swept in a graceful curve down to the intricately tiled floor of a vast room filled with work tables and an assortment of statues, columns and massive moldings. People were sitting at various tables, intent on their work.

"There are six vaults down here, each filled with items waiting for restoration. There are different areas for rugs, tapestries, manuscripts, furniture, paintings, and the marble you see here."

"His collection must have been enormous, to judge by all this," Maggy said.

Harry laughed. "This is just a fraction of Hearst's original collection. He owned half a dozen estates on this scale, each of them filled with treasures. And huge warehouses with crates of artwork that were never opened. Most of his art collection was sold off in the late thirties. Now so many of the pieces here are in need of restoration, it's hard to decide which ones to work on first. Conservation is painstaking and very expensive."

"But the castle must generate a tremendous income with all the tourists that pass through here."

"It does, enough to be the only self-supporting State Park in California. But it still doesn't cover all the restoration work that needs to be done," Harry said. They passed through an archway into another huge vault.

"The vaults are controlled for temperature, humidity and light, and we have an X-ray unit to examine paintings and furniture. We use ultra violet light on ceramics to detect earlier restoration work that can't be seen in normal light. Some of the people you see here are artisans who reproduce artwork and create original designs to blend with the castle surroundings, just as Hearst did. The Sienese Palio banners in the Refectory are good examples. The originals are over two hundred years old and far too fragile to be on display."

They passed into a smaller room with tables covered by vases and pottery of all sizes and colors.

"Are these the 'old pots' that Nancy said you like so much?" Maggy asked.

"Exactly. And that's not such a bad description, either." He pointed out a round ceramic jar decorated with black figures of winged lions with human faces. "This piece is a Corinthian pyxis from—"

"Pyxis?" Maggy interrupted.

"That term refers to its shape, essentially a round box with a lid. It's dated to about 600 BC. Some of these are reproductions, but many of them are authentic. The oldest piece in the collection is a Baring amphora from the eighth century BC. Most of the Greek vases in the collection are on display in the main library upstairs."

"What is it about the vases in particular that interests you so much?" Maggy asked.

Harry looked at her quickly, his brows drawn together in a frown. He didn't look pleased with her question. "Why do you ask?"

Maggy shrugged, surprised at his reaction. "I'm just curious. Is it a secret?"

"Hardly." He guided her around an assortment of carved marble arches and pedestals as they walked back toward the stairs. "You did say last night that you were dangerous to those who kept secrets."

"No I didn't. You said dangerous, not me."

"Would it please you to find out I had a dark secret?"

What an odd question. Maggy wasn't exactly sure what they were talking about. "I was just curious, really. Was that your field of study before you started here as curator?"

He considered her question for a while before he answered her.

"Yes. It was probably one of the reasons I was hired. Hearst's collection of Greek vases was the largest and finest in the world until he sold a portion of it to the Metropolitan Museum of Art. The truth is that I've been interested in ancient pottery for a very long time. Every piece has a story to tell, Maggy, if you make the effort to study it. Each one has it's own secret."

Maggy blinked as they walked out into the bright sunlight. She felt a little shiver run through her as Harry took her hand in his. "I haven't forgotten your request," he said. "Let's see the Neptune Pool."

Chapter 3

❖

$\mathcal{B}$eatrice looked out beyond the white marble pillars to the Pacific Ocean sparkling in the distance. The deep blue was echoed in the cloudless expanse of sky, contrasting brilliantly with the golden hills cascading down to the sea. She heard the cry of distant seagulls carried along on the soft wind that brushed against her skin.

As she trailed her feet slowly through the clear water she admired the fourth century Roman temple opposite and the colonnade of pillars that seemed to embrace the huge pool. Light refracted through the water to turn it a shimmering turquoise, so it seemed the water itself glowed. Such a glorious place!

At the First Level of Heaven, what she had learned was the sensory plane, she saw every object and being with a heightened awareness. Physical and spiritual essences combined to give a depth of color, light and vibrancy that transcended anything perceived by mortal senses. She

looked at the smooth ivory skin of her hands and arms and was amazed at
the unearthly beauty that radiated from her own body as well. Her many
years in Heaven had still not accustomed her to this dazzling display.

Beneath her angelic light, she was much the same as she had been in
life. Still tall, a large woman with deep brown, wavy hair swinging to her
shoulders. Her eyes were an unusual, cornflower blue, deep-set and
expressive, quick to laugh or cry. She had a generous mouth, with full lips
that were most comfortable in a smile. That smile held a trace of irony,
with an off-center lilt, so that one side curved up more than the other.
Even in repose her face attested to that now, as the left side of her mouth
was framed by a distinct line. Laugh lines crinkled around her eyes as well,
giving her the look of a vibrant woman in her mid-forties. Youth carried
with it the grace of physical perfection, but she preferred the lived-in face
of middle age, where character begins to etch itself on the surface.

Her strong, voluptuous body was now transformed with an angelic
beauty. Not incongruously, she was wearing an ordinary, blue cotton sun-
dress with a loose skirt that was inelegantly bunched up around her thighs
as she sat at the edge of the pool, trailing her feet in the cool water. The
sight of her at this moment would have blinded all but a very
few mortals..

Since her death sixty years earlier, Beatrice had grown to accept her lot
as an Angel of the First Level. She felt the benefits far outweighed the few
liabilities she had encountered so far. Though she remembered few details
of her mortal life, she knew with certainty that she had loved life passion-
ately and that this Heaven, so close to earth, suited her admirably.

Despite the fact that she could experience neither hunger nor thirst, she
felt a sudden wish for the pleasure of a cool drink. Her thoughts focused
on the image of her favorite cocktail, a concoction of crushed ice, brandy,
cream and nutmeg. Almost instantly, a crystal goblet materialized on the
marble tile beside her, icy condensation frosting the outside of the glass.
With a contented sigh she took a sip of the Brandy Alexander and let the
sweet, frozen liquid melt slowly on her tongue. Alcohol, food or drink

would have no effect on her, but the sensation of taste was sometimes a sweet indulgence, a reminiscence of human life.

The Roman columns lining the Neptune pool reminded her of a Maxfield Parrish scene, with its heady play of sunlight and shadow. She sensed the massive height of San Simeon castle behind her. As often happened, she had a sudden flash of memory from her time on earth. So odd, the things she remembered.

She had a vivid impression of William Randolph Hearst, only she had called him W.R. And the lovely Marion, always at his side. Without knowing details of her relationship with them, her mind was instantly filled with tantalizing bits of their history. She had been their guest at the castle. She remembered a lively, glittering group of celebrities and artists that had joined her there in life. Wouldn't W.R. be surprised to know his castle was a favorite spot for angels? Especially when some of his enemies had accused him of being the devil incarnate during his lifetime. She remembered him as a larger than life figure, and knew he had inspired great admiration and animosity in equal measure. Of all his palatial dwellings scattered across the globe, he had loved San Simeon best. She thought it strange that she had never seen him here, in Heaven's image of the dream he created on earth. But mysteries abounded in Heaven as well as earth. And angels often chose to be unseen, even in the First Level.

Beatrice wondered how many of her fellows were even now wandering about the grounds. She felt somewhat solitary and nostalgic today, so she had hidden herself away from the common plane where all angelic creatures could see each other. She was as invisible to them as they were to her. With the slightest wish on her part she would instantly materialize among them, but she was content by herself just now. Privacy and solitude were highly valued blessings in Heaven, a place that could sometimes get rather crowded. With a far greater effort, Beatrice could wish herself into the mortal world, where she would see groups of tourists trailing through the estate, led by tour guides rattling off the curious history of San Simeon.

After living for sixty years in the First Level, she seldom ventured into the flat, colorless mortal world unless she was compelled to do so by her responsibilities, or the occasional longing to see a simple human being once again. Like other angels, Beatrice loved all mortals without conscious thought or effort, as naturally as she radiated light or floated through the air.

But she had no yearning to see any of them now. She gazed at the faint disc of the moon barely visible in the late morning sky overhead. The ubiquitous moon, hinting of the night to come even on a day such as this. Beatrice began to sing in a rich contralto voice as she twirled her drink in her hands. She imagined the orchestra playing and music began to form in the still afternoon, framing her voice with a sultry richness. The notes she sang seemed to glide into the air around her with a shimmering, almost visual quality.

It had to be Moonglow
Way up in the blue,
It had to be Moonglow
That led me straight to you.

As she sang, Beatrice had the strangest sensation that someone was listening to her. She looked around suddenly, expecting to see someone standing on the far side of the pool, or above on the terrace behind her. Of course, no one was there. No one could enter her solitary corner of Heaven without an invitation.

She thought of the music again and the words welled up inside her and poured out into the morning air. As she sang, she caught a glimpse of another time she had sung this song here at the castle. At a magnificent party with more than a hundred guests; she had been pulled onto the makeshift stage for an impromptu performance. What a thrilling night that was!

We seemed to float right through the air,
Heavenly songs seemed to come from everywhere.
And now when there's Moonglow
Way up in the blue,
I always remember that Moonglow gave me you.

Beatrice felt the subtle change in air pressure and heard the slight whooshing sound that told her she had an unexpected visitor. She sensed his identity immediately, though he was standing behind her out of sight, and her heart lifted.

"Ah, Beatrice! A voice to make the angels weep," he said as she turned to greet him. She saw the one being who had the power to enter her solitary place, and the last one in the world she expected to see.

"Roland, darling! How marvelous to see you after all this time." She stood up, shaking the water off her feet as she ran to him and clasped him in a warm embrace. How good it felt to hold him again! "You haven't changed at all in fifty years," she said.

"Nor have you, my dear. Though fifty years or fifty decades wouldn't make that much difference, as you know."

"Yes, of course. But I just can't get used to our sense of time here. I still think of it in the old way."

"It does take time," he said with a grin.

"I can see your jokes haven't improved either." Beatrice stepped back to take a good look at him, to see if his appearance could offer some clue to this altogether unusual visit. He was a slender, beguiling youth of about twenty, just as he had been the last time she saw him. His blonde hair was sleek and shining above rather disconcerting gray eyes that were much too deep to look into directly. Eyes that spoke of vastness; that could pull you in if you looked at them too long. They were the only thing about him that belied the impression of innocent, perfect youth. He was the same height as Beatrice, with a lean, muscular body that radiated a dazzling light even stronger than hers. She could swear he was wearing that same linen robe the last time she'd seen him; it's brilliant white seemed to change colors subtly as he moved.

In short, he looked exactly as he had when he first welcomed Beatrice to Heaven sixty years earlier. Roland was a teaching angel who lived in a higher level of Heaven. Beatrice never knew exactly where he lived, or what that Heaven was like. When she had asked him, he told her he could no more describe it to her than she could describe the First Level to a living mortal.

"I give up!" Beatrice exclaimed. "I'm absolutely thrilled to see you again, but I thought we said our last good-byes. You were very clear that I'd have to get on here without you."

"Sometimes things don't go as planned, Beatrice, even in Heaven." He sighed and took her arm as they walked slowly away from the pool. He flashed a smile at her. "You've done very well these years without me."

"I've been more than content. This place suits me just fine. And I've gotten a kick out of my human charges, exasperating as they can be."

"You've done very well with them. As a Guardian Angel you are exemplary." He looked troubled. "All except for one, I'm afraid."

"One? But who? If any one of them had gotten into trouble, I'd know it instantly. I'm sure of it."

"This is most unfortunate, even unbelievable. Someone has been—" he hesitated, a frown marring his perfect features. "—overlooked."

She gasped. "No! That's impossible."

"I would have agreed with you, had I not seen the effects only moments ago."

"What effects? Please tell me everything."

Again he sighed, and sat down on the balustrade overlooking the tawny hillside, pulling her down to sit beside him. She had never seen him at a loss for words like this. "She is a young woman who is now not thirty yards from where we sit, walking along beside the pool in the mortal world. She is visiting the castle with a tour group."

Beatrice was dumbfounded. "You must be joking. I'd know if one of my mortals was nearby."

"As I said, this is unprecedented. The only way I became aware of her myself is this—" again he hesitated, as though he had difficulty grasping the thought.

"She heard you singing just now. Think of it! A mortal heard you singing in Heaven!" He looked at her closely. "The moment she heard your first note, a ripple of awareness passed through to us above. The bond with you is clear."

"I can't believe it," Beatrice said quickly. Then her brows drew together for a moment while she reconsidered. "Oh! I must have sensed her presence just now when I thought someone was listening to me. Then when you arrived, I just assumed it was you."

"No, dear. I was only alerted when I felt her listening to you."

"But if she's mine, yet I've been unaware of her—then she's had no one?" Beatrice asked with disbelief.

Roland nodded. "I'm afraid so. It's hard to comprehend."

"Not hard—impossible! Every mortal on earth has a guardian angel."

"The fact remains that Maggy Lane has lived on earth for thirty years with no angel to care for her in any way. Despite this lack, she has survived the tragedies of her life, the loss of her parents and grandparents, with great strength." He paused for a moment, considering. "Apparently she hasn't needed our help," he added.

"Oh, piffle! Every mortal needs help." She stood up suddenly. "I must see her at once."

"Of course, Beatrice. But first take a moment to reflect on this. You know that angels can freely visit the mortal world, though it is sometimes painful." He waited until he got a reluctant nod from her.

"But for a mortal to perceive any part of Heaven seems to fly in the face of nature. You've spent the better part of sixty years learning the laws of Heaven, but this—this is something different. It seems the very fabric of

Heaven has been affected in some way. Two natural laws have already been broken."

"That's exactly why I must go to her and try to put this right."

"Impetuous as always! Nonetheless, I suggest you proceed with caution. Imagine that a mortal suddenly found the laws of gravity suspended. You can't predict what will happen any longer."

"Dear Roland," She placed her hand gently on his cheek for a moment and felt his love and concern radiating out to her. "You know I'll be careful. But I must see her for myself before I can do anything else. Not a molecule will be disturbed on the mortal plane, I promise."

She raised her hand in farewell, and vanished.

* * *

As they came down the steps toward the Neptune Pool, Maggy caught her breath in wonder. The mid-day sun flattened and intensified the colors of the scene before her, so she seemed to be looking at an artist's rendering rather than physical reality. The brilliant aqua of the pool was hatched with geometric designs of black tile inlaid on the bottom surface. Alabaster Roman-Grecco statues gazed serenely out through the colonnades curving around the pool. Neptune presided over all from his temple facade directly opposite. Between the pillars vistas of rolling hills gently unfolded to meet the ocean below. Each colonnade seemed to frame its own perfect view.

"It's no accident the view is so magnificent from this spot," Harry's voice broke into her thoughts. "The pool began on a much more modest scale, but grew to this size after twelve years of renovations. Hearst firmly believed that you can create a Heaven on earth, with enough effort."

"He succeeded only too well," Maggy said. "It's even more spectacular than I imagined." They walked down another set of stairs and she saw a white marble Venus surrounded by mermaids.

"Miss Morgan designed this as a waterfall, so Venus would appear to be rising up out of the water," Harry said. Even though the fountain was turned off, Maggy easily pictured the way it would look with water cascading around the magnificent statue.

"This was my grandmother's favorite place on the ranch. She used to come here in the early mornings before the household was awake. She described it to me so well. Seeing it like this—it's as though her words have come to life."

Harry looked at her thoughtfully for a moment. "It's extraordinary, when you think of it, that this place is exactly as it was then. That would have been over sixty years ago.

"Anna started working here when she was eighteen. That was in 1936. She stayed here until sometime during the war."

"You called your grandmother Anna?"

"I called her Nana up until I was seven. But then I went to live with her and I insisted on calling her Anna."

His look was a question.

They walked along the terrace under the colonnades in silence. "I lost my parents in a car accident when I was seven," Maggy said. "I barely remember them. Anna raised me."

"That must have been hard for you."

Maggy smiled. "It was at first. But she was always there for me, and my grandfather too."

"You must wonder about the time she spent here."

"Reading the diary brings Anna closer to me than ever. But not the same Anna I knew. She was just a girl when she worked here. Her mother was a teacher, so Anna was well educated and she read a great deal, but she'd never traveled far from Cambria. Then to suddenly see all this," she waved her hand toward castle. "No wonder it made such an impression on her."

"It made a similar impression on everyone who visited here, regardless of how worldly they were. George Bernard Shaw came up with my favorite description. 'This is the way God would have done it, if he had the money.'"

As they walked closer to the pool, Maggy realized her hands were tingling. She noticed she was a little breathless, almost shaky. With sudden apprehension she began rubbing her hands together as a wave of adrenaline washed over her. Oh no, not again! She told herself to stay calm, nothing was going to happen. She wasn't losing her mind. She looked at Harry and realized he had been speaking. He didn't seem to notice anything wrong. She heard a whooshing sound behind her and felt a slight change in air pressure. She turned to look back toward the pool.

Maggy was dumbfounded at the lovely apparition that appeared in front of her. Harry and her surroundings faded away. The woman was standing at the edge of the pool, her blue dress floating about her. A strange and wonderful light radiated from her, and with it a feeling of such love that Maggy's heart ached to feel it.

But the expression on the woman's face was one of utter dismay as she looked at Maggy. "Oh, no! You can see me, can't you?" Her voice was gentle and rich, with a hauntingly familiar quality.

Maggy nodded dumbly as she basked in the sparkling presence before her. Though there was no heat radiating from the extraordinary being, Maggy felt that she was showered in sunlight that made the ordinary day grow dim. Suddenly, Maggy knew the woman's voice. "It was you! You were singing just now!"

"Yes, that was me, I'm afraid."

"Oh, but it was the most beautiful thing I've ever heard. Thank you so much!"

If anything, the woman—or being, whatever she was—looked even more upset. Maggy was moved almost to tears by the beauty of this creature, the love shining from her, and her obvious discomfort.

"Is something wrong?" Maggy blurted out. "I want to help you if I can." She paused for a moment and then smiled. "Beatrice. That's your name, isn't it? I know you."

"Yes, I am Beatrice." The woman, as perfect as an angel, came close to Maggy and touched her cheek softly. Elation coursed through Maggy's spirit at the brief contact. "But this should never have happened. I'm sorry, Maggy."

"But what has happened? I don't understand."

Beatrice gazed directly at her with a look of such regret that Maggy felt tears well up in her eyes. Finally Beatrice smiled. "I must go. Good-bye, my darling." As quickly as she had appeared, she vanished before Maggy's eyes.

At the moment that Beatrice disappeared, it seemed that all light was taken with her. There was an echoing drop in air pressure that Maggy felt pulling her forward. For the first time in her life, she crumpled to the ground in a dead faint.

Chapter 4

❖

*B*eatrice didn't go back to the First Level, where she was sure to see Roland again. After the disastrous events of the last few minutes, she simply wasn't ready to face him. Instead she stayed in the mortal plane and winked into existence just a few miles down the hill from the castle. The remains of a mile-long pergola built by Hearst dominated the ridge where she stood. Pillars marched down the hill in pairs that supported open rafters, which had once been covered with a canopy of blooming vines and espaliered fruit trees. They now stood faded and unadorned. Beatrice thought Roland might follow her here, but saw no trace of him. She didn't know whether she was disappointed or relieved to postpone that encounter.

What a balled up mess! Poor, darling Maggy. Seeing an angel like that, without a plan or purpose. A mistake, Beatrice had told her! Oh, it was a mistake all right, and she'd made it even worse. She paced down the hillside in a distracted fashion and tried to calm down so she could think the whole thing through.

Before she had gone five steps, an angel materialized in front of Beatrice with a booming sound, he was moving at such speed. His white hair stood out from his head as though charged with electricity, his white robes swirled around him. The expression on his face was furious, righteous anger fairly radiating from his eyes. Though he was the same height as Beatrice, he seemed to loom over her.

"How dare you! That was the most reckless display I've ever seen! Do you think this is a game? How could you appear to her like that, without even thinking of the consequences? God knows what damage you've done to both of them!"

Beatrice gaped at him. She felt terrible enough already, but to be accused in this wretched manner was too much. And by a total stranger!

"If anyone is reckless, it's you!" she shouted. "Throwing accusations around when you obviously don't know what happened." She paused, and her shoulders sagged as her brief anger passed. "The trouble is, I don't know what happened either. I suppose you were there and saw everything?"

"Of course I was there. Though I had the common decency to remain invisible to mortal eyes."

"I never dreamed she would see me. I should have suspected something like this would happen. Believe me, I didn't choose to be seen by her. I only learned of her existence just now—and it seems I'm her guardian angel."

The hostility left his face as he studied her. "Perhaps I may have judged you too hastily. I tend to react strongly if I think one of my charges is threatened. Harry is mine, you see." He took her hand in his. "My name is Ambrose. And you were Beatrice Page when you lived on earth. I recognized you the moment I saw you."

Beatrice was puzzled. "You remember your mortal life? You must be a new angel, if you still have that luxury. But how can you remember me, when I lived ages ago?"

"I've been slower to forget than most angels, it's true. My memories are far from complete, but I know as a young boy in the 1930's I listened to a famous singer named Beatrice Page. My parents allowed me to see you perform at the Waldorf-Astoria in New York. Now, let's sit down and see if we can make sense out of this."

They sat without ceremony on the ground as Beatrice poured out her story to him. She still had trouble believing it herself. "In a way your were right, Ambrose. I should have expected trouble, since I already knew Maggy could hear my singing in the First Level. Roland warned me to be careful, but I never for a moment expected anything like this."

"And who is Roland?"

"He was my teacher when I arrived in Heaven. He's the one who told me Maggy could hear me singing, even when I was in the First Level."

"Well, then. There's no use wishing it hadn't been done. We must figure out why this strange bond exists between you and Maggy, if we are to fix it. But first we need to see what damage your visit has done."

"Maggy must be terribly upset," Beatrice said slowly. "She didn't seem to fear me. I had the strangest feeling that I knew her, but not in the normal way we sense the thoughts and emotions of our earthly charges. She wasn't revealed to me clearly, yet I felt such closeness to her. It was the strangest feeling, as though we recognized each other."

"There's no doubt she knew you. She called you by name." Ambrose raised one bushy eyebrow. "Most extraordinary! I agree with you that she was unafraid; quite the contrary, she seemed galvanized with joy at seeing you. However, after your abrupt departure she was overcome by the whole experience. She fainted away." He paused at Beatrice's anguished exclamation.

"Please try to be calm. She's a strong young woman and Harry is taking care of her as we speak. I fear the damage may be with him as well as Maggy. This has created a most unfortunate situation."

Beatrice looked at Ambrose in surprise. She honestly hadn't given a thought to the young man with Maggy. "What do you mean?"

"Harry was shocked. I don't know that I've ever seen him this deeply upset before."

"But why should he be upset? He didn't see me!"

Ambrose looked at Beatrice as though she was being willfully obtuse. "Because he's never had much experience with mental illness. You don't know Harry. He's affable enough on the surface, but I've never seen a man who is more shut off from the rest of the world. I've despaired of ever finding a way to help him. Much to my surprise, he began pursuing Maggy in a way that is very unlike him. I was quite elated at this turn of events. Now, in the space of one hour, he's seen her hear voices that aren't there, speak to invisible beings, and then faint dead away. He thinks she's mentally unstable, of course."

"Oh dear. You're right. And what must Maggy be feeling? If only I could go to her and offer comfort without being seen." Beatrice looked back toward the castle, her eyes shadowed. She turned back to Ambrose suddenly. "Why is Maggy so important to him?"

"I'm not sure yet. Whatever was happening between the two of them has been changed irrevocably by your untimely appearance."

"Roland will be terribly disappointed with me. Impetuous, as always! I've really loused it up this time."

Ambrose hesitated. "Don't blame yourself, Beatrice. I believe the higher angels sometimes lose touch with mortal failings, or even the trials we face in the First Level. No one could know what would happen. I propose we work together to solve this puzzle."

"Marvelous! Since I can't go to Maggy without being seen, I'll need your help just to get close to her," Beatrice said as they shook hands to seal their bargain.

"I'll do my best where Maggy is concerned, though I lack the insight of a true bond with her, like I have with Harry," Ambrose said. He looked down the rolling hills to the bay of San Simeon below. "If you wish, we can meet here in the mortal plain to discuss what we have learned. This pergola is a pleasant spot, and it's unlikely Maggy will stumble upon you here."

Beatrice cast a skeptical glance at the bare columns of the pergola. It didn't seem that pleasant a spot to her, but it had its advantages. "I doubt that Roland will look for me here, since I've never seen him in the mortal plane. For now, I'd rather not ask him for help. I need to solve this myself. Thanks, Ambrose. I appreciate your help more than you know." She stood up and brushed the dirt from her hands. "There must be a reason behind all this. But where do we look for it?"

"I too suspect a larger purpose at work. And you are somehow tied to the center of it. You and Maggy." Ambrose stood beside her, his chin resting in his hand as he thought. "Are you sure you have no memories from your mortal life? Did you ever visit this place when you lived?"

"I know I spent time at the castle. Earlier today I had a vivid recollection of a party at the castle under a full moon, the scent of flowers in the night, jewels sparkling, the orchestra playing over the laughter of the guests. I remember Marion Davies teasing me relentlessly. She pulled me to the stage to sing Moonglow." Beatrice came back to the present with an audible sigh. "That's all. The rest is gone. I might have come here often, but I don't recall anything else."

"You don't remember any others? Did you visit here with any family or close friends?"

"I don't know," she said. "Any other memories are insubstantial. The more I try to grasp them, the more they fade away, like a dream on waking. You must have had the same feeling yourself."

"I know our first days in Heaven are spent remembering every event in our mortal lives. And I know that once the process of forgetting begins, we are not encouraged to recall those years on earth. But this is a completely different situation from the normal ways of Heaven. If you're going to help Maggy, you must try to remember."

Chapter 5

*M*aggy opened her eyes to find a crowd of people looking down at her. She looked at them with some confusion. "What happened? Who are you?"

"It's OK, Maggy." She turned her head to see Harry's blue eyes looking anxiously at her. "You fainted. I'm afraid you hit your head when you fell."

"That's ridiculous! I've never fainted in my life." Even as she protested, Maggy had to admit it looked bad, since she seemed to be lying on the ground with no recollection of how she got there. As her eyes focused more clearly, she saw the crowd of people was really just Harry and two women.

"You may not have fainted before, young lady," said the woman leaning over her, "but you were out cold just now. Your pulse is normal." She held up a finger and moved it slowly from left to right. "Just look at my finger. That's it."

"I'm fine, really. I'm sorry to have caused all this trouble." Maggy sat up and winced as the motion caused a sudden pounding in her head.

"You should be examined more thoroughly," said the woman.

Harry squeezed Maggy's hand. "Do you feel well enough to move? I'd like to get you inside where you can rest comfortably. There's a tour group coming through here in ten minutes or so."

"Yes, let's go. I'd rather not be lying on the ground when they come." Maggy leaned on Harry as he helped her up. "I'm OK, though. I can walk by myself."

"Maybe. But Jean will come with us to take another look at you, just to make sure." Harry indicated the woman who had helped her. "She's the nurse on duty today."

They went to a small room on the lower floor of one of the guesthouses, where Maggy gratefully reclined on a plain sofa. This room looked more like an ordinary office than part of the castle. The nurse couldn't find anything wrong with her, but advised her to see a doctor when she returned home.

When they were alone, Harry pulled a chair up close and looked at Maggy questioningly. "Are you ready to talk about what happened?"

Maggy was uncomfortably aware of the sympathetic tone of his voice. She sat up a little straighter. She wasn't about to let anyone treat her as a child or an invalid, regardless of what had happened.

"Yes, I want to talk about it now, before I have time to really think about it and convince myself that it didn't really happen. I know what I saw. I was a little confused when you were all standing over me. But I remember everything now. Just tell me this, Harry. Did you see anyone?"

"I'm sorry, Maggy, I didn't. You walked over near the pool and spoke as though someone was there, but I didn't see anyone."

Maggy sighed. "I was afraid of that. I saw a woman, an incredibly beautiful, unearthly woman. She had dark hair and a blue dress—they both seemed to be floating around her. And she was radiating light; I know it sounds crazy, but the most dazzling light seemed to shimmer all around her." Maggy stopped and leaned forward. "It was the same woman I heard singing earlier."

"I gathered that from what you said."

"Oh, right. Look, I know this couldn't have happened. It must sound crazy to you. But it did happen! Not only did I see and hear her, but I recognized her. Her name is Beatrice."

Harry was absolutely still for a long moment, until Maggy finally turned away from him. It was no use. He didn't believe her.

"Who is Beatrice?" he asked.

"I don't know anything more than that. Just Beatrice. Who, or what she is—it's a mystery to me."

"Are you sure the name Beatrice doesn't mean anything to you?"

"I've never known anyone named Beatrice. And I'm positive I've never seen anyone like her." She laughed softly. "That's hardly a surprise."

"You got a nasty bump on the head when you fell. I think you should see a doctor while you're here, rather than wait until you return home. If there's something physically wrong with you, you need to take care of it right away."

"You mean if there's something wrong with me that would account for what I saw. Do you think I had a seizure?"

"It's not impossible. This could be the first sign of an illness that should be diagnosed and treated. It would be best to rule out any physical causes first."

"And then? If there's nothing physically wrong with me?"

"I don't know. Maybe overwork or stress could explain it. Or maybe it just can't be explained." He gave her hand a reassuring squeeze, though he still looked worried. "Why don't you rest here for a little while. I'll check back on you in a half hour or so."

"One other thing you should know," Maggy said. "She was very surprised and upset that I could see her. She kept saying something was wrong. Very wrong."

"On that point, she and I are in agreement." Harry's fingers brushed briefly against her face in a strangely comforting gesture. Then he left her alone with her thoughts. Her head still ached and her eyes were slightly sensitive to light, even in this dimly lit room. She closed her eyes and tried to relax the tension in her body. Had she really imagined the whole thing, as he suggested? She was glad she'd been reluctant to tell him about her emotional response to Beatrice, and the love she had felt radiating from her. He really would have thought that was crazy!

Well, it wasn't crazy; it was real. It was a profound and fantastic event that she had been privileged to witness, and she wasn't going to let him or her own skepticism convince her otherwise. She didn't need a doctor to tell her there was nothing wrong with her. There must be a reason, or at least an explanation, behind Beatrice's sudden appearance. Maggy would simply find out what it was.

Once the decision was made, she immediately began to feel better. This was territory that she understood. She would attack this problem just as she would any other research project, although it was true she'd never investigated visions or apparitions before. Maggy pulled a pencil and notepad from her purse and frowned in concentration. She would start with the assumption that Beatrice had once been a real person who could be found. She had her name, her physical description, and a possible connection with the castle. And maybe a connection to Maggy, herself. She knew that Beatrice had a voice that was more beautiful than anything she'd ever heard. And she knew that Beatrice liked the song Moonglow. That was hardly a wealth of information, but it was enough to start.

Maggy's fingers itched to get at her computer, where she could access on-line databases from libraries and universities around the world. She'd have to give Carol a call and ask her to help. She wondered what her friend would think of all that had happened this morning. At least Carol knew her, and knew that she wasn't some flighty mental case.

Without waiting for Harry, Maggy left the office and hurried down steps that she was sure led to the bus loading area. Instead she ran into another tour group. One of the guides escorted her in the opposite direction and put her on the next bus down to the visitor area. Well, so what! Who could blame her for getting a little lost after what she'd been through? Maggy was more determined than ever that Harry was wrong. She was going to prove to him that Beatrice was real.

* * *

"You've been through hell, haven't you?" Carol's familiar voice said over the phone. "Or, I should say, the opposite of hell from your description." Maggy could picture her sitting in her kitchen, twining the phone cord around her fingers.

"She was other-worldly, and more. I didn't tell Harry this, but I could feel love radiating from her like a physical touch. It was the most profound experience I've ever had. Anna would have said she was my guardian angel."

Maggy suddenly realized the significance of what she had just said so thoughtlessly. Of course Anna would have thought Beatrice was an angel. Anna had always been a believer. After what Maggy had witnessed this morning, the notion didn't seem as farfetched as it had before.

"It's far more likely than you having a hallucination. I've never known a more pragmatic person than you. And I mean that in the worst possible way."

Maggy laughed. "You love this, don't you? It's sure a switch from our usual roles."

"You said it. You're such a doubting Thomas, I'd just about given up hope. You gave be a terrible time when I joined the Church of New Enlightenment, remember?"

Actually, Maggy had though Carol was joining a band of crackpots. "Come on, that's not fair. They believed in seances, reincarnation and spirit guides," Maggy said.

"Maybe so, but you just saw an angel! What's more, I believe you really did."

"Thanks, Carol. For a while I was beginning to doubt myself. You must admit it sounds crazy. Harry certainly seemed to think so."

"What does he know? He's only just met you. And who is he anyway? It's very interesting you seem to care so much what he thinks."

"I don't really. Well, maybe I do a little. He was the museum curator for several years. He's just in town temporarily, and staying here at the Beach House Inn. I met him last night. I have an appointment with him to discuss Anna's diary."

"And?"

"And what?"

"Maggy, you haven't told me anything about him! Sometimes it's like pulling teeth to get anything out of you. What's he like?"

"Oh, all right! He's perfectly charming in an annoying way, and he makes me nervous and ridiculously tongue-tied. There. Are you happy now?"

"Yes, thank you."

"And you're going to stop giving me the third degree about Harry?"

"No, of course not! You've only told me that you like him more than you think you should. I want to know why. And don't just give me that tall, dark and handsome bit."

"He's not tall, dark, and handsome. He's blonde. I don't know how to describe the quality he has. He doesn't take things seriously; he's too busy being amused. And he seems fascinated by everything he sees."

"Fascinated by you, I bet."

"Oh, Carol. You've always been my biggest fan. But really, I don't know what to think about him. Especially after what happened today," Maggy said, and then laughed suddenly. "Well, that sure distracted me from my real troubles. I need your help on this, Carol. I want you to find out whatever you can about my angel, if that's what she is." Maggy explained her premise about Beatrice and quickly read down her short list of known data points.

"It's not much to work with. But I'm sure I can expand on that list and shed some light on your mysterious Beatrice."

"Do you realize I'm asking you to prove the existence of an angel?" Maggy asked. "After all the discussions I had with Anna on this very subject, she could never convince me. I don't know why this is happening to me! But I know what I saw."

"Why do you have to prove Beatrice is real? Isn't it enough that you saw her?"

"There's more to it than that. I don't know exactly."

"Never mind," Carol said. "I know why. Harry."

"Not just Harry. When I saw Beatrice, she was terribly upset by the fact that I could see her. She said it shouldn't have happened. But it did happen, and I want to find out why. I want to help her if I can."

After she hung up, Maggy thought again about Anna's certainty that angels were as real as the sun rising each morning. She wondered if they had each been blessed with the same vision. Maybe it ran in the family. Her smile was tinged with regret as she picked up the diary.

Anna's Diary—October 14, 1936

Today marks my third month at the castle. Some of the wonders I see each day have become almost routine. Yet I must confess to being a bit star-struck by the famous guests that visit here so often. My only contact with the real world is my weekly visit to father, and even then I spend the time weaving fairy tales for him about life at the castle. Only my fairy stories are nothing but truth.

When I lived at home we looked forward to a special outing to see a movie at San Louis Obispo. Cambria is much too small to have its own movie theater. But how we loved those festive trips, especially when mother was alive. Now I can see a new film almost every night in Mr. Hearst's private theater, if I wish. Most of these films are so new they haven't been released from the studios yet. There are two showings each evening at 7:00 and 11:00pm. Mr. Hearst allows household staff to attend the early showing in the theater with its overstuffed, velvet loge seats and crimson silk-covered walls. Fifteen-foot, gilt-painted caryatids hold bouquets of electric lights that dim when the film is shown. This evening some of us attended the 11:00 showing of the Katharine Hepburn movie 'Sylvia Scarlett,' right along with Mr. Hearst and his guests. Cary Grant was so dashing in his role and even more so in person, for he was sitting just a few rows in front me. There were only two dozen guests tonight, so I sat with some of the kitchen staff in the huge loge seats in the last row. The audience can sometimes be quite ruthless with nasty comments about a film, but all of them agreed that this effort was marvelous and sure to be a smash hit.

I'm becoming familiar with quite a few famous faces. Marion Davies invites many of her film-star friends for weekend visits at the castle. Charlie Chaplin is a frequent visitor, and always clowning with everyone, even those of us who have work to do! Last week I escorted Prince Louis Ferdinand of Liechtenstein to his rooms at "A" House. What a handsome man he is! Then I had Emma show me on the map exactly where Liechtenstein is, since I certainly didn't remember it from my geography class.

Welcoming the guests is my favorite duty. No matter how exalted or famous they are, each one of them is quite dazzled by the castle and the accommodations. After I settle them in their rooms, I show them the controls to the radio and music selections. There is a phonograph in one of the basement vaults that plays the latest musical recordings throughout the day, and I make sure each guest has a list of that day's entertainment. They can also tune in to six different radio stations from San Francisco or Los Angeles. I make sure they have the card listing the day's menu and dining hour, and the title of the evening film. If a guest forgets to bring the smallest necessity, they just let me know. The castle has almost anything they can ask for, toiletries, bathing suits, riding clothes, boots, a barber, even a beauty salon.

Some guests can still find fault, however. Emma told me that one of them complained when he wasn't permitted to bring his own valet to the castle, but had to make do with one of us. Another was quite disconcerted when she was denied breakfast in bed, not even so much as a cup of coffee. Mr. Hearst doesn't approve of breakfast in bed. He says if people don't get up and get dressed they might waste away hours that could be better spent outdoors.

Some guests are not famous, but are even more fascinating in their own way. Mrs. Page is like that, with her dark beauty and her kind voice. Emma said that she's a widow. She has come here several times, and sometimes stays in "A" House. She usually comes with her two friends Mr. Winter and Mr. Orcutt. She and Mr. Orcutt are older, perhaps the same age as Miss Davies. Mr. Winter is quite young though, I'd say he is only a few years older than I. The three of them are often together. Mr. Winter is more handsome than any of the film stars that visit, his hair brushed with gold from the sun, and eyes bluer than the Pacific. Even more handsome than Prince Louis Ferdinand. Mr. Winter is in every respect a fine gentleman, and just as nice to me as Mrs. Page. Neither of them ever look at me as though, by being a servant, I'm somehow less than a person. Or worse, as though I'm invisible. I have unfortunately seen this behavior in many of the other guests. I suppose I shouldn't be surprised. But Mrs. Page and Mr. Winter always have a warm smile for me and can spare a moment for conversation. I look forward to their visits with pleasure.

Maggy closed the diary slowly, reluctant to leave Anna's world of 1936. She noticed the time and realized the Clarks would be expecting her for dinner soon. A good thing, since she had completely forgotten to eat lunch.

This time Maggy was careful to take the left turn at the end of the hallway, which took her directly to the dining room.

* * *

Harry drove down the hill from the castle in a black mood. What in the hell was that all about? The truth was he was furious with himself. Why hadn't he called Maggy's bluff right away? But she had caught him completely off guard. The last thing he'd expected from her was the scene she'd created. It was almost as if he believed she was actually seeing something, some vision. And that was impossible.

As a researcher, she was wasting her life. She could be the darling of millions as an actress. The whine of his engine told him he'd forgotten to shift gears. Cursing under his breath, Harry slammed into fourth and straightened out from a hairpin turn he'd taken too fast.

He thought of the way he'd reacted to her as she stood there by the pool, talking to thin air. The hair had stood up on the back of his neck as he watched her. Her face—he'd never seen that expression on anyone's face before. Even now it got to him. She got to him, period. When he'd met her earlier at the Roman pool, he'd wanted her to reveal herself to him. He'd stared at her as though he could will her to tell him the truth. Instead, he'd found himself lost in those artless, green eyes. He had resisted an overwhelming urge to pull her into his arms, to part her delicate lips with kisses.

He took a deep breath and relaxed his foot on the gas pedal. He'd better think this through before he saw her again. His initial reaction to her act had been on a gut level. He'd been worried about her, for God's sake! And then she'd taken off without waiting for him. Probably didn't want to press her luck any further.

As he turned out of the visitor parking lot onto the highway, an unwelcome thought occurred to him. What if it wasn't an act? He didn't think for a minute that she'd seen anything real, but what if she'd really had some kind of seizure? He'd called Nancy before he left to make sure Maggy had gotten back to the inn in one piece. Apparently nothing was wrong with her.

No, it had to be an act. That was the only explanation. How else could she have come up with the name Beatrice? It couldn't be a coincidence. If he was going to find out what her game was, he'd have to be more careful in his dealings with her.

* * *

"Maggy, there you are," said Nancy Clark cheerfully. "Please sit down and join us. You must tell us about your tour this morning, and what you think of Mr. Hearst's ranch."

There were two more people at the table that Maggy hadn't met, which left the only vacant place next to Harry. She took it reluctantly, aware of his intense gaze following her. Well, so what if she'd left the castle without telling him? She straightened her shoulders and turned to face him.

"It was fantastic," Maggy said. "I didn't have a chance to thank you, Harry, for showing me the restoration vaults and the Roman pool."

"And the Neptune pool, don't forget," he added, his eyes unwavering. She felt the beginnings of a blush on her cheeks, he was staring at her so pointedly.

"Where are my manners!" Nancy said. "You know Liz and Brian Sorenson, but you haven't met our guests from Boston." Nancy introduced the Wrights, an older couple visiting their grown children in Monterey. Maggy realized with relief that no one else had noticed Harry's behavior, or the tension between them.

Conversation drifted in a pleasant buzz that required little attention on Maggy's part. She concentrated instead on the hearty meal that Nancy had prepared, a rich Belgian beef stew prepared with caramelized onions and dark beer.

Harry spoke to her quietly. "Why didn't you wait for me? I was worried when I came back and you were gone."

"I just felt restless," Maggy said. She was glad that he was the one who seemed a little unbalanced now. "I decided to come back on my own, since I had some phone calls to make."

"How do you feel now?"

"Fine. Thanks for your concern, but it's really unnecessary. In fact, I spent part of the afternoon reading Anna's diary."

"Oh?" Harry said and leaned back in his chair, the intensity in his eyes replaced by a speculative look. "What did you find?"

"I simply found—Anna. Her life at the castle was filled with hard work, but it was also a great adventure."

"Have you decided yet about donating the diary to us?"

"Yes, I think it should go to the state museum. But not until I've read all of it. Some things that she's written might be private."

"That's wonderful, and I understand completely. Perhaps I could begin studying the diary as soon as you're through?"

"The volumes aren't very long. I can finish the first one and let you have it tomorrow."

"Good. I'd like to show you our staff library tomorrow, if you're interested. Not quite as impressive as the Gothic Library at La Casa Grande, but it's a treasure trove of information about the castle itself."

Before Maggy could answer, a cheerful voice called out, "Everyone look this way please. And smile!" Mrs. Wright had stepped back from the table and was about to snap a photo of the little group.

Harry abruptly stood up and was at her side in two strides. "This is your vacation, so you should be included in the picture. Please, allow me."

"You'll never get Harry in a picture, anyway," Nancy said. "I don't know why a good-looking man like you is so camera shy."

"You flatter me shamelessly, Nancy," Harry said with a smile, as Mrs. Wright sat down next to her husband. "Now, everyone ready?" He took two photos and handed the camera back to Mrs. Wright, amid much good-humored chatter.

As the group began to say its good-nights, Harry helped Maggy up from her chair, his hand lingering on her arm. "Will you meet me tomorrow? I promise our library is a researcher's dream."

"I'd love to see it," Maggy said, all too aware of his touch and the way he bent toward her as he spoke. They made arrangements to meet at the visitor center the following morning. Maggy went to her room much relieved from her earlier state, but no less determined to find the mysterious Beatrice.

* * *

Beatrice was at that moment standing beneath a profusion of lush grapevines that covered the espalier several feet above her. Flowering peach trees scented the evening air with a subtle perfume. She sipped a Brandy Alexander absently, and was hardly aware of the perfection of the scene around her. She stood under the pergola where she had met Ambrose earlier, though this structure was in the First Level of Heaven, rather than the mortal plane. A faint luminance radiated from every growing thing around her. The full moon illuminated the ocean below. She remembered her agreement to meet Ambrose in the mortal plane. With a regretful sigh, she focused on the glass in her hand and caused it to disappear. Then with a deeper concentration, she willed herself into the mortal plane.

The light suddenly dimmed and objects became dull before her eyes. Where the pergola had been a leafy garden, it was now bare and falling into disrepair. The moon above would no doubt please a mortal eye, but to Beatrice it was a pale echo of its Heavenly twin. A cloud drifted over the face of the moon, and the surrounding hillside fell into deeper shadows.

"Beatrice! At last you're here. I have much to tell you," said Ambrose with some impatience. His white hair was neatly combed, and he had replaced the white robes he wore during their last encounter with khaki slacks and a plaid shirt. He looked like a kindly grandfather or uncle, quite unremarkable except for the faint glow that surrounded him.

"I'm glad you've learned something. I'm afraid I haven't made much progress. I haven't spoken to Roland yet. Maybe I'll have to ask for his help after all."

"I see no reason to bother him. I have even more cause to suspect that this dilemma has something to do with you, Beatrice. Maggy has a very strong connection with the castle. Her grandmother, Anna, lived here in the thirties. She worked here as a housemaid. Do you remember her?"

"I've told you, Ambrose, my memories are sporadic. I scarcely remember my hosts. It seems to me there was a small army of household staff," Beatrice said. They began walking along the wide bridle path, which was illuminated by the light emanating from their bodies.

"I want you to try harder, Beatrice. She was just a girl when she worked there, barely eighteen years old. She resembled Maggy a good deal. Didn't Maggy seem at all familiar to you?"

Beatrice paused. "It did seem as though I had seen her before. I was so shocked by my meeting with her, I didn't notice it at the time. But, yes, there was something familiar about her. Perhaps her voice, or the way she smiled at me so beautifully."

"That's better. Now, try to think of that, but let yourself drift back. Try to remember that face back in 1936."

Beatrice closed her eyes and pictured Maggy's sweet smile. She held that image and journeyed back to the furthest limits of her memory, and then strained to reach even further. For a moment she saw another face, very like Maggy's, framed with light brown hair. Then it was gone.

"I'm sorry. I almost remembered her. I must have known her, but there's nothing else. It's just beyond my grasp."

Ambrose began walking again and kicked a small rock off the path. "Blast! Well, don't worry yet, Beatrice. We still have another avenue open to us. Anna left a diary of her experiences at the castle. Maggy is reading it now and will pass it on to Harry when she's done. She wants to donate it to the museum. Perhaps the diary will offer some explanation of your bond with Maggy."

"Maybe something in the diary will help me remember," Beatrice said hopefully. "What happened to Anna?"

"She lived a good life. Anna died last year when she was in her late seventies. You might have rubbed shoulders with her in Heaven and not recognized her."

"Perhaps. Or she could have passed the First Level altogether and gone directly to a higher level. She could have even gone back to earth immediately to start a new life."

"At any rate, she isn't here now to help us."

"What about Harry? Does he still think Maggy is suffering a mental breakdown?"

"He's still worried about her, but I think he's withholding judgment for the time being. He's extremely interested in Anna's diaries. From what I can see, that interest extends to Maggy herself."

Chapter 6

❖

Anna's Diary, December 10, 1936

I've just returned to the castle from my weekly visit with father. I can see his health is failing, though he remains uncomplaining. I feel terrible when I leave him, and yet I'm happy to be back at the castle. I know we depend on the income I receive from my job at the castle, but I still feel guilty. He has no one to look after him now, just Mrs. Sulley. She is a godsend, but she is only a neighbor, not family. There are no other positions to be had anywhere near Cambria or San Simeon, so I would have to leave him one way or another. Still, it hurts us both.

We've begun a routine with our visits, where I regale him with tales of the castle and one famous guest after another. Often we laugh together like two children at the antics of Miss Davies' visitors. Mr. Hearst does his best to keep them in check, but they're sometimes filled with too much vitality for their own

good. Or, perhaps, with too much whiskey. Two drinks are served at the dinner hour and no further spirits are offered. Emma told me that all the staff
know about Marion Davies' fondness for liquor, and Mr. Hearst's efforts to
keep her and her guests in check.

It's a brave soul who disregards Mr. Hearst's strict rules about drinking to
excess. The guilty parties go back to their rooms and find their bags packed and
a car waiting to take them down the hill at once. Some favored guests will get
a second chance, however. Not long ago, in the throws of an alcoholic revelry,
these particular visitors made a midnight raid out to the gardens, where they
clothed the Water Nymph, the Three Graces, and other nude statues in various pieces of borrowed underwear. Much to my delight, I saw the stately sculptures myself early the next morning, with satin panties and lace brassieres modestly covering them. I was relieved that the culprits were not sent down the hill.
Instead, when they went to the Refectory for dinner, they were banished to the
end of the table, far from the other guests. Carefully arranged on the table in
front of their place settings was a pile of empty whiskey and gin bottles. The
warning was a little joke from Mr. Hearst, but the point has been taken,
I think.

I was very pleased to welcome Mr. Winter back to the castle last week. He's
here this time without Mrs. Page or Mr. Orcutt. I believe he has some business
with Mr. Hearst, something to do with Mr. Hearst's art collection. Emma told
me there are several huge warehouses near the pier in San Simeon filled with
treasures waiting to be installed at the castle. I find this truly amazing, since
every one of the rooms I've seen is already bursting with artwork, tapestries,
antique furniture, even antique carved ceilings overhead. Emma just smiled
and said, "That must be why he keeps building."

There may be some truth in that. I've grown so used to the sound of hammers pounding and workmen shouting to each other, I scarcely notice it anymore. It's just part of life here at the castle. Miss Morgan is often here, consulting with Mr. Hearst and quietly directing construction in her role as architect. Building has apparently gone on non-stop for the past seventeen years,
almost from the time I was born. I believe perfection has already been

achieved, but Mr. Hearst must not agree. Perhaps his notion of perfection is that it can always be made more perfect. If that's true, his castle might never be completed.

December 11, 1936

Everyone is buzzing with the news. Today, King Edward VIII of England announced he is abdicating the throne to marry an American divorcee, Wallis Simpson. Yesterday his resignation was read to the House of Commons, and today he spoke in a radio broadcast to Britain and the rest of the world. Emma and I stopped our cleaning to listen to his voice on the radio. The words were riveting.

"I have found it impossible to carry the heavy burden of responsibility and to discharge my duties as King as I would wish to do without the help and support of the woman I love."

To give up a kingdom for love! It's the most wonderful, romantic gesture I've ever imagined, despite Emma's arguments. She was quick to point out that he will still be quite horribly rich, even if he must resign himself to being merely the Duke of Windsor instead of King. Many of his British subjects think he's a traitor to have chosen Mrs. Simpson over England. They must believe that duty takes precedence over love. I think their opposition only makes his action more brave and magnificent. My only worry is that Mrs. Simpson has been divorced twice. I don't know much about love, but two failed marriages don't bode well for the future of the third. No. That couldn't be true. She must be worthy, for him to make such a sacrifice. Like a fairy tale come to life.

This is the kind of love that I wish for in my heart. A love that transcends all obstacles of wealth or position. I wonder if I'll ever know such love, or meet such a man. I've often wondered what he would be like, and if I would recognize him instantly when we meet. Will he be handsome and kind, like Mr. Winter, or perhaps someone that I might not notice on first acquaintance? I must admit that my thoughts turn to Mr. Winter often. He is like a scattering of sunshine on a gray day.

*Enough of these childish musings. I must be about my work. It is too easy
to dream in such surroundings, and think that anything is possible.*

Maggy finished reading the last page of the diary and sat pensive for a
moment, staring out the window at the shore, shrouded now in mist. She
agreed with every word Anna had written, but recognized that times had
certainly changed since 1936. What a tumultuous era that was, with the
world just recovering from the agony of a global economic depression, and
poised on the brink of World War II.

And what a grand gesture King Edward made in giving up the throne.
He could have taken a socially acceptable wife, and kept Wallis Simpson
as his mistress. Edward would have gotten away with it in his day, without the press prying into his private life. In the thirties, a wife would have
been forced to look the other way rather than create a scandal, particularly
if she was the Queen of England. Then Maggy vaguely remembered something about King Edward being a Nazi sympathizer, that he'd been forced
to give up the throne for that reason. Love for Wallace Simpson was just
a cover.

Anna had been thrilled with the romance of it, but time had revealed
the fairy tale for what it was.

She closed the diary and put it down on the desk next to several books
that had been there when she arrived. She felt suddenly very alone. Earlier
she had glanced through the journal that was left on the little writing desk
in her room. The Clarks kept a similar journal in each of the guest rooms
for their visitors to share any thoughts or discoveries with other guests.
Apparently most of them were on their honeymoon or celebrating a wedding anniversary and all were deliriously in love, even if their writing skills
left something to be desired. Though her best friend had been happily
married for several years, Maggy seldom felt like the odd-man out. But
now she felt an unexpected loneliness that threatened to overwhelm her.
She had been successful in denying it, but it was a familiar ache that had

been with her ever since Anna died. She had no family left, no parents, no husband or children. She was, quite simply, alone.

Maggy looked back sadly to her time with Jason. She had wanted to be in love so much that she had ignored those nuances, the little warning signals that told her something was wrong. She must have known that open confrontation would have ended their affair, so she said nothing. She took the coward's way out with Jason. But she'd never do that again. She would insist on honesty, no matter how much it might hurt. And someday she'd find a man who believed the same way.

God, how melodramatic she was being! She was no better than eighteen year old Anna, yearning for an all-encompassing passion, for a man who loved her enough to give up a kingdom for her. Or at least enough to build a life together, since she wasn't likely to run into any royalty soon.

Maggy closed the diary abruptly and put it in her purse to give to Harry. She had other things to think about than the dismal state of her love life. She had a mystery to solve, and she was hopeful that the resource library Harry mentioned might prove a fertile hunting ground. At least she'd be taking action instead of waiting for Carol to call her back. She was also curious to find out what Harry thought about Anna's diary.

As Maggy headed out to her car for the short drive up the coast to the Visitor Center, she saw the countryside was blanketed by a layer of mist that drifted in wispy tendrils with the wind. She could smell the salt air and hear the surf breaking to her left on Moonstone Beach Drive, but the ocean was invisible. Weather guaranteed to frizz your hair. She turned on her headlights as cars loomed out of patches of dense fog ahead.

A good day for the blues. She rummaged in her purse for one of her tapes and put on an old Harold Arlen song that was so depressing it usually had the reverse effect on her mood. She sang at the top of her voice.

I got a right to sing the blues,
I got a right to moan and sigh,
I got a right to sit and cry

Down around the river.
A certain man in this old town
Keeps draggin' my poor heart around
And all I see for me is
Mi-ser-y.

Sure enough, Maggy felt the corners of her mouth twitching in a smile. How could you be depressed singing the blues? She felt much better.

As she parked at the Visitor Center, Harry appeared by her window. "Hi, Maggy. Foggy days must agree with you. I bet this weather seems just like home."

"I'm afraid you'd lose that bet. We don't get this kind of fog in Portland, mostly just rain."

"You look lovely, despite the gloomy weather." He held the door for her as she got out of her car. "We'll have to take my car up the hill since they won't let us on the private drive without a permit," Harry said as he led her to a Landrover parked nearby.

He drove leisurely up the same narrow road the bus had taken yesterday, its hairpin turns treacherous now in the pockets of dense fog. While he concentrated on the road ahead, Maggy found herself studying him intently. He was wearing faded jeans and a light green T-shirt, hardly the look you would expect for a museum curator. Former curator, she corrected herself. His sandy hair was sun-streaked and just as unruly as the first time she'd seen him. He wore the same glasses, perched on a straight nose. Everything about his face was strong and distinct, particularly the high cheekbones and clean line of his jaw. She noticed well-defined muscles in his arms and wondered what an art historian did to keep so fit. She felt a sudden urge to touch the blond hairs glistening on the golden skin of his forearms.

Maggy suddenly snapped out of her reverie and looked up to find Harry watching her. She felt an embarrassed flush heat her face, but found it impossible to look away. He held her look for a long moment. This time he didn't tease her or make some smart remark. Instead he pointed out a break in the mist ahead.

"Look off to your right. Those aoudads are descendants from Hearst's zoo," Harry said, pointing to three large animals that resembled mountain goats with magnificent curved horns. "Along with zebras, tahr goats and elk, they're the only animals that could thrive here without care. When he sold off the zoo in the thirties there were over six hundred animals in his collection."

Maggy was grateful for the distraction from the uncomfortably intimate glance they had shared. "At least now we won't be stopped here on the road by a buffalo or lion or some other creature," she said.

"Good point. It was common in those days to wait for an animal that blocked the road, much to the irritation of Hearst's guests. You had to pass through three gates, whose sole purpose was to separate the different species of animals. Since some of the animals were dangerous, it wasn't always safe to leave your car. He meant it when he said animals have the right of way."

They drove below the first guest house and the lower terrace of the Neptune Pool and then turned left to a parking lot next to a large double-wide trailer.

"I didn't notice this when I took the tour," Maggy said.

"That's why we keep it hidden. It would spoil the ambiance, don't you think?" They walked into a single long room that was filled with bookcases on every side. In the center were tables, some holding computer terminals. Maggy could see newspaper and magazine racks as well as an old-fashioned card catalogue.

"We're in the process of transferring everything to computer," Harry said. "As you can imagine, there are always more important uses for funding, so it's a slow process."

"But well worth it, just for the ease of doing computer searches."

"You'll get no argument from me there. This is the definitive resource for information about the castle. There's so much material that none of the tours can possibly include it all. The tour guides delve into whatever interests them, so they can give their tours a personal touch."

"I could see that in my tour yesterday," Maggy said.

Harry stopped by one of the tables and turned toward her. "Are you feeling better today? No lingering effects from your experience by the Neptune Pool?" he asked.

"No, I'm fine. I'd like to look through the material here to see if there are any references to my grandmother," Maggy said. She didn't want to tell him that she was really looking for Beatrice, not Anna. Not when she had so little information to go on.

"Okay. You can use this station." Harry quickly showed her the database they were using, one that she was already familiar with. "You'll also find personal letters, photographs, and documents from the castle operation, as well as newspaper and magazine articles." He indicated shelves of oversized books containing documents and photographs.

"Thanks, Harry. This is wonderful."

"Did you remember to bring Anna's diary for me?" Harry reminded her.

"Oh, I forgot! I mean, I have it right here. I just forgot to give it to you. Sorry," Maggy said as she took the diary from her bag.

Silence descended on the room as Harry read the diary and Maggy started to formulate queries about Beatrice. After a number of failed attempts, she decided to look for material on Anna. Two entries came up immediately. The first was a listing of household staff in 1936–37. The second was a photograph.

Maggy looked up the call letters and found a large scrapbook filled with carefully labeled photographs. She turned to page 97, but was disappointed to find no picture of Anna there. She checked her call numbers again, but there was no mistake. She leafed through the large book, fascinated by pictures of Clarke Gable and Carole Lombard dressed as cowboys, and Claudette Colbert dressed as an Indian maiden. Just as interesting were photos of the huge staff Hearst needed to run his ranch. She saw the zoo veterinarian holding a tiny lion cub, and a domestic staff member reaching up to feed a baby giraffe with a milk bottle. There were photographs of electricians, chauffeurs, the head gardener Nigel Keep, construction workers, and a host of artisans. One picture showed Prince Louis Ferdinand of Liechtenstein with the head housekeeper. Maggy looked closely at the photograph. Anna was right, this guy was a knockout.

She turned the next page and there was a picture of Anna, sitting in a lawn chair by the pillars of the Neptune Pool! The woman sitting next to her was identified as Emma Sunderson. Anna smiled into the camera, a hand shading her eyes from the sun.

Maggy called Harry over to see her discovery. "You resemble your grandmother quite a bit," he said.

"Do you think so?" Maggy hadn't really thought of it before.

"Yes. Especially your smile." As he spoke he touched her shoulder. She wanted suddenly to lean into his touch, to get closer to him. Instead she stood quite still. She turned the page of the scrapbook, not really seeing the photographs. She felt him stiffen and drop his hand from her arm.

As her gaze focused on the photographs, one image suddenly penetrated her consciousness with a jolt. It was Beatrice! She gasped and clutched Harry's arm.

"Harry, it's her! That's a picture of Beatrice."

"You mean the woman you saw—"

"Yes, yes, it's her. What does it say about her?"

"Guests for a convivial weekend at San Simeon include David Niven, Charlie Chaplin, Norma Shearer, Beatrice Page, Edward Orcutt and Logan Winter."

"Anna wrote about her. Mrs. Page! Harry, do you realize what this means?"

"No, I don't—"

Maggy was giddy with excitement. "Oh, it means all sorts of wonderful things. It means I'm not crazy and I didn't imagine her. It means that she was a real person. She looked exactly the same, only—filled with light somehow." She stopped suddenly as she realized the enormity of what she had just said. "Anna was right all along. There is life after death! My God!"

Maggy looked at Harry. "You have to believe me now. This proves that I didn't just make her up out of thin air. She's real."

"There are still all kinds of rationale explanations for what happened. Maybe you saw a photograph of Beatrice long ago and forgot it, or maybe Anna mentioned her to you." He turned his blue eyes full on hers. "The photograph proves Beatrice Page was a real person, beyond a doubt." He took her hand. "I want to believe you, Maggy, more than you know."

"But you don't." Maggy realized she had been holding her breath, as she let go a sigh of disappointment. Why had she thought he'd believe her?

"I'm sorry," he said, and leaned forward to brush his lips against hers ever so gently. She didn't want to respond to his touch, but a shiver went through her. For a moment her heart seemed to stop beating. She looked up at him quickly, her feelings a mass of contradictions. She put some distance between them and turned back to look at the photograph.

"I'd like to make a copy of this, if it's all right," she said. "And also the staff list from that period."

"The photo won't reproduce well on our copy machine, but you're welcome to use it," Harry said and showed her the combination fax copier next to the computers. After she had made a passable copy, Maggy looked at the faded images again.

"What year was this picture taken, does it say?" she asked.

"Yes, it's here. May, 1936."

"So that would have been just before Anna started working at the castle."

"If your grandmother knew Beatrice Page, maybe you know something about her even if you don't realize it. Something troubling enough to have caused your vision." Harry closed the photo album.

"I don't want to argue with you, since you don't believe me anyway," Maggy said. "This is the last time I'm going to tell you—I wasn't hallucinating. I think Beatrice appeared to me for a reason. Maybe I can figure it out if I learn more about her life. Anna wrote about Beatrice's friends, Mr. Orcutt and Mr. Winter." She took the album from Harry. He seemed in a hurry to put it away, but Maggy wasn't done yet. The copy she had made wasn't nearly this good. She studied the picture of Orcutt. He was just as tall as Beatrice, with dark hair and piercing eyes that looked black in the photograph. He was standing close to her with his hand on her arm. It seemed a possessive gesture to Maggy.

"Anna wrote that Orcutt and Beatrice were older, as old as Miss Davies. That would be late thirties, maybe even forty. But Winter was much younger. I think Anna had a crush on Mr. Winter, from the way she wrote about him," Maggy said. "Too bad you can't see him very well in this picture." Winter was several inches taller than Orcutt, but standing behind him and turned away from the camera. His face was blurred as though he had been moving when the picture was taken. There was an impression of light-colored hair and little else.

"Logan Winter," Maggy said. "That's odd. Are you related to him, by any chance?"

Harry leaned closer to look at the photograph. "You mean because his name is Logan? Not to my knowledge. I've traced the Logan name back a few generations in my family, but I've never heard it used as a first name."

"I wonder who your namesake was, for Anna to think so highly of him?"

"Your guess is as good as mine, Maggy." He closed the large book again and placed it back on the shelves, then turned to give her an inquiring look. "So, where do we go from here?"

"I'm going to find out everything I can about Beatrice Page and her two mysterious friends. Come on." She went back to the computer and entered a query on Beatrice Page. The message came back "No entries found." She typed in the names Edward Orcutt and then Logan Winter. Both queries came up empty.

"That's funny. It doesn't even list the picture we found already. And we know from Anna's diary that they were frequent guests here." Maggy said.

"Perhaps the material covering them hasn't been transferred to the database yet," Harry suggested.

"Then it should still be in card catalogue, shouldn't it?"

A thorough search of the old file cards failed to turn up any of the three names.

"I think it's odd that they aren't listed here at all," Maggy said. "And Anna's picture wasn't in the book where it was listed in the database file. Could someone have tampered with these records?"

"It's possible, but I doubt it. We have a sophisticated electronic security system to protect against theft and vandalism. There was a terrorist bombing here in the seventies that destroyed a small part of one of the guest houses."

"That was after Patty Hearst was kidnapped, wasn't it?"

"Yes. That's when the security systems were put in place. The safeguards in the library aren't nearly as elaborate. But it's more likely that a simple filing error was made. There are thousands of documents on file here."

"You mean a series of filing errors, all related to the same group of people," she said. "And you think a coincidence like that is more likely?"

"More likely than a visit from a ghost."

Maggy's face colored at his words. "She wasn't a ghost. She wasn't some moaning, shattered spirit haunting the castle grounds. She was glorious! Anna tried to convince me that we all have guardian angels, but I didn't believe her for a minute."

"You believe she was an angel?" Harry looked genuinely shocked. Maggy felt a little better, but she didn't see why it made any difference to him. Ghost or angel, he still didn't believe any of it.

"Yes, that's exactly what she was. And it doesn't really matter what you think about it." She was feeling better by the moment.

"I've never been much of a believer," Harry said. "If it were true, then angels haven't been much help to us, given the misery and horror on this earth."

"I'm not trying to solve the meaning of life, Harry. Angels must have their troubles, too. Beatrice said I wasn't supposed to see her, that something was wrong."

Harry ran a hand through his hair in frustration. "I didn't experience what you did, Maggy. All rational thought goes against it. More than that, I can't say."

Maggy smiled at him, somewhat mollified. "I don't really blame you. If our situations were reversed, I probably wouldn't believe you either."

Harry returned her smile. "I'm glad you're not holding it against me. I hope you'll let me help you. Maybe together we can find something that will make me change my mind."

"You don't believe that for a minute, but thanks," Maggy said. Even though he thought she was crazy, the notion of him helping out didn't bother her after all.

Chapter 7

❖

*M*aggy hung up the phone and drummed her fingers impatiently on the desktop. "Damn! Of all the times for Carol not to be home!"

She had an hour to kill before Carol would call her back. She didn't feel like waiting in her room at the inn, charming as it was. She suddenly realized she was starving. She'd had only coffee this morning and it was already past lunch time.

Maggy decided to walk along the beach to a little restaurant she'd seen earlier. The mist had all but burned away, leaving the day sunny and warm with a fog bank hovering far on the horizon. She waved to Mr. Clark as she walked through his garden and crossed the street to the well-marked trail along the beach.

Her thoughts were racing as she walked slowly past low, rocky cliffs with occasional wooden steps leading down to the beach. More than anything, she wished she could talk to Anna about the remarkable events that had happened. Not just because Anna might know something about Beatrice, but for her insight into Maggy's own heart. Anna had been mother, father and best friend to Maggy from her earliest memories. No one could ease a wound, or help untangle a difficult problem like Anna. Just by listening, and believing in Maggy's ability and common sense, she had made Maggy feel strong.

Strangely enough, Harry was having a similar effect on her. The fact that he didn't believe her made her want to prove him wrong. Well, not just prove him wrong, though that would be pleasant. What she really wanted was to share this newfound wonder with him. This absolute conviction that real angels coexist with us. What was it about Harry that made her feel this way? They'd known each other for less than two days! But she had to admit, the two days since they'd met were far from ordinary.

Her feelings for Harry were far from ordinary. She might as well face it. Despite her best intentions, she wanted to get closer to him. The kiss he had brushed against her lips had filled her with such yearning, she'd been afraid to move.

Up until yesterday, she had been just like him. She was notoriously short on faith, especially when it came to supernatural events, spirits, or angels.

And there was that word again. Angel. Her mind filled with the vision of Beatrice showering light in the darkness of day, and the loving touch of her hand. What she had seen couldn't possibly be real, yet she felt a certainty that she had never experienced in her life. Trying to describe it in rationale terms was like trying to describe the color violet to someone who had been blind since birth. Maggy offered up a little apology to her grandmother, wherever she might be. Anna had tried to tell her.

She crossed back over the road to the little restaurant, a small, two-story house with weathered clapboard siding. Like all the other buildings she had seen on Moonstone Beach Drive, it was well tended. A garden of low growing ground cover with bright yellow flowers bordered the entryway.

After a leisurely lunch of clam chowder and salad, Maggy felt her impatience return. She could barely wait to tell Carol what had happened, and enlist her help again.

She saw the requisite hour had passed, so she quickly paid her bill and covered the quarter-mile back to the inn in record time.

"Carol! You're home finally," she said with relief.

"I am allowed out of the house occasionally."

"Come on, I've been dying to talk to you. You'll never guess what happened. I found Beatrice!"

"Well, I found her too. But you first," came Carol's surprising answer.

Maggy explained to her about the photograph, and the lack of any reference to Beatrice in the library database.

"Well, that fits with what I've been able to uncover, which is much more substantial, if I do say so myself," Carol said.

"I'm at a little disadvantage here without my computer, you know."

"No excuses. Prepare to be amazed while I run and get my notes." Maggy could hear Carol talking to her husband in the background. "I'm back. Now, this is what I found. Beatrice Page was a widow, formerly married to Maxwell Page who was a successful lyricist and composer. She was a popular singer with quite a following, apparently performing a lot of her husband's material as well as current hits. She sang on several of the national radio shows—you know, the thirties version of MTV. I have it here somewhere." Maggy heard papers rattling.

"Here it is. She was on Manhattan Merry Go Round and the Ed Sullivan Show, and a whole list of other shows. They moved to Los Angeles from New York in 1930 and worked in radio and films until he died in 1934. She dropped out of sight after that. No children. Beatrice had a brief comeback as a singer just before she died in 1937. She was 43." Carol stopped. "Well?"

"Whew. I'm impressed, I have to admit. Wait, when did you say she died?"

"May, 1937."

"That's awfully close to the time Anna was writing about. Did you find out how she died?"

"Let's see." Maggy twisted the phone cord while Carol searched back through her material. "Here it is. 'Death of singer ruled accidental.' It seems she had an accident while—oh, my God! I didn't notice this before."

"What?"

"Maggy, this is weird. She died in a riding accident at Hearst Castle. I don't like it."

Maggy was stunned. "She died here?"

"Not in Cambria. She died at the castle. There aren't any more details; just that it was a fall, some kind of riding accident."

"I don't understand. What can it have to do with the fact that I saw her?"

"I have a bad feeling about this, Maggy," Carol said. "I want you to be careful."

"Carol, be serious. That happened almost sixty years ago. I think you're over reacting. But it is possible that Anna knew something."

"What about the fact that all references to Beatrice were removed from the library at the castle."

"I didn't say they were removed, they just weren't there," Maggy said.

"Oh, really?"

"Okay, okay. Something doesn't make sense here, I'll admit. If it will make you happy, I promise I'll be careful."

"Good," Carol said, somewhat appeased.

"You'd better see what you can find out about Edward Orcutt and Logan Winter. They were friends of Beatrice who always came with her to the castle."

"My pleasure. Is that Orcutt with two t's? And Winter as in season?"

"Yes on both counts," Maggy answered.

"Okay. So, how's Harry?"

"Just as cynical as I used to be."

"You mean he doesn't buy it that you saw an angel? What did you expect?"

"Yeah, I know," Maggy said. "I just wanted him to believe me. He was there when it happened."

"He didn't see anything, right? Hey, I only believe you because I know you. A stranger would have to think you had a seizure or something. And he just met you!"

"I know. He wants to help me find out more about Beatrice."

"Uh-oh. I feel responsible for this Maggy, goading you into a romance again."

"You don't have that much influence on me. Don't flatter yourself! Besides, nothing much has happened yet. Just a kiss."

"Just a kiss? Just a kiss! You're in trouble, girl. When you say nothing much has happened yet, I worry."

"There's nothing to worry about, for Heaven's sake."

"Yeah, right. And Heaven is where Beatrice is."

"Carol, come on. Beatrice died in an accident. But even if it wasn't an accident, it was sixty years ago! So let's see, I should be worried about a possible murderer who would have to be at least eighty or ninety years old. Is he going to cane me to death? Get a grip!"

Carol laughed. "Okay, you win this time. Don't rule Harry out, just because he doesn't believe you. I'd wonder about any guy who'd believe a wild tale like yours, at least on the first date. I keep saying there are men out there as decent as my David. Maybe he's one of them, but you don't know that yet."

"I know, I know. I'll be careful."

Maggy hung up the phone and looked out her window absently. Carol's news troubled her more than she cared to admit. But why should it be so upsetting? She knew that Beatrice had died. And the news clipping said it was an accident. There was probably nothing more to it than that.

Maybe Anna's diary would offer a clue, or at least some insight into what Beatrice had really been like when she was alive. Maggy took her suitcase from the closet and put it on the bed. Odd. She could have sworn she left the side compartment unzipped. She'd just opened it to get her sunglasses before she went to lunch. And now it was neatly closed. A chill ran through her as she thought of someone coming into her room, going through her things. Well, of course the hotel maid had straightened her room and made the bed. But she had been back to the room for a few minutes after that and the suitcase was open. She was sure of it.

She surveyed the room thoroughly, but noticed nothing else out of place. She went into the bathroom and looked carefully through her few belongings there. Her gaze fastened on the counter as she tried to make sense of what she was seeing. Her silver bracelet and earrings were lying where she had left them, but they were smashed and twisted completely out of shape. Maggy picked up the heavy bracelet in disbelief. It would take tremendous strength to bend the metal to this unrecognizable lump.

There was no doubt someone had been here. Someone who was stealthy enough to leave little trace of his presence, but angry enough to do this. She put down the bracelet quickly, it's cool weight suddenly unpleasant in her hand.

The diaries! Maggy went back to her suitcase and opened the side compartment. She looked through maps and guidebooks, but didn't find either diary. Wait, she had taken the first two volumes with her. She looked quickly in her purse and found the second volume that she was still reading. She'd given the first volume to Harry. But where was the last volume? She searched her suitcase again. Had she put it in that compartment? She couldn't remember for sure. It wasn't there.

She searched her entire room, but could find no trace of it.

She sat down on the bed for a moment, as disbelief was slowly overtaken by a simmering rage. How dare someone smash her jewelry? And far worse, take Anna's diary! With that thought, Maggy stormed from her room and went to the front desk. Nancy came out at once to greet her, the smile vanishing from her face when she saw Maggy's expression.

"I want to report a theft. Someone's been in my room. My diary is missing and he smashed my jewelry!"

"Oh no! My dear, I'm so sorry. Nothing like this has ever happened to us here. You'll want to file a report with the police, I imagine. Let me make the call for you." After a short conversation, Nancy said an officer would be there within the hour.

"Can you let me see your room?" Nancy asked.

They walked quickly back to Maggy's room, where she showed Nancy the second volume of Anna's diary that she had been reading.

"They took a volume just like this, but not this one?" Nancy asked.

"Yes. There were three volumes. I loaned the first volume to Harry and I had the second one with me. The third volume is missing."

"Are you sure you had the last diary in your suitcase?"

"Well, yes. I think so. But someone was definitely here in my room." She showed Nancy the bracelet. "I left it on the bathroom counter when I went out about one o'clock. Did you see anyone unusual here after that?"

"No, no one. John and I were the only ones here this afternoon. Except for Harry, of course. But you came in with him, didn't you?"

"No, he dropped me off at the Visitor Center."

"Oh, well." Nancy shrugged her shoulders. "I didn't see anyone suspicious, but maybe Harry saw something. You should ask him."

Their conversation was interrupted when Nancy's husband John came into the room, followed by a police patrolman. Maggy made her report to Officer Trent, who filled out a form for her to sign. He was polite, but skeptical. "There's no evidence of forced entry, ma'am. Someone would have had to use a key to get past this lock, unless you left the window open. Even so, there's no sign that someone got in through the window. If a diary has been stolen, there's not much chance we'll get it back. We have a hard enough time recovering stolen cars, or other items of value. Sorry."

After they left, Maggy paced her room. Had the diary been in her suitcase? She was sure she had all three volumes with her. Maybe the officer didn't take this very seriously, but someone had been angry enough to smash her bracelet. Something was going on, and not just sixty years in the past.

Maggy picked up the remaining volume of Anna's diary and began to read.

Anna's Diary—January 13, 1937

I spent the Christmas holidays at home with father. It was wonderful to have time with him again, though it bothers me to see him so frail. The man I once thought invincible, with endless optimism about the future. Now there's a hollowness to him, as though when mother died she took the best part of him with her. After a week at home, memories of my life at the castle began to seem unreal, like a fantastic story far removed from my normal life. I hated to leave father again last week, but he insisted that I go. Mrs. Sully came over from next door to reassure me that he would be well taken care of. We worry about each other too much.

I had a happy reunion with Emma, who said she missed me while I was away. She complained that the castle had been empty and very dull, since Mr. Hearst spent Christmas at his mansion in Santa Monica. They call it the Beach House. Emma told me he owns six estates as large as San Simeon, including St. Donat's castle in Scotland! Though I can't believe they are as grand as the Enchanted Hill. After six months of employment, there are still many rooms I have yet to visit.

Now it seems as though I never left La Cuesta Encantada. This morning I worked in a portion of the main house I've never seen before, called quite fittingly the Celestial Suite. It is a room high up in the tower, a hundred feet or more above the terrace. Its octagonal shape allows windows to give a breath-

taking view in every direction. As though you are standing in Heaven, looking out over the earth. There is no glass in the tall, arched windows, but they're
each covered with a gold-painted screen carved in intricate designs. The whole
room looks like it has been splashed in gold, from the gilt-painted ceiling to the
flaxen drapes between each window, to the buttery velvet bedspread.

Directly above is one of the two great bell towers which make La Casa
Grande seem like a Spanish cathedral, and the guest cottages far below resemble a small village clustered around it. The twin towers hold dozens of large
bells that are rung on Sunday. I sometimes hear them ringing on my day off,
when I'm at home with father. Their music floats all the way down to
Cambria.

Much as this room is like a celestial haven, I think its proximity to those
bells would make it very unpleasant on a Sunday morning. I wonder that
guests don't come away with their eardrums ruptured. I'll have to ask Emma
about this.

I was delighted to see on the guest list for tomorrow the names of my two
favorite visitors, Mrs. Page and Mr. Winter. Though Mr. Orcutt will arrive
with them, I can't include him as a favorite. He seems pleasant enough, but
he's always impatient with me or tends to disregard me altogether. Perhaps it's
just my pride that makes this seem such a fault. He is their friend, so he must
be a better person than I suppose.

I do look forward to seeing Mrs. Page and Mr. Winter. They're assigned to
their usual rooms in Casa del Mar, so I'll be sure to see them again when I do
my chores there.

January 15, 1937

Never would I have dreamed such a hideous turn of events! How could I
have been so mistaken in my opinion of Mr. Winter? Now my future rests in
his hands, to toss away like so much rubbish if he wishes.

It happened this afternoon. My hands still shake as I write this entry...

Maggy's eye widened in shock as she read Anna's account of her confrontation with Mr. Winter. He had attacked her physically and accused her of stealing something from him. Maggy couldn't believe it. As she read on, her fury mounted. That bastard! She slammed down the diary. How dare he touch her, let alone accuse her grandmother of stealing! Anna was the most honorable person Maggy had ever known. She paced the length of her room furiously. And to accuse her when her position made her completely powerless! He was probably so rich he'd never had to worry about anything so mundane as being fired from a job.

She slowed her pace as she realized the implications of what she had read. This was serious trouble. Why had Anna never mentioned a word of it to her? Could this have had something to do with Maggy's own predicament? Something to do with Beatrice?

Maggy was surprised that Winter had changed character so abruptly. Though she obviously hadn't known him well, Anna had seldom been deceived by anyone. She'd always been a perceptive judge of character, even with very little evidence to base her conclusions on. She hadn't cared much for Jason, though she hadn't made a big issue of it. Anna seemed to see right into people. Well, apparently not always, Maggy amended. Winter must have been a fool or worse to treat Anna that way. Both he and Orcutt sounded like bad news. Still, she wondered if something could have really been stolen out of Winter's room. If so, what was it?

Maggy remembered with a jolt what had just happened in her own hotel room. Was history repeating itself? What if there was some connection between Mr. Winter's theft and her own? No, she was being paranoid. There was really nothing to indicate the two were related, or even that Winter's theft had anything to do with Beatrice.

Anna's diary, far from providing answers, seemed to be raising even more questions. Maggy sat down and picked up the slim volume again. She began to read in earnest.

Anna's Diary—January 17, 1937

It's been two days, yet no outcry has been raised. Mr. Winter remains in the same rooms at "A" House, where I go to perform my duties with great apprehension. Mrs. Page is also a guest at Casa del Mar. She looks at me strangely, perhaps because she has noticed the change in my behavior. She said I looked very pale and asked if I felt ill. I wish I could confide in her, but I can't bring myself to do it. What if he has told her his suspicions? Somehow, I don't think he has, though I believe he still suspects me of being a thief. The ugly bruises on my arms are reminder enough of his contempt.

Our paths cross frequently, more so than with the other guests. He seems to be wary of me, watching, deliberating, but he hasn't spoken to me. He hasn't denounced me to Mr. Hearst. I wonder what holds him back. I've been told that he and Mrs. Page will leave in two days time. Will he accuse me? I pray each day that I won't be forced to leave.

I can't bear the uncertainty any longer. I must speak to him before he leaves. Somehow I must convince him that I am not a thief.

Chapter 8

❖

"There you are, Harry," Steve Liggett sat down at the work table next to Harry, careful not to get dust on his carefully pressed slacks. The museum curator was dressed impeccably, as usual. Even when they attended graduate classes together at UC Berkeley, Steve had shunned the student uniform of worn jeans and tee shirts.

"I've been meaning to ask you about that woman's diary," Steve said. "What was her name?"

"Maggy Lane." Harry wasn't feeling particularly sociable. He continued writing notes as he examined the Attic kantharos cup on the worktable, the same piece he'd been working on unsuccessfully for the past two days.

"Well? Is it something we can use?"

Harry put down his pencil with obvious reluctance and turned to Steve. He supposed he did owe his friend a report. "I've started to read the first volume of three diaries. The author was very young, and as you know, she worked here as a housemaid. It's extremely descriptive and romantic. It almost reads like a gothic novel."

Steve was silent for a moment. Harry looked at his friend and immediately regretted his honest response. Steve was no doubt figuring out an angle to exploit the diaries.

"That's good news," Steve said. "I've been looking for something with a broader appeal than the usual guidebooks. This might be just the thing. If it's that good, we could throw a little publicity in. I have some marketing ideas—"

"Slow down, Steve! You always have marketing ideas," Harry shook his head.

"You never had these problems when you were curator. Attendance has been dropping each year. I've got to generate more interest in the castle."

Harry clapped his friend on the shoulder. "You've done a great job already. The living history tours are sold out, aren't they?"

"The numbers are still down though. That's the bottom line. We need revenue for restoration. The cost is astronomical!"

"I doubt this little diary is going to change any of that," Harry said carefully. The last thing he wanted was publicity for Anna Lane's diary.

Steve looked doubtful. "It sounds perfect. I'm not questioning your judgment, but I'd like to read it myself. Get a feel for it."

Harry laughed. "The hell you're not. But you're the boss now, so I'll let it pass."

After Steve left, Harry sat with the Greek portrait cup in front of him, oblivious to it and the muffled conversations coming from the next vaulted work chamber. The air circulation system clicked on, but he didn't move a muscle.

His meeting with Maggy this morning had taken over his thoughts, leaving him in a state of confusion. He could swear she believed everything she told him. She seemed so damned sincere, despite his arguments against her.

How could he have forgotten that one photograph? He thought he'd removed every reference to Beatrice Page and her friends from the archives long ago. Seeing it had made his blood run cold. He'd tried to put the album away before she got a good look at it. Maggy could be persistent, he was finding out.

He wanted to believe her. Hell, he wanted her period. Again he'd had to fight the urge to hold her close, to press her body against his. All he'd allowed himself was the faintest touch of his lips to hers. The thought of it filled him with fire. She'd put him in an impossible position. He could tell her any number of things about Beatrice Page, but he didn't think it would help her. Not if she really was as genuine as he wanted to believe. And if she wasn't...

He let the thought trail off unpleasantly. He hated to think she had an ulterior motive. There were too many things he didn't want her, or anyone else, to find out.

* * *

Beatrice walked along the promenade of the Neptune Pool, idly taking in the scene before her as she thought about Anna Lane. The fog bank that drifted up toward the top of the hillside was shot with sparkling light that gave an impression of vivid colors, yet when she focused her attention on it, it seemed a dazzling, pure white. As the mist flowed around the pool in thin wisps, lights appeared all around her. The first time she had seen this phenomena, she'd fallen to her knees and wept at the sight of such unearthly beauty. It was common for new angels to spend much of their time weeping, joy literally streaming from their eyes at the sights they beheld.

But now Beatrice wasn't contemplating the weather. She was trying to push her mind in a direction that angels in the First Level rarely ever took. She was trying to remember her mortal life and a young woman named

Anna. It was impossibly vexing. True, she had enjoyed the spontaneous bits of memory that sometimes popped into her mind unbidden. But before Ambrose had asked her to recollect her life, she had never attempted this willful, almost painful remembering. It was not going well. Not only did she have no coherent memory of her life, she had little recollection of her arrival in Heaven or her early days here. Roland told her that the first year or so was spent in remembering the life just past, learning and evaluating the experience so it could be properly let go. Forgotten.

Beatrice must have learned that lesson well. She could remember every moment of each day she had spent in Heaven, except for that first year. She could instantly picture the faces of each one of her earthly charges, each success or failure they'd experienced. But hard as she tried, her own life was a void, less substantial than the sparkling fog that flowed past on idle currents of air.

She would just have to try harder, focus her mind more clearly. Maybe if she thought of Maggy that would help. Ambrose said she resembled Anna. Beatrice wondered for a moment how Ambrose knew that. There was her mind, trying to distract her again. She thought of Maggy, thought of her radiant smile and heart-shaped face, her blonde hair curving away from her forehead. Keeping that image in her mind, she pushed her mind back as far as she could reach, trying to remember another smile, another era. Time seemed to stop while she pushed herself to the limits of her ability. She was adrift, floating on the edge of memory.

She saw her! Anna was standing before her, as clear in her memory as a living being. Her light brown hair was short and wavy around her face, her hazel eyes crinkling in a smile of pure pleasure. She was holding a deep, midnight blue gown in her arms. "Oh, Mrs. Page!" she said, as she looked down at the dress quickly, a reverent look, as though to reassure herself the dress was real. "Thank you so much for your great generosity. You're so kind to me!" As she held the dress up in front of her and whirled around slowly, she became less substantial, as though a gauze curtain had been placed before her. Within moments she had faded away.

"No!" Beatrice cried aloud. "Not yet! I must learn more about her."

Beatrice looked around her present surroundings with a start. She had walked out to the middle of the Neptune Pool, completely unaware of her actions. She was standing on the surface of the water, before the great temple facade with its magnificent sculpture of Neptune. "How thoughtless of me," she mused as she walked back over the water toward the edge of the pool. Fortunately, there were no other angels present to observe her social gaffe. Unsure of the results her experiment would bring, she had again hidden herself away from the common plane of the First Heaven. A wise decision. Though all angels could walk on water as easily as they could soar through the air, few ever did. It would be presumptuous.

Nonetheless, she was elated at her small success. She had actually seen her! Now she knew exactly what Anna looked like. What a sweet smile she had lighting up her face. And Beatrice knew that she had given Anna a blue gown, one that had brought that very smile to her lips.

It was a good start. Beatrice was eager to share this with Ambrose, and wondered if he had learned any more on his own. She slipped back to the common plane of the First Level, and saw twenty or thirty angels enjoying the fog that was still drifting past the Neptune Pool and up toward the higher terraces. Angels of varied ages and era of dress were talking quietly in groups, or strolled by themselves past the colonnades. She hadn't really expected to see Ambrose here, but she was disappointed just the same. She cast her mind out through the First Level, searching for him.

She waited while her mental message sped outward to circle the entire globe, all in the space of a few moments. There was no response to her call, no sense of his presence anywhere.

"Where could he be?" she wondered. Her call should have reached him, even if he was sojourning in the First Heaven of India, or England, or China. She tried once more to locate him, still with no success.

She remembered that they agreed to meet on earth instead of the First Level. Reluctantly, she willed herself to the mortal world, appearing instantly on the hilltop where the ruins of the pergola stretched out ahead of her for a short distance before they disappeared into the fog. Here the fog was simply a blanket of impenetrable gray, with no life, no visible spark of light save from occasional rays of pale sunlight filtering through.

Beatrice leaned back against a cool pillar and closed her eyes in concentration. Again she sent her call out to Ambrose, though with much greater difficulty through the heavy atmosphere of earth. After fully ten minutes of searching for him, she opened her eyes. She could find no trace of him anywhere on earth.

"Ambrose!" she shouted and stamped her foot in a fit of temper. A futile gesture, since her mental summons had gone unanswered. But she felt a little better for the outburst. Where was he? She had thought her powers sufficient to search all of Heaven and earth for any being. This was the first time she had ever come up empty-handed.

She would have some questions for Ambrose the next time she met with him.

Anna's Diary—January 18, 1937

Another day has passed with no solution to my problem. Though Mr. Winter still watches me, I've had no opportunity to speak with him. He could talk to me privately any time he wished, for I work at my tasks alone most of the day. Yet he hasn't approached me. He's never alone, but always with Mrs. Page or another of Mr. Hearst's guests.

His delay in accusing me has given me hope. Perhaps he still might change his mind. Or perhaps it was all a mistake, and he has found whatever was so precious to him that he thought was stolen. Yet if that were true, he wouldn't leave me in fear like this. He couldn't be so cruel. Then I remember his face when he accused me. I don't know what to think.

I had further bad luck when I overheard a terrible argument, one that I sincerely wish I hadn't heard. Perhaps Mrs. Page, despite all her wealth and kindness, has even more troubles to bear than being a widow.

Last night I went to the late film showing in the theater at eleven o'clock. I was so distracted by my private thoughts and worries that I became quite agitated. I suddenly felt claustrophobic, even in such a large, dark room. I barely remember what story was unfolding on the screen before me, it all seemed so far removed from my impending ruin. I had to escape. Fortunately, I was sitting next to the aisle in the very last row, so no one noticed me leave.

I passed the alcove where the carillon organ sat silently. Before I turned the corner I heard a man's voice just ahead. I slowed my footsteps, apprehensive. He was almost shouting, his words venomous. A woman's voice answered him, much softer. But I could still hear every word in the stillness of the hallway. I recognized her immediately, and the man with her must have been Mr. Orcutt.

"Maxwell is dead and you belong to me now. I've waited years for you. I've been more than patient. And this is how you repay me?"

"I never promised you anything, Edward. I don't understand what I've done to get you worked up like this."

"I want you to stop seeing Winter. He's at least twenty years younger than you are! It's humiliating."

"But Logan was Maxwell's friend, just as he is mine. And yours too, or so I thought. What's wrong with you?"

"God, Beatrice! I am not Maxwell! When will you stop punishing me for that? But I care for you more than he ever could."

"Edward, I don't love you. I'll never marry again. I've told you this before."

"You will! You will come to see it my way. But I don't want you seeing Winter. He's making you look like a fool."

Mrs. Page's response was lost on me as I realized their voices were growing closer. I was horrified at what I had heard, but how much worse if they knew I had heard them! I looked around in a panic for some escape, but there was just the corridor along which I had come. I stood rooted to the spot for several seconds, undecided. Then I began to walk forward, as though I hadn't been riveted in place by their conversation.

I turned the corner and almost collided with Mr. Orcutt. "You fool! Look where you're going!" he said to me. His breath had an unpleasant smell of alcohol.

"Edward, be quiet please. Can't you see you're frightening her?" I was relieved when Mrs. Page stepped between us. "Don't pay any attention to him, dear," she said to me.

Mr. Orcutt looked at me with distaste. "Were you spying on us? Is that it?"

"No, sir. Of course not," I answered with a twinge of guilt. I hadn't intended to overhear them, but I had nonetheless.

"Don't be ridiculous, Edward. You're getting upset over nothing. Absolutely nothing." She pulled him past me in the direction of the theater. After they were out of sight I leaned against the wall, shaking all over. Was I now to be accused of spying, as well as theft?

But then my thoughts became more rationale and I calmed myself. Mrs. Page wouldn't let him cause trouble for me over something so small. Poor Mrs. Page, to be insulted so meanly by someone who was supposedly her friend.

And what of Mr. Winter? Could her relationship with him be more than the friendship I had assumed? It had never occurred to me, I suppose because of the difference in their ages. But Mrs. Page is still lovely, far more beautiful than women half her age. Perhaps Mr. Winter is in love with her too, just as Mr. Orcutt claims to be. At the thought I feel a small flicker of discomfort, which I find quite unsettling. Even after the horrible way Mr. Winter accused me, I must still harbor some hopeful feeling about him. I pray that he will see his actions were all a mistake.

January 19, 1937

I am so happy I feel I could float up to the ceiling! I will not be accused! In fact, Mr. Winter has put in a good word to the head housekeeper for my excellent service. Or, I should say Logan has, for he has asked me to use his first name, since he now numbers me one of his friends.

This morning I finally found an opportunity to speak to him, just after I'd finished my duties at Casa del Mar and was heading along the terrace back to La Casa Grande. I met him there, walking toward me with his head lowered and hands in his pockets. He would have passed me unaware if I hadn't stopped him.

I'd hardly begun my defense when he interrupted me. "I'm glad to see you, so I can apologize for my actions the other day," he said. "I was terribly wrong, I see that now. I hope you'll forgive me, though the anguish I must have put you through is inexcusable."

The very words I longed to hear! I'm ashamed to say that, now that my case was truly won, the relief was so great it caused my knees to buckle. His hand shot out to steady me and he helped me to one of the low, stone benches nearby.

Once I had regained my composure, I asked him hesitantly what was missing from his room, and if he had found it again.

"No. It's gone." He slumped on the bench beside me. "It was a very valuable vase that's been owned by my family for a great many years. Far older and more valuable than any vase in Mr. Hearst's great collection." He turned to me suddenly, his eyes catching the light as he looked at me. "Did you see it? A small, round vase," he held up his hands to indicate the size, "fired a deep blue color. It had faint symbols carved around the base."

"No, I've never seen it," I replied.

"Even when you prepared my room? Perhaps you saw it, but didn't notice it particularly."

"No. I'm sure I didn't see it. I unpacked your suitcase after you arrived that day, just as I have on every other visit."

"You wouldn't have unpacked this. It was on the dresser, on a piece of blue velvet."

"I remember the velvet, like a dresser scarf, with gold trim. I noticed you had moved the silver dish from its normal place on the dresser. But there was nothing on the dresser besides the scarf."

We looked at each other. It must have been stolen. There was no doubt of that now.

"Did you bring the vase for Mr. Hearst?" It seemed the only reason he would bring such a valuable piece with him on holiday.

"For Hearst?" He seemed surprised at first. "Oh, yes. I was going to offer it to him. But now that it's gone, I'd appreciate it if you didn't mention it to him or his staff."

"Shouldn't you tell them? It's only been four days. Maybe the police—"

"No! I don't want a scandal with Hearst or his guests. I don't want him to know about this."

"If you're sure," I said. How ironic that I had lived for days in fear of the police coming, and now I wanted him to send for them.

"I'm certain. No police." He leaned forward, his hands gripping the front edge of the stone bench. "I suppose anyone could have walked into my room and taken it."

"Yes. The rooms aren't locked here. I've never seen a key."

We sat quietly for a moment, the sun warming us. The scent of lavender and newly turned earth came from nearby gardens around us.

He broke the silence finally. "I'm sorry I frightened you, Anna. More sorry than I can say. The shock of my discovery drove me to it. There's no excuse for my behavior."

"It's done now, sir. I'm only glad that you know I wouldn't steal anything."

"One look at you would convince any sane person," he said. "Do you mind if I call you Anna?"

"Of course not," I said with a smile. All the guests referred to me by my first name, but I felt very grand giving him permission to use it.

"Wonderful. Then, Anna, it's only fair that you should call me Logan, since we are friends now. Is it a deal?"

We shook hands on our bargain.

I've not only escaped certain ruin, but I've gained a friend as well. I knew that Mr. Winter was a decent man, and that his fury must have been caused by some terrible mistake. It was just my misfortune to be the closest and most obvious target for his suspicion. The vase he spoke of must be very dear to him, *to have roused his passion so violently. I wonder what hardship forced him to bring it here, to offer it up for sale to Mr. Hearst.*

We all have our treasures that we consider beyond any price. Mine is a small locket given to me by my mother before she died. It is more valuable to me than any diamonds or pearls. But that's easy for me to say, because the locket has no great monetary value. I'll never be put to the test.

I can see that he feels this loss deeply, even though he would have sold it to Mr. Hearst if it hadn't been stolen. It must be worth a fortune. I'll do whatever I can to help him find it. During my tasks each day throughout the castle I see a great many things. Perhaps one day I may see a mysterious blue vase.

Maggy's reading was interrupted by a knock on the door. She had been so engrossed in Anna's tale that it took her a minute to get her bearings. She could hear the subtle rhythm of the surf outside, and noticed that the last glimmers of daylight had disappeared. Another short knock at the door brought her to her feet.

Harry stood there, grinning at her. "Hi. I was afraid you'd gone out."

"Nope. Here I am."

"I thought I might take you to dinner this evening, since Nancy doesn't cook on Saturday night. That is, if you haven't eaten already."

"No, that would be great. I mean, no I haven't eaten and yes, let's go to dinner."

As usual, she was dazzling him with her wit. Maggy laughed suddenly and Harry joined her. Her nervousness disappeared as quickly as it had come.

"We can go to Robin's in Cambria," Harry said. "The food is great, and the building is interesting too. One of the construction foremen from the castle built it as his home in the twenties."

"Always the tour guide, aren't you?" she teased.

"Bad habit. Been trying to break it, but no luck so far. Just let me know when I get especially boring."

"Don't worry. I tend to nod off and snore loudly when the conversation gets dull."

"Somehow I got the impression you were interested in everything."

"Funny. That's just what I thought about you," Maggy said.

They drove the short distance to the restaurant in Harry's Landrover. It was a white stucco, Spanish-style building with lovely stained glass windows set in arched mahogany frames. A garden surrounded the building and creeping vines framed the entryway and windows.

They sat at a small wooden table in a quiet alcove. A piano played in the next room. Maggy thought it was a Cole Porter tune she remembered from one of Anna's old records.

"Have you found out anything else about Beatrice Page or her friends?" Harry asked.

"Yes, I have. She died at the castle in 1937. An accident of some sort. And Anna knew them all! She wrote about them in her diary."

"Interesting. But not very conclusive, if you're looking for a reason why she appeared to you."

"No, it doesn't explain anything yet. But it can't be just a coincidence."

They ordered two glasses of wine and the evening special, black bean burritos with salad. As promised, the wine was excellent. Maggy twirled her glass absently between her hands. "Anna also mentioned that something was stolen from Logan Winter. Taken from his room."

That caught Harry's attention. "Did she say anything else about it? Was it ever found?"

"She described it. It was a blue vase, very valuable. But I don't know if it turned up again, or if he ever found out who took it. Maybe there will be some mention of it in a later entry." Maggy sipped her wine slowly, feeling uncomfortable as she thought of a thief in her own room, handling her things.

"There's something else, isn't there?" Harry asked.

In a rush, Maggy told him about the third volume of the diary that had been taken from her room, and the way her bracelet and been crushed. He took her hand in his, his brow furrowed.

"Maggy, this worries me. I don't like to think of you in any danger."

"It's pretty unnerving, I admit. Did you see anyone when you came back this afternoon?"

"I was there about 1:30 to pick up some work I'd left in my room. But I didn't see anything unusual."

"I can't believe anyone would want to hurt me."

"Smashing your bracelet the way you describe it—it sounds like a fit of rage to me. Maybe the thief didn't find what he was looking for."

"But the diary is gone. What else could there be? I certainly don't have anything worth stealing."

Harry rubbed his thumb gently over the back of her hand, looking at her intently. "Maybe not. But I'll feel better when we know who was in your room and why."

He smiled at her suddenly, the tension relaxing from his face. "I think that's enough worrying for one night. Do you like to dance, Maggy?"

They went into the bar, where the piano player was just coming back from a break. He began to sing a sultry version of "Sentimental Journey." The room was dimly lit by candles on the tables, and almost deserted. One couple danced slowly to the music.

"Cambria closes up by ten o'clock most nights," Harry said. "Not exactly a hotbed of wild living."

He took her into his arms and they moved slowly with the music. One song followed another, and their conversation drifted comfortably, until they stopped talking altogether. She felt as though she belonged there, breathing in his clean scent, her forehead brushing against his cheek. Almost without volition, she moved closer to him. Every inch of her body was aware of him. She closed her eyes and drifted to the music, feeling like they were the only two people in the world.

"Maggy," he whispered into her hair. He cupped her chin in his hand and looked into her eyes, then dropped his gaze to her mouth. Slowly, he leaned down and pressed his lips against hers. It seemed so natural, so right. His hand went to the back of her head as she welcomed his kiss. She pressed against him and felt his tongue brush hers, perfectly, then deepen into her mouth. Her whole being was concentrated on his kiss and the surge of heat that washed over her. He pulled away from her, a look of consternation barely masking the passion in his eyes.

She looked around, suddenly aware of her surroundings again. Embarrassment tinged her already flushed cheeks. Fortunately, no one seemed to be paying any attention to them.

He took her hand. "I think it's time to go. What do you say we walk back along the beach trail? We can leave my car here. It's not far and I think we could both use some fresh air."

They walked for several blocks along the sidewalk before coming to a stand of Monterey pines that marked the beginning of the public trail. The night was clear and crisp. The moon lit their way and made the stars look pale above them. Maggy's heightened senses took in every detail of her surroundings. A breeze came in from the ocean, bringing with it a salty dampness and the sound of waves lapping against the rocky sand. She was acutely aware of Harry walking beside her in silence, his hand warming hers. She wondered what he was thinking.

"They say you can see moonstones on the beach on a night like this," he said. "They look like ordinary white pebbles in daylight, but at night they reflect the light of the moon, so you can find them glowing on the sand."

"Can you really? Have you ever tried to find any?"

"Honestly? I don't know. I've never tested the theory."

"Let's look now. I don't think I've ever seen a moonstone."

They went down the first set of steps that lead to a small, crescent-shaped beach, enclosed by low rocky cliffs on either end. They walked along the shore, shoes in hand, testing the angle of the moonlight on the wet sand. The tide was out, so they continued to the next small cove, hidden by jagged rocks that looked like they had been thrown down by a giant's hand.

Maggy glanced at Harry, at his tousled hair that was damp from the ocean. She smiled at the urge she felt to run her hands through it. From almost the first moment she saw him, she had resisted that impulse. She didn't feel much like fighting it anymore. "Tell me about your life, Harry. I don't really know anything about you, except that you were the curator at the castle, and as Nancy said, you go off on adventures."

"There's not much to tell. You know I'm fascinated by ancient pottery. That's what Nancy meant by my adventures. Sometimes I'm called on to verify the authenticity of a piece, which might be in San Francisco, or London, or anywhere. Since large sums of money are at stake, several experts will testify on the same piece."

"What about your personal life, away from work?" Maggy had a horrible thought. "You aren't married, are you?"

Harry laughed. "No. Far from it."

"Have you ever been married?"

He didn't answer for a moment. His face was shadowed in the moonlight. "Yes. A very long time ago."

"What happened?

"She died."

"I'm sorry," Maggy said. Perhaps this was the pain she'd sensed in him earlier. She looked at his face again, but couldn't make out his expression. "Can you tell me about her?"

"No, I can't. As I said, it was a long time ago. I've been alone for years. It's suited me very well." He stopped walking and looked directly at her. "Until now."

Maggy felt her breath catch in her throat. He took a step toward her and traced the curve of her cheek with his hand. "I don't know what to do about you, Maggy," he said, his voice husky.

She leaned toward him, drawn inexorably closer. He swept her into a fierce embrace. His lips bruised hers in a passionate kiss, his tongue searching. She reveled in his touch, pulled him nearer as her arms went around his shoulders. His hands pressed her hips closer and she felt him against her, hard and impatient. God! She wanted to make love to him. She had never felt this fury of need before.

They parted and looked at each other, breathless. She laughed unsteadily. "I think we'd better start walking again if we're ever going to get back to the inn."

He smiled at her and released her slowly. "We haven't found a moonstone yet."

She had completely forgotten they were looking for them. "No wonder, if this is the way you look." They started walking again, hand in hand.

"Are you always so practical?" He had that amused tone in his voice. She knew he'd have the same expression in his eyes, even though she couldn't see him clearly in the moonlight.

"I try to be." She didn't feel the least bit practical, not with him walking beside her. They turned and made their way up the beach toward the next short stairway to the road.

"Have you finished reading Anna's diary yet?" Harry asked.

"No, but I'll probably finish it tomorrow."

"Will you let me see it then?"

"If you like." They walked through the gardens to the side door of the inn. Harry unlocked the door with his keys. A simple gesture, but to Maggy's heightened senses, it seemed incredibly intimate.

At her door she fumbled with her keys, her hands shaky. He took the keys from her and opened the door. His look burned into her, but now there was something more than passion in his gaze. He stood slightly apart as he handed the keys back.

"I don't want to say goodnight," Maggy said, suddenly hesitant. Why was he standing a step away from her? Had he changed his mind? She reached out a hand to him. He took it in a fierce grip and pulled her close.

"Maggy. Beautiful Maggy," he whispered as his fingers touched the planes of her face. He tilted her head up and kissed her with a gentleness that made her forget everything. All she knew was this man, his arms pulling her closer, his mouth covering hers.

"Come inside," she murmured.

He put both hands on her shoulders and pushed her carefully away. Maggy didn't understand what he was doing. She still burned with his kiss, his touch.

"I want you more at this moment than anything on earth," he said, his voice ragged. "But it would be a mistake for both of us. Goodnight, Maggy."

He left her standing in the doorway, her fingers pressed to her lips.

* * *

Harry returned to his room and flipped on the lights impatiently. He walked to the window and turned on the lamp by the writing table. The spacious room felt claustrophobic. His thoughts were filled with Maggy, with her warmth, her scent, and what he'd almost done to her.

He had to get out of there, the air was so close it was difficult to breathe. He quickly changed into running shoes and sweats and headed back to the beach trail. When he reached the hard-packed sand by the water, he ran as though he was pursued by demons, as though his life depended on it. As though he were running from death itself.

Finally he stopped, bent over with his hands on his knees, gasping for air. Maybe now he could think rationally. He turned and started walking back the way he'd come, oblivious to the night breeze cooling his damp skin, his heartbeat gradually slowing as his body recovered.

An ironic smile crossed his face as he thought of his plans to seduce Maggy tonight, to gain her confidence, and finally learn the truth about her elaborate performance at the castle. He tried to put his finger on the exact moment when things had changed, when he lost control of the situation.

Maybe it was when she asked him if he'd been married before. A common enough question; one he'd answered many times, in many different ways. He'd only told Maggy the truth, but the simple question had opened a door in his mind. No, not the question itself. It was Maggy asking the question.

He found himself thinking, not of his wife, but of Marie.

Maggy had sparked those painful memories for the second time. And then, as Maggy had invited him to spend the night, he suddenly became afraid for her. He knew then his plans for casual seduction were impossible. The fire between them went deeper than that.

He stopped walking as another, more shocking thought occurred to him. He had told Maggy he wanted her more than anything else on earth. Those words had been thoughtless, but they had been true. The realization left him numb. He wanted her more than he wanted the elusive goal he'd spent a lifetime searching for.

He stood there for an endless moment, trying to see a solution. But it was no use. He had saved them both from a liaison that would ultimately bring untold pain. He straightened resolutely and continued walking along the trail, determined to keep his emotions in check. There would be no seduction. That was a dangerous luxury he wouldn't allow himself. It would be more difficult than he imagined, but he wouldn't give up his primary goal. He needed to find out what Maggy knew.

* * *

Maggy woke early the next morning to bright sunlight streaming in through the window. She peeped out from under the covers, reluctant to leave the dream that was already fading from her consciousness. The night before came to her in a flood of memory. Her face burned with embarrassment.

It had been the most wonderful night of her life, up until the moment Harry had rejected her. She'd thought he wanted her as much as she wanted him. Maggy had hardly recognized herself, she'd been so willing. Willing? Face it, she'd thrown herself at him.

What did she really know about him? After all, she had known him a grand total of two days. Maybe he thought she jumped into bed with any guy who bought her dinner and twirled her around the dance floor. No. He wouldn't think that. There was more to what happened between them than simple lust. The overwhelming attraction she had felt for him was like nothing she'd ever experienced before. But had he felt it the way she had? Why had he left her so abruptly?

She turned on the shower and then pulled clothes out of the closet to wear, scarcely noticing what they were. She felt tears sting her eyes as she remembered the joy she felt last night, and the doubt that had replaced it. They never found any moonstones on the beach either. Maybe she hadn't found anything she'd hoped for last night. Maybe she was inventing Harry the same way she had invented Jason, convincing herself he was what she wanted him to be. She dismissed that thought almost the moment it formed in her mind. Harry was nothing like Jason.

But why was he so secretive about his past? What was he hiding? Maggy had a horrible thought. Could Harry have stolen the diary from her room? He hadn't made any effort to hide his interest in the diary. But why would he steal it when she was going to give it to him anyway? Unless he didn't want her to read it.

She was suddenly afraid she had made a terrible mistake.

Chapter 9

❖

$\mathcal{B}$eatrice materialized on the hillside near the pergola, happy to see her surroundings bathed in pale sunlight. Even this paltry illumination lightened her mood considerably and made her earthly surroundings less oppressive.

A quick glance showed her that Ambrose was nowhere to be seen. Rather than search for him, she decided to simply wait. She sat down gracefully, her long skirt a vivid splash of yellow on the ground around her. She saw several zebras and tahr goats on the slope below her. One zebra nipped another playfully on the neck and then raced away, but couldn't get the other to give chase.

Beatrice laughed and called out to the animal silently. It raised its head and listened intently, its nostrils quivering. After a moment's hesitation it trotted up the hill toward her. It stopped a foot away from her and again pricked its ears, listening.

"Aren't you a fine, lovely creature?" she crooned, admiring the bold striations of its coat. The zebra couldn't see or hear her, but could sense her presence nonetheless. Beatrice ran a hand over its coat, feeling the warmth of a muscled shoulder. She leaned her head against its neck and stroked a velvety muzzle. After standing peacefully for several seconds, it nipped at her and tossed its head.

"I can see that you have a highly developed sense of humor for a zebra," Beatrice said with a grin. "Would it extend as far as offering a ride to a very well-behaved angel?" She grasped a handful of coarse black mane and climbed astride the animal. A mischievous, off-center smile lit her face as she leaned down to whisper in its ear. "Let's run!"

Soon they were racing down the path of the pergola at a full gallop, Beatrice's yellow skirt bunched above her knees and streaming out behind her. Elation coursed through her, for she felt the animal's joy as well as her own. They ran past the old zoo enclosures and on down to an open hillside. She could see a tour bus going up the road far to her left. She imagined the tourists exclaiming over a lone zebra galloping down the hill. Of course, they wouldn't see her. Unless one of them was Maggy.

Beatrice spoke to the zebra again and they slowed down to an easy trot. Thank heavens, she didn't sense Maggy's presence anywhere nearby. They turned back up the hill, the zebra content now with a slower pace. "All right, then. You've had your fun, so now we can behave with a measure of dignity." She patted its neck affectionately.

When they neared the columns of the pergola, Ambrose appeared suddenly in front of them. The zebra whinnied and reared up in alarm. Beatrice slipped quickly down from its back and spoke soothingly in its ear, but even this had no effect on the shaking animal.

Ambrose raised a hand toward the zebra and it backed up, eyes rolling. To Beatrice's astonishment, it turned and bolted away from them.

"Whatever possessed it to run away like that?" She asked.

Ambrose walked up to her, hands outstretched. "I have no idea. I would have appeared with more caution if I'd known you were cavorting with wild beasts."

"Don't be absurd. You can scarcely call these placid creatures wild."

"If you say so. With the number of tourists passing through here, I wouldn't think a stray angel or two would frighten them." Ambrose seemed amused.

"It's true animals can sense our presence far easier than mortals can. But they love to be near angels."

"They love to be near you, my dear. Don't think every angel has the same talents you have. I've never been fond of animals and I'm sure they sense that when I'm near. But no harm done."

Beatrice turned suddenly, hands on hips, as she remembered she was still quite irritated with him. "Where were you yesterday afternoon?"

"Why, let's see. Yesterday I was gathering information to help us solve our dilemma. And I was worrying about Harry and his infatuation for your young lady."

"But where were you? Why didn't you answer my call? You must have known I was searching for you."

"No, I didn't realize. I find solutions come to me more easily if I leave the common plane of Heaven and retreat to complete solitude. Isn't that true for you as well?"

"I suppose so," she answered, somewhat mollified.

"I have a great deal of news for you. I observed Maggy and Harry unearth a photograph of you from your days at San Simeon. Maggy has learned even more about your mortal life."

Beatrice still felt very little curiosity about her life. Except for the few moments of recollection she had experienced, it seemed that Ambrose was speaking of a stranger. "Does anything point to a connection between us?"

"I suspect you are the only one who can answer that question, Beatrice."

"So you keep telling me. I did remember Anna yesterday, just for a moment. That's why I was looking for you."

"Then you've made some progress. Perhaps this will help you remember more." A black and white photograph slowly materialized in his outstretched hand. "Maggy found a photograph like this in the library at the castle. It was taken in 1936."

Beatrice took the picture and looked at her own smiling face. She hadn't looked in a mirror or seen her own image in years, but knew somehow that she had changed little from the woman in the photograph. "I still don't remember."

"Look at the man standing next to you. Edward Orcutt."

She studied the dark-haired man, unsmiling, his hand on her arm. "No. Nothing."

"You disappoint me, Beatrice. He was very close to you. You must remember something about him."

"Wait!" Beatrice grasped his arm. "Not him. The other man. I can't really see him in this picture, but I remember him. His fair hair and, like this picture, he was always in motion. Doing something or going somewhere. I think—I think I was very fond of him." She looked at Ambrose questioningly. "Who was he?"

"His name was Logan Winter. The three of you were friends and often visited the castle together."

"I was right about him then."

"Perhaps. I learned something else that could be important, but I don't want to alarm you."

"Very little can alarm me, Ambrose, given my current occupation."

He took her hand in his. "You died here at the castle a year after this photograph was taken."

Beatrice looked at him, speechless.

"It seems you had a fall from a horse. A terrible accident." He watched her intently, waiting for her response.

"It's no use. I don't remember."

"When I saw you riding that creature just now, you looked as though you were an expert horsewoman. You and the zebra moved as one."

"It seemed natural to me. I didn't give it a thought. I still don't remember my mortal life—or death."

"But I think you will."

"You're right, Ambrose. I have to know what happened."

Chapter 10

*A*nna's Diary—January 29, 1937

We have so many guests here this week, I've hardly had a moment to myself. We've been working extra duty to take care of them all, even though Mr. Hearst has brought in more staff from his Los Angeles estates. Fortunately, those workers have been here before so they're familiar with the castle routine. In addition to the extra maids and valets, five waiters from the Ambassador Hotel in Los Angeles have come to assist in serving and also to give our waiters a little polish, to make sure everything is done just so.

Mr. Hearst and Miss Davies have invited sixty people to their party tonight, a smaller number than summer house parties. Their guests have been arriving over the past three days, and most of them will stay for several days after the event. Such preparations! The kitchen staff is working night and day, with huge deliveries of food and produce arriving hourly. The ranch itself provides much of the beef and poultry, and the greenhouses supply some of the produce even in January.

We're lucky to have an unexpected gift of warm weather this week, some days reaching as high as eighty degrees. Today has been a balmy day as well, and preparations are underway to stage the party on the great terrace overlooking the Neptune Pool. I can't think of a lovelier setting, even with early nightfall, since alabaster globes will illuminate the grounds with electric light.

There's no time to write now with all the tasks left to be completed. If I finish my work in time I hope to see some of the festivities myself.

January 30, 1937

A wonderful night! I will add it to my list of special memories about this place.

Early evening found me with Mrs. Page in her room, helping her as she decided which gown to wear for the party. I was quite flattered that she asked for my help, so I lingered in her room in spite of the many chores still awaiting my attention. She showed me four gowns, each one more magnificent than the last, making the decision terribly difficult. I'd never seen such fine, elegant creations and found it impossible to choose between them. Each one fit her perfectly and the different colors complemented her dark hair and creamy skin.

But the fifth gown! It was a deep, midnight blue, of a texture that seemed to glow with subtle shades as the light struck it. The color darkened her blue eyes and made her skin seem even whiter. The soft fabric hugged her waist and hips smoothly, flowing from a daringly low neckline. I fastened the back for her and she twirled around in a circle, the full floor-length skirt swirling out around her, then draping against her body as she stopped moving.

"Anna, you needn't say a word. I can see from your expression that this is the dress I must wear tonight," she said.

It was the most beautiful gown I had ever seen, and I was quick to tell her so.

Our preparations were interrupted by the arrival of Mr. Orcutt. He complemented Mrs. Page and then noticed me suddenly, as though I hadn't been standing right there the whole time. With a cold look, he told me my services were no longer required. How I dislike that man!

Mrs. Page said I should stay, but the last thing I wished was to cause an argument between them. Besides, I had a long list of chores still to finish. I left them and went to check in on the other guests in Casa del Mar.

Several hours later I was able to relax. Emma and I rested on the upper balcony of "C" House, where we had a clear view of the festivities. The party was in full swing on the terrace above the Neptune Pool. The weather was holding, though it promised to be chilly later in the evening. Globes atop classical columns competed with the full moon to light the scene below. A stage had been set up for the Tommy Dorsey band and I could hear strains of familiar melodies floating on the air.

"Look! That's Clark Gable dancing with Jean Harlow," Emma said. Emma was well informed about our Hollywood celebrities. "Miss Harlow has been very ill, but she seems much better now."

"Emma, you don't have to point out Clark Gable to me. Even if I'd never been to a movie theater before, I couldn't miss seeing his films once I got here!"

"I know.. But isn't it exiting to see them together, just like one of their pictures, like "Red Dust," or "Hold Your Man."

I had to agree with Emma, as usual. The guest list read like a Hollywood gossip column in one of Mr. Hearst's newspapers. And no wonder, for one of the guests was Louella Parsons, whose scandalous reports I've read myself with guilty pleasure.

Emma regaled me with stories of her new boyfriend, a young landscaper who works closely with the head gardener Mr. Keep. I was surprised to see this new side of the usually cynical Emma. She was completely infatuated with this young man, James, undoubtedly the brightest and handsomest fellow ever to walk the earth. When I suggested that she might come down to earth herself, she just laughed at me.

"Oh, Anna! I'm sure I will soon enough. But let me have my fun now. Don't spoil it for me."

She left then, her face flushed and glowing, to meet James. I leaned against the balcony and listened to the buzz of the crowd below, and hummed along as the band played "Little White Lies."

My duties were finished for the evening. Rather than go up to my room, I decided to go down for a closer look. The terrace was surrounded by paths and gardens where I could sit unobserved. It was too lovely a night for sleeping!

I found a perfect spot for my vigil, just off the terrace away from the main paths. The housekeeper wouldn't be pleased to find me there, so I tried my best to keep out of sight. I saw Mrs. Page, resplendent in her blue gown, dancing with Mr. Winter. Logan, I mean. I wondered if Logan was really in love with her, as Mr. Orcutt feared. They made a striking pair, with his fair head bent ever so slightly to her dark one, for she is a tall woman. They looked happy together, her face turned up to his in laughter.

I recognized Errol Flynn dancing with an auburn-haired beauty who looked familiar, but lacking Emma's expertise, I didn't recognize her. I smiled to see Charlie Chaplin entertaining Miss Davies and a small group in his usual fashion.

Then Mrs. Page was walking to her table with Mr. Orcutt, his arm around her shoulder possessively. It was none of my concern, but I disliked seeing him with her anyway.

"Are you a lookout for enemy troops, by any chance?" said a voice right beside me.

I started with surprise, an excuse rushing to my lips. Then I saw Logan's blue eyes crinkling with laughter at my embarrassment.

"I thought it must be a serious campaign, since you were observing everything with such concentration," he teased.

"I'm so glad it's just you!" I said. "If Mrs. Redelsperger found me spying on the party like this, I'd really be in trouble."

"Well, Anna, you've put me in my place. Since it's 'just' me, I guess you have nothing to worry about."

I smiled, but felt shy in front of him. He looked as glamorous and polished as any of the guests. His black tuxedo made his hair seem even fairer in the moonlight. I still wore my uniform, wrinkled and dirty from my long day's work. Suddenly self-conscious of my poor appearance, I shrank before his amused scrutiny. I certainly hadn't expected anyone to see me tonight.

"Don't worry, Anna. I'd never squeal on a friend." He soon had me laughing at the antics of his famous acquaintances, so I forgot what I was wearing and that I was an interloper here.

"That's better," he said. "You have a beautiful smile, Anna. I think you should use it at every opportunity." He looked out at the crowd of people. "You do have an excellent vantage point here. Very well-chosen."

We saw a small commotion in the crowd near the bandstand, but couldn't quite make out what was happening. Then Marion Davies pulled Mrs. Page up the steps to the stage, against her strong protests.

Miss Davies stood at the microphone, her captive's hand firmly in her grasp. "Ladies and gentlemen, I'm happy that I've finally persuaded," here there was laughter from the crowd, "— I've finally persuaded Beatrice to sing for you! I know you've all missed her just as much as I have. Remember her name — Beatrice Page. She's going to be the next musical sensation!"

Logan clapped his hands enthusiastically, forgetting that I was trying to be unobtrusive. I quickly asked him to please be quiet or I'd be discovered. "Sorry, Anna. I'm amazed! I never thought Marion would convince her to sing. You're in for a rare treat."

Mrs. Page spoke to Tommy Dorsey for a moment and then turned to face the crowd, a smile on her lips.

"This was a favorite song of my husband, Maxwell, whom many of you knew and loved."

The opening notes of Moonglow drifted on the air, the audience suddenly hushed with anticipation. Then she began to sing. Her voice was the most remarkable sound I'd ever heard, the notes pure and full of resonance. I'd listened to the popular tune many times before, but it had never struck me as a powerful or emotional song. Now I could hear the love in her voice for her hus-

band, the joy she had found with him. When she stopped singing, the last note seemed to hang suspended in the air and then was gone. Just as her husband was gone. I felt tears come to my eyes as the crowd sat in silence. Then a roar of applause rose up from them, a deafening show of approval.

When the crowd quieted she sang several more songs, her blue gown swirling around her as she swayed to the music. She was glorious! I believe every man present fell in love with her at that moment. Marion Davies looked on with a happy smile at her friend's success.

When she finished singing and stepped down from the stage she was surrounded by the glittering crowd, showering her with accolades.

"Didn't I tell you she was marvelous?" Logan said to me.

I'd almost forgotten he was standing next to me, I'd been so transfixed by her performance. "You're right about her, Logan. She has the most beautiful voice I've ever heard. Far better than any of the singers I've heard on the radio."

Logan took my arm and we sat down on a marble bench nearby, secluded from the noisy crowd on the terrace.

"Beatrice sang professionally during her marriage," he said. "She was a rising star then, more successful every year. You might have even heard her perform on the radio. But then Maxwell died and she swore she'd never sing again. Said she didn't have the heart for it."

"But she must! Her voice is a gift that should be shared with the world."

"I agree with you wholeheartedly, Anna. I think Marion was very clever in insisting that she perform tonight."

"She seemed to love singing for us. She was like a magnet drawing everyone in with the magic of her voice."

"Yet she couldn't bear to listen to Moonglow until tonight, let alone sing it."

"She must have loved her husband very much."

I saw the glimmer of Logan's smile in the moonlight. "They had a very generous kind of love. Instead of shutting others out, their happiness spread out to everyone who knew them." Logan was silent for a moment, then frowned. "He was only 45, a vibrant, brilliantly creative man. He'd barely begun living."

"What a strange way of putting it. He was almost twice as old as you are, after all. Not a young man."

Logan looked at me with an odd little smile. "Anna, you're too young to see it yet. Maxwell's life was far too short. Many people just begin to realize their potential by the time they reach middle age."

I thought that might be true for some, but Logan himself seemed quite perfect in my eyes, despite his odd notions about age. I wasn't happy that he thought I was 'too young to see it.' I wanted him to see me as a woman, not a child. He was only a few years older than I, but he acted as though there were a vast gulf of experience between us.

"Did you know Mr. Page well?" I asked him.

"We worked together, Maxwell, Edward and I. And Beatrice, of course. We grew to know each other well."

"You were business associates?"

"Maxwell and Edward were partners. Maxwell and Beatrice wrote and performed the music and Edward managed the business. The music business could be brutal back when they started. Edward had a knack for sorting it all out. He knew which syndicates to contract with and got top dollar for them. I helped produce some of their tours later on. But we all revolved around Maxwell ultimately. Even Beatrice. Max was the glue that held us together."

"You still miss him," I said quietly.

I don't know quite how it happened, but I found myself telling him about mother and how much father and I have missed her during the past two years. "She was sick for a long time before she died," I said. "We knew, father and I. She hadn't much time left. But then she was gone and no amount of time could have prepared us for it." I spoke without hesitation, as though I'd known him for years.

"Since she died father has been—it's hard to describe. He's diminished from what he was. Nothing I do for him can make up for his loss."

"Nor should it. It's too heavy a burden for you, Anna. You had to go through your own grief for your mother. You shouldn't try to make your father give up his."

I started to argue with him, but before the words left my mouth I could see there was some truth to what he said. I had wanted father to be strong, to be the same man he had been before. "Maybe you're right, Logan. I haven't been able to talk to anyone about this before. Thank you."

"There's no need to thank me. We must help each other when we can, Anna." He stood and looked over the fan palms that had hidden us from view. "Now I must offer my congratulations to Beatrice. That is, if I can fight my way through that crowd of admirers," he said.

"Of course."

I tried not to feel disappointed that our conversation had come to an end so soon. After he left me to join the revelry of the party, I turned away to walk along the terrace toward La Casa Grande, my feet scarcely touching the ground as I went. I felt lighter, happier than I had in a long time. Partly because the responsibility for my father's happiness didn't rest so heavily on my shoulders. And partly because of Logan himself. His easy manner, his kindness, his quick laughter.

That night I dreamed of his fair head leaning close to mine, with the sultry voice of Beatrice Page floating on the air, weaving a spell between us.

Maggy put down the diary, stunned that her grandmother had heard Beatrice sing the very song that had started this mystery! She sat holding the closed diary in her lap, oblivious to the breeze that blew across the patio, her lemonade untouched on the table beside her. Instead of the weathered shingles of the inn or the pale, morning light splashing over the beach in front of her, she pictured Beatrice as she had seen her standing by the Neptune Pool. That image blurred in her mind with the Beatrice that Anna described in her diary, as she appeared sixty years ago singing "Moonglow" to an adoring crowd, her blue gown swirling around her. Maggy felt a strange sense of dislocation, as though Anna's dream had become her own.

She shivered, and then quickly dismissed her fanciful thoughts. She had to keep well grounded in reality, despite her extraordinary experience. Or rather, because of it. Another image nagged at her for a moment, just out of reach. It was Anna, wearing her only evening gown to a party when Maggy was just a child. A blue gown, shot with iridescent threads. Maggy knew that dress very well. Could it be the same one? The idea seemed preposterous, but filled her with curiosity.

Maggy was also consumed with curiosity about Logan Winter. Who was he? Why hadn't Anna ever mentioned anything about him? Or for that matter, about any of these fantastic events? She had told many stories about her life at San Simeon, but not a word about Beatrice or Logan.

Logan. The man was a mystery. It sounded like Anna had been well on her way to falling in love with him. But she had married Michael Lane, not Logan Winter. Despite her intense infatuation, it seemed nothing permanent had come of it.

Another thing that struck Maggy was the way Anna wrote about Logan. Funny, it almost seemed as if she was describing someone just like Harry. And the coincidence of their names. What were the odds that they just happened to share the name Logan? The possibility of a connection between Harry and this mysterious shadow from the past made Maggy feel decidedly uncomfortable.

She looked through her handbag for the photocopies she had taken at the staff library Saturday morning. Could it only have been yesterday that she stood there with Harry close beside her, shocked to see a picture of Beatrice? So much had happened, it seemed like a month had passed since that first whisper of a kiss. Or rather, so much hadn't happened.

"Snap out of it, girl!" Maggy thought and shook her head, annoyed with herself. She'd better stop mooning about Harry and start finding out what really happened to Beatrice back in 1937. And what was going on right now.

She found the photograph and put it on the table next to Anna's diary. He had been right; the copy wasn't very good. But that wasn't what interested her now. She looked at the list of staff employed at the castle during the time Anna worked there. July, 1936 through the end of 1939. There were literally hundreds of names. No wonder the Hearst Corporation turned the property over to the state after Hearst died. It required a small army to run the place.

If she was going to get anywhere, she'd have to narrow the focus of her search. Maggy studied the list carefully and drew a line at January 1937, the date Logan had accused Anna of stealing something from his room. Then she turned to the next page and drew a line after May 1937, when Beatrice died. Something extraordinary had happened during that five-month period that had yet to be resolved. She was sure of it.

Now her list was slightly more manageable. She counted a total of 87 names. The ranch hands were listed on a separate payroll document, so this only included staff that worked on the main castle grounds: carpenters, laborers, electricians, artisans, secretaries, gardeners, cooks and other household help, even a zookeeper! The list seemed endless, yet the chances of finding anyone still living in the area were not great, she knew. Or living anywhere, for that matter. Even the youngest person on the roster would be close to eighty now. Most of the names she was reading would have moved away or died decades ago.

But that was no reason not to look. Maggy was determined to find someone who was actually there, someone who remembered Anna.

Her first course was the obvious one. She took out the local phone book and began looking up last names. The book was so small, even now that the little town was a flourishing artists' colony, it gave some indication of Cambria's size sixty years ago. It wouldn't surprise her if every person who lived in Cambria had worked at the castle then.

She exhausted the Cambria names in less than a half-hour without success. The section for San Simeon was larger. After another hour of calls, she was ready to give it up for awhile and see if Nancy was still serving breakfast. She was famished, but the last thing she wanted to do was run into Harry this morning. Maggy looked at her watch. It was only ten o'clock. Maybe just one more call.

"Cora Owen?" A man's voice answered, very loud. "Lord, I haven't heard that name in fifty years or more."

"I'm looking for the Cora Owen that worked at Hearst Castle in the thirties."

"Yep. That's my sister Cora. I'm Tom Owen," Maggy winced at the volume of his voice and held the receiver away from her ear.

"But she buried two husbands since those days. She's Cora Bishop now. What do you want with her?"

"My grandmother worked at the castle in the late thirties and I'm hoping your sister will remember her."

"She might. Course, her mind wanders a little now and then. What was your grandma's name? Maybe I knew her myself."

"Anna. Anna Lane. Her maiden name was Cummins. She worked as a housemaid at the castle."

"Anna Cummins. No. Can't say I remember. But I didn't see much of those folks up the hill. Us ranch hands didn't mix with them. Cora might've known her though. She cleaned house up there for years."

Maggy felt her excitement growing. Even though there was no mention of Cora Owen in Anna's diary, there was still a chance that they knew each other.

"Where can I find your sister, Mr. Owen?" she asked.

"She's at Sunday service now. Her friends will bring her home by 11:30 I imagine."

"You mean she lives there with you?"

"Well, of course. She couldn't bring herself to give up this house of hers, so I help her look after things."

"That's wonderful. Do you think I could stop by to meet her?"

"Don't see why not." He gave Maggy directions to his house in the countryside between San Simeon and Cambria.

She hung up the phone with a feeling of real accomplishment. Now she was getting somewhere!

Chapter 11

❖

With more than an hour before her appointment with Cora Bishop and her brother, Maggy had plenty of time to find something to eat. She wandered into the dining room, where she was disappointed to see Nancy clearing away the last traces of breakfast.

"There you are, Maggy. I was beginning to wonder if you or Harry would turn up this morning."

Maggy felt the beginnings of a blush creep up her cheeks. She told herself not to be an idiot.

"I haven't seen him this morning," she said. "Am I too late for breakfast?"

"No, you're just in time. I have ginger pancakes and fresh orange juice."

"Thanks, Nancy. I'm starving!" Maggy said. "Here, let me take some of those." She helped Nancy carry the dirty dishes into the kitchen.

Soon she was ensconced on a stool at the kitchen counter, her hands wrapped around a mug of steaming coffee, while Nancy poured batter on the griddle.

"How long have you lived in Cambria?" Maggy asked.

"We've been here about ten years, John and I. We came here for our anniversary and fell in love with the place. We decided then and there that we'd move here after we retired."

"You call this retiring? You work all the time!"

"It's not really work if you're doing what you enjoy. Me with my cooking and John with his gardening. Besides, Harry sees that we have plenty of help for the heavy work. And we both love having guests."

"Harry helps you?" Maggy was confused. "I thought he was a guest here."

Nancy looked disconcerted for a moment. "Oh. He is. But he knows everyone in Cambria."

"Talking about me again, Nancy?" came a familiar male voice from the hallway behind them. Maggy felt her pulse quicken as he walked into the room, awareness prickling her senses.

"Oh, get on with you, Harry. We have better things to do than talk about you!" Nancy's affectionate smile belied her words. "You're looking cheerful this morning for such a slug abed."

"I am cheerful, and deeply offended at the same time. I've been working for hours."

"On Sunday morning? That's the trouble with you. You'll never find a wife if you keep working day and night."

"Nancy, for the last time—I'm not looking for a wife." Harry turned to Maggy with a conspiratorial grin. "There's no pleasing this woman. First I'm lazy, then I'm a workaholic."

Maggy had regained her composure enough to comment. "You're not the only one who's been working this morning." She was still embarrassed about last night, but maybe she was over reacting. Her other doubts about him didn't seem as substantial now that he was standing in front of her.

Harry zeroed in on her immediately. "Have you made progress on your research project?" As he spoke he took two glasses out of the cupboard and looked at her quizzically. "And would you like orange juice?"

Maggy laughed despite her irritation with him. "Yes and yes."

Nancy swatted Harry with her potholder as he poured the juice. "Sit down now, Harry. How can I get breakfast ready with you underfoot, running around my kitchen as though you own the place!"

"I surrender. Just bring me whatever you want, Nancy. That's what you usually do anyway."

Nancy brought them two plates stacked high with pancakes, each accompanied by fresh peach slices. Maggy breathed in the scent of sweet ginger and melting butter.

"I'm so hungry. This is wonderful!" she said after the first bite.

"That's what I like," Harry said. "A woman who isn't afraid to eat. Even after you wolfed down your dinner last night."

Maggy was tempted to swat him herself. "Some men have been killed for lesser remarks than that. Until you've been on a diet yourself, don't throw stones."

"What did I say? That was a compliment! Nancy, help me out here."

Nancy had watched this exchange in silence, a smile slowly spreading across her features. "Not on your life. I can see that you've met your match, Harry." She untied the apron from around her waist and hung it up neatly. "There's more coffee if you want it. And don't wash up your dishes, just leave them in the sink. Remember, Harry, you're a guest here."

He held up his hands as though to ward her off. "Okay, Nancy. I promise; no cleaning of any kind."

After Nancy left, Maggy got up to pour another cup of coffee. Harry studied her as she sat down next to him. "So what secrets did you uncover this morning?" he asked her casually.

"No secrets yet. But I have an appointment to meet Cora Bishop an hour from now." Even though it hadn't taken much detective work,

Maggy was more than a little proud of her success. She waited expectantly for Harry to ask who Cora Bishop was.

"That's fast work. She's a good find; she worked at the castle from about 1930 right up to World War II."

"You know about her already?"

"Sure. I interviewed her as part of a video series I did about five years ago. 'The Living History of Hearst Castle.' We included everyone we could find who had worked at the ranch. Quite a few of them have died since then, so we were fortunate to capture their memories when we did."

Maggy tried not to let her disappointment show. "I don't suppose any of them said anything interesting about Beatrice?"

"A few of them might have mentioned her. But Hearst entertained hundreds of guests at the castle over the years, and his employees had as many stories to tell about them. I would have told you if I remembered anything important. You know that, don't you Maggy?" He didn't smile, but watched her reaction closely.

"I'm not sure," she said, all pretense gone as she returned his look.

He stood up abruptly and took their dishes to the sink. "Would you mind if I go with you to visit Cora? You might succeed in learning something from her that slipped by me before. I wasn't looking for Beatrice when I interviewed her five years ago."

"I—no, I don't mind if you come." As Maggy said the words, she realized they were true. She wanted him to come with her, doubts be damned!

"Good. Let's hope Cora's condition hasn't deteriorated since I last saw her. She had periods when she was perfectly lucid, with an amazing ability to recall events. At other times, she confused the past and present. Couldn't quite remember what year she was living in. I think she was eighty-one when I talked to her."

Maggy did a quick calculation. "She would have been older than Anna then. About twenty-six or so when Beatrice was at the castle."

"And about eighty-six now, don't forget."

* * *

A half-hour later they were on the road traveling east from the town of San Simeon, Maggy at the wheel of her rental car. With Harry giving directions, she was free to relax and enjoy the countryside as they drove down a two-lane highway through rolling pastures, clusters of buildings giving way to open spaces and an occasional farmhouse. Majestic live oak trees raised bare limbs to the sky, still graceful without their summer finery.

"When are you going back home?" Harry asked.

"I'm leaving on Thursday," she answered. "That only gives us three days, well four, counting today, to solve this mystery." She didn't add that it only gave them four more days together, but the unspoken words hung in the air between them.

Harry leaned over and gently brushed her hair back where it had fallen against her cheek. "Sometimes you hide behind that gorgeous sweep of hair, Maggy." His touch burned her skin, but she managed to remain outwardly calm as she glowered at him.

"I do not! My hair just falls in my face sometimes." As she spoke, her hair came loose from behind her ear to fall across the right side of her face in a shining curtain.

"I have a proposition for you," he brushed back her hair again, his fingertips lingering against the back of her neck. "Stay here Thursday. There's a private party at the castle that night, a benefit for the State Parks and Recreation system. It's a rare opportunity to see the castle as it was before, full of music and life."

"Is that an invitation?"

"Of course it is. I want to be there with you when you see it. There will be about a hundred guests, all dressed in period evening clothes from the thirties. Like a costume party."

"Darn! And I didn't bring my ball gown."

"You won't get out of it that easy," he said. "I have at your disposal the entire docent's wardrobe. You can borrow any gown that strikes your fancy." He leaned closer. "Say you'll come, Maggy."

"All right, I'll come! And hope Carol doesn't kill me for being gone so long." She smiled at him and shook her head, causing her hair to fall down again. "Thank you, Harry. It sounds fascinating."

"It will be, now." He pointed out a white-painted farmhouse on the right, shaded by several ancient oak trees. "That's Cora Bishop's house."

As they pulled into the driveway, a man came out of the house to meet them. "Well, hello there Harry!" he said, surprise evident in his voice as they shook hands. He offered a lean, work-roughened hand to Maggy. "And you must be Miss Lane. Come on in. Cora's expectin' you." They followed him into a warm, over-furnished living room, family photographs and knick-knacks covering every surface.

"Here's the girl I was telling you about, Cora," he said to his sister. She was sitting in one of the armchairs, a flowered dress covering her ample form. The face above her lacy collar was flushed and good-natured, deep wrinkles emphasizing every feature. Her thin, white hair was neatly pinned up in a French twist. She didn't look a day over eighty.

"There's no need to shout, Tom. I can hear perfectly well. Come in here, you two." She looked at Harry quizzically for a moment. "I know you, young man. Just a minute, it will come to me."

"You were kind enough to let me interview you five years ago," Harry volunteered.

"I remember! Thank you for sending us a copy of that video picture you made. It took me back, seeing those faces. And you put in some photographs from when we were all youngsters up at the castle. Yes, it took me back."

"That's why I wanted to talk to you, Mrs. Bishop," Maggy said.

"Please, call me Cora, dear."

"Cora, then. And my name is Maggy." She felt a little awkward calling such an elderly woman by her first name. "My grandmother worked at the castle in the late thirties. I wondered if you knew her. Her name was Anna Lane. She was Anna Cummins before her marriage."

"Anna. Of course I knew her. There weren't so many people living in Cambria or San Simeon then, and everybody knew everybody. But she was a few years younger than I was, so I didn't know her from school. Her family was dead poor, I remember. Everyone was poor in those days, unless you were lucky enough to work up on the hill."

"Do you remember her working with you up there?" Maggy asked hopefully.

"The castle, you mean? Mr. Hearst didn't like to call it the castle, you know. He always called it the ranch. What a place it was! So many people, and comings and goings. Such excitement. It was a marvel up there. Like Shangri-La, I always thought." The whistle of a tea-kettle came from the next room, interrupting her reminiscences. "Oh, you must have some tea with us," she said.

"You stay put, Cora, and entertain your guests. I'll fetch the tea, or there's fresh coffee if you want," Tom said just as loudly as before.

Maggy and Harry both asked for coffee and Tom disappeared into the kitchen.

"The man is deaf as a post," Cora said. "And just as obstinate." Despite her words, she smiled proudly as she spoke of him. "Tom worked at the real ranch, tending cattle and such. He'd ride fences and sometimes ride out to fix the telephone lines. Mr. Hearst would put out a telephone line in the middle of nowhere, just so he could send his orders to those news-paper chiefs when he went on one of his horseback rides. Now where was I?"

"You were talking about the castle, and if you knew Anna there," Maggy reminded her.

"We were both housemaids, but Anna worked mostly at "A" House with Emma Christenson. That was the House of the Sea, don't you know. Every house had a name. I worked in the main house most days. Anna kept to herself, but she was a lovely young thing. A kinder person you never saw.

"We were all star-struck then, with the celebrities we took care of. I remember when David Niven came with his wife, and Anna was so exited. She was new then. I think that was the first movie star she ever saw."

"Was she friendly with any of the guests?" Harry asked.

"We didn't have much time to get friendly with the guests. We worked a full day's work, let me tell you. But we were treated with respect, especially by Mr. Hearst himself."

Tom came back into the room with a tray and mugs of coffee and tea. Both were brewed so strong they were pitch black. Maggy added a healthy amount of cream to her coffee and found it as good as the Starbuck's coffee she got at home.

"Maggy, is it?" Cora said to her suddenly. "Turn your face to the light so I can see you better."

Feeling self-conscious, Maggy put down her cup and moved closer to the old woman.

"You're the image of your grandmother. Different color hair, but the same fair coloring and shape to your face. Just like Anna. She was a lovely girl." She fell silent.

"Did she become friends with any of the guests?" Maggy repeated Harry's earlier question.

"Oh, she did. We all had our favorites among the guests. I was always exited when Clark Gable came to visit. But Anna worshipped that singer, Beatrice Page, more's the pity. Of course, everybody loved her, especially when she started up singing again. And there was her friend, what was his name? He was such a fine-looking young man, always had a laugh or kind word for everyone." She looked at Harry while she spoke, and a confused expression came over her.

"Winter. That's your name, isn't it?" she said to Harry.

"No, Cora," Harry said gently. "I'm the fellow who interviewed you for the video tape. And this is Maggy, Anna's granddaughter."

"Well, of course I know that!" Cora said quickly as she looked back at Maggy.

"We think Anna knew Beatrice Page and her friend, Logan Winter," Maggy said. "Did Anna ever tell you about an object that was stolen from Mr. Winter's room?"

"Stolen? Why if anything were stolen, it would have been a scandal! With all those rooms filled with riches. You had to have a card with your picture on it to be let in the gate down below. No one would dare steal anything from Mr. Hearst!" Cora seemed shocked at the very idea.

Maggy was beginning to worry that their visit wasn't going to turn up any new information. "Can you remember anything else about Anna, or about her friends?"

"Well, Anna was very friendly with that young man," she looked from Maggy to Harry again. "I saw her talking with him myself more than once. She didn't speak of him though. When we took our meals, she always talked about Beatrice Page. There was another one who came with Mrs. Page, Orcutt was his name. Why she brought him with her I don't know. He was a mean-spirited man. Bad temper, and he always had liquor. We worried when the guests got ahold of liquor, lest we be blamed for getting it for them. Mr. Hearst couldn't abide drunkenness.

"Then there was that terrible business with Mrs. Page. Anna took it real hard when she got killed. It was a shame, such a talented lady. Such a beautiful voice she had. We never knew what really happened. There were all sorts of rumors and gossip, but they said it was an accident. Poor Anna wept for days afterward."

"What were some of the rumors you heard?" Maggy asked.

"Well, they said maybe it wasn't an accident. There was a lover's quarrel between her and Mr. Winter. I never believed that for a minute." Cora looked at Harry as she spoke. "I knew you wouldn't hurt her."

"Cora, I'm not Winter. My name is Harry Logan. I was the curator at the castle. Do you remember our interview?" Maggy was impressed with Harry's patience as he spoke to her.

"Logan. Yes, Logan Winter. I knew you wouldn't hurt anyone. He was kind to you, Anna." Maggy realized with a start that Cora was speaking to her, confusing her with Anna. "We could tell that you were sweet on him, even though you would never speak of it."

Tom stood up and went to Cora's side. "That's enough recollecting for one day, Cora."

Maggy picked up her bag and took Cora's hand in hers. "Thank you for seeing us today, Cora. We appreciate your help."

"It's good to see you again, Anna. Nice of you and your young man to visit me after all this time." Cora said, and patted Maggy's hand. She looked at Harry again with a troubled expression. Then her eyes cleared and she smiled. "I know what's wrong! It's those glasses. You don't wear glasses, Mr. Winter!"

* * *

Maggy pulled into her parking place at the Beach House Inn and turned off the engine. The lot was empty except for Harry's dusty Landrover parked nearby. She looked at him sitting next to her and smiled. "Well, that was a little unnerving, Mr. Winter."

"I warned you that might happen," Harry said. "Cora was better a few years ago when I interviewed her. She had lapses, but recovered quickly if you reminded her of the present."

"I can see why she might have confused me with Anna. There is a resemblance between us, as you've pointed out. But where did she get it into her head that you are Logan Winter?"

"Maybe the name Logan set her off," Harry answered. "I don't know, Maggy. I've seen her confuse her brother Tom with her dead husband, so I wouldn't worry about it."

"Interesting that there were rumors of a love affair between Beatrice and Logan Winter. Do you think he could have had something to do with her death?"

"Apparently he was with her when the accident happened. But the inquest ruled it accidental death. No, I don't think they were lovers, or that he was responsible for her death."

"How do you know that?" Maggy asked, surprised that he had such a strong opinion. "Did you find a record of what happened?"

He hesitated before answering. "I'm sure I saw a newspaper account of it at one point or another. It was all public record, after all."

"But there wasn't any record of it at the resource library. That's what worries me. And if they were having an affair I doubt if that was public record."

"Do you really think Beatrice is haunting you? To avenge her murder? You said yourself that she wasn't a ghost."

"I know I did. And I meant it. I still believe she's an angel. I don't know if her death was accidental or not, or if it's the reason she appeared to me, but I'm going to find out." Maggy looked at Harry with a trace of uneasiness. "You changed the subject very conveniently. I get the feeling you know more about this than you're telling me."

"I want to solve this mystery as much as you do, Maggy," he said. He shook his head wearily. "Maybe more, in fact. That reminds me, have you finished with the second volume of Anna's diary? There's still a chance that I might catch something in it that wouldn't mean anything to you."

"No, I have another few pages left to read. But I don't understand you, Harry. Why would you want to solve this mystery more than I do? It doesn't really have anything to do with you, except through me. Does it?"

The muscle in Harry's cheek worked as he clenched and unclenched his teeth. He looked out the window unseeingly. Whatever was troubling him was making Maggy increasingly nervous.

"What is it?" she asked. "What are you hiding from me?"

Finally he turned to her. She was surprised to see anguish in his eyes as he reached a hand up to brush her hair away from her face. "I don't know what to say." His fingers traced a path along her cheek, touched lightly on her mouth. The contact made her senses reel, even as warning signals were flashing in her mind.

"All I know is this," he said. With a groan he reached out for her, crushing her to him in a fierce embrace. His lips pressed against hers, demanding, impatient for her response. She reacted to him instantly, her arms twining around his neck, pulling him closer. His tongue brushed hers, sending fiery pulses charging through her body.

He pulled away from her a few inches, his eyes intense with arousal. And something more. She couldn't read what was in them.

"You feel it too," he said, his fingers once again caressing her cheek. "But can I trust you, Maggy?" Without another word, he left her abruptly. She sat alone in the car, completely bewildered by his actions.

Chapter 12

As soon as Maggy returned to her room she dialed Carol's number, anxious to see if her friend had managed to dig up anything on Beatrice's companions. She listened impatiently to the phone ringing on the other end and tried not to think about Harry's strange behavior and the way she reacted to him. But her mind wasn't cooperating. She couldn't think about anything else at the moment.

Despite her doubts about him, all it took was a touch, or not even that, just a certain look from him and she was lost. But now her doubts had come back full force, intensified by his unexpected response to her questions. Why couldn't he confide in her? Why couldn't he trust her?

"Hello," Carol's cheery voice snapped her out of her reverie.

"Carol, I'm so glad you're home," Maggy said.

"Hey, that's the same way we started our last conversation. And where else would I be, when I've spent the whole weekend digging through ancient history for you!"

When Maggy didn't respond in kind, Carol's voice softened. "Are you okay, Maggy?"

"Yeah, I guess so," Maggy said. Now wasn't the time to tell Carol her fears. "Just a little preoccupied. But I'm dying to find out what you learned. And thank you for helping, Carol. Really."

"No problem. As usual I got some dazzling results. First we have Edward Orcutt. He was a business partner of Maxwell Page. Maxwell did the creative stuff, composing and lyrics, Beatrice did the performing, and Edward Orcutt did everything else. He managed all the bookings, copyrights, publishing deals, film contracts, everything. He went to college with Maxwell, which is probably how they met. After Beatrice died in 1937, he went on to act as business manager for quite a few Hollywood celebrities. And he had the good sense to invest in real estate. He was a rich man when he died in 1971.

"Did he ever marry?"

"Not for years. He finally married in 1956. They had a child in 1958, a boy. Let's see, here it is. Miles Orcutt. Wow! Daddy must have been in his sixties."

"Interesting," Maggy said, thinking of the argument Anna had overheard between Edward and Beatrice. She quickly described it to Carol. "Maybe he really loved Beatrice. Maybe it took that long for him to get over her."

"Well, not many people loved him. Several of his clients tried to sue him unsuccessfully. They claimed he cheated them, but none of them could prove it. On the other hand, he was extremely litigious himself. And he usually won."

"Anna disliked him from the moment she met him," Maggy said.

"Well, then we know he was a jerk," Carol said seriously. "This history doesn't disprove it."

"What about Logan Winter?" Maggy asked. "Anna felt very differently about him."

"He wasn't so easy," Carol said. "I couldn't get a complete picture of him or where he came from. Apparently, he just appeared out of nowhere. Hearst bought art from him in the late twenties and he had a fortune in his own right, but I couldn't find out where his money came from."

"Wait a minute," Maggy interrupted. "Are you sure we're talking about the same person? Anna said he was just a few years older than she was. That would have made him early or mid-twenties, tops. That's too young for this to be the same guy. He'd have to have been a major art agent before he was twenty!"

"Anna could have been wrong about his age. Hey, maybe he had a baby face when she knew him, but he was really 35. No, this is your man. And he wasn't an art agent, he was a collector himself. He was playing in the same league as Hearst, but he bought and sold discreetly, on a small scale."

Maggy was silent for a moment, trying to reconcile this image of Logan Winter with Anna's description. "What about Beatrice? How did he know her?" she asked.

"I found a reference to a film he financed for Beatrice and Maxwell in 1930. I believe he backed more of their ventures after that. It's likely that Marion Davies introduced him to her Hollywood friends."

"I don't know, Carol. It seems like we have a few pieces of the puzzle and the rest are missing."

"I know what you mean," Carol said in an aggrieved voice. "I've run into one dead end after another. And finally, I lost his trail altogether. Can you imagine? There was one possible reference that he might have fought in World War II, but I couldn't find anything conclusive. No estate left behind, no wife or heirs. He just disappeared and his fortune disappeared along with him."

Maggy laughed. "I can tell this just drives you crazy, Carol."

"You bet it does! I'll keep digging around though. Even if it was sixty years ago, there's bound to be some evidence of what happened to him."

"I'm glad I was able to provide such a challenge for you. Wouldn't want you to get bored," Maggy said.

"You're treading on thin ice, girl. And you owe me big time for my missed weekend. You can start paying me back by telling me all about Harry."

Maggy felt her mood sink the moment she thought about him. "Carol, I think I'm in over my head with him."

Carol's voice lost its bantering tone immediately. "Okay, tell me everything."

Maggy quickly told her that Harry invited her to a private party at the castle on Thursday where everyone would wear clothes from the twenties and thirties. "I agreed to go with him even though I'll have to borrow a dress. Apparently the museum keeps a wardrobe of costumes for the docents to wear." Maggy said.

"Well, I can see how that's a bad thing. You'll be away from your desk for one more day and I'll have to cover for you! Come one, Maggy, quit stalling. What's really going on?"

"I invited him to sleep with me last night," Maggy said reluctantly.

"Of course you did. Any fool could've seen that coming from the way you talked about him." Carol replied. "And?"

"No, that's just the point. He turned me down. Said it would be a mistake for both of us. But the way he kissed me! Carol, I know he wants me. And as for me—all he has to do is look at me and I want to drag him to bed."

"Well, now I am surprised," Carol said. "You mean he wouldn't sleep with you on your first date? Isn't that your usual tune, Ms. Conservative?"

"But this isn't a usual situation where you can take your time and get to know each other. He said it would be a mistake. I don't know what to think about him. I don't think I can trust him."

"Maggy, slow down! Okay, it's a bit unusual for a man to turn down an offer like that, coming from a woman like you. By the way, I'm amazed at you, you wicked girl. Maybe he likes you more than you realize."

"No, it's more than that," Maggy said. She told Carol about their visit with Cora Bishop. "When I asked him what he was hiding from me, he got terribly upset. He said he couldn't tell me anything."

"You're right, Maggy. It sounds like he's holding something back. But remember, you're still practically strangers. Maybe he doesn't know if he can trust you yet."

"That's just it. There's no time left. I'm only going to be here until Thursday. Well, Friday, if I go to the party with him Thursday night. Then we'll never see each other again. I knew there wasn't a chance for anything more. He was right when he said it would be a mistake."

"Really? If he invited you to spend the night, would you turn him down?" Carol asked.

"You see right through me, as usual," Maggy said with a shaky laugh. "But something else happened. Someone was in my room. He took the last volume of Anna's diary and smashed the silver earrings and bracelet you gave me."

"Are you serious?"

"Unfortunately, yes. I discovered it right after I talked to you yesterday. I filed a police report, but they said there isn't much chance of getting it back."

"This is too weird, Maggy. Who would break into your room?"

"It wasn't a break-in. Someone must have used a key."

"But why?" Carol asked.

"Maybe somebody else thinks Anna's diary is important, I don't know. I had the other two volumes with me, so they only got the last one."

"This worries me a lot more than your problems with Harry," Carol said. "Just suppose Beatrice didn't die accidentally. And now somebody doesn't want you to find out what really happened."

"You mean the eighty or ninety year old murderer?" Maggy was still skeptical.

"Whoever. Somebody was in your room, Maggy. What if you had walked in while he was still there?"

"I don't know, Carol. You're not helping to cheer me up, you know."

"I don't want to cheer you up. I want you to be careful, damn it. Now, who knew about Anna's diary?"

"Just the curator of the museum. And Harry, of course. But I'm donating the diary to the museum, so there's no reason for either of them to steal it."

"Unless there's something in it that he—whoever he is—doesn't want you to see. You still haven't read it all yet, have you?"

"I'm just finishing the second volume," Maggy said slowly. "Harry knew I hadn't read the diaries yet. I told him."

Carol didn't have anything to say for a moment, and Maggy felt her dread increase.

"You don't think Harry took the diary, do you?" Carol finally asked.

"I can't believe he would do that," Maggy said, feeling sick now that the words were spoken. "But he did come back to the inn yesterday afternoon. He said he had to pick up some work he left in his room."

"Are you sure nobody else knew about it?" Carol asked.

Maggy tried to recall her actions from the time she arrived on Thursday night to Saturday, when she noticed the diary was missing. The grim expression on her face relaxed suddenly. "Yes! I'd forgotten. Harry and I talked about Anna's diary at dinner on Friday night. Any of the others could have overheard us. The Clarks were there, and the Sorensons, and a couple from Boston."

"I just thought of something else," Carol said. "The museum curator could have told dozens of people about it, for all we know. It wasn't a secret."

"You're right," Maggy said with relief. "I think we're getting each other paranoid."

"Maybe. But now you have a handful of possible suspects, including Harry. A little healthy paranoia might keep you from getting hurt. And I'm not talking about your love life. I mean really hurt."

"Okay. But I don't know what precautions I can take, except to get to the bottom of this as quickly as possible."

"You could come home now," Carol said. "Forget the whole thing."

"I can't. Not yet. I have to find out about Beatrice, and the only way I can do that is to stay here."

"Oh well, I had to give it a shot, even though I knew you wouldn't give up," Carol said. "But at least admit the real reason you're staying."

"I've told you, Carol. I'm going to find out what happened to Beatrice, and why she appeared to me."

Carol's voice took on the tone she used when her children were trying to get away with something. "So you've said. But there's no real reason why you can't conduct research here. If you came home you could actually do the work yourself instead of having me do it for you. Not that I'm complaining," she added quickly as Maggy started to protest. "Just so you know why you're staying."

"God, Carol! I'm not staying just because of Harry. You're so annoying sometimes."

Maggy was troubled after she hung up the phone. Though she had been quick to argue with Carol about her motives for staying, she had to admit that her friend was probably right. As usual. Maggy shook her head and marveled, not for the first time, at her friendship with Carol that had spanned almost fifteen years. Trust Carol to be the one who made her really face up to herself, whether she wanted to or not.

It was hard for her to admit how important Harry had become to her, and how much it hurt to have doubts about his motives.

She found the diary exactly where she had left it that morning, hidden away in her suitcase. Maybe Anna's words from long ago would help her out of her dilemma.

Anna's Diary—February 2, 1937

It's been three days since the party. Emma and I have had our hands full seeing to the guests still remaining. Logan left early Saturday morning, but he made a special point to look me up and say a quick good-bye. Emma saw this exchange and had a few foolish comments to make. I begged her to drop the matter. She's become a good friend, and when she saw that I was serious, she stopped her light-hearted teasing at once.

Mrs. Page left the castle this afternoon, still happy and glowing with pleasure from her success Friday night. I helped her pack her suitcase and lingered with her in her room, while we talked about many things. Later I was surprised that she had confided such private feelings to me, but at the time I felt a strong rapport with her. And the gifts she gave me! I told her they were much too valuable, but she insisted that I keep them both. A surprising afternoon on all counts.

I started folding her things and putting them in her cases, and found myself telling her how beautiful her singing had been on Friday, and that I'd watched her from my vantage point in the gardens.

"Thank you, Anna," she said with a smile. Then she was thoughtful, as though she was remembering something dear. "It's been much too long. I love to sing more than anything on earth, and I'm happy that I've found my voice again."

Then she asked me to sit down on her bed for a moment. "I've been wanting to apologize to you, dear, for the way Edward spoke to you the other night. He can be a terrible lout sometimes," she said. I thought that was an understatement, though I certainly didn't say so.

"I should apologize to you, Mrs. Page," I said instead. "I didn't mean to eavesdrop, but I couldn't help hearing him. I'm so sorry."

"Nonsense. You did nothing wrong." She sighed and shook her head. "He's always been a difficult man, but he's gotten much worse since Maxwell died. I think Max had a good effect on him. Maxwell and I both appreciated all that Edward did for us, for our careers."

"How did he help you?" I asked, my curiosity getting the better of me. Though Logan had already told me a little bit about Mr. Orcutt, I wondered if Beatrice might have seen it differently.

"Maxwell didn't have a head for business at all, but he was a brilliant composer and lyricist. You probably know many of his songs. I could sing, but I was never known for my practical nature. So Edward came along and organized us. He took care of all the business details, made sure we met the right people, signed the right contracts. That's when we began to have real success. We owed him a great deal."

"But your talent is what made you successful." I said.

She smiled at me indulgently. "Anna, there are any number of talented people who never become successful. Maxwell and I didn't care that much about money or business. We just weren't any good at it. Edward made the difference for us."

After hearing her voice and seeing her perform, I thought she was far too modest. Of course, I didn't know what it had been like for her when she was starting out, but I still thought she overestimated Mr. Orcutt's contribution. It might have been prejudice on my part, for I disliked him as much as ever.

"And now?" I asked her.

"Now? He's delighted that I've decided to go to work again. That's the one thing that Edward and Logan can agree on. They both want me to sing again. It was impossible before." The expression around her eyes only hinted at the grief she must have felt when her husband died.

"I understand how you feel, Mrs. Page."

"Do you, Anna? You're very young to know about such things."

I answered her slowly, remembering. "When I lost my mother I couldn't bear to be reminded of our happy times together, when we were a family. It only made it more painful. But now I treasure those memories. In a way, they bring her back to me."

She reached over to squeeze my hand. "Exactly. And that's why I'm finally able to sing again." She stood up and went to the closet. "Now, shall we finish packing? I have far too many clothes for one woman. Edward insists that I keep buying the latest fashions. God forbid I should ever be seen in a dress from last season!" she laughed.

"I know it isn't my place to ask you, m'am," I hesitated, embarrassed at my audacity. "Will you marry him?"

"Marry Edward?" She turned to me with several gowns in her arms. "No, dear. As I've told him many times, I'm never going to marry again. He will have to accept it sooner or later. Then perhaps he'll get over these jealous delusions he is suffering from."

I smiled happily at her words. Happy for her sake because she was safe from Mr. Orcutt. And for my own, because she and Logan could not possibly be lovers.

"Are you a good seamstress, Anna?" she asked, looking at me closely.

"Very good, indeed. I'll be happy to mend something for you. I can do alterations as well, though there might not be enough time to finish before you leave today."

"You can take all the time you want," she said and held up the blue gown she had worn at the party. "This is for you. I want you to have it." She held it against my shoulders and eyed it critically as it draped over my uniform.

I was speechless with surprise.

"You're quite a bit smaller than I am, and you'll need to hem up the length. But I think it will look beautiful on you."

Words of gratitude tumbled out of my mouth so fast that she laughed and held up her hand to stop me. "Nonsense. I know how much you admire this dress, so it pleases me to give it to you."

I held up the rich fabric over my plain uniform and looked at myself in the mirror. She was right, it did suit my fair coloring. It was a gown that would make any woman beautiful.

"I have just the thing to go with it," she said as she looked through one of the drawers in a 16th century dresser. "Here they are." She had a brown jar in her hands, which she brought over to me. Inside was a long string of pearls that she held up near my face.

"Yes, these suit you as well. And they set off the color of the gown beautifully."

"Mrs. Page, I couldn't possibly accept these. They're much too valuable," I protested, even as I looked admiringly at their luster next to my skin.

Her answer was even more surprising. "Anna, I don't want to keep them. Someone gave them to me as some sort of joke the last time I visited here. I'm very annoyed with that person, whoever it was. He left a note saying that they were a gift from Logan. But Logan denied that he gave me any pearls. So there you have it. An anonymous gift. I've never learned who the culprit was."

I was shocked. "But they're real, aren't they?"

"Yes, they certainly are. And quite lovely. But I don't want them. I want you to have them, along with the dress."

I put them back in their little jar, slowly comprehending that she was determined. Such generosity as hers was far from typical, even among the rich. Especially among the rich, I had learned.

"I don't know what to say," I stammered.

"Say you'll accept these gifts. To celebrate my successful comeback. To please me."

At last I agreed to her wishes, and my delight came bubbling to the surface. I couldn't believe my good fortune to have met and become friends with such a woman. We continued our conversation in high spirits, chatting like old school chums, while I helped pack away her many belongings.

I didn't think it strange at the time, but later I wondered at the ease I felt with her, the newfound closeness. Almost as though she were the sister I never had. This, despite the years between us, for she was nearer my mother's age than mine. And I think she felt this bond as well. She asked me to call her by her first name, just as Logan had done in the name of friendship.

She left late this afternoon with Mr. Orcutt. Miss Davies and Mr. Hearst saw them off on their journey back to Los Angeles. I suspect from her manner that Miss Davies dislikes Mr. Orcutt as much as I do, but she is kind to him nonetheless. Doubtless because of her fondness for Beatrice.

I look into the small mirror over my bureau at my reflection. The pearls glow against my skin. The blue gown is hanging in my closet as I write this, with pins to mark the new seams I will set in. I can't wait to show father my new finery. The pearls must be worth a great deal of money, and will go a long way toward easing our financial worries. The gown, though. That I will keep.

I wish Logan could see me in my brilliant gown, and the pearls as well. Perhaps then he would look at me differently. If I finish the alterations before his next visit—

No. Such thoughts are nonsense. By no stretch of the imagination could I wear the gown here at the castle. And there is no other place where I would ever see Logan. These fantasies of mine are just that, silly daydreams. I won't think of them anymore.

Instead I will remember Beatrice and her kindness.

Maggy was incredulous when she closed the diary. The blue gown that Anna described, that Beatrice had worn, was at this moment tucked away in a garment bag in her own closet in Portland. She'd been right, it was the same gown!

Maggy had seen her grandmother wear it once, years ago. It had been a fancy party for the grown-ups. It must have been their thirtieth anniversary, when Maggy had been six or seven years old. To her adoring eyes, Anna had been transformed into a fairy princess that night.

Then another thought occurred to her. She quickly reread the last entry in the diary. Those must be the same pearls that Anna had given her on her 21st birthday. Maggy still wore them on those rare occasions when she dressed up. What had Anna said about them? That they were a gift from a dear friend, but she wouldn't say who had given them to her. Maggy had assumed it had been an old boyfriend and that's why Anna wouldn't tell her. But the friend had been Beatrice!

How had Anna managed to keep the pearls, when she obviously intended to sell them? And what had happened between Anna and Logan?

She couldn't believe the story would end here, when so many questions remained unanswered. Damn! If she only had the last volume! When she had glanced through the journals shortly after Anna's death, Maggy had seen entries as late as 1938, or maybe later. She couldn't remember exactly. Nor could she remember when Hearst and Marion Davies had closed up the castle. She knew the castle was thought to be vulnerable to air attack by the Japanese during World War II, so they had moved to Wyntoon, a smaller Hearst estate even more remotely located in the northern forests of California. But Anna hadn't gone with them.

Maggy berated herself for not reading the diaries as soon as she found them among Anna's belongings. Now she might never know what was in the missing volume.

Chapter 13

$\mathcal{H}$arry surveyed the scene of chaos before him, unable to make sense of it. Old newspapers and magazines were strewn on the floor, some of their pages torn. Not a single book remained on the shelves. They were tossed randomly on top of each other around the small room.

"This is the way we found it this morning," Steve Liggett said, his voice echoing Harry's feeling of bewilderment. "A security guard thought he heard something this morning, and this is what he found."

"He didn't see anyone?"

"No. And the door was still locked. It's the damnedest thing. He said he heard somebody crashing around in here."

Harry felt a chill pass over him. Maggy's room had been locked too, but that hadn't stopped someone from destroying her jewelry. Could it be the same person? As he looked at the wreckage, he was afraid whoever had done this was losing his control. This room had been destroyed in a rage.

"I hope the computer is still intact, or months of work will be lost," Steve looked at the computer lying on its side on the floor.

"Here, I'll help you get the monitor," Harry said. Together they put it back on the table. It sat crookedly on its base, a large crack running across the glass screen.

Steve looked around the small library helplessly, his meticulously groomed form at odds with the disorder of his surroundings.

"I don't get it. How could anyone get in here?"

"And more importantly," Harry asked, "why?"

"No kidding," Steve scratched his head, the uncharacteristic gesture leaving his hair rumpled. "There's nothing here of any value to a thief, no antiques or artwork. Just photos and records." His frown deepened. "It might take weeks to figure out if anything is missing in this mess."

"It seems to me there are two possibilities," Harry said slowly, as though he were thinking out loud. "The thief was looking for something. Either he found it, and left this wreckage so we wouldn't know what he took."

"Or what?"

"Or he didn't find it, and just lost his temper."

Steve gave a sharp laugh. "I'd hate to see this guy if he got really mad!" He walked to one of the windows that looked out to the driveway. "I still don't see how anybody could get in here. The roads are gated and guards are posted twenty-four hours a day. Tour guides sometimes use the library on Sunday, but we might not have discovered this until tomorrow if the guard hadn't heard something."

"I'll see what I can find out," Harry said as they locked the door of the library behind them.

"Thanks, Harry. If we find anything missing, I'll let you know."

Harry walked back to the landrover unseeingly, his mind in a black cloud. He had been right to be afraid for Maggy. But he'd been afraid of the harm he could do to her himself. Now he had proof there was someone else in on the hunt. He'd had hints of it before, when he followed a promising lead only to find someone had beaten him to it.

If Maggy was in danger, as he suspected, then he had no choice. He had to warn her, and the only way to do that was to tell her the truth.

* * *

"Why do you think Anna's diary is so important?" Beatrice asked Ambrose. They were standing in their usual meeting place near the abandoned pergola. Beatrice strained her eyes to see him in the shadowy light of the earthly sun. He was wearing white robes again today, which made him look like a well-fed Roman citizen arguing his case.

"Because it might answer some of our questions," Ambrose said as he paced back and forth in front of her. "There's a chance that Anna observed something. If that's true, she probably didn't place any significance on it. But she might have written about it in her diary. I found out from Maggy that the first two volumes didn't contain anything helpful."

"But you think the third volume will be different?"

"If we could only find it!" he fumed.

"Please hold still," Beatrice said. "You're making me dizzy."

"It's this inactivity! It's driving me to distraction."

"But you say the last volume was stolen out of Maggy's room. Who could've done that?"

"I never said it was stolen." Ambrose started pacing again, much to Beatrice's irritation. "Maggy's convinced someone broke into her room, but I'm not."

"Then where's the diary?"

"I don't know. Maybe the foolish girl misplaced it. She could have left it somewhere accidentally and not even realized it."

"In a pig's eye." Beatrice said. "And I'd never call Maggy a foolish girl. She's quite the opposite. Ambrose, please stop pacing this minute!"

He came to an abrupt halt. "I have an idea. Come with me." Ambrose grabbed her wrist and they both disappeared, only to reappear instantly on a sidewalk 700 miles north of San Simeon.

"I wish you'd told me before doing that," Beatrice said, snatching her hand away from him.

"No time to waste," Ambrose replied with a satisfied grin. "Let's see if we can find that diary."

"Here? Where have you brought me?"

"Oregon."

They stood in a residential neighborhood on a meandering drive. A light rain fell around them, with no trace of sunlight to lighten the dark afternoon. Rain dripped from fir trees and leafy rhododendrons and the damp air was rich with the smell of earth and pine. A sharp contrast to the dry California coast they had just left. Maggy's house was a small, single-story structure with a large front window overlooking a small wooden deck. The blue-painted trim was echoed by the verdigris wind chimes that tinkled softly in the wind.

They started toward the house when the sound of a car door slamming nearby caught their attention. A woman got out of a station wagon parked in front of the house and walked up the drive. She didn't carry an umbrella, and misty rain formed dewdrops on her curly dark hair. She unlocked the front door and walked inside.

"Who was that?" Beatrice asked.

"Unless it's a very well-equipped thief, it must be Maggy's friend Carol," Ambrose said. "Let's see what she's up to."

When they materialized in the living room, Carol was just coming out of the back hallway, carrying a large garment bag over one arm. She paused to turn out the light, leaving the hall in mid-afternoon darkness. Ambrose walked very close to her, his robes brushing against her legs, as he eyed the bag suspiciously. "What is she taking, I wonder?"

Carol suddenly froze and looked around her, as though she was listening for something. She walked further into the living room and paused again. "Is someone there?"

"Ambrose, she can feel our presence. Leave her alone for Heaven's sake. We're the trespassers here."

"She's entirely too sensitive to angels," he said. He watched as Carol shivered and retraced her steps back down the hallway. She came back a moment later, shaking her head. After another slow look around the room she picked up the keys from the counter and walked out the front door with a decisive stride. The door lock clicked behind her.

"What exactly are we doing here?" Beatrice asked him. Though she agreed with Ambrose that they had to do something, she wasn't sure that searching Maggy's house while she was gone was the right thing to do.

"I told you. We're looking for the diary," he answered. "There's a good chance that she just forgot it, and then jumped to conclusions when she couldn't find it in her room."

"Really, Ambrose, you're making her sound like a hysterical female. Maggy wouldn't have just imagined that someone was in her room. I don't buy it."

"But you don't know that much about her. You're hampered in your powers, Beatrice. You can't see into Maggy's heart with perfect insight. Besides, she had every reason to be hysterical. She saw you, remember?"

"Oh, all right," Beatrice said. "But I do feel a bond with her. It's a different sort of closeness than I feel with my other mortals. It's very personal, as though she touches a chord in me. Yet at the same time, she's obscured. I can't see beneath her surface."

"Yes, that's all very interesting, but it's not why we're here." Ambrose surveyed the living room with its vaulted ceiling and brick fireplace. While he wandered away, Beatrice was drawn to a large painting in an ornate mahogany frame near the fireplace. A moody, stylized portrait of a woman in shades of pearl, gray and black, gazing off to her left with half lowered eyes. It was a gorgeous piece, but evoked a feeling of profound melancholy.

"Here's a good place to look," Ambrose said from the other room, a small dining alcove that adjoined the kitchen to their left. He walked to a large, white-painted bookcase that took up one wall of the airy little room, illuminated by full-length windows on the opposite wall. He looked carefully over the titles of dozens of books. Some were older hard covers and college texts, but most were paperbacks.

"Blast! It isn't here," Ambrose said. Beatrice scarcely heard him, as she absorbed the peaceful harmony of her surroundings. The clean, white walls were adorned with brightly colored prints and pastel watercolors, counterpoint to the dark painting that dominated the living room. A collection of multi-colored glass spheres was placed at eye level on the bookcase, so each one caught the dim light from the windows. How they would sparkle on a sunny day! There was a spacious feel to the place, even though the rooms were small. A fichus tree in one corner of the room reached up toward the vaulted ceiling. Beatrice noticed it had just been watered. By Carol perhaps?

"There's nothing here," Ambrose repeated. "Let's try the other rooms."

"Just a minute," Beatrice said. She picked up a framed photograph of a young girl and a woman, leaning together companionably. Smiles wreathed their faces. The girl was probably ten or twelve, with the coltish look of adolescence. Her long hair was so fair it looked white. That must be Maggy, Beatrice thought. And the woman was much older, her brown hair faded, but still soft around her face.

Beatrice recognized her! Even though this Anna was at least sixty years old, the smile was the same. She ran her fingers over the glass, and remembered sitting with a much younger Anna on a bed amidst a confusion of colorful clothes. And talking about—what? There was a feeling of loss, and grief. There had been a deep understanding between them. But she remembered elation as well. She put down the photograph and went to look for Ambrose, eager to share this memory with him.

She found him in a large bedroom, looking into the drawers of an old, maple dressing table. It's round mirror reflected the simple furnishings of the rest of the room. Beatrice could see her own indistinct reflection in the glass. She felt decidedly uncomfortable as she watched Ambrose shuffling through Maggy's possessions. She didn't feel quite so eager to confide in him about her newly found memories of Anna.

"Perhaps we should leave, Ambrose. I don't feel right about this."

"You'll be a great help to Maggy, if you let a little thing like this bother you," he said. He dropped a sweater back into the drawer and turned to look at her, his forehead creased in a frown. "Really, Beatrice, you act as though angels aren't the worst eavesdroppers in creation! Who has privacy from them? Whose innermost thoughts aren't spread out like so much dirty laundry for a guardian angel to see?"

"What's wrong with you, Ambrose? You can't really feel that way!" Beatrice cried. The subtle light radiating from her grew brighter as she moved across the room toward him. "You know it's nothing like that!"

Ambrose backed away from her, shading his eyes. "I know. You're right, of course. Forgive my outburst, Beatrice, and calm yourself. I'm just discouraged because the diary doesn't seem to be here." He closed the drawer and stood up. "I looked in her study at the end of the hall too. Nothing. I was sure it would be here."

"Well, you've made a mistake. It looks like Maggy was right."

"You mean someone stole it from her room?"

"What else could have happened to it?" Beatrice asked, her light fading as her temper cooled.

"I'm afraid Maggy has suspicions, rather ugly suspicions about Harry," Ambrose said. "That's one reason I hoped to find the diary here."

"She thinks Harry took it?"

"As I said, she suspects him."

"But you know otherwise, don't you? He's yours, after all. As you so rudely put it, his innermost thoughts are spread out before you like dirty laundry."

"Touché. I deserved that."

Beatrice sat down on the bed, her shoulders slumped. She looked out the French doors at the falling rain. "If only I could go to Maggy myself. If I could touch her spirit again, perhaps I could find some purpose to all this."

"That's impossible, and you know it. She'd see you just as plainly as she did before. Besides, she doesn't know anything."

"Maybe not consciously," Beatrice said. She flashed an intense look at Ambrose. "Well? Are you going to answer my question about Harry? What do you know about him?"

"I know that he and Maggy are about to become lovers. At first I thought a romance would help both of them, but now I'm not so sure."

"Oh, swell! And you haven't bothered to tell me about this until now? Didn't you think it was important? What's wrong with you?" She jumped up off the bed and glared at him. Before he could answer she continued. "And you still haven't answered my question about Harry. Did he steal the diary?"

Ambrose stood his ground under her barrage of questions. "What's wrong with me Beatrice, is you. You have a tendency to let passion guide your actions. I've been slow to tell you about Maggy and Harry's affair for fear that you might act impulsively again. I don't want you interfering in some way that will hurt him."

"Then tell me about Harry. Convince me that Maggy's fears about him are groundless."

"Of course they're groundless. Harry didn't break into Maggy's room, nor did he steal the diary from her." He raised his hand to forestall her reply. "The diary isn't his main concern."

"What is, then?"

"Maggy, of course."

"I don't believe you, Ambrose. Don't just brush aside my questions. Tell me about Harry." Beatrice found her patience with him and was near the breaking point. "I want the truth."

"What do you know about truth, Beatrice? You have no reason to doubt me, yet you question everything I say. The fact is you don't know what you're dealing with!"

"Why don't you tell me? What are we dealing with?" A fierce light emanated from her body once again. Ambrose squinted against its painful brilliance. Her eyes focused on him intently, unwavering, willing him to answer her.

Ambrose wilted before her eyes. "It's the cup! The Angel's Cup!" His angry voice rang out. "I warn you, Beatrice! You'll regret this knowledge."

"What cup? What are you talking about?"

"This time you've pushed me too far," Ambrose said. "You'll get nothing more out of me."

"Oh, stop being so melodramatic. What does a cup have to do with Maggy, or Harry, or me for that matter?"

He seemed to reconsider for a moment, and then a knowing look came to his eyes. "I'll tell you this much about Harry. He'll stop at nothing until he finds the Cup."

Before she could say another word, he vanished.

* * *

"That miserable coward!" Beatrice fumed as she paced back and forth on the terrace by the Neptune Pool. She had wasted no time leaving Maggy's house after Ambrose' abrupt disappearance. Now she was back in the First level, oblivious to the other angels casting curious glances in her direction. They kept their distance from her as she stalked by the pool like a caged lioness, a thunderous expression on her face, sparks of light flashing from her as she moved.

Why was Ambrose being so difficult? He had promised to help her solve the riddle surrounding Maggy, yet he'd deliberately withheld details about Maggy and Harry's relationship. And now he wouldn't tell her anything about Harry, except that drivel about a mysterious cup.

Beatrice had considered following him when he disappeared so suddenly, but realized it would do no good. Ambrose was telling her just what he wanted her to know and nothing more. Well, fine! He hadn't been much help anyway. She'd just have to continue without him. But it galled her that he had thrown her a crumb of information and then run away like a petulant child.

The Angel's Cup. She stopped pacing and ran her hand absently through her hair as she thought. Maybe there was something to it after all. The name was tantalizing. She had heard it before somewhere, not on earth, but right here in Heaven. It was part of an ancient folk tale, or angelic myth, something she had heard in passing. Something about an angel's cup. An amusing story, nothing more.

She realized with some chagrin that the time had come to enlist Roland's help. It was pride that had driven her to solve the puzzle on her own. At least she was honest enough to admit to it. But Maggy's welfare was more important than a little misplaced vanity. Beatrice noticed the host of angels around her and their curious gazes. Ambrose' cruel description of angels as prying busybodies came suddenly to mind. Even as she bristled at the unfairness of it, she thought better of meeting Roland in plain view of her fellow angels. Who were, after all, blessed with a perfectly natural curiosity.

Beatrice faded out of existence on the common plane and appeared in the same spot by the pool in her own solitary corner of Heaven. She relaxed her shoulders and took a deep breath, then closed her eyes and sent out her plea to Roland.

"You can open your eyes now, Beatrice."

He was standing right before her, a gentle smile illuminating his handsome young face. She felt her spirits rising just at the sight of him. "Roland, thank you for coming," she said.

"What, are we so formal now, so reserved that I'm to be deprived of an embrace?"

"Never!" She laughed and threw her arms around him, basking in his presence. "I've missed you!"

"Just so you haven't been avoiding me, my dear." His eyes sparkled mischievously.

What a fool she was! Of course he knew she'd been doing exactly that. "Roland, I need your help."

"I gathered as much from your summons. I'm yours to command." He bowed deeply before her.

"This is serious," she said. Suddenly at a loss for words, she sat down on the tiled edge of the pool, dipping her feet in the cool water. He sat beside her and waited in perfect stillness.

"What can you tell me about the Angel's Cup?"

"Seheiah and the Cup of Long Life," Roland said. "We spoke of this when you were a new arrival here. You've forgotten your history lessons, it seems."

"But we studied so many things, each one of them more astonishing than the last. I just remember there was something about a cup, some ancient myth. I guess I wasn't paying attention at the time." She lifted her chin and turned to face him, her off-center smile disarming. "Sorry, teacher."

"He was one of the first angels. Seheiah never lived as a mortal, and was fascinated by the concept of mortality. Life, shadowed by inevitable death, intrigued him. He came to believe that a mortal lifetime was far too brief. He became the angel of long life, visiting mortals on earth to let them drink from the cup of life.

"During one of these visits, so the story goes, a mortal stole the cup from Seheiah. This mortal wanted to live forever. But that was not to be his fate."

"What happened to him?"

"After a millennia of life, he found immortality had begun to pall. He died by his own hand. The cup was never recovered in Heaven. There are rumors that it has been passed down from one mortal to another over the centuries."

"But why do you say rumors? Don't you know, Roland? Is this simply a myth, or does Seheiah's Cup really exist?"

"Seheiah is the only one who could answer that question. No one knows where, or even who he is. The existence of the cup is a mystery. It resides in Heaven's blind spot, presided over by Seheiah himself, and hidden to all the Levels of Heaven. Mortals who have touched it have disappeared from our sight, even their memory forgotten."

"Maggy! That would explain why she has no guardian angel!"

"But she does have an angel now, my dear. You."

"You're right, I suppose," Beatrice said and gave a frustrated kick, sending water cascading out over the surface of the pool. "But I think Seheiah's Cup exists on earth, and might be the key to this mystery."

She reached out to Roland and gave him a quick hug. "Thank you for the history lesson, professor."

"Is there anything else I can tell you, Beatrice? Or anything you wish to confide in me?"

She stood and pulled him up beside her. "No. Maggy is my charge and I have to do this on my own. But it's good to know you're there, Roland."

"Now I can add stubbornness to your list of attributes," he said. "Good luck, my dear." He brushed a kiss on her cheek, gave her a quick smile and disappeared with only the slightest ripple of air to mark his passing.

Beatrice wondered why she hadn't told him about her ill-fated alliance with Ambrose. She sometimes felt that Roland knew everything about her, whether she told him or not; that he could solve any problem with a snap of his fingers if he wanted to. But he preferred to let her find her own way, like an indulgent parent watching a toddler's first steps. Well, she wouldn't ask him for any more help.

Enough about Roland, and Ambrose too, for that matter. Now she was completely on her own. She couldn't go to Maggy, but there was one person she was very anxious to visit. Both Maggy and Ambrose had expressed doubts about Harry's motives. Beatrice would have to make sure Maggy was nowhere near, but she was determined to see Harry for herself.

Chapter 14

Maggy stood before the mirror in her room, a long black skirt held up to her waist. She looked critically at the small, ivory flowers printed on the fabric, the color matched by her Anne Klein pullover. Yes, it would do. She slipped into the skirt and looked at her watch again. Now she was definitely late for dinner. Still, she went into the bathroom and rifled through her cosmetic bag. A little rose-colored lipstick, a quick touch of powder, her favorite scent behind her ears. Better.

She couldn't put it off any longer. Her heart raced at the thought of seeing Harry again. She tried to think of the questions she wanted to ask him. Instead, she pictured their last meeting, and the anguished kiss that had driven all thoughts from her mind. No, enough of that. This time Maggy would get some answers.

She walked down the now familiar hallway to the dining room, the hum of conversation and laughter greeting her.

"Sorry I'm late," she said.

"You're just in time, Maggy," Nancy said. "Let me introduce our new guests." Maggy saw that the Sorensons were gone, replaced by two middle-aged women. She couldn't quite concentrate on their names as Nancy introduced them. Harry's chair was empty. The tension in her shoulders drained away, along with her excitement.

Nancy had prepared another sumptuous meal, a raspberry chicken entree with rice and asparagus. Maggy found she had little appetite. Nancy eyed at her closely.

"Are you feeling well, Maggy? You look pale."

"Oh, I'm fine, really. Just a little distracted this evening."

"It's a shame Harry couldn't join us for dinner," Nancy said. She turned to the woman sitting next to her. "Harry could answer Mrs. Jame's questions about the castle and Mr. Hearst."

"Please, call me Sylvia," the woman said as she reached for the salt shaker. Her bracelets jangled as she moved, and a multitude of gaudy rings sparkled on her fingers. Her face was colorfully painted, crimson lipstick applied outside the edges of thin lips. "I visited the Vanderbuilt estate, Biltmore it's called. The dining room was just the same as the one at Hearst Castle, with the banners and the long table and the huge fireplaces. I wondered who copied whom." She continued to speak between bites of food. "And how much it cost Hearst to build that great monstrosity. Someone said ten million, but that seems awfully low to me."

"I don't know," Nancy's husband John answered. "But Harry might drop in later. He'd probably know."

"I'm sure he would," Nancy added. "As I've told Maggy and the Wrights, he was the curator at the museum and knows all kinds of things about the castle and its history."

The conversation continued to swirl around Maggy like waves on the shore, sometimes drawing her in, sometimes leaving her to her own thoughts. Thoughts that centered uncomfortably on Harry's strange behavior that morning.

"Will you have coffee with your dessert, Maggy?" Nancy's voice brought her back with a start.

"That sounds good," Maggy said. "Can I help you?"

"You and Harry, always volunteering to help. If you insist on it, dear, you can carry in the cups and we'll leave John to entertain our guests."

Maggy followed Nancy into the kitchen, which smelled of fresh-brewed coffee. "I'll just heat up the cobbler in the microwave while you get the cups," Nancy said and pointed to the cabinet over the sink.

Nancy spoke quietly as Maggy stacked the cups on a tray. "I don't know what's bothering the two of you, but I've never seen Harry in such a temper as he was this afternoon."

Maggy looked at Nancy as she set the timer on the microwave. "Really?"

"Yes, really. He said he wouldn't be here for dinner, and just paced around the kitchen like a tiger in a cage, growling at me for no reason that I could see." Nancy looked at her pointedly. "Maybe I'm seeing the reason now."

"Me? I don't think so." Maggy's normal reticence faded away as Nancy's teasing look changed to one of genuine concern. "Everything was fine this morning when we went to see Cora Bishop. When we got back, I got the idea that he hasn't been completely honest with me. He didn't deny it."

Nancy leaned against the counter and folded her arms across her chest as she studied Maggy. "One thing you should know about Harry. He's a deep one, with reasons that I've never understood for some of the things he does. But he's a dear friend, almost like a son to me. I'd like nothing better than to see him find happiness."

She leaned close to Maggy and gave her arm a pat. "From what I've seen, you've turned him upside down. He doesn't like it, but he's bound to confide in you, given time."

"That's just it. We don't have any time! I'm leaving this Thursday. Or maybe Friday."

"A lot can happen in a few days," Nancy said. "I think you should give him the benefit of the doubt."

The microwave beeped and Nancy took out a steaming cobbler. The aroma of sweet cherries and pastry began to revive Maggy's appetite. Or perhaps it was Nancy's advice.

As they returned to the dining room John called out to them. "Better bring another plate for Harry."

Maggy put the tray down on the table and glanced over at him reluctantly. His blue eyes caught hers in a smile that made her shiver.

"Sit down, both of you. I'll get it," Harry said and sauntered into the kitchen. Maggy wondered at his composure. He seemed completely recovered from his earlier anxiety.

When he returned, Sylvia James immediately buttonholed him with her questions. He took his place next to Maggy.

"Hearst did spend about ten million dollars for the castle and its furnishings, including all the artwork displayed there," Harry said. "But you have to remember, many of those were Depression dollars, when the average annual salary was about $1,700."

Maggy thought of her grandmother's salary of $1.00 a day. Anna had been happy to get it.

"So who was richer, Vanderbuilt or Hearst?" Mrs. James asked.

"Vanderbuilt's fortune was bigger than Hearst's by far," Harry said. "But Hearst himself earned about $50,000 a day. In today's dollars, that would be about $350,000. Yet he still came close to bankruptcy in the thirties."

The conversation moved on to Cambria's best shopping, and Harry turned to Maggy. "Will you come for a walk with me? We need to talk."

"Now?"

"Right now." He took her hand and they made their excuses. Nancy beamed at them as they left the warmth and noise of the dining room behind.

They crossed the road to the trail by the beach, but this time walked in the other direction toward a stand of Monterey pines, away from town. Maggy looked to her left at the waves rolling against the sand, and felt the wind blowing through her hair. She looked at the man walking beside her silently, wearing faded jeans and a shirt that could use ironing, his blond hair tossed by the wind. Some of the tension from that morning had returned. She could see it in the way he walked. He looked dangerous. Dangerous and absolutely wonderful.

"I'm sorry for the way I acted this morning," he said.

She didn't say anything, waiting for him to continue.

"I didn't know what to tell you about myself." He stopped walking and took her hands in his. "Your hands are cold," he said and kissed them gently, one after the other.

Maggy smiled as his touch filled her with elation.

"Tell me the truth," she said.

He bent close to her, his voice a whisper. "I don't want to lose you, Maggy. I'm afraid that you might be in danger." With her hand clasped in his, they began to walk again.

"I'm sorry I couldn't tell you this before. When I was the curator here I learned about a vase that once belonged to Logan Winter. I believe it's very ancient, even older than the Egyptian statues of Sekhmet in Hearst's collection. I became obsessed with finding it. I've spent years researching its origins."

"Tell me about it," Maggy said.

"I believe Winter's vase was called by many different names. The two most common were the Angel's Cup, or Seheiah's Cup. If I'm right, it would be far more valuable than anything Hearst possessed. Its origins are surrounded in myth and legends of angels and devils. It's believed to be a deep blue color, but not very large." He held his hands out to describe its size, about five inches in diameter. "Like early Minoan pottery, it has incised decorations around the base. That would identify it as Pyrgos, named after a site in Crete, dating to about 3000 BC."

"You've been searching for this treasure all along?" Maggy asked with a feeling of trepidation.

"It's more than treasure," he said. His voice barely contained his excitement. "If Winter was right about it, this cup predates the Pyrgos ware that it resembles. He claimed to have a translation of the decorations incised on its base. Not decorations, but inscriptions.

"Who drinks the cup of mortal life,
Rests unseen in Heaven's shadow.
Behold the color of life,
Behold the gift of life,
Behold the secret of Immortality."

Maggy felt the words pass through her with a terrible finality. "What does that mean?"

"I haven't been able to figure it out exactly. It's a religious reference, of course, but it's hard to interpret since the origin of the cup is unclear. It could be referring to an afterlife."

"Or to immortality itself," Maggy said.

Harry looked at her. "Maybe. If I'm right about it, the vase is beyond price. I believe Winter had it, and it was stolen from his room."

That name again. Logan Winter! Maggy had suddenly had enough of him. "If it was so valuable, he shouldn't have had it," she said. "It should have been in a museum. What right did one man have to own it? Just because he was rich? He treated it so carelessly it was stolen, and he blamed Anna for it!"

He stopped walking and turned to face her. "Times were very different then. Winter and other collectors like Hearst saved countless pieces of art from destruction."

"Well, he didn't save this piece. He lost it." She didn't care for Harry's defense of the mysterious Winter.

"True. It was stolen from him. He never recovered it, but I'm hoping I'll have better luck."

Maggy suddenly realized what he was really telling her. The knowledge hit her like a blow, making her feel numb.

"Why did you lie to me? You said you didn't know anything about Winter." She added unsteadily, her voice barely above a whisper. "Or Beatrice."

He ran his hand through his hair in a now familiar gesture of frustration. She could see the muscles in his jaw clench, as he fought his internal battle. "I was afraid, Maggy. By the time I knew you, it was too late. I'd already deceived you. I was afraid to lose you."

"That doesn't answer my question. Why did you lie to me in the first place?"

"Because someone else is looking for the vase. I don't know who it is, but I've seen evidence of it. Then I learned you were coming here with Anna Lane's diary. I didn't know if you were here to donate the diary, or find the vase for yourself. I had to find out."

"Have you found out then? Do you know if you can trust me now?" She threw the words at him like weapons. "Have you decided I'm not a liar?"

Without waiting for his answer, she turned and ran along the path away from him, her vision blurred by tears. What a fool she'd been!

"Maggy, wait damn it!" He caught her by the arm and turned her to face him. His eyes were fierce as he held her. "You've got to hear me out. Someone vandalized the docent's library last night. I'm afraid you might be in danger. Believe me, I never meant to hurt you."

"You didn't? You knew I'd seen Beatrice. You knew it was her the moment I described her to you. And you told me I was overworked, imagining things."

"I knew you were describing Beatrice. But I also knew Beatrice had been dead for sixty years. At first I didn't know what to believe about you,

Maggy." His finger traced the line of tears along her cheek. She jerked away from his touch and wiped her hand over her eyes.

"I'm learning about you the hard way, Harry. You lied to me from the beginning. You've been using me to get your precious vase, or cup. Whatever it is, I don't care. Just leave me alone!"

She turned away from him and hurried back toward the inn, praying he wouldn't follow her again. When she reached the road, she looked back to see him standing in the distance where she had left him.

Maggy let herself into her room, her hands shaking as she turned the key. Nothing had prepared her for the ache she felt at Harry's betrayal. How could this hurt so much? She'd only known him for a few days, yet it felt as though a part of her had been ripped out. She threw herself on her bed and was surprised when she couldn't cry. Oh, great! She could humiliate herself in front of him by crying, but now she couldn't even get that relief.

Her eyes fell on the second volume of Anna's diary that she had finished reading that afternoon. She had left it on the floor beside her bed. No wonder Harry was so interested in the diary, if he thought it might lead him to the vase he was looking for. Just an old piece of pottery. She thought of the first evening she'd arrived, when Nancy had introduced Harry and said how much he loved those old pots of his.

Damn him! She got up off the bed and turned on the gas fireplace. She held her hands up to the warmth, her face bathed in flickering light. Someone else was looking for the cup. Not a ghost, or an angel, but a real person. Maybe it was the same person who had stolen the last volume of Anna's diary from this very room. Why had they smashed her jewelry as well? Wouldn't it have been smarter to just take the diary? A chill passed through her as she thought of that small act of violence.

He might have lied to her, but Maggy was positive that Harry would-n't hurt her. He might break her heart, but he wouldn't hurt her. She laughed ruefully at her thoughts. She still couldn't seem to get warm. Her hands and feet were like ice. With a weary sigh, she went into the bathroom and turned on the shower. That would warm her up. Maybe she could sing a show tune, like the one from South Pacific, and wash Harry out of her system. But she didn't feel much like singing.

After a steamy hot shower, she started to feel a little better. She wrapped herself in her long terry robe and sat in front of the fireplace again. Her thoughts turned to Beatrice as she had appeared to her at the Neptune Pool. Her angel. Maggy pictured the glowing image and it brought a measure of serenity to her.

A knock at the door interrupted her thoughts. She was instantly wary as she stood up and went to answer it.

Harry stood there, looking at her with a hunger that was frightening in its intensity. "Don't shut me out, Maggy. Please." He stood perfectly still, waiting.

She couldn't turn him away. Without relaxing her stance, she stepped aside and opened the door for him. He closed it behind him, his blue eyes shadowed in the light from the fire.

"I didn't betray you, Maggy. I never would."

"How can I believe you now, after what you've told me?"

He moved closer to her, but didn't touch her. She felt as though an electric charge was emanating from him, drawing her closer. She resisted it, and stood absolutely still.

"When I told you I wanted to believe you, it was the truth." He leaned forward as though to touch her, then dropped his hand in a resigned gesture. "But I couldn't. The only rationale explanation was that you knew about the vase, and invented the whole scene with Beatrice. I had to find out why."

"You never believed any of it?" Maggy didn't know what she'd expected. Certainly not this.

"Something happened to me, Maggy. The closer I got to you, the harder it was to believe you were my adversary. More than that," he touched her face gently, "I fought against the feelings I had for you. That's why I left you last night.

"Now I have to believe you saw Beatrice, just as you described her." His hand dropped from her face as he looked at her, his eyes troubled. "You see, it's too late for me. I've already fallen in love with you."

Maggy stared at him, her eyes wide with shock. When she didn't pull away, he bent toward her and pressed his lips against hers gently, as though he was afraid she might disappear. The contact sent a thrill spinning through her body, just as his words had sent her spirit soaring. She leaned closer to him and opened her lips slightly as his tongue brushed against hers.

With a groan, he pulled her tight against him, his hands crushing the terry cloth of her robe, his tongue probing her mouth. Maggy's arms went around his shoulders, her hands caressed the back of his neck. She was flooded by sensations from his kiss and the length of his body pressed against hers.

After a moment, she pulled away from him to look into his eyes. What she saw there made her shiver with desire. "I was furious with you, Harry. But now I don't know."

"Trust me in this," he said.

"I must be crazy to believe you, but I do. All of it."

He picked her up and carried her to the bed, where he tumbled down beside her, still locked in an embrace. "I can't bear to let you go, even for a second," he whispered. Then his lips were on hers again, kissing the corner of her mouth. His tongue teased open her lips and deepened into a passionate, fiery kiss.

Maggy pushed him away long enough to unbutton his shirt. She ran her fingers through the thatch of blond hair on his chest, then caressed the smooth skin on his back as she hugged him closer. She was lost in a sea of sensation as first his hands, then his lips caressed her everywhere.

His touch burned her breasts, tracing fire down the length of her belly until he slowly stroked between her legs. Her eyes flew open as she felt him press his fingers against her; his light caress sent sparks of feeling tingling out from her center. She felt him pressing against her thigh through the jeans he still wore, and she was crazy with impatience.

"Here, let me help you out of those," she said with a shaky grin. Her hands were unsteady as she unfastened his belt buckle and they both pushed his jeans out of the way. Her robe had disappeared.

She reveled in the warmth of his body covering hers. "I love you, Maggy," he looked down at her and brushed her hair gently away from her face. With his eyes on hers, he entered her with one deep, slow thrust. She gasped and moved up to meet him, to pull him ever deeper inside her. They moved together, slowly, each thrust sending jolts of pleasure through Maggy's body, each one building until she cried out as they overwhelmed her, flooding out from the center of her body in a wave of fire. She clung to his shoulders as the climax shook her.

"God, Maggy!" he gasped her name and came into her in a fiery rush.

They lay still, their breath quieting as Maggy slowly came back to herself. She stroked his hair, his wonderful, unruly hair, a smile of pure joy on her face.

Harry kissed her gently, and pulled her next to him while he put his arm around her shoulder. "Don't scare me like that again, okay?" he whispered. "Seeing you walk away from me on the beach—you don't know what it did to me."

"Then don't lie to me again, Harry." The severe look she gave him was undermined by her rumpled appearance and the feeling that glowed in her eyes. "You don't know what that does to me."

His embrace tightened around her shoulders. "I've lived my life without confiding in anyone. This is new for me, Maggy. It's not easy."

She ran her fingers over the hair gleaming on his well-muscled chest, her heart aching for him. "Don't you trust anyone? How can you live like that?"

"I haven't had much success with trust in the past. Life has taught me to depend on myself."

"Do you trust me?" she asked.

He turned to look at her closely. "Promise me one thing, Maggy. Remember what I've told you tonight. If I disappoint you, it won't be because I don't love you."

"Why would you disappoint me?" His words convinced Maggy that he hadn't told her everything. At least not yet.

"I hope I never will. But promise me that you'll give me the benefit of the doubt. And remember that I love you. Okay?" He kissed her again, his lips lingering on hers.

"Okay, I promise. Besides, that's just what Nancy said about you. She said I should give you the benefit of the doubt."

"You were talking about me, the two of you?"

"No, of course not," Maggy said with a contented smile. "I have better things to do than gossip about you."

"I'm glad to hear it."

"She thinks the world of you, you know."

"Nancy? Not that you'd know what she thinks, since you don't gossip with her." His laugh was so quiet she could barely hear it. "Nancy and John are good friends."

Maggy squirmed out of his embrace and leaned over the edge of the bed, unconscious of the picture she presented to him. She pushed herself back up and brushed the hair away from her face so she could see him. "Here, I want you to have this," she said and handed him the second volume of Anna's diary.

"You're sure?"

"Of course I'm sure, Harry. I want to help you find your treasure." Her words were muffled by his embrace and the quick kiss he planted on her lips.

She sighed when he released her to look at the diary. "I've read everything in that volume, and I don't think there are any clues there," she said. "Anna tried to help Winter find his vase, but she didn't have any luck. At least she didn't say anything about finding it."

"Thanks. Maybe there's something here that will help."

"And while you're reading it, you can keep Beatrice in mind. See if you can figure out anything that would explain my angel." Maggy nestled closer to him under the covers.

He turned out the lamp and kissed her hair. "Beatrice might be your angel, but I have mine right here." She smiled at him in the darkened room. "I don't feel very angelic at the moment."

He laughed as he leaned over her. "Good." His kiss put all thoughts of angels out of her mind.

* * *

Maggy woke to bright sunlight streaming in through the window shades. Memories of the night past flowed over her like a lovely dream. She stretched her arms over her head and turned to see if Harry was awake.

The smile died on her lips when she saw the sheets pulled up neatly, the space beside her empty. He wasn't there. She sat up slowly, her body feeling sated and sore from their night of lovemaking.

She searched for her bathrobe and found it thrown half under the bed. She quickly wrapped it around her and padded into the bathroom. He was really gone. Harry certainly had a thing or two to learn about intimacy.

Maggy sat down on the bed and sighed. He had even smoothed out the pillow, so there was hardly any evidence to show he'd been there at all. She couldn't believe it. He said he loved her. Why would he disappear without a word?

Now she saw what she had missed before; a small gray box on Harry's side of the bed, half hidden under his pillow. A velvet jeweler's box. She picked it up slowly.

Inside was a delicate gold ring. The polished center stone was milky white, almost translucent, with two small diamonds on either side.

A moonstone! She had been so disappointed when they hadn't found one on the beach. Maggy slipped the ring on her finger and held up her hand to admire it. It fit perfectly.

A soft smile touched her lips as she thought about him. Harry obviously had more secrets that he wasn't telling her about. But she could live with that for the time being. Whatever he was hiding, he'd tell her about as soon as he could. If they had enough time.

Well, she wasn't going to worry about that either. He loved her. She knew it was true as certainly as the she knew the sun was shining in the sky. He might still break her heart, but it wouldn't be because he didn't love her. She laughed suddenly, a feeling of pure joy bubbling up inside her. She didn't care how reckless she was being, falling in love with a man she barely knew. It was crazy! But crazy things had been happening to her ever since she got here.

As Maggy took her shower, she decided on her course of action for the day. She would do her own investigating, and the place she'd start was the accident that took Beatrice's life. Though someone had removed all traces of Beatrice from the resource library, there would have been coverage in the local papers. She'd simply try the library in San Luis Obispo. The thought of getting back to work was exhilarating.

Within an hour Maggy was driving over the coast range toward San Luis Obispo, Nancy's directions to the library written in her notebook. She wasn't so much driving over the coast range, as through it by way of a long, flat valley, with hills rising up abruptly on either side. Clouds cast occasional shadows over the countryside, alternating with brilliant sunshine. Just the kind of weather she loved.

Traffic got heavier as she entered San Luis Obispo. Like many cities, this one tried to solve its traffic problems with an endless number of one-way thoroughfares. After consulting her map and backtracking several times, she finally pulled into a public parking lot in front of the city library.

Maggy entered a large, two-story structure and saw the usual assortment of notices, pamphlets and local news weeklies stacked in the front
lobby. She walked past the front counter where several people waited
patiently in line. A quick look revealed a row of computer terminals to her
right. She settled in at one of them and started her query
regarding Beatrice.

After a few minutes she had several citations to check in the San Luis
Obispo Daily Telegram, which had apparently printed all sorts of stories
about Hearst Castle and it's famous guests. The one that interested her
particularly was dated May 16, 1937. Singer dies at San Simeon Castle.

"I have all the microfiche reels you asked for except CS-35," the clerk
said as he handed her three cassettes. "Someone must be using that one.
You might find it by the microfiche readers if they forgot to turn it
back in."

Wouldn't you know the very article she wanted was the one missing?
Could someone have tampered with files here as well? She found the
machines and loaded the first cassette. The tiny print raced before her eyes
until she found the call numbers. There. Marion Davies hosts Gala Event.
A picture of Marion Davies standing before a microphone, holding
Beatrice's hand.

This was the night Anna had written about! When Marion Davies convinced Beatrice to sing again. The article must have been in the society
section, as it was concerned with naming the famous guests and describing their designer clothes. No mention of Logan Winter. But the writer
loved Beatrice and predicted she would have a successful comeback.
Maggy put a quarter in the viewer to make a copy of the article and went
on to the next story.

Death of Singer Ruled Accidental
*Today the San Luis Obispo County Coroner found the death of popular
singer Beatrice Page to be an accident. Mrs. Page was pronounced dead at*

5:37pm on May 16 at the guest cottage of San Simeon Castle, where she was taken after sustaining severe injuries in a fall from a horse.

Present at the scene of the accident were Edward Orcutt and Logan Winter, both of Los Angeles. Mr. Winter was cleared of any wrongdoing for his actions in transporting Mrs. Page back to the castle for medical treatment.

The horse ridden by Mrs. Page, owned by W. R. Hearst, suffered a broken leg in the fall and was destroyed. Beatrice Page leaves no survivors. Her husband, well-known composer Maxwell Page, died in 1934.

A private memorial service will be held in Los Angeles at the Four Seasons Chapel on May 20.

Maggy didn't know what to make of this chilling account. She was filled with a strange awe, almost a reverence, when she thought of the beautiful woman she had seen by the Neptune Pool and realized this was a matter-of-fact description of her death. Beatrice hadn't really died. She had gone on to another life. Just as Anna had, and every other person on earth must have.

She looked back at the article and wondered what had happened that day so long ago. Beatrice was with her two friends, whom she must have trusted above all others. There was no reason to suspect her death wasn't an accident, horrible as it might be. Maggy made a copy of the article to take with her and loaded the last microfiche cassette.

This story was different, since there were several photographs accompanying the text. The subject was the king himself, W.R. Hearst. Hearst's 71st Birthday Fete. She checked the date–April 29, 1934. Hearst had loved to give parties, and the grandest of them all were for his own birthdays. Maggy smiled to herself. Now there was a brave man, to make such an uproar over a 71st birthday. The article was several pages long, comprised mostly of photographs of the rich and notorious, all dressed in elaborate costumes provided by Hearst. She saw David Niven as a policeman, with Cary Grant and his wife trailing along in the role of unsuccessful burglars. Greta Garbo in chaps and a ten-gallon hat. Bette Davis looked gorgeous in an evening gown trimmed with feathers, standing next to Charles Lindbergh.

Though it was fascinating to see these glimpses into the world that Hearst had created, Maggy wasn't learning anything new about Beatrice. She scrolled impatiently to the last page of the article. The second photograph caught her eye immediately. Marion Davies, hamming it up as a lovely clown, stood next to Beatrice. There was Edward Orcutt again, and the man next to him—Maggy stared at the photograph in shock. It must be Logan Winter, but it couldn't be!

The photograph was grainy and hard to see clearly. She adjusted the focus knob on the viewer and squinted at the screen. The resemblance to Harry was unmistakable. The same blond hair and strong jawline, the same high cheekbones. Harry had to be related to Logan Winter after all, in spite of his earlier denials. Perhaps Logan Winter was his grandfather. Another lie that he hadn't bothered to correct! God, he was the most irritating man. Why couldn't he just trust her and tell her what this was all about?

Maggy's mind raced over possible scenarios that this new information presented. Maybe Harry was trying to find his grandfather, not just the vase. Carol said Logan Winter had disappeared without a trace after the war. She just didn't have enough information. Logan Winter would have to be in his eighties by now.

Maggy jammed her quarter into the microfiche machine and pressed the button to get a copy of the damning photograph. This time she would get the truth out of Harry if it killed her. She gathered her copies together and took the cassettes back to the counter. The clerk directed her to pay phones by the front door.

"I believe Harry is in the Restoration Vault this morning," the curator told her to her great surprise. She hadn't expected to find him so easily. "It will take a little while to get him to the phone. Can he call you back?"

"No," she said. "Please deliver a message to him for me. It's very important that I meet him this afternoon." She didn't want to see him at the inn.

Neutral territory would be better. "I'll be at the Visitor Center at one o'clock. Please tell him it's extremely urgent."

* * *

Maggy glanced at her watch again and saw the moonstone ring sparkling on her finger. She wouldn't let it sway her from her purpose, no matter how much the gift meant to her. She had arrived at the Visitor Center a few minutes early. Now she idly watched the tourists wandering through the gift shop to her left. On her right the ticket counter had a red digital display showing the next available tour departure. She sat on a bench in front of a low palm tree, tapping her fingers against the wooden planks. One of the tour guides had mentioned the price tag for the Visitor Center in 1987 was ten million dollars, just what Hearst had paid for San Simeon and all its treasures. Times have certainly changed, she thought wryly.

She saw Harry walking toward her through the stream of tourists, his blond hair unruly as usual. She fought a spontaneous smile at the sight of him. But she couldn't fight the feeling that swept over her, bringing a flush to her cheeks.

"Hey, Maggy," he said and sat down next to her. His look told her he was thinking the same thing she was. Well, she wasn't about to be distracted. She was going to get some answers from him whether he liked it or not.

When she didn't respond, he held his hands up in supplication. "I'm here as requested. What is it, Maggy?"

She pulled the photocopy from her handbag and gave it to him wordlessly.

He looked at it and grew solemn, his jaw clenched. He looked up at her. "What do you want to know?"

"I want to know everything, Harry. Who are you?" She tried to keep her voice neutral, but she could hear a pleading note and the questions came tumbling out. "You can't tell me you don't know about Logan Winter, you're obviously related to him. You must be his grandson, or some other close relation. There's no other explanation. Why won't you tell me?"

He remained silent, tension evident in the set of his shoulders. He seemed to be fighting an internal battle with himself. "I don't know if you're ready for this. But there is another explanation." He took her hand and slowly rubbed his thumb against her palm. "You're wearing my ring," he said and brought her hand to his lips. She sat mesmerized at his touch and the sound of his voice. "I'm trusting you with my life," he whispered.

He stood up, drawing her with him. "Come on. I want to show you something."

They took Maggy's car back to the inn, barely speaking during the short drive. Maggy felt as though she was in a fog, every sense focused on Harry and what he was going to tell her. They went down the hallway away from her room to Harry's room. He opened a desk drawer and took out a metal case, about the size of a cigar box. He dialed several numbers on a small combination lock to open it.

"This photograph was taken in January, 1936," he said and handed it to her. She took it gingerly, afraid of what she might see. Unlike the pictures in the article, this one was sharp and clear. Beatrice stood on the terrace of the Neptune Pool with Edward Orcutt and—her heart raced suddenly as a jolt of adrenaline rushed through her. She looked at Harry uncomprehendingly.

"Yes, Maggy. I am Logan Winter."

"But, that's not—I mean, it's impossible," she choked. She looked at the black and white photograph again, her eyes growing wider. He was looking at Beatrice with a familiar half-smile on his face, seemingly unaware of the camera. The clothes were different, a double-breasted suit and tie. His fair hair was shorter, parted on the side and combed back from his face in the style of the thirties. There were no glasses either. But it was Harry.

"I don't normally allow my picture to be taken, but sometimes it can't be avoided," he said. "I had to remove this photo from the staff library at the castle."

"You took it?" She looked at him as though he was a stranger. Was this some kind of weird joke? It was far from being funny. "Next you're going to tell me that you're eighty years old, I suppose," she said shakily. "How old are you?"

"A little older than that, actually." His eyes pleaded with hers, though he didn't make a move to touch her again. "I've aged considerably since I lost Seheiah's Cup."

Maggy found it difficult to breath. "You're saying that you knew Anna? You knew my grandmother? She was your maid?" Maggy's face was white with shock. She couldn't believe it. She just couldn't.

"Damn it, Maggy! This is why I didn't want to tell you."

"I—" she stopped speaking, unable to continue. In the space of a moment, her whole world had turned upside down. She felt her grip on reality was tottering precariously. "I can't deal with this now. I just can't." Maggy ran from the room.

Chapter 15

*M*aggy closed the door to her room and locked it. She stood with her back against the door, her breath coming in gasps as though she had run a race. Why had she locked the door? Did she think Harry was going to follow her down the hall and break into her room? Beat her with his cane? After all he was eighty years old. No, older than that, actually.

She fought the nervous laughter that threatened to choke her, put her hands over her face and tried to slow her breathing. Now wasn't the time to get hysterical. She was going to cool down and think about this. Calmly and rationally.

After a moment she dropped her hands and sat down on the bed. Okay. There could only be two possibilities. Either Harry was lying to her, or he really was Logan Winter, a man who was eighty or ninety years old. One more horrible possibility occurred to her. Maybe Harry just thought he was Winter.

No. Whatever he was, Harry wasn't crazy. The certainty of that thought startled her. It had a familiar ring to it. Two days ago she was determined to prove to Harry that she wasn't crazy herself. She believed she'd seen an angel. Why was it so hard for her to believe that Harry was Logan Winter? Which was more fantastic?

He could have faked that photograph easily enough. If Tom Hanks could shake hands with President Kennedy on the movie screen, it should-n't be difficult to alter a simple photograph. But why? And if he were lying about this, he might be lying about everything, including his feelings for her.

That thought threatened to destroy the iron grip she had on her emo-tions. She wouldn't think about that now. Damn, she should have stayed with him and asked more questions instead of running off like that! He had mentioned the cup that was stolen from Winter, or stolen from Harry sixty years ago. She shook her head as the words formed in her mind. She felt like she had fallen through the looking glass. But what did the cup have to do with it?

With sudden resolve, Maggy reached for the telephone. For the first time in their long friendship she wouldn't be able to confide in Carol, but she could ask for her help. She dialed their office number and almost cried at the sound of Carol's familiar voice.

"Lane-Smith Research, may I help you?"

God! How normal that sounded. "I sure hope you can," Maggy said.

"Hey, I'm beginning to think you miss me. We just talked yesterday, you know. Are you on vacation or what?"

"Or what. Definitely or what."

"Uh-oh. Well, I've got plenty to tell you anyway, so it's good you called. You first."

Maggy hesitated. This was going to be hard. "I can't explain everything to you now, Carol. But I need to get everything you can find about Harry Logan. Everything."

"Are you sure about this?" Carol's voice was serious, without it's usual humor. "You know this can be sticky when it's personal."

"I know. But I mean it. Everything. His parents, where he was born, school, scandal, marriage, children, work—everything. I have my reasons, I just—" she swallowed. "I'll tell you more when I figure this out."

"That's okay," Carol's voice was like a soothing balm coming over the wire. "What are friends for? I'll just pretend he's a politician and I'm a muckraking journalist. If he can be brought down, I'll do it!" She paused. "But I hope he wins my vote, kid, because something tells me he already has yours. Am I right?"

"You wouldn't believe me if I told you."

"You sound miserable enough to be in love."

"I don't know, Carol. I just don't know."

"It's my turn now, and I have some very good news for you."

"I could use some, believe me."

"I was at your house yesterday watering your plants, not that they needed it, by the way. Guess what I found in plain sight right by your bed?"

"If you don't tell me I'm going to strangle you with this phone cord."

"Okay, sorry. But this is good. It was the diary! The one you said was missing! You must have forgotten to bring it with you. You were in a terrible rush when you left. You barely caught your flight."

"You're kidding," Maggy said.

"As usual, your wit just knocks me out. No, I wouldn't kid you about this. This is serious."

"But someone was in my room. I was sure it was stolen!"

"I don't know about that, Maggy. The diary was here."

"But the bracelet was smashed—"

"Maybe whoever it was got pissed off when they didn't find anything. Who knows?" Carol said, the voice of rationality.

"Wow! I don't know what to say." Maggy twisted the phone cord around her fingers, her mind racing.

"A simple thank you will do nicely."

"Do you have the diary now?"

"Nope. I sent it off to you by Fed Ex this morning. You should have it tomorrow. But I think you've gotten me a little spooked."

"What do you mean?" Maggy asked.

"When I was leaving your house, I had the weirdest feeling. Like somebody was in the room with me."

"Maybe it was Beatrice," Maggy said.

"No way. It was scary. I even went back to check the other rooms. But nobody was there, of course."

"Hey, you're the iron woman. Nothing bothers you."

"Well, this did. I'll be happy when you're back home," Carol said, uncharacteristically serious.

"I don't know how to thank you for all the help you've given me."

"Don't worry, I'm adding up all the ones you owe me from this trip," Carol said in her usual flippant voice. "I'll never have to buy lunch again!"

"I mean it, Carol. You're the best." Maggy felt tears come to her eyes.

"Hey. We've been there and back, remember?" Carol said gently. "Now don't get all emotional on me."

"Sorry. I've been on an emotional roller coaster lately."

"Did you change your flight to come back on Friday?"

"Not yet."

"Aren't you going to that party with Harry? Or is that something you can't talk about?"

"I want to go, but now I'm not sure. About anything."

"If you want to go, then go. Since when are you sure in love? That's why it's so damn awful!"

"This is different. Besides, you were sure with David," Maggy reminded her.

"Yeah, but not until after we were married. Some days I still have doubts." Carol laughed. "I've cried on your shoulder enough times over him. You just conveniently forgot."

Maggy hung up the phone and felt comforted by her friend's good humor. No matter what happened, Carol was always on her side. And she was good at her job. If anyone could find out about Harry, Carol would.

She was right about the party, too. Maggy was going to see this through to the end, regardless of the consequences.

* * *

Maggy got into her car and headed for Cambria, relieved when she didn't see Harry on her way out of the inn. Relieved and disappointed at the same time. Not that she had a clue what she would say to him when she did see him again. She drove down the main street of Cambria, past dozens of colorful shops and art galleries. Off to her right she saw heather and blooming marigolds surrounding Robin's Restaurant where Harry had taken her for dinner on Saturday. It seemed a lifetime ago.

On impulse she stopped at the Chamber of Commerce and asked if any castle tours were still open that day. She was in luck, with a seat vacant at 3:30 on tour number two. She still had about an hour to kill before then. Maybe she'd feel better if she had something to eat. Funny, she had to keep reminding herself to eat on this trip. She hadn't lost her appetite like this since the breakup with Jason.

After grabbing a sandwich at Lynn's Bakery, Maggy drove north toward the castle. Her thoughts returned to Harry and his bizarre story. Could it be true? Was there a chance, even a tiny chance that he could be Logan Winter? If angels were real, what other impossible things might be possible? No wonder he'd asked her to give him the benefit of the doubt before. She sighed disconsolately. He'd also warned her that he might disappoint her.

She found her way to the departure platform for her tour just before the bus closed its doors. As she rode up the hill she let the babble of voices from the tourists fade away and felt the 1930's music on the loudspeaker wash over her. She tried to imagine Harry driving up this same hill sixty years ago, maybe with Beatrice sitting beside him, or even Edward Orcutt. No. It was no use, the whole idea was making her head ache.

A bright young woman welcomed them with the usual admonitions, and again instructed them to deposit chewing gum in the receptacle before starting the tour. This time they climbed three sets of stairs that opened out directly on the Neptune Pool. Even with a crowd of people around her, Maggy felt the serenity of the place easing her jangled nerves. A cool breeze blew up from the west, lifting her hair and carrying the scent of the ocean. Maggy looked to the far side of the pool, where Beatrice had materialized before her out of thin air. She wished that Beatrice would appear again in all her radiant glory. But she felt no tingling awareness as she had before, heard no haunting melody over the buzzing voices of tourists.

They entered La Casa Grande by a side entrance, just as they had on the first tour, to protect the ancient tile mosaic from the pounding feet of thousands of tourists. She walked through the Assembly Room and the Refectory for the second time. Maggy looked at the opulent furnishings and exquisitely carved fireplaces with a feeling of frustration. What was she doing here? What did she hope to find?

Their tour guide led them through the Morning Room with its view toward the back terrace, and then through the billiard room, where she was again struck by the rich colors and medieval pageantry of the Gothic mille fleurs tapestry. The guide pointed out the "thousand flowers" that the artist had woven into the background almost five hundred years ago.

Finally, they took one of the winding, tower staircases to the second floor, which Maggy hadn't seen on her first tour. She admired the Simon Vouet painting that was placed on the ceiling of the bedroom. Maggy listened intently as their guide told the story of the painting. Endymion attained immortal youth and beauty through his nightly trysts with the goddess Selene as he slept eternally in his cave. He gave up life itself for an endless half-life. The vivid figures in the painting seemed lit by sunlight from above. Maggy shivered despite the warmth of the room.

They passed through the last cloister bedroom, also called the Della Robbia room for its highly glazed ceramic sculptures from the famous workshops in Italy. Then they entered the part of the castle Maggy was most anxious to see, the south wing which housed the servants' quarters.

The rooms were small in comparison to the rest of the castle, but Maggy knew they had seemed large enough to Anna and the others who had worked here. She remembered that Anna had written she felt comfortable in her own room; that it was simple enough to remind her of home. Many of them were furnished beautifully, echoing the overall style of the castle. Some were smaller and furnished quite simply with art-deco style furniture. One of these very rooms was where Anna had lived for five years of her life. Where she had dreamed of Logan Winter.

Whatever revelation she had hoped for didn't come. Though the furnishings remained, these rooms were empty of any trace of their former occupants, unlike much of the rest of the castle, where William Randolph Hearst had left his forceful personality in every room.

They descended through another of the towers and walked along the Esplanade with its distant views of the coastline, and its grand displays of rhododendrons, azaleas and citrus trees and bright purple lantanas, blooming even in autumn. Maggy paused by the four statues of Sekhmet, the lion-headed goddess of war and battle. The tour guide told them this was Hearst's oldest piece, dating back to 1300 BC. But not nearly as old as Seheiah's Cup, Maggy thought. If any part of Harry's story could be believed.

Ahead was the entrance to Casa del Mar. Anna had called it "A" House, where she had done most of her work. As with the other guest cottages, the walls were draped with a riot of climbing greenery. Maggy thought it might be bougainvillea, but didn't know for sure.

In the lobby they passed beneath the gilded wood coat of arms and mitre of a sixteenth century bishop. The architect, Julia Morgan, had designed the rest of the ceiling to match it flawlessly. The rooms were dominated by carved wood and red velvet, relieved by a panorama of gilded windows looking out on views of gardens and landscapes that were so perfect they seemed unreal. Maggy looked at the seventeenth-century canopy bed. This could be the room where Beatrice had stayed, where she had been brought after the accident. Perhaps she had died on this bed.

The group was herded through two adjoining bathrooms with shower stalls instead of bathtubs. Maggy thought of Anna's description of Logan Winter when he attacked her as she was scrubbing the floor. Could Harry have been the man who frightened Anna so much that she expected to be sent to jail?

Damn it! This was getting her nowhere! Nothing she saw here could help her make sense of Harry's fantastic claim. She would have to accept the fact that he was lying to her for some reason that she couldn't begin to understand. Maggy suddenly felt exhausted as they filed out of "A" house and walked toward the tennis courts.

The rest of the tour passed in a blur to her, her heart a lead weight in her chest as they passed through the eerie beauty of the Roman Pool. She climbed back on the bus gratefully and closed her eyes.

* * *

As Maggy's bus wound around the drive down the hill, Beatrice stood in Heaven near the temple facade of the Neptune Pool. She cast her awareness out into the mortal plane and found the person she sought. He was very close by.

She disappeared from the First Level and reappeared instantly in small room in one of the guest cottages. The room was plain and furnished with several desks and a couch. It didn't look anything like the rest of the castle, but more like a drab office. Sitting at one of the desks was a fair-haired man, wearing a rumpled shirt and faded denim pants, intently reading a slim volume. She moved closer to him, and caught her breath.

Logan! It was Logan. There was no doubt. He was her best friend, Logan, whom she couldn't picture clearly until this moment. Now she looked at his familiar face, hardly changed at all in sixty years. Though she couldn't see his eyes, she knew they were a brilliant blue. She wanted to see them again, and willed him to look up at her.

He didn't move a muscle, oblivious to her presence. Beatrice supposed she should be thankful for that. She walked closer to him, and ran her hand along his cheek tenderly. At this he stopped reading and looked up in surprise. His blue eyes surveyed the empty office for a moment, and then resumed reading.

Beatrice sat next to him, soaking in his presence and the faint stirrings of memory that came to her in tantalizing glimpses. Logan had comforted her when she was lost in a sea of grief. Their friendship had been forged then, but she couldn't remember what caused her pain. She remembered a great camaraderie and a profound peacefulness when she was with him.

But Logan should be at least eighty years old. This man was Logan, but now he went by the name Harry. He appeared to be about thirty-five, a man glowing with vitality even as he sat quietly reading. She watched him as he turned another page of the book. It must be Anna's diary.

Then the tale of Seheiah's Cup was real, and Logan, or Harry, must have had it at one time. That's the only way he could have lived for sixty years with barely a sign of aging. Did he have it still? Or was he looking for it?

Beatrice wondered what connection had grown between Logan and Maggy. Ambrose said they might be lovers. She hoped it was true, and leaned toward him a second time, gracing him with another brief touch of her hand. She saw his muscles relax ever so slightly at the contact. Her memories were maddeningly incomplete, but she knew that Logan had never been at peace. His friendship had brought her solace, yet he had remained fundamentally alone. She had sensed a deep privacy in him that held others at arms' length. Even her. She knew somehow that their friendship had been as special to him as it had been to her. But she had never been able to breach his wall of reserve.

It must have been the Cup that set him apart from the rest of the world. Who could he share such a secret with? No wonder he had felt alone. Beatrice hoped that Maggy could help him find what he was looking for.

She left him and returned to the First Level, to sit in one of the celestial suite bedrooms high in the towers of la Casa Grande. These rooms had always been a sort of joke to most of the inhabitants of the First Level. But Beatrice loved them, as she did the rest of the castle. She looked out the filigreed wood coverings of the windows to the sun setting in the distance as she thought about what she had seen.

One thing bothered her. Ambrose claimed to be Harry's guardian angel. If Harry had possessed Seheiah's Cup and the legends were true, then he couldn't have an angel. He would have been hidden to all but the ancient angel Seheiah himself.

Beatrice sighed as she passed through the window and allowed herself to float down from the tower toward the gardens below. It seemed that every answer brought with it a host of questions. The next time she saw Ambrose, she'd get the truth out of him one way or another.

* * *

Harry closed the last page of Anna's diary and put it down on the desk in front of him with a bitter sigh. How blind he'd been. Anna had clearly taken his offer of friendship as something more than he'd intended. He'd thought of her as a sweet, precocious child. Her brief companionship had always lifted his spirits. Even reading her words had offered comfort of a sort, as though a cool hand had touched his forehead. A harsh laugh shook him. How little she had really known about Logan Winter.

If he had told her the truth, as he'd just told Maggy, would she have run from him, too? Looked at him with fear, as though he'd changed into a freak of nature, or a lunatic? He felt sick when he remembered Maggy's expression.

The ringing telephone broke into his thoughts. He stared at it blankly for several moments, letting it ring. Finally he picked it up, remembering that he'd let Steve know where he was.

But it wasn't Steve. He sat up straighter as he listened to the voice on the phone.

"Are you sure?" he said, his grip tightening on the receiver.

"Yeah, I'm sure. A newcomer has been sniffing around the auction houses. He's interested in artwork from Crete, circa 3000 BC, and he's not particular about its provenance. This is way out of his sphere. The guy's loaded, but he's not a collector. Sounded like the kind of activity you wanted to hear about."

"Who is it?" Harry asked.

"Miles Orcutt. His daddy left him a real estate fortune. He does some real estate dealing himself, strictly big ventures. He definitely doesn't have to work for a living."

"Thanks," Harry said. "I appreciate the tip."

"You've done all right by me before, Mr. Logan. Pleasure doing business with you."

Harry replaced the receiver and sat motionless. He could have sworn Edward Orcutt knew nothing about the Cup. But this could be no coincidence. He must have pieced something together before he died, enough to let his son carry on the search.

He stood up abruptly. It was too soon to talk to Maggy, to reason with her. But he wouldn't waste any time finding Miles Orcutt. Particularly if he posed a threat to Maggy.

Chapter 16

*M*aggy woke late the next morning after a sleepless night. She hadn't seen Harry since their talk the night before. If anything, she even felt worse today. She didn't want to see him, afraid of what they would say to each other.

She got up and showered, then pulled on some jeans and a T-shirt. She wandered into the empty dining room to find all the breakfast things cleared away. A clatter of dishes came from the kitchen as she poked her head in cautiously to see who was there.

"Good morning, Maggy," came Nancy's welcome voice. "You can fix yourself some cereal if you like. Afraid you missed pancakes this morning."

"Sorry I overslept," Maggy said. "Cereal is plenty. I'm not very hungry."

Nancy wrung out a sponge in the sink and wiped down the countertop. "I wish you and Harry would straighten out whatever's got you both in such a state. He stormed out of here this morning without even a cup of coffee."

"Coffee sounds good," Maggy said, hoping Nancy would drop what seemed to be her favorite subject.

"Help yourself. You don't have to tell me anything if you don't want to. It's just my nature to worry."

"Thanks," Maggy threw an appreciative smile in her direction as she poured herself a cup of coffee.

"Oh, you had a Federal Express delivery this morning. I didn't know if I should wake you or not."

Maggy froze, her cereal spoon in midair. "That must be the last volume of my grandmother's diary. My friend sent it to me yesterday."

"You sit still. I'll get it for you," Nancy said and went down the hall toward the guest lobby. She returned a minute later with a blue and white Federal Express package.

Maggy tore it open and saw the familiar bindings of Anna's diary. "Yes, this is it! Thanks so much." She stood up to leave.

"Well, at least take your coffee with you, dear," Nancy said.

Maggy went back to her room with the diary in one hand and her coffee cup in the other. She sat down near the window and looked at the last volume of Anna's diary. The date of the first entry filled her with dread. Only two weeks before Beatrice died.

Anna's Diary—May 1, 1937

I've not written anything for months, so I will make up for it now. Since Beatrice Page left the castle after her triumph at the party, it's been something of a let-down. I still feel a special closeness with her, ever since she gave me the gown and pearls.

And wonder of wonders! My father has fallen in love and is going to marry Mrs. Sully, our neighbor who has been looking in on him for me! That brought home to me how self-centered I've been, to not even notice such a thing hap-

pening to my own father. All I noticed was that he seemed to be getting better, and seemed much happier than he'd been in a very long time.

Mrs. Sully was left an income by her late husband, and her mortgage is paid off as well, so father can rest easier now without financial ruin looming on the horizon. They will move into her house to live after they are married. Mrs. Sully turned bright red when I walked in for my weekly visit and found them in an embrace! I had to reassure her that they have my blessings. I've told him to do as he wishes with the house, for I don't think I will live there after I leave the castle.

But I don't plan to leave any time soon! Even when the days pass uneventfully, it's a marvel to live here. Mr. Hearst and Miss Davies have been gone for a month, traveling in Europe with a dozen guests in tow. The castle has been empty of all but household staff. But it's far from quiet. There's still hammering and constant noise from the construction crews. This is so ever-present that I only notice it when they stop for their lunch break, or lay off for the evening. Then the quiet is deafening.

Julia Morgan comes every weekend to oversee the construction, even though Mr. Hearst is not here to meet with her. She climbs the scaffolding without a qualm, always neat as a pin in her business suit. Her eyes never miss a thing. I'm told she and Mr. Hearst exchange wires just as often as though he were here in California, regardless of what country he's passing through on his journey.

And such wonderful news I've heard about Mrs. Page! I'd have to be blind and deaf not to hear her name, she's grown that successful. I've read about her singing engagements in Mr. Hearst's papers and in Louella Parsons' gossip column. Mrs. Parsons even mentioned Logan as her escort to a nightclub performance in Los Angeles. It's only been a few months since she came back to her old life, yet she has performed with Benny Goodman's band in several cities, and I've even heard her sing on the radio.

I tuned in to the Chase and Sandborn Hour, as I usually do on Sunday evenings. I couldn't believe it when Eddie Cantor introduced her, and then I heard her wonderful voice coming over the radio. I was thrilled that father could hear her sing while I described her to him. Her voice over the radio was-

n't half as lovely as it is in person, but still so beautiful it made me wish more than anything to see her again. I hope she comes back soon, and that Logan will come as well.

Not that I've been idle or bored all this time. Emma and her boyfriend James insisted that I meet a friend of his, Michael Lane. Michael is an apprentice electrician, learning his trade here at the castle from Mr. Eubanks.

I was reluctant to meet him, because it seemed so awkward with Emma and James in love, and Michael and I absolute strangers. We met after dinner on the lower terrace. For once there were no more chores to be done with all the guests gone. James had the good sense to drag Emma away, so Michael and I could get to know each other without our friends listening to every word we said. We strolled along "C" Terrace, where the staff often relaxes before the evening chores begin. We drifted away from Mrs. Redelsberger and the others until we were quite alone. On one side was the Pacific Ocean stretched out below us, rimmed with gold from the setting sun, and on the other side Neptune was presiding over his magnificent pool.

Michael cleared his throat and smiled at me. He's only a little taller than I am, so I look at him right at eye level. But he's solid and strong, not slight by any means. Fine brown eyes and brown curly hair. Working man's hands, with cuts and scrapes everywhere.

"What does an electrician do to bang up his hands so much?" I asked him finally, when it seemed that he would never speak.

"I get pretty banged up while I'm learning. It's rough work sometimes, just keeping the power and telephones working. This," he pointed to a scar along the side of his hand, "was when we had a line down during the storm last February." He held up a blackened thumbnail. "And this was when I decided to nail myself to a post instead of the wire I was stringing." He looked at his hands as if seeing them for the first time. "I guess they do look pretty bad." He seemed embarrassed.

"Nonsense," I said quickly. "It just shows that you work for a living. My hands aren't that lily-white either." I showed him my own hands, clean but red and chapped from all the detergents I used every day, the nails short and bare.

His hands dwarfed mine as he clasped them gently. "Your hands are beautiful, Anna. They should be wearing gold and pearls, at least."

I didn't know what to say to that, he seemed so serious. I felt a little awkward again when I took my hands from his. "Mrs. Eubanks was my schoolteacher in Cambria, did you know that?"

That got us talking about life in a small town like Cambria, and what it was like in San Francisco where he comes from. Soon we were laughing and feeling much better with each other.

He's a fine man, very down-to-earth. He knows exactly what he wants in this life, a quality I've always admired in others, since it's difficult for me to look into the future with anything resembling certainty. He told me that he pestered his friend James to introduce us, because he'd seen me working at the castle. I was flattered and completely taken by surprise. I don't think I noticed him at all until Emma mentioned his name to me.

The four of us have gone into town together, but mostly Michael meets me after dinner if we're both free. It was all very pleasant until now.

Now father and Mrs. Sulley are hovering over me with excited questions about him, because he called on me unexpectedly last week when I was spending my free day at home. I wasn't happy with him for putting me on the spot like that! But father and Mrs. Sulley loved him. They treated him like visiting royalty.

The next time I saw Michael he surprised me as I was polishing silver in the pantry. He was repairing the radio wiring for one of the guest rooms, so he was far from where he should be.

"Are you a guest now, free to wander around the castle whenever you choose?" I asked.

"I knew you were working in the big house today, Anna. I just wanted to see you for a minute."

"Well, I don't want to see you. Not after you invited yourself to meet my family, without even asking me. I don't want father to get the wrong idea about us. He's had enough disappointments in his life."

"What wrong idea will he get, Anna?" His voice was strained, and I realized how mean my words had been. I liked Michael and I'd been flattered by his attention. But I hadn't thought seriously about him until he met my father.

"He probably thinks that we'll be announcing our engagement any day now."

"Would that be so terrible?"

"Michael, be reasonable. We've known each other such a short time, not even two months. I don't know what I feel for you."

"Anna. Look at me." He sat down close to me on the kitchen bench. The expression in his dark eyes was one I'd never seen before. Then he leaned forward and kissed me. I was so surprised I didn't move. He didn't stop, but drew me even closer. At last he pulled away and I realized I'd been holding my breath. I let it out with a little gasp as his eyes locked on mine.

"I love you, Anna. I'm as certain of that as I am of anything in the world. One day you'll see it too." He touched my face with his rough hand, the lightest caress. Then he was gone.

I sat frozen at the table for a long time, my thoughts in a turmoil. At last I looked at my surroundings again. I found the polishing cloth where it had fallen on the floor and resumed my task.

Maggy sat with the diary open on her lap, her mouth curved in the hint of a smile, lost in her own memories. She remembered the feel of her grandfather's big hands as he swung her up on his shoulders when she was little. He had always seemed huge to her, big and happy, a man with a gentle heart. How funny to realize from Anna's description that he hadn't been a tall man. Maggy had always thought he towered to the sky. He had died when Maggy was ten years old. The loss was wrenching, almost worse than the loss of her parents.

Poor Anna, Maggy thought. How much harder it must have been for her. But they had gotten through it somehow. Maggy gently ran her fingers over the words written by her grandmother. She didn't know if she would be able to give this volume to the museum. It touched her so deeply. To them, it was just a little bit of history, an interesting footnote. It would be lost with all the thousands of papers documenting the castle and its people. But to Maggy, it was a glimpse into the lives of two people who meant everything to her.

She sighed at her morose thoughts. Why all this sadness? Her grandparents had lived a full life together. True, they suffered great losses, but they had more happiness than most people hope to find. They'd had more than thirty years together.

The muted ringing of the phone snapped her out of her reverie.

"Hey, Maggy," Carol's voice sounded like she was in the next room. "Did you get it?"

"I'm reading it right now. Thanks so much for sending it."

"Enough about that," Carol dismissed her friend's thanks offhandedly. "You wanted to know about Harry."

Maggy felt her body tense with apprehension. "Yes. What did you find?"

"He's pretty much an open book. When he was hired to be the curator at San Simeon they published a complete biography on him. I've checked out everything that I could." She paused and Maggy could hear the sound of papers crackling. "This isn't exactly chronological, but here goes. Harry Logan—graduated from UC Berkeley in 1981 with a degree in architecture and fine art. Spent five years at Oxford, where he became a recognized expert on Greek vases and antiquities. Hired as curator of San Simeon ten years ago. Resigned three years ago. Teaches graduate courses at UC Berkeley. Never married. Parents Ira and Janine Logan, deceased. Date of birth–August 13, 1958."

Maggy sagged back in her chair as Carol stopped reading. He was lying to her about everything! Not just his fantastic story about Logan Winter, but even about his marriage. She had felt such sympathy for him when he said his wife had died! Damn him!

"Hello, Maggy. Are you there?" Carol asked.

"Yes, I'm just..." Maggy felt like she was choking.

"Are you okay? Not what you wanted to hear, I take it?"

"No. I don't know what I expected, but this is—," she took a deep breath to try to calm down, "it's just a let-down." She tried to think rationally about the information Carol had just given her.

"There's something about that date," Maggy said finally. "What is it?"

"He was born in 1958," Carol said. "Let's see, that would make him about eight years older than you. Finally, you're interested in an older man!"

"He doesn't look that old," Maggy said. Then she realized where that train of thought might lead, and gave herself a mental shake. Carol didn't know the half of it. "No, really," Maggy said impatiently. "I'm serious about this. That date is familiar."

"I know! That's the same year that Edward Orcutt's son was born, remember? What was his name?"

"I don't think you mentioned the son's name. Strange that he and Harry would be born the same year."

"Whoa down, now," Carol said. "It doesn't seem that strange to me. So what if they were born in the same year?"

"Maybe it's just a coincidence," Maggy said in a small voice, the anger she had felt earlier replaced by a sick feeling of defeat. Harry had lied to her.

"Do you want to tell me what this is all about?"

"I don't know, Carol. The whole thing is so fantastic. I feel like a real jerk."

"Well, I won't let that one just lie there. Tell me. You'll feel better."

Maggy knew Carol was right. "Harry told me that he was Logan Winter. He, himself. That he knew Anna when she was eighteen years old."

"I thought Logan Winter was in his twenties then."

"He was."

Now it was Carol's turn to be speechless. "Okay, let me get this straight. Harry told you he's this mystery man, which would make him about eighty years old?"

"No. He said he's older than that."

"You're making my head spin, girl. Did he have any explanation? Any proof?"

"A photograph of him and Beatrice."

Carol snorted. "That's nothing! Anything else?"

"No. He mentioned Seheiah's Cup, that was stolen out of Winter's room."

"Oh, I get it. So this cup is like in that movie, Indiana Jones. What was it supposed to be? The Holy Grail or something? The fountain of youth? What does he take you for?"

"An idiot, I guess," Maggy said quietly. She fought the tears that were welling up, but knew that Carol could tell by her voice.

"I'm sorry, honey. I shouldn't have said that. I forgot that we aren't operating in a normal world anymore. Once Beatrice made her appearance, everything changed."

"That's what I thought, too. I've been trying to believe him, but I just can't. And now, with what you've found out, I have to face the truth."

"But why would he lie to you? Especially such a stupendous lie?"

"I don't know."

"Sure I can't convince you to come home?"

"No. Not until I find out why he did it." Maggy was positive about that, at least.

"Well, I don't like it. I'm worried about you."

Maggy laughed. "That's your job, you know. I think the only danger is to my pride. And I've gotten a lot tougher than I look. So don't worry, okay?"

After she hung up, Maggy wondered if she was trying to reassure Carol, or herself.

She picked up Anna's diary where she had left it on the bed.

Anna's Diary—May 8, 1937

    The castle is buzzing with activity again! Miss Davies and Mr. Hearst returned early last week. Emma said they toured all of Italy, even south as far as the city of Pompeii. The sights they must have seen! All of us have been rushing to see that everything is perfectly prepared for them. The air fairly crackles with excitement, now that the lord and master is home.

    My own wish has been granted as well. Last night I welcomed Beatrice Page back to the castle, to stay in her old room in Casa del Mar. I was so happy to see her again. She gave me a great hug when we met, and warmed me with her brilliant smile. I had to tell her straight off how I'd been listening to her on the radio, and how happy I was for her success.

    "Thank you, Anna. I've been blessed ever since the night Marion forced me to sing. It's been wonderful. Come, help me unpack my things and I'll tell you all about it."

    I could see right away that she was more relaxed than she had been before. At the same time she seemed bursting with high spirits. Fortunately, Mr. Orcutt wasn't with her to cast shadows on her happiness.

    I spent almost an hour with her in her room while she told an amazing story of her whirlwind tour, performing in New York and Los Angeles, and even in San Francisco. She was the voice that every band leader wanted, at least for the moment.

    "I feel truly alive when I'm singing to an audience," Beatrice said. "This is the first real joy I've known since Maxwell died. I can express my feelings at last, instead of keeping them all bottled up inside."

    I was well aware of her almost magical ability to draw in an audience, to make them feel what she was feeling.

    "When I heard you sing, it was like you were singing just for me," I told her. "I think everybody who heard you felt the same way."

    I looked for Logan to arrive, but didn't see him among the guests who came last night. It seems a very long time since I've seen him. When I think of Logan,

I wonder what his life must be like away from the castle, which is just a holiday for him, a respite from his real life. Faced with that blank wall, I find my thoughts turning to Michael and our encounter in the pantry last week. His kiss that turned me upside down.

I've scarcely seen Michael since then. I've grown used to his company, and I miss our comfortable times together. I'm afraid those times are over, now that he's made his intentions clear. The few times I've seen him, I've grown terribly nervous and felt my heart racing. I want to speak to him, but I don't know what it is I want to say. Do I love him? Is this how love feels? If so, it's a nervous, unpleasant feeling. I don't think I care for it.

May 9, 1937

Logan arrived today! He must have driven up in his own car, or I would have been told when to expect him. As it was, he caught me completely by surprise. He passed me on the terrace as I hurried to "A" House on an errand for one of the guests. Before I knew it he'd gathered me up in a hug, just as Beatrice had. I was so happy to see him again! He's just as he was before, flashing his ready smile at me and asking how I've been all this time. His eyes are even bluer than I remembered, his hair very blond against tanned skin. I didn't have much opportunity to speak to him, for my duties are heavier now that the castle is teeming with guests. I have to run just to keep up with them all.

I knew he would be busy all evening with dinner and socializing, and then the evening's film would be shown at 11:00 or so. The nightly routine is a command performance required of all Mr. Hearst's guests. Logan said he would find time to visit with me later, to tell me all about his adventures with Beatrice over the past two months.

He looked at me seriously for just a moment and said the strangest thing. "You look different, Anna. I believe you've grown up since I last saw you." To my great annoyance, I felt a blush creep up my cheeks at his remark, disproving his compliment. But I feel absurdly flattered anyway. I've always wanted him to see me as a grown woman, and now it seems that he does.

This afternoon I welcomed many famous guests that I've only read about before. Charles Lindbergh was a great hero of mine when I was a child, so it was thrilling to meet him today. He is even taller than Mr. Hearst! Then I greeted another arrival that gave me no pleasure at all. Mr. Orcutt looked at me as though I had already committed some offense. He went immediately to Beatrice's room when he arrived. I hope he doesn't spoil this visit for her.

Logan was true to his word, and he found me late this afternoon just as I was carrying the last of the soiled bed linens back to the big house. He waited while I delivered them to the laundry room, and then we walked on the Esplanade to the south side of the castle, where guests and staff were less likely to wander.

"Anna, I wish you could have seen Beatrice perform at the Waldorf-Astoria in New York," he said as we strolled in the warmth of the slanting sunlight. "She captivated everyone. They are a hard crowd to please, believe me."

"She told me a little about her tour, and I read about it in the newspaper. Your name was there too, in Louella Parson's column."

"No doubt," he said, not looking very pleased. Then he turned to me with an eager expression. "Have you managed to find out anything about the vase that was stolen from my room?"

"I'm sorry, I haven't heard or seen a thing. It's as though it never existed."

"It was too much to hope for," he said. He expression was grim when he spoke. He seemed almost to be talking to himself. "I'll learn to live without it, for whatever time I have left."

"I beg your pardon?" I asked him, mystified by his remark.

He saw me again clearly, and the weary expression left his eyes. They crinkled up in a warm smile. "It's nothing at all." He laughed a little, though I didn't know what he found so amusing. "You know, Anna, you're like a spring breeze, scented with flowers and new grass. Seeing you helps blow the cobwebs from my mind. Thank you."

This did little to explain what he was talking about, but I didn't care. Soon we spoke of other things. He told me about some of the places he had traveled, and I told him how quiet the castle had been without Mr. Hearst and Miss

Davies. I don't know exactly how it happened, but I found myself telling him about my friends Emma and James, and then Michael's name was on my lips.

I stopped talking, embarrassed that I had been rambling on so much.

"I think Michael is a very lucky man," Logan said.

May 10, 1937

Mr. Orcutt is determined to cause trouble. He's like a powder keg awaiting a match, with his resentments all too visible. I don't understand how he can work with Beatrice and Logan when he feels such jealousy.

For the second time I was unlucky enough to overhear him in a temper. This morning I was hurrying through my cleaning rounds. When I entered Beatrice's room I immediately heard angry voices. Beatrice was nowhere to be seen, but Mr. Orcutt's voice was unmistakable. It was too late to back out, for I was in plain view of them both. But they didn't notice me right away.

"I'm telling you, Winter. Leave her alone. You've caused enough damage already."

"Come on, Edward. You're way off base here," Logan's voice was calm, but I could tell he was angry.

"Am I? Do you think I don't know what's going on between you?"

"Nothing is going on between us, except in your fevered imagination."

Mr. Orcutt acted as though he hadn't even heard Logan. "She's twenty years older than you, for God's sake! You're making a damn fool of her, and you aren't even worth the dirt under her feet!" He was shouting now, and trembling with rage.

"Orcutt, you should be careful when you make accusations," Logan's voice was no louder, but heavy with the contempt. "Whatever Beatrice and I are to each other, it doesn't concern you."

They were both tensed, ready for the first blow. I must have made some sound then, for they turned to me at the same time.

"I'm sorry, I—I've come for the room," I stammered.

"It's you again," Mr. Orcutt said. "Always spying, showing up where you're not wanted."

"That's enough," Logan said. "I suggest you leave, Orcutt. Now."

The look he gave Logan was dark with hatred. "I'll leave you with your little friend, then. But this is far from over, Winter."

When Mr. Orcutt was finally gone, I felt terribly relieved. "I'm sorry I rushed in like that. I didn't think anyone was here."

"No, Anna. You have nothing to be sorry for."

Logan walked over to where I stood by the door. "Are you all right?"

"Yes. It's just that—" I wasn't sure how to continue.

"Come over here." He took the clean bed linens from my hands led me to a sofa near the window. "Sit here for a moment and calm down. I'm sorry you had to witness that. It was just bad luck that we happened to come looking for Beatrice at the same time."

"This isn't the first time I've seen him like this," I said. "He frightens me."

Logan's face was shadowed, his eyes dark as he looked at me. "I don't know what we're going to do about Edward. He was a different man when Maxwell was alive. You'd hardly recognize him." He looked out the window toward the ocean far below. He didn't seem to focus on the view, but on his own thoughts instead. "His obsession with Beatrice has gotten worse over the past few months."

"I heard him speak the same way to Mrs. Page. It was terrible." I described the argument I'd overheard at the theater. "Why can't he accept the truth? She told him plainly enough. She doesn't love him." I said.

"We all knew that he adored her, right from the start. But that's often the case with Beatrice. Loving her comes as naturally as breathing the air." I knew exactly what he meant. "There was never any doubt that she and Max were absolutely faithful to each other. Orcutt was just another one of her fans, albeit a business partner as well."

"Did he always hate you, even then?"

"No, we got on fairly well at first. I could appreciate his keen business sense and his connections in the music world. They owed a great deal of their suc-

cess to him. He appreciated my financial backing, at least in the beginning. We were both part of the magic circle that Beatrice and Maxwell drew around them." He turned from the window and sat beside me on the sofa.

"Then Max died and everything stopped. Beatrice retired from public life. Edward hovered over her constantly. I think she depended on him without ever really knowing he was there. He must have assumed all along that she would marry him."

"She said she'd never marry anyone. I heard her."

"Yes, I know," he said. After a moment or two, he took my hand in his. I couldn't help but notice how different his hands were from Michael's. Graceful and smooth, with no calluses or scraped knuckles. "I'll leave you to your work, Anna. Please don't worry about Edward. Beatrice and I will work this out."

After he left I threw myself back into my work. I changed the bed linens and cleaned the floors. Dusted the lovely old furniture and art pieces, and scrubbed the tiles in the bathroom. No matter how hard I worked, I could still see Mr. Orcutt's face, twisted with malice, his eyes black and piercing. I wasn't afraid for myself, but I felt a terrible forboding for Logan.

Chapter 17

Beatrice sat on the ground with her back resting against the pillar of the ruined pergola. She twisted a piece of dried grass in her hand as she looked down to the Pacific. Morning light was breaking through majestic clouds overhead, shooting sunbeams like spotlights through the mist and shadows. It still looked dim and colorless to her, spoiled as she was by the colors of Heaven. But she scarcely noticed as she waited impatiently. She sent out another call to Ambrose, daring him to show his face to her.

"Dear Beatrice!" Ambrose materialized before her with a clap of air like distant thunder. She was not impressed, her displeasure evident on her face.

"Oh dear. You're still angry with me," he said as he sat down beside her. "We really should make it up, you know. We'll do much better if we work together. I'll start by apologizing for not telling you about Harry."

Beatrice said nothing, just looked at him with obvious skepticism.

"You saw him, didn't you?" Ambrose asked, unperturbed by her silence. "Did you recognize him?"

"Of course I recognized him!" She said. "He's Logan! And you have a lot of explaining to do."

Ambrose seemed to wilt a little before her angry stare. "All right. What do you want to know about him?"

"It should be obvious, shouldn't it? Why didn't you tell me who he was? Even more important, how can I believe that you're his guardian angel? He must have the Cup, so that means he doesn't have an angel!"

"I'll tell you everything, my dear. Please, just be patient. This hasn't been easy for me." He pulled a handkerchief from his robe and wiped his forehead with it. Beatrice thought this a foolish affectation, but said nothing.

"I didn't tell you about Logan because I was worried about you. You had forgotten your mortal existence, just as we all must strive to put that behind us. I knew you had to remember some events from your life, but I didn't want those memories to hurt you." He turned to her with a hesitant smile. "You're not quite as invincible as you'd like to believe, Beatrice. I was only trying to protect you."

He could see this argument was having no appreciable effect on her.

"I was suddenly made aware of Logan's existence on January 15, 1937. The day Seheiah's Cup was stolen from him. The day I became his guardian angel. You can imagine my confusion, to have a full-grown mortal thrust upon me like that. And not an ordinary mortal! I sensed right away that he was older than he appeared. He's hardly aged at all since then either. Still a picture of glowing vitality." His voice lost it's injured tone as he leaned toward her. "It's been difficult for me to reach him."

Beatrice held up a hand to interrupt his story. "I still don't see why you couldn't tell me. How could remembering any of this hurt me?"

"Oh dear. I didn't want to tell you this, Beatrice," Ambrose said slowly. He looked as though he was in pain as he spoke. "Harry—, that is, Logan was obsessed with finding Seheiah's Cup once it was stolen from him. I've always known the Cup was an evil thing with the power to twist a man's life, play on his weaknesses. Yet he had to find it again! He would stop at nothing then, and he'll stop at nothing now. He fears death too much." He shook his head and covered his eyes with his hand.

She could see now that his pain was genuine. "This wouldn't have hurt me, Ambrose. I would have tried my best to help him, just as you've tried to do."

"That's not all. You see, Logan was responsible for your death."

Beatrice looked at him, uncomprehending.

"He was remorseful. He tried to save you, but by that time it was too late."

"I don't believe you." Beatrice said quickly. "Logan wouldn't have hurt me!"

"You forget, Beatrice, I know his thoughts intimately. He has thought often of the day you died. It tortures him, twists in him like a knife."

"Go on," she said finally.

"When the Cup was stolen from him, he suspected everyone. He even attacked Anna, thinking she was the thief. She wrote about that in the second volume of her diaries."

"I saw him reading it yesterday at the castle," Beatrice said.

"Then you know I'm telling you the truth."

She had an impression of what Anna had written, true enough. But Beatrice was still not convinced. "I know that you can't lie in the sense that mortals understand," she said. "But I question your interpretation of events, Ambrose. Just because you're an angel, doesn't mean you're right about this. Logan couldn't have hurt me, I know it."

"The Cup has poisoned his mind, especially back then when it had just been ripped out of his grasp. He was desperate to get it back! Even though he loved you, he began to suspect that either you or Edward had stolen it."

Nothing he said caused even a glimmer of memory to surface in Beatrice's mind. The past was an impenetrable wall, with only the tiniest chinks broken through. Vague, spontaneous memories of Anna and Logan. She didn't even remember what Edward looked like.

Beatrice stood up suddenly, unable to contain her anguish and frustration. "If only I could remember!"

Ambrose followed her as she strode down the abandoned bridle path, heedless of her direction. He caught up to her and clasped a hand on her arm.

"Beatrice, stop. I believe it's too painful for you to remember."

She turned on him, her eyes flashing dangerously. "How do you know so much about what happened, Ambrose? You are privy to Harry's true emotions, of course, but how do you know all the details of what happened?"

Ambrose took a step backwards. "Simply this. I was his guardian from the day he lost the Cup. I was there when you died, Beatrice. I witnessed everything with my own eyes."

Chapter 18

*A*nna's Diary—May 14, 1937

Michael Lane is the most unreasonable man I've ever known! I'm so angry with him, and disappointed as well. And angry with myself, for missing his company so much over the past week that I was yearning to see him again. But I barely caught a glimpse of him until last night.

After dinner I joined the rest of the staff at "C" terrace, as usual. I looked for Michael, but didn't see him among the familiar faces. I tried not to show my disappointment, as Emma and some of the other girls gossiped about our famous guests. We'd been there about fifteen minutes, and some were starting to leave for the evening chores. Suddenly, Michael was at my side. I was so happy to see him! But my smile faded when I saw his stiff shoulders and unsmiling face.

"I need to talk to you, Anna. It's important."

Emma and the others exchanged glances and left us. He took my hand abruptly and we walked down a path toward south side of the castle, where no one could see us. The light was beginning to fade, but I could still make out his curly hair and dark eyes. He looked like a thundercloud.

"What is it, Michael? What's wrong?"

"When you told me about your friend Logan Winter, I thought he was old, like Mrs. Page."

"Mrs. Page isn't that old." I rushed to her defense, as though he had insulted her. "And what difference does it make?"

"Anna, you don't know what you're doing to me. When I see you with him, it tears me up inside."

"Is that why you've stayed away from me for days?"

"I was giving you some time to think about things. I wanted to talk to you, but I was afraid I rushed you too much already."

"I wanted to see you, too," I said softly, my heart hammering away in my chest.

He swept me into an embrace that fairly lifted my feet off the ground. Then he kissed me as I've never dreamed of being kissed by a man, so that I forgot where I was. I forgot everything, except his touch and his arms holding me.

"I love you so much, Anna," he whispered to me at last, and caressed my cheek with his big hand.

"I love you too, Michael," I said. I was afraid I might burst with the happiness I felt.

He released me and took my hand. We turned toward the castle, for he knew I had to get back to work.

"Then you won't see him again," he said. A statement, not a question.

"Logan? Of course I'll see him again. He's my friend."

Michael stopped as though he'd been struck. "You can't see him! You love me."

"I do, and you've no reason to be jealous of Logan." The moment I spoke the words, I knew they were true. Any fantasies I'd woven about Logan had

died with that kiss. Even before tonight, with Michael's first kiss that had caught me unaware as I sat polishing silver.

"I won't allow you to see him!" he said, looking as though he couldn't comprehend what I just told him.

"Oh, are you my father, that you can give me orders? Even father doesn't tell me who I can or can't see!" I snapped, wishing I could shake some sense into him.

"The two of you together, whispering and laughing. I've seen it, Anna."

"Have you been following me?" Now I was just as angry as he was. "How dare you order me around! How dare you spy on me!"

"You're mine, Anna. I can't stand the thought of you with another man. Especially him!"

"What do you know about him? Nothing! But that's not the point. How could I ever love a man who doesn't trust me?" I struggled to keep the tears from falling as I turned and ran away from him.

I had experienced the heights of joy and been plunged into misery all within the space of ten minutes.

May 16, 1937

Tragedy! I can't believe what I write on the page, nor can I see clearly through my tears. But I must write it, or I will die with grief.

Beatrice is dead! My dear friend, no—more than that somehow. I feel as I did when mother died. The shock of it hurts so. She lies in her bedroom now, where Logan carried her, his face contorted with fear and grief.

None of us know what really happened. A large group went out riding this afternoon with Mr. Hearst. Logan, Beatrice and Mr. Orcutt left the others to take a different path. I don't know what happened to their groom.

Logan came in not an hour ago, with Beatrice in his arms. The back of his shirt collar was soaked with blood, but he seemed unhurt, his attention focused entirely on Beatrice. Her face was white, a trickle of blood seeped from the corner of her mouth. The side of her head was bruised horribly, and swelling. Her leg was twisted at an unnatural angle. All the while Logan was shouting orders, sending everyone scurrying in his path. "Get the doctor here at once! She's taken a blow to the head."

He laid her gently on the bed, then looked up at me. I don't know if he even recognized me. Miss Davies' nurse came into the room. It was then I saw Mr. Orcutt standing by the door, his face pinched with shock. He stared at Beatrice and Logan, his eyes unwavering. But he didn't move toward them. Just stood, deathly still, at the edge of the room.

The nurse bent close to Beatrice and examined the wound on her head. She turned to Logan. "Her injuries are more serious than I can attend to, sir. The doctor has been sent for, but he's on another call right now. We've sent a rider out to find Mr. Hearst—"

"She needs medical attention!" Logan cut her off in mid-sentence. "Hearst can't help her!"

"I know that, sir," she placated him. "Another doctor from San Luis Obispo is on his way here now. "

"When?" I saw her wince as Logan grasped her arm. "When will he get here?"

"Not more than an hour, sir, perhaps and hour and a half," from her voice I could see what Logan saw. This was a death sentence for Beatrice.

"No!" he shouted. "We must do something for her now! We can't let her die."

He bent close to Beatrice and took her limp hand. "Beatrice. Listen to me. You must hang on! Don't leave us. Live!"

The minutes passed as we stood watching helplessly. I don't think he was aware of anyone else in the room as he spoke to Beatrice. He brushed the hair away from her forehead gently, tears running unheeded down his face. "My darling, I would save you now if I had the Cup. You must drink from the Cup." He muttered the same words over and over.

Then he raised his eyes, blankly at first. Finally, his gaze focused on me. He ran to me and grabbed my shoulders in a painful grip. "Anna! Have you found the Cup? It's the only thing that will save her. Have you found it? Please God, say you have!"

"I'm so sorry, Logan," I could barely speak through my tears. "I've found nothing."

He pushed me away and went back to her bedside. His shoulders sagged as he kneeled beside her. He took her hand once again and bowed his head.

The next minutes seemed to last an eternity. The only sound in the room was Beatrice's strained breathing. She stirred slightly, her breathing changed. Logan leaned near to her. I think she spoke to him.

The vigil continued. No one in the room moved, or spoke. We waited, filled with dread. Then her labored breathing stilled. I heard Logan whisper in the shocked silence. "God, no."

Then Orcutt leaped into the room, tearing at Logan like a madman. "You killed her!" He shouted in a frenzy, spittle flying from his mouth. "It's your fault she's dead!" His fingers were like claws as he tried to strangle Logan where he leaned against the bed. At first Logan didn't respond to the attack. Finally, he whirled and struck Orcutt a ferocious blow to the chest. It knocked the wind out of him, and he crumpled to the floor, weeping and gasping for air.

"Stay away from me, Orcutt, or I'll kill you," Logan said in a voice that sent chills up my spine. Mr. Orcutt staggered to his feet, still breathing hard. His face softened for a moment as he looked at Beatrice. Then it closed tight, all expression erased. He said in a quiet voice, barely audible even in the hushed silence, "You'll pay for this, Winter." Then he stumbled out of the room, still in obvious pain from the blow he received.

In the midst of this madness, the doctor finally arrived. There was little for him to do. He examined Beatrice's body. He tried to comfort Logan with the news that even he could not have saved her; her injuries were too severe. She would have died in any case. The doctor pronounced Beatrice dead at 5:37pm.

I can't believe this has happened. Only this morning I spoke to her. Just for a minute, as our paths crossed on the terrace in front of Casa del Mar. She was brimming over with life and good spirits. She asked me about the dress she had given me, and I told her I was almost finished with the alterations; that it would be perfect when I was done. Her smile had warmed me like a splash of sunlight.

Chapter 19

$\mathcal{M}$aggy looked at the faded writing in the diary, unable to go on reading. She touched the page where streaks of moisture had caused the ink to run. Those were Anna's tears.

Maggy wished Anna could have seen Beatrice as she shimmered by the pool last Friday, radiant and compelling. More than alive, even after decades had passed.

Her thoughts turned inevitably to Harry. Now he wanted her to believe that he was this person. Logan Winter, who caused so much trouble for Anna, and God knows what he did to Beatrice. Maggy closed the diary, her thoughts troubled. To be fair, Logan did everything he could to save her. But it wasn't enough, was it?

Anna's account confirmed one thing. Logan believed Seheiah's Cup would save Beatrice's life, that it would have healed her wounds. Maybe Harry heard about this somehow, and that's why he thought up his crazy story. Maybe that's why he wanted the Cup so badly. He really believed it could make you live forever.

A sharp knock sounded on her door, bringing her abruptly back to the present. She didn't really want to see anyone now. The most important thing was to finish reading the diary, no matter how painful the rest of the story might be.

When the knock repeated, she stood up and went to answer the door, muttering under her breath at the interruption.

Maggy felt a jolt go through her when she saw Harry standing in front of her. He was the last person she expected to see, after the way she left him. Now she felt completely unprepared, off-balance.

"Don't run away from me again, Maggy," he said as he braced the door open with his arm.

She felt heat rush to her face at his words. She had run away from him the moment he'd told her his 'true' identity. She wasn't normally a coward, and it rankled that she hadn't faced him right then.

"What do you want?" She asked him, her voice much stronger than she felt with him standing only inches away from her.

"I want your undivided attention for a few hours. Just hear me out, okay? Then you can call the state authorities and have me committed if you want."

His blue eyes drew her in. She pulled herself back consciously, though she could see his lips curve up in the tiniest smile at her momentary lapse.

"This isn't funny," Maggy said quickly.

"It's far from being funny," Harry said. "I'm deadly serious."

"Okay. I'll hear you out. But I won't believe you, Harry. What you claim is impossible."

"I'll refrain from any mention of angels at that remark," he said without a trace of humor. She resisted an urge to strangle him. "All I ask is that you listen to what I have to say. I may surprise you, my darling."

Maggy gave him a sharp look at the endearment. The same words Logan had used when he spoke to Beatrice as she lay on her deathbed.

Don't be silly, she thought. It's a perfectly ordinary term, used thousands of times every day.

"Are you hungry? Have you eaten lunch yet?" he asked.

"Lunch? Already?" Maggy hadn't been aware of the morning passing, she'd been so engrossed in Anna's diary.

"It's almost one o'clock. I'll take you to lunch. We can talk there."

Instead of driving into Cambria as she expected, Harry turned north on Highway One toward San Simeon.

He spoke of inconsequential things, smoothing over her less than enthusiastic responses. When he mentioned the party on Thursday, she didn't say anything. He let it pass. Maggy looked up at the castle visible on the crest of the Santa Lucia hills, even from this great distance. She could just make out the tall palm trees, like a series of giant flags reaching to the fourth floor, with the two massive towers extending even higher. Maggy wished she could attend the party on Thursday. See the castle alive again, as it was when Beatrice was there. Filled with music, couples swaying as they danced.

She pushed the thought away. It couldn't happen. Not now.

Harry turned off the highway at the town of San Simeon, a mile before they reached the visitor center for the castle. He drove through the little beach town, past strip malls and gas stations. It was like a hundred modern towns, saved from the commonplace only by the sweep and murmur of the ocean nearby. It had once been a bustling seaport where Hearsts treasures were unloaded and stored in nearby warehouses. Finally Harry pulled into the driveway of a single-story Spanish style house with a red tile roof, reminiscent of the cottages at the castle.

Maggy looked at him in surprise as he turned off the engine.

"What are we doing here?"

"This is where we're having lunch," Harry said. He reached into the back seat for a basket that Maggy hadn't noticed when she got in. "A picnic, actually."

"You were very confident that I'd come," she said.

"Not really. I don't know what to expect from you, Maggy."

Harry opened the front door with a key and flipped the light switch on. The entryway was a colorful pattern of inlaid tiles. White walls were trimmed with beautifully detailed dark wood moldings. Harry led her into a living room that had sheets spread over the furniture. Obviously, no one was living here.

"Whose house is this?" she asked.

"Mine. I bought it in 1945 after the War."

Maggy stiffened at his words.

"You said you'd listen. Don't judge, Maggy. Just listen."

He took the sheets off of a large sofa, a rich green fabric covering the overstuffed cushions. It looked old to Maggy, but she was certainly no expert.

"I'll light a fire while you set out our lunch, okay?" Harry smiled at her.

Maggy opened the lunch basket and saw the feast Harry had brought, roasted chicken and fresh crusty bread, salads, cheeses, two sinful-looking truffles. A bottle of Chardonnay and two crystal wine glasses. She looked at him suspiciously.

"Did Nancy make this?"

"Don't blame her. She's a terrible romantic. She thinks you're wonderful, by the way."

"You probably haven't told her your little secret," Maggy said.

"No. I haven't told anyone but you. At least in this century."

She gaped at him. She couldn't help it.

"Here," he said as he handed her a glass of wine. "You look like you need this. Let's eat some of this before we start. Nancy will be very disappointed if we don't touch our lunch."

Maggy took a sip gratefully, and sat on the sofa. She was hungry in spite of the apprehension that was building inside of her. They both ate some of the chicken and delicacies Nancy had prepared, but it wasn't a comfortable meal. The wine helped to relax some of her tension.

"Okay. Tell me," Maggy said.

He didn't sit down, but poured himself another glass of wine and stood by the fireplace. "As I said I bought this house in 1945. I lived here when I was curator at the museum, but it's been empty since then."

"Before you go on, I have to tell you that I know about you already," she stopped him, hating to hear his lies.

"Oh? What do you know?"

"I know that you were born in 1958, that your parents were Ira and Janine Logan. You graduated from UC Berkeley in the eighties, and you did a stint at Oxford. You never married."

"Been doing your homework, I see," he spoke lightly, but his hand tightened on the wineglass he was holding.

"I had to," Maggy said in a small voice.

"I suppose you did." He turned away from her and faced the fire. She could see his face in profile as he spoke. "I did attend Berkeley and Oxford, just as you discovered, for the express purpose of getting the job as curator here."

"So you could look for Seheiah's Cup at the castle," Maggy said.

"Yes. Everything else is a facade that I built for myself." He looked at her again. "It's the face I show the world, Maggy."

She didn't say anything, just sipped her wine. And waited.

"I was born in England in the Year of our Lord 1588." Maggy gasped and made a move to object, but he held up his hand before she could speak. "No, hear me out, no matter how incredible it sounds. Just listen, as you promised.

"It was an auspicious year. The height of the Elizabethan Age, with the Spanish Armada defeated and broken, and Shakespeare headed for triumph in London. I was the eldest son of Sir John Daubeney of High Wycombe. We had a fine estate called Barrington Hall, won for the family by my grandfather's service to Elizabeth I, before she was queen. That was during the blessedly short reign of Bloody Mary. My father had little taste for intrigue and he developed a keen ability to escape the notice of royal eyes. From childhood I was betrothed to the daughter of Sir Robert

Sidney, our close neighbor and friend. He sent her to live with us on her tenth birthday. We would marry in five years' time. Marie was a willful, beautiful girl, who knew me better than I knew myself. We considered ourselves blessed, for we were very much in love."

Maggy recovered from her earlier shock when she felt a strong, primitive reaction to his words. She resisted the feeling, and looked at him more closely as he spoke. His voice was changing, the rhythm and cadence were strange. He didn't seem to see her or his surroundings.

"We loved each other fiercely, and did our best to remain virgins until our wedding night. But the blood ran hot between us, and we lay together once. Despite our inexperience, it was a night of love I thought I'd never know again." He looked at her suddenly and the pain left his face for a moment. "I was wrong," he said pointedly.

She couldn't help the small thrill that grew in her at his words and the look in his eyes. It only made her feel worse.

"Two months before our wedding, fever broke out in London. Soon the sickness had spread to High Wycombe. Barrington Hall was closed tight for fear the Black Death would take us, as it was claiming thousands in the towns and villages around us. But wealth and stone walls were no protection. Within a fortnight, Marie and my mother both lay dead. My prayers had gone unanswered. Their bodies were burned on a pyre along with others of our household. I watched the black smoke of that fire rise to the heavens, and I knew why my prayers had been futile. There was no one there to hear them. My faith was gone, burned to ashes and dust like the bodies on the pyre before me.

"Father was crushed with grief for my mother. The whole country was plunged into mourning, for we had also lost our great queen. James I was a poor replacement. The next year passed by without meaning or purpose, for I could not bring myself to care what happened. Father understood my despair well, and allowed me to leave Barrington Hall and its bitter memories. My younger brother, Charles, took my place at home and I wandered the land.

"My only companion was my servant Walter. We traveled through many cities in Europe, always heading south. For someone who hated death as much as I, it is ironic that I found myself on the battlefield, fighting against our old adversary. Spain had been defeated by Elizabeth the year of my birth, but now fought against James. It was a strange choice of profession. Though I was quick and strong, I was a poor marksman due to less than perfect eyesight. I made up for that lack with a disregard for my own safety. Death was my enemy, and I taunted him at every opportunity. I gained a reputation for taking our wounded from the field, regardless of the danger. Sometimes they lived.

"I survived, despite the risks I took. On the battlefield I met an old man, Gamal. It was a foreign name, though he spoke without accent. He claimed to be from the Holy Land. He never told me how he came to be so far from home. He must have been almost fifty, which seemed ancient to me. I thought it strange he had no scars or injuries, and even all his teeth! Unusual for such an old man. He had been watching me, he said. Then he told a strange story, one that was so fantastic I didn't believe it. I thought he must be mad.

"He said he had chosen me because I hated death, but did not fear it. I was the one he had been looking for to receive the gift. He didn't want to know my name, should his resolve weaken when the pain of age or injury took him. It made no sense to me, but I listened.

"He pulled out a cup, non-descript and dusty. It wasn't worn with age, but smooth and perfectly formed. Yet my first impression of it was that it was very old. He held it reverently in two hands. "I was born during the time of Caesar," he said. "The Cup was given to me by a stranger passing through our village. He had grown weary of life, as I have done at last.

"You will take this gift—Seheiah's Cup." He handed the cup to me. It was heavy in my hands, but warm. For some reason that I didn't understand, I felt less wary of him. As though I had known him for many years. But I still thought he was mad.

"Drink from it once every third year and you will never age. How old are you boy?" he asked me.

"You are mistaken to think me a boy," I said, affronted. My boyhood had died long ago, taken from me when the plague swept through our village. "I'm an old man of twenty-three."

"Gamal smiled at me wryly. 'Time will correct that misapprehension.'

'The Cup will cure any mortal injury or illness,' he continued. 'When you drink, recite the incantation as it is written here.' He pointed to the strange marks cut around the base of the Cup. In a singsong voice he chanted, 'Who drinks the Cup of mortal life, Rests unseen in Heaven's shadow. Behold the color of life, Behold the gift of life, Behold the secret of immortality.'

"He made me repeat that verse several times until he was convinced I had memorized the words. 'The years will not touch you now,' he said. 'Blessings upon you, brother.'

"He left me then. Later I tried to find him, but he had disappeared. I never saw him again. I didn't believe Gamal, but I kept the Cup. I thought his story was amusing, even if it was the raving of a madman.

"Seven weeks later came the battle of San Sebastian. I was wounded during that route. What a charnel house it was." Harry pressed a hand over his eyes, as though to rub away the sights he was seeing.

"You see, Maggy, the Cup also heals the mind, the memory. While I had it in my possession I could remember any day of my life perfectly, in minute detail. This uncanny power has diminished slightly since 1937, thank God! I've learned that forgetfulness can be a blessing.

"My injury was not severe, an arrow through the fleshy part of my thigh. Others had recovered from worse. But in three days time the wound was gangrenous, putrid with infection. I had seen enough wounds to know I'd not survive this. My page went for the field surgeon, who wished to amputate my leg. I knew that would be fatal as well. I preferred to die a whole man. The physician was content to bleed me and leave me to my fate.

"In three more days the infection had spread up through my groin, my leg blackened. I remembered Gamal's Cup that would heal any injury or disease. I was a dead man already, but I thought I would put his Cup to the test. I never believed for an instant that he had spoken the truth.

"My page, young Walter, filled the Cup with water and brought it to me where I lay. He lifted my head so I could drink.

"In that first instant I knew Gamal had spoken the truth. The healing water coursed through my body with an energy that was overwhelming. The pain vanished, replaced by a feeling of unlimited vitality. My fevered body cooled on the sweat-soaked litter where I lay. I drank the rest of the water, holding the Cup in my own hands, and recited the verse as Gamal had told me.

"I threw off the blanket that covered me and unwrapped the foul bandages from around my leg. It was clean and whole, as I knew it would be. There was no wound, no infection.

"Walter looked at me with awe and made the sign of the cross. He also made a sign to ward off evil, though he tried to hide that from my view. Despite his fears, he was my most loyal companion. He grew resigned to serving a master who never grew a day older. I offered the Cup to him on several occasions, but he would never drink from it. I watched as he grew older, imperceptibly at first. Then his body changed more with the passing years. He died forty years later, an old man of fifty-five, taken by the plague that had spared him as a boy. Still loyal to me, a youth of twenty-three, unchanged in any way. Walter did not despise death, as I did. Nor did he fear it. He welcomed it!

"But I am ahead of my story. Gamal was right when he said I hated death. I used the Cup to save injured men on the battlefield. I had the sense to hide the Cup itself, and I mimicked many of the accepted medical treatments of the time, which amounted to bleeding and administering healing plasters. Fortunately, with the Cup I didn't have to perform amputations. It worked far too well to go unnoticed. The men were either awed as Walter was, or afraid of me.

"I had forgotten about the doctor who had left me to die. One night I collapsed on my sleeping mat in utter exhaustion. Walter was nearby, and must have sounded a warning that caused me to move slightly. I awoke to a hideous pain in my chest where the good doctor had plunged a knife into me. No doubt his aim would have been more deadly if I hadn't moved.

"This attack cost the doctor his life, for Walter slit his throat before he was able to speak. I don't know if he meant to steal the Cup or simply destroy it.

"I barely had the strength to repeat the words as Walter held the Cup to my lips. The chant wasn't necessary, as the Cup had healed my wounds before without it, but I felt bound to honor Gamal's instructions. When my strength returned, I thought for the first time about the dark side of the Cup."

Chapter 20

"*I* turned my back on the battlefield without regret, and returned at last to my ancestral home. But I had returned too late. My father and brother were both dead. Charles left behind a young widow. Lettice and her son, Logan, barely three years old."

"Logan!" Maggy said.

Harry looked up at the sound of her voice, his eyes focusing on her face.

"I've taken that name many times through the years. A penance, perhaps. Or a reminder that love can lead to destruction."

"Lettice became my wife." Harry paused at a small movement Maggy made, momentarily distracted from his story. "Yes, Maggy. I was married, just as I told you. I told you the truth as much as I could. Not something I've grown used to doing over the years." He took another sip of wine and continued.

"What began as a duty changed as the years passed. I grew to love the boy and his mother after a fashion. Not the passion I had felt for Marie, but love just the same. They were the last remnants of my family. I shared the Cup with Lettice right from the beginning, but told no one else. We lived peacefully for twenty years, the secret of the Cup ours alone. She seemed content to keep her youth and beauty. I devoted myself to the running of my estate, and it prospered. As Logan grew older he became restless and impatient with our life at Barrington Hall. He refused all of the young women who were eager to wed him. When our son was twenty, he left home to join the East India Company. He was gone for nine years.

"He came back a man of thirty, to greet his uncle and his mother, who hadn't aged a day since his third birthday. We should have told him about the Cup, that much is clear.

"He had heard rumors about our unnatural youth before he left, but familiarity and love had blinded him to the truth. We were simply his parents.

"Yet he couldn't deny the evidence of his own eyes. He thought it the work of the devil. He reviled his mother, refused to speak to me. He left Barrington Hall to lodge in the town, where we expected him to denounce us. But he was silent.

"Lettice went to him the next day, determined to win back his affection. I had seen her face when Logan accused us, the way she looked at me, and I feared what would happen. I was right to be afraid. A fool would have seen it, how the rumors had affected her over the years. The curious looks, the sudden silences when we entered a room. But I was blind to it all. Her son convinced her that she'd been led astray by Satan himself. It wasn't Logan who denounced me to the Church, but Lettice. My wife.

"They had betrayed me. Yet I knew they were wrong. My faith in the devil had died along with my faith in God. There was nothing evil about the Cup, no trace of the demon in it's healing powers. The only evil was in what people would do to possess it, or what they would do to destroy it.

"Walter and I left that night, taking the Cup with us. I was fortunate that my servant had proved more loyal to me than my own family. I learned that the Sheriff came with a warrant for my arrest the next day. My execution would have been swift and merciless, had my luck not held.

"So I began a new life. Walter and I lost ourselves in the teeming city of London. The year was 1636. My chronological age was forty-eight, but my physical age had not changed since I first tasted from the Cup. For ten short years, Walter was my companion. When the plague next came I urged him to leave the city, for I knew he would not drink from the Cup. But he refused to leave me. I played the part of a young physician, and saved many lives with the Cup. This time I was wary with my ministrations, so no one would guess the real cure. I went to great lengths to remain anonymous. But Walter I could not save. He was a stubborn man."

Harry stopped speaking, the firelight flickering over his features in the dim light of the room. "After Walter died, I was truly alone.

"I stayed in London for almost twenty years, until the Great Plague of 1665 swept through the city like a holocaust. Nothing had prepared me for the fury of this pestilence. I saved countless hundreds with the Cup, but thousands more died. I fought against death with every fiber of my being, but even with the miracle of Seheiah's Cup, my efforts seemed puny in the face of such virulence. I wondered why I continued to fight. Why did I rail against death? I finally realized that it was not these strangers I longed to save, that I could never defeat my true enemy. I could never bring back my mother, or my beloved Marie, both dead for sixty years.

"When the plague finally spent itself, I put away the Cup and put away my doctor's robes. I left London, and went from city to city, living in each for a decade, or possibly two. Never long enough for my perpetual youth to be questioned.

"Then I began a quest, which has lasted to this day. To find the origins of Seheiah's Cup. I had to understand what it was, and why I had been chosen.

"I became a scientist. I examined the Cup in every detail. I copied the inscriptions around the base, hoping to discover the language they were written in. I had only Gamal's word that the translation he had given me was correct. I wanted corroboration.

"I tried to chip off a bit of the Cup, to identify what material it was made of. Nothing could scratch its surface. Not a knife blade, not even a diamond broach.

"The most astonishing test was the simplest one. It looked like fired ceramic, but the Cup felt heavy, as though made of an unusual material. When I placed it on a balance, the mechanism didn't move. It had no weight at all! I picked it up again, felt its heaviness in my hand. I put it back on the balance, which showed that it weighed the same as empty air.

"But what had I really learned? I already knew the Cup had properties that defied science and religion. This merely confirmed it."

Harry turned to Maggy, his smile self-deprecating. "For the most part, I've failed to discover anything revealing, even after centuries of study. Seheiah was mentioned in the Cabala as an angel who protects against fire and illness, and who governs longevity. That is all I found. Despite that reference, and the miracle of the Cup itself, I could never bring myself to believe in Heaven, any more than I could believe in the devil. Each time I tried to share the secret of the Cup, I was—" he paused, as though searching for words. "—disappointed."

Maggy didn't know what to think, much less what to say to him. "What about Logan Winter?" she asked finally.

"One of the many names I've used over the years. By the time I became Logan Winter I had amassed a great deal of wealth. Money was never an object in itself, but it was necessary each time I created a new identity for myself. I'd developed a love for art of all kinds, first discovered when I began to examine ancient pottery. I became a collector, much like Hearst was, though I'd been at it far longer.

"Then through my connection with Hearst, I met Beatrice and Maxwell. I was enchanted with them, with their world. For all the gaiety and excitement they created, I felt a peace with them that had long been missing from my life. I decided I would risk sharing the Cup with them. Before I could act on that decision, Maxwell was struck down. I was | too late.

"Then the Cup was stolen from my room at the castle. I'd taken it there to perform the ritual, as I had done every third year for almost four centuries. But I'd grown careless. That morning I set out the Cup on a piece of blue velvet with gold edging. It occupied a central place in my room, on the dresser which I'd cleared of everything else.

"I returned to my room in the early afternoon to find it had disappeared. The blue velvet was undisturbed, without a mark to show it had been there. I went mad with shock, and not a little fear. I had no idea what would happen to me if I didn't drink from the Cup. Would I suddenly age hundreds of years in an instant? Crumble to dust? I was in a frenzy to find the Cup. That was when I found poor Anna and treated her so badly.

"Fate was kinder to me than I deserved. As the days passed, I began to realize that I would live, unchanged for the most part. I've hardly aged ten years since 1937." He paused and tapped the glasses he wore. "My short-sightedness returned about twenty years ago. The first reminder of mortality." He drank from the wineglass and set it back on the mantel. He continued to stare into the fire as he spoke.

"I felt I was to blame for Beatrice's death."

Maggy went cold at his words.

"Beatrice and I decided to return from our ride early that day. We left the group about two-thirds of the way from our destination. Edward was quick to follow us. I think he had passed over the edge between reason and madness, his obsession with Beatrice was so great. I didn't realize that until later. Always too late.

"We rode for about a half-hour, Beatrice and I talking quietly, very much aware of Edward's silent presence behind us. Seeing us together again, ignoring his threats as though they were nothing, must have goaded him past all endurance.

"He erupted in a explotion of anger, his attack completely unexpected on my part, despite all his warnings. His riding crop slashed the back of my neck. Beatrice screamed at him to stop, but he was past all hearing. Invective spewed from his lips, but I couldn't make out any words. His murderous intent was clear.

"The horses were shying wildly as he continued his attack. I tried to hold his arm, but couldn't get any leverage on the moving horses. Beatrice tried again to intervene, and his whip cracked down across the face of her horse like a gunshot. The animal was off, running sightlessly, its eyes blinded.

"Edward and I froze with horror, watching as the great horse ran flat out, mad with panic. She was an accomplished rider, but her skills were useless. I raced after her as soon as I could move, and watched the horse go down heavily, Beatrice still on its back.

"The horse had fallen on her leg, but the worst injury was the head wound. My only thought was to get her back to the castle, to a doctor.

"But no doctor could have saved her. Those were the longest minutes of my life, watching her gasping for breath as I knelt beside her, help-less as a child. Before she died, she whispered one word. 'Maxwell.'

"With all my heart I cursed the thief who had stolen the Cup, and taken her life along with it. I had failed to save Maxwell, and now Beatrice as well." He looked straight at her, his blue eyes deep, fathomless. "Through my own carelessness I lost the one thing that could have cured her injuries. The Cup would have saved her, Maggy."

She looked at him standing there, his blond hair gleaming in the light from the fire and the afternoon sun, filtering dimly through closed cur-tains. She remembered the scene Anna had described when Logan brought Beatrice to the castle in his arms. It all fit. He described it perfectly, as though he had lived through it himself.

Her eyes opened wide in shock as she realized what she was thinking.

"I can see it in your eyes, Maggy," he said and moved to sit beside her on the sofa. "You're beginning to believe me."

"I…" she felt tears come to her eyes suddenly. She lifted a hand to caress his face, his dear, handsome face, with only the slightest beginnings of laugh lines around the eyes. Could it really be so old, and not show any evidence of all those years? "It's hard to believe, Harry."

"But you do believe me!" he waited tensely, blue eyes riveted on her, until she nodded almost imperceptibly.

"Thank God!" He swept her into an embrace that took her breath away. She reveled in the feel of his arms around her, his heart beating close to hers. The tears came unchecked now, streaming down her face as she wept for him. For all his losses, his disillusionment. The loneliness he must have felt. She wrapped her arms around him and felt his shoulder relax as the tension left his body. Finally, she pulled back and looked at him, trying to understand.

"Harry, why? Why did you do it, year after year, when it set you so apart from the rest of the world?"

He stroked her face gently, his eyes devouring every feature. Then he brushed her hair back where it had fallen across her cheek and tucked it behind her ear. She smiled at the gesture.

"I've asked myself that question a thousand times." He leaned back again and clasped her hand as he spoke. "I've lived eight life spans without finding the answer. I could say that I love life, with a fascination that is untiring. I thrill to the changing seasons, the scents of different cities, the dry wind of the desert, the ocean mist. I've tasted all these things with heightened senses, perfected by the Cup.

"But that wouldn't be enough, would it? Even that would pall over the years. It's the people of this world that fascinate me, Maggy. My curiosity has always got the best of me. In this marvelous and terrible world, what will happen next? What fantastic discovery will suddenly turn the world we know upside down? I've seen it happen countless times, and each time life settles down to a new status quo, as firmly embraced and taken for granted as the one that had been discarded. The enormity of the drama I've witnessed has lacked only one thing—someone to live it with me. Someone who can share my view. But as I said, my efforts to share the Cup ultimately failed.

"On only two occasions did I consider giving up the Cup. During the Great Plague of London in 1665, and the day Beatrice died."

"But when Beatrice died, you didn't have the Cup any longer," Maggy said.

"Up to that point, I had been searching for it everywhere. I thought it only a matter of time until I found out who had stolen it. When Beatrice died, I stopped searching. I no longer wanted to find it. I didn't know how much time I had left, or how fast I would age. But it didn't matter anymore. I went to England and enlisted. Strangely enough, I survived that war as well, even without the Cup."

"Something must have changed your mind," Maggy said. "You said you've been trying to find Seheaih's Cup for years now."

"I don't know what changed. Perhaps it was the war that did it. Death was everywhere. My old adversary. I fought it just as I always had. When the war was over, I found I wanted to live. I still missed Beatrice, but I took up my search for the Cup again."

"And that led you back to San Simeon, and finally to Anna's diary," Maggy said thoughtfully.

"I thought she might have written something that I had missed, a small detail that might shed light on what happened to the Cup. It can't have simply disappeared off the face of the earth!"

"Maybe it did."

He looked at her with a shocked expression on his face. "I suppose it could have. Its very existence is a mystery." He considered it for awhile, then shook his head. "No. I can't operate on that belief. It just doesn't make sense."

"I agree," Maggy said. Then she had another though that made her decidedly uncomfortable. "I don't think Anna would have appreciated you reading her private thoughts about Logan Winter!"

"Probably not. When I read the diaries, I was astounded that she had feelings for me. I never intended to mislead her. After I scared her to death with my accusations, I simply wanted to reassure her. That was when I got to know her. She was a lovely girl, filled with curiosity and wonder."

"But she did care for you."

"I never knew it. When she told me about her friend Michael, I could see what I had missed before. Not a girl, but a woman."

Maggy hesitated, afraid of the answer she might get. But she had to know. "Did you love her, or Beatrice?"

"Love? Love is dangerous for me, Maggy. I've learned to fight against it, almost as much as I fight against death. I married again in 1749, and in 1856. Each time I offered the Cup to my wife. Giselle wouldn't drink from the Cup. I watched her grow old, bowed with arthritis and finally dementia. What we now call Alzheimer's disease. She died in 1780."

"You were married for thirty years?"

He nodded. "My third wife willingly drank from the Cup. She was a great beauty of 29 when we married. But I misjudged her completely. She took several lovers during our marriage. She must have told the last one about the Cup, for he devised a scheme to steal it. Her loyalty to me surfaced at the wrong moment, I'm afraid. He murdered her savagely and took the Cup, leaving bloody footprints on the carpet where he walked to the door."

Maggy started. "Seheiah's Cup was stolen from you before?"

His expression was grim. "I found him and recovered it. He stood trial for murder, and was executed for his crime. No one believed his fanciful tale about the Cup of Life. The courts of England were swift in those days."

Maggy could hardly take it all in. She found her head spinning at these fantastic stories that seemed more appropriate for children to scare each other with around a campfire. Not to be discussed calmly over a glass of wine.

"Are you all right, Maggy?" His voice was gentle.

"Yes, I'm fine," she said, her head clearing. "But you didn't answer my question about Anna and Beatrice."

"The answer is no, I didn't love either of them in the way you mean. I didn't trust myself to love anymore. There were brief affairs over the years. But I had learned it was safer to seek out friendships. That was what I had with Beatrice, and I hoped with Anna, too."

"Anna did forget you soon enough when she met my grandfather."

Harry let out a short laugh. "So you see, Maggy. I'm entirely resistible. Your grandmother had the good sense to throw me over."

"She was always a very wise woman," Maggy said, feeling a little better. "She's the one who convinced me that your story is true, Harry."

He turned to her in surprise. "How could Anna do that?"

"I just read in the last volume of her diary—"

"What? I thought that had been stolen from your room."

Now Maggy had the grace to look sheepish before him. How embarrassing! "I was wrong about that. I accidentally left it at home and my friend Carol sent it to me. But I still believe someone was in my room. No matter what you say, you won't convince me otherwise."

"Calm down, my darling. Tell me how Anna made you believe me."

She felt warmed by the simple endearment, and realized she no longer had to prove anything to him. "Anna described the day of the accident, how you carried Beatrice in your arms. How you kept talking about the Cup."

"Then I owe Anna a debt I can never repay," Harry said, and kissed the palm of her hand.

A thrill coursed through Maggy's body at the touch of his lips. She took her hand away and tried to concentrate on her next words, despite the sensations that his touch evoked in her. Damn! He could be distracting.

"Anna wrote that Edward Orcutt accused you of killing Beatrice. You didn't mention that."

"Edward was lucky I only hit him once. He could never accept responsibility for his actions. He couldn't accept the fact that Beatrice didn't love him. Nor that his jealousy led to that last, hideous confrontation. But it was my fault, ultimately. I should have prevented it."

"No, Harry. You couldn't have known what would happen." Maggy leaned toward him, offering comfort. "You did everything you could."

His lips found hers in a kiss that was at first tender, accepting the warmth she freely gave. Then her mouth opened under his and his tongue reached deeper, sending fire racing through her. Her skin felt hot where their bodies were strained together, her breasts pressed against his chest, their arms entwined. The moment seemed to go on forever.

"This is what I've fought against for so many years, Maggy," he whispered to her, as he leaned back to cup her face in his hands. "From the moment I saw you at the inn, tearing off in the wrong direction—" he put a finger to her lips to silence her objection. "And then later when you saw Beatrice, your face glowing with light. I love you, my darling. No matter what happens."

Then she was lost in his kiss, the past forgotten in the blinding sensation of this moment. All that existed for her was the glory of this man, as she held him closer, felt the muscles of his shoulders flex through the cotton of his shirt, and then the warmth of his skin as the shirt disappeared. His hands caressed her body, the curve of her breast. He kissed her and smoothed his hands over the flair of her hips, pulling her closer.

Then they stretched out on the old sofa, clothes scattered heedlessly, naked skin touching the full length of their bodies. Maggy twisted to get closer as she felt him straining against her belly. She opened her body to him and gasped as he entered her slowly, the movement causing ripples of feeling to radiate out from her core, until he was deep inside her. She met him eagerly, each movement sending her further out of herself, until she was all sensation, all feeling. She cried out as the climax overtook her, her body shuddering. The aftershocks reverberated through her for a timeless moment and finally left her drained and satiated.

But Harry was not through with her yet. Maggy's eyes flew open to look at him. As she did, he thrust once more, deep within her, his blue eyes locked on hers. This was a new place, a new feeling, deeper still. Somewhere she'd never gone. "Come with me, Maggy," he whispered.

At his words, and his movements deep inside her, the second climax ripped through her, breathtaking in its intensity. He poured himself into her as she cried out his name, while waves of feeling pulsed through her body, sending her flying off into space.

* * *

Maggy opened her eyes a short time late, at first not knowing where she was. Hardly knowing who she was after that experience! Harry's arm was wrapped around her, his body warm against hers. The sight of his face, unguarded now in sleep, made her heart turn over. God! She loved him. And she believed him, believed he was born in 1588. They both must be crazy.

She gathered her clothes and started to dress quietly.

"Now that's a pretty sight," he said, as she hooked her bra in back. He leaned over to kiss her shoulder.

"You know, Harry, I've been thinking," Maggy said. She looked at his beautiful body, sprawled out beside her on the couch. "And by the way, I could think much more clearly if you got dressed." She handed him his jeans.

"You're a cruel woman," he said.

"You said that life's mysteries drove you to keep using the Cup. You always wanted to see what came next?"

"Yes. That's true."

"And you didn't have faith in religion—Heaven or Hell?"

"Not since—well almost from the beginning."

"But now you know that I've seen Beatrice! You know there's something more after we die. I know she's an angel, but even if you can't believe that, you have to acknowledge that death isn't final."

"Okay. I'm with you so far."

"Harry, aren't you curious? Don't you want to find out what comes next? After we die?"

She could see him turning it over in his mind. "You're saying that death isn't the enemy."

"Maybe not." She shrugged. "I don't know. It seems to me that if you live forever, you might be missing what comes next. Maybe the most important part."

"Maggy, you amaze me," he said. "I guess I'll just have to get used to that. But you have an advantage. You saw Beatrice."

As he leaned down to pick up his shirt, Maggy looked startled.

"What's this?" She traced the white scar that covered the back of his neck. She hadn't noticed it before.

"The only wound I've had that the Cup didn't heal. It happened when Edward caught me with his whip."

She was shocked at the size of the scar. "He must have almost taken your head off."

"That was his intention," Harry said grimly.

Harry left her back at the inn, after she agreed to let him see the last volume of Anna's diary as soon as she had finished reading it. He returned the first two volumes to her solemnly, and then brushed a kiss on her lips, light as a whisper.

Chapter 21

$\mathcal{B}$eatrice paced back and forth briskly, wearing a path in the dried grasses where she walked. She paused for a moment by one of the pillars that reached toward the afternoon sky.

"You may have been there on the day I died, but I still don't believe that Logan killed me," she said.

"My dear," Ambrose said quickly. "He didn't kill you, he didn't strike you down himself. I said he was responsible for your death. His obsession with the Cup is what caused it."

"Explain!"

"That day you all went riding with Mr. Hearst. But the three of you decided to leave the rest of the group. You'd been riding together quite amiably, for about a half-hour, when Logan turned the conversation to the missing Cup."

"Seheiah's Cup."

"Of course. I believe he had spent so many years lying about his life, that he almost believed the stories he told. He almost believed he was the charming persona that he presented to the world. And why not? People were drawn to him, to his physical beauty and vitality. They accepted him at face value, never suspecting that he had an unnatural secret life. But when he lost the Cup something snapped inside him. He tried to hide it, but it was barely contained beneath the surface." Ambrose placed his hand on her arm to stop her pacing.

"He asked you both several questions about it, about what each of you were doing on the day it disappeared. You were shocked that he hadn't told you about this theft before. He was, after all, your dear friend."

"I know he was," Beatrice said.

"But he suspected you, that's why he hadn't said anything sooner. Edward Orcutt was incensed that Logan was all but accusing you. They came to blows, and Logan used his whip on Edward. Logan was like a madman, and Edward was unable to hold him off. Edward was cut several times by Logan's whip. When Edward finally struck back, his whip snapped around Logan's neck in a terrible blow. You foolishly tried to intervene, putting yourself in terrible danger. Logan's blows caught your horse and it bolted. You died from those injuries, Beatrice."

Beatrice didn't say anything, just stood silently for a long moment. Much of what Ambrose said had the ring of truth. His eyes were heavy with remembered pain. He had seen it himself, after all. No wonder he hadn't wanted her to remember this ugly scene.

"But you've described an accident, Ambrose. Logan didn't intend to harm me!"

"Of course he didn't, my dear. He was horrified at the outcome of his attack. He did everything he could to save you. But without the Cup, he could do very little. He accused Edward of causing your death, but he really blamed himself."

"Poor Harry," Beatrice said at last. "He's lived with this guilt for sixty long years. I wish I'd known. I would have tried to help him."

"You wouldn't find him an easy man to comfort, my dear. After your death, all that was left for him was the Cup. His desire for it has blotted out everything else for him."

Beatrice was overwhelmed with a feeling of such anguish that she turned away from Ambrose. She sat down on the ground and covered her face with her hands.

"I'm sorry, Beatrice. I know this hurts you," Ambrose said gently.

"I don't remember anything from that day. But I know that while Harry lived as Logan Winter, he was my true friend. When I saw him at the library, I had a fleeting memory of terrible sorrow."

She looked up suddenly as a new thought occurred to her. "Isn't it strange that I have no recollection of Edward? He figured so prominently in my life, yet I can't even picture his face, or remember a single word he spoke to me. Not a single emotion, nothing. As though he never existed."

For a moment, Ambrose looked stricken at her words. Then he smiled at her gently, his eyes filled with sympathy. "He loved you, from what I observed. Perhaps that's why you don't remember. The ties were too strong. You don't remember Maxwell, do you?"

The name brought with it a sense of joy that was tantalizing, ephemeral. But she couldn't remember a man, or see a face. "No," she said.

"Well, then. Maxwell was your husband, whom you loved to distraction. So you've forgotten those who were most important to you, Beatrice. Just as Heaven requires."

Everything Ambrose said made sense. But it left her with a terrible feeling of emptiness.

"I wonder why Logan thought you might have taken the Cup," he mused. "Perhaps you saw it somewhere at the castle, but didn't recognize its value?"

"How could I know what I saw?" she said. "I've forgotten everything important."

"Despite its danger, I think the Cup holds the answer to Harry's troubles. If we can find it ourselves, we might be able to help him. Try to remember it, Beatrice. It was a small, round vase, with marks engraved around the base. A deep green color. It had a look of great age."

Try as she might, nothing came to her mind. "I'm sorry," she said for what seemed the thousandth time. "I just don't remember."

* * *

Maggy was sitting in Nancy's kitchen the next morning, sipping a cup of steaming coffee. She had slept through breakfast, thanks to Harry keeping her occupied late last night and then slipping off to work without waking her. Again. She smiled at the thought of the note he'd left her.

Darling Maggy,
You look like a beautiful and very contented golden cat curled up on her pillow. I hope you will let me take you to the docent's wardrobe today, so you can choose a gown to wear to the party tomorrow. I'll be back at 2:00, in case you can go.
Love, Harry

Nancy sat down on the kitchen stool next to her and leaned her elbows on the counter. "It may be none of my business, but I can't help noticing that you look especially happy this morning. Couldn't be because of Harry, now could it?"

"Is it that obvious?"

"Well, all I know is this past week, when one of you looks like a thundercloud, so does the other. And when Harry left this morning, he was walking on air."

Maggy smiled in spite of herself. "I guess I'm walking on air, too. And I guess I'll be going to the party tomorrow at the castle after all."

"That's wonderful! Harry was kind enough to wrangle invitations for John and I. We'd never be able to afford them otherwise, not at $500 a plate! Such a grand affair I believe the governor will be there, and some Hollywood people as well. Just to add some glamour and remind us of what it was like before. We're both thrilled to be going."

"I am too," Maggy said.

Nancy leaned toward her with a conspiratorial air. "I'm so glad you and Harry have made up. He's done so much for John and I. We've worried about him for years, hoping that he would find someone."

"That's the second time you've mentioned how Harry has helped you. What has he done, if you don't mind me asking?" Maggy had gotten the distinct impression that Nancy did mind.

"Oh dear. Now I've put my foot in it," Nancy said with a frown. "It's just that Harry has asked us not to speak of it. I never have until now." She patted Maggy's hand. "But it's different with you, Maggy. I know you love each other. It shines out of you both like a beacon.

"When John and I first came to Cambria ten years ago, we stayed here at the inn. Harry was a guest here too. He hadn't taken the job as curator yet, I believe he was making the final arrangements. Well, John and I fell in love with the place. We dreamed of moving here, but knew we could never afford to buy a house, much less find a way to earn a living in this little town, not at our age."

Maggy was perplexed. "But you have this inn, which must have cost a small fortune."

"Not yet, but soon we'll own it outright. You see, Harry owns it. He bought the inn and then gave us a lease option on it, since he didn't want us to use our life savings on a down payment. A hefty percentage of our monthly lease goes toward the purchase price. He won't tell us what he paid, but I bet it's more than he's getting from us. By the time we actually buy it from Harry, there won't be that much left to finance. And he makes sure we have all the help we need to run the place. His only condition was that we always have a room for him here when he needs it. As if we wouldn't, after all he's done!"

Maggy stirred her coffee, completely surprised by Nancy's confession. "That was awfully generous of him," she said.

"I'll say it was. To help us like that, two strangers! We couldn't believe it. It was like a gift from Heaven. So you can see why we want the best for him."

"Of course."

"But not just because of what he's done for us. We've grown terribly fond of him, just like he was our own son."

Maggy wondered what Nancy would say if she knew her 'son' was over 400 years old. "Well, I've grown fond of him myself," she said.

"You make a lovely pair, the two of you, both so fair and graceful. You make me remember how it is to be young and in love," Nancy said with a wistful look on her face.

"Not as young as you think," Maggy replied. This conversation was getting entirely too sentimental for her, though she was happy Nancy had confided in her. Here was yet another side to Harry that he kept hidden away. He was full of surprises, she thought.

* * *

"Are you ready?" Harry asked as soon as she opened her door.

"Yes. All set," she said. He looked at her jeans and Reeboks skeptically.

"You look absolutely beautiful," he said and leaned over to kiss her. Her body responded instantly, reminding her of their night of unrestrained lovemaking. "But certainly not like the Duchess of Windsor off to choose her gown."

"That's good, because I have no intention of looking like a duchess or a movie star until tomorrow night." Maggy smiled at the prospect of being Cinderella for one evening.

"I guess you knew her," she said thoughtfully as they drove toward the castle.

"Who?"

"The Duchess of Windsor. The one Anna wrote about."

"I met her and the Duke at the castle, yes."

"Their romance is what started Anna daydreaming about you. You know, kings and commoners, sacrificing all for love."

"It was a wildly romantic act that shocked the world back then," Harry said. "Yet they didn't seem that happy when I met them. They had that grand gesture to live up to."

"And you knew all the others. Clark Gable, David Niven, Jean Harlow. Marion Davies and Hearst."

"Yes, I met all of them. I didn't know any of them particularly well, except for Marion and Hearst."

"It takes some getting used to."

"Why would that be any harder than accepting that I knew people from the seventeenth century?"

"Just that I've grown up hearing about them from Anna. She told me about all the famous guests that visited the castle. Except she never told me about you, or Beatrice."

They were silent for a while as they drove up the winding road. A comfortable silence. She looked at him openly now as he drove, loving the strong contours of his shoulders and arms, the clean line of his jaw. She caught movement out of the corner of her eye, and saw a young zebra kicking up its heels in the distance while the older ones grazed.

"In Hearst's day, we would have gone down to the basement to try on costumes," Harry said. "He had hundreds of them stored there. You could dress as a fireman, a sheik, cavalry officer, just about anything. Some people thought he had half the MGM wardrobe department in his basement."

"Where are we going now?" Maggy asked.

"This building used to house the construction crew." He pulled up in front of a cement block building, hidden from view of the castle grounds by the rise of the hill and a screen of vegetation. "We have a much smaller selection than Hearst provided. But we don't need to keep quite the assortment he had; just authentic clothes from the twenties and thirties. We usually have only a dozen docents in costume at the same time, scattered throughout the castle."

To Maggy's surprise, they entered a busy office with phones ringing and people hurrying about their business. Harry guided her down a hallway to the back of the building and into a room with several racks of clothes hanging neatly. Each costume had a label above it, with a description and a date. Maggy saw that they ranged from the early twenties to the mid-forties. Beneath the dresses, gowns and men's suits, a shelf held dozens of shoes. Capes and coats were on another rack.

"Paquin, Lelong, Worth," Maggy read the labels aloud. "Valentina. I don't know much about fashion, but these designers must have cost a fortune, even back then."

"They did," Harry agreed. "All of these have been donated to the museum. Go ahead, try anything you like," Harry said with a sweep of his hand.

Maggy felt like a kid in a candy store. She loved this era of clothes, and had been more than delighted when many of the old styles had come back in fashion. She examined long gowns with ecru lace trim, some with shoulder pads and pinched waists, some with tiny shoulder straps and plunging backs. Taffeta, silk, brocade, velvet, crepe; every fabric imaginable, with exquisite hand beadwork and appliqués enhancing the designs. There were fur coats that would outrage animal rights activists, and feathered capes that looked like they came straight from Las Vegas. Everything was in excellent condition, though she could tell that all the clothes were very old. Maggy didn't know where to begin.

Finally she picked out two gowns and held them up for Harry's inspection.

"Very nice," he said as he eyed the cream-colored Lanvin with pearl beadwork around the neckline, and a teal confection of crinkled taffeta that would bring out the green in her eyes. "You have excellent taste, in spite of your weakness for jeans. There's a fitting room over there."

After modeling the two gowns, Maggy decided the teal gown fit much better, thought it was still a little loose in the waist. The snug bodice was square-cut with wide shoulder straps and flared out to a draped skirt that reached to mid-calf. She turned in a quick pirouette to see the skirt twirl out around her. Not nearly as beautiful as Anna's blue gown, she thought, but it will have to do.

"Yes, the green is definitely it," Harry said as he admired her choice. She tried on several wraps to go with it, but found nothing that would match. She settled on an unusual long coat made of fine, black wool that completely covered the dress.

"I'd better wear my own shoes," Maggy said, "or I'll really feel like Cinderella."

"Nice, comfortable shoes, I hope. I plan to dance with you tomorrow until you beg for mercy," Harry said.

"In that case, my Reeboks will be perfect," Maggy said sweetly. As she was hanging up the coat, he spun her around and kissed her, teasing her mouth with his. She couldn't resist him. Soon they were locked in an embrace, straining against each other. When he pulled away from her slightly, they were both short of breath, and Maggy's body was tingling all over.

"That will teach you to threaten me with Reeboks," he said, and then ducked when she landed several good punches, despite the fact that she was collapsing with laughter.

Harry dropped her off back at the inn, both of them in high good spirits. He kissed her once more at her door, as though he couldn't keep from touching her. That was fine with Maggy; since her hands had a mind of their own where he was concerned. Just now she was running her fingers gently over the back of his neck, returning his kiss wholeheartedly.

"I've got business in San Francisco tonight," Harry said, pulling back at last. "I'll be back tomorrow evening for the party. Can you be ready by seven?"

"I'll be so glamorous you'll hardly recognize me," Maggy said. She already had some ideas about how she was going to fix her hair and makeup to match the gown lying across her bed.

After Harry was gone she held up the designer gown once more. After looking at it from several different angles, she sighed. Too bad she hadn't asked Carol to send Anna's gown. She and Anna had been exactly the same size, so it fit her perfectly. Oh well, it didn't matter.

That reminded her of the diary she'd been reading when Harry knocked on her door yesterday. She'd finish reading it now, without any further interruptions. Hopefully, she could find something that would help them all.

Anna's Diary—May 18, 1937

The coroner's inquest has ruled that Beatrice died accidentally. All of us who saw Logan bring her in were questioned by the police. It's been like a horrible dream that goes on without end. This morning I woke with the same crushing sense of loss, but for a moment I couldn't remember what had caused it.

Logan and Mr. Orcutt were detained by the police until the ruling today, so now they are free to go. What will they do now, without her?

Poor Miss Davies was devastated by her friend's death. Mr. Hearst was terribly angry with the newspaper stories of the other papers, full of speculation that it might not have been an accident.

Her body was taken from the coroner's office and sent to Los Angeles today, to be buried beside her husband. I wanted to go to the funeral day after tomorrow, but father begged me not to. He's been very upset by this, for my sake. He can see how hard it is for me.

I've seen Logan in passing. He walks like an old man, hardly noticing his surroundings. Like a ghost passing through the world without touching it. My heart aches for him. Michael I haven't seen at all.

I've been going about my tasks with a fury. It seems to help, if I concentrate very hard on the work at hand. But this afternoon I stumbled on another horrible scene. I had put off going into Beatrice's room as long as I could. Mrs. Redelsperger asked me to pack up the rest of her belongings, the ones the coroner hadn't already taken. When I entered her room, I saw Mr. Orcutt there, bent over a bureau drawer and holding her fine, silky lingerie in his hands. Blouses and sweaters were strewn haphazardly about where he had let them drop.

A cold fury rose up in me. "What are you doing?" I asked him, barely able to contain my anger.

"Nothing that concerns you," he said in his usual sneering voice.

"How dare you touch her things?" I shouted at him now, all caution forgotten. "Get out of this room at once!"

"Who do you think you are, you stupid bitch!" He stepped toward me, shaking his fist and then jabbing his finger at me. "If not for you and your shoddy work, none of this would have happened!"

His words hardly registered on me I was so angry. I backed away from him, my eyes never leaving his face. He was tight as a coiled spring, malevolence pouring out from him. I put some distance between us. "I warn you, Mr. Hearst will know of this. You'll never show your face here again!"

He seemed to recover his composure. "Go ahead, you little fool. I have no wish to return here." Then he left me alone in her room, a confusion of clothes strewn about, with dresser drawers half open. I looked around at the mess he had made. Her jewelry case was open, but I couldn't tell if anything was missing from it.

It was then that I realized what he had said to me, something about doing shoddy work. What could that have to do with anything? Especially when it was completely untrue? I took pride in my work and no one had any cause to complain. I loved everything about the castle and its priceless art treasures. I loved the modern art-deco touches and other startling contrasts that Mr. Hearst delighted in. I knew every piece in each one of my rooms, and treated them all with great care. Not a spec of dust ever marred their beauty. What could Mr. Orcutt have meant by his strange accusations?

I decided that he must be having some kind of nervous attack that was affecting his mind. But I still wondered if his dreadful temper and irrational fits of rage could have led to Beatrice's death. Then I remembered all the things I'd heard him say to her, and to Logan. No, he would never have hurt Beatrice. He would have done anything to hurt Logan, but not Beatrice.

I continued to think about the three of them as I started to straighten the room and pack up Beatrice's belongings. As I touched her clothes, inhaled her perfume that still lingered, she seemed so close, as though she had just stepped out of the room for a moment. It was hard to believe that she was really dead. That her lovely voice was gone forever.

This evening after I finished dinner, I crossed paths with Logan and asked to speak to him. There was still an hour before the guests gathered in the Assembly Room for cocktails before dinner, so I thought we might have some time together. I've been so worried about him since Beatrice died. His absent gaze and half-hearted attempt to smile did little to ease my fears.

We sat outside in the evening air, in a hidden corner of the South terrace. The twin towers of the castle loomed behind us in the dusk, as the globes lighting the grounds flickered to life. The scent of lavender reminded me of happier times when we had met together in these gardens. If I didn't know him so well, I'd think this was a different man altogether. There was no spark left, none of the wry amusement or self-deprecating charm that had been so natural to him.

Now that I had him next to me, silent and waiting, I didn't know what to say to him. How much greater his loss must be than mine! How presumptuous of me to think I could help him.

I cleared my throat hesitantly, building up my courage. Still he was silent beside me. He seemed unaware of my presence, or his surroundings.

"I miss her," I said stupidly. I didn't know those were the words that would come. As soon as I spoke I wished I could take them back.

He turned to me then. I could see the moment when he recognized me, when the vagueness left his eyes.

"Anna. Poor Anna." He took my hand in his. "Of course you miss her."

Then he seemed to forget me again, forget that he held my hand, that we sat together on the terrace with beauty surrounding us.

"I'm worried about you, Logan," I said. This was the true reason I wanted to see him. I wanted some reassurance. "Are you going to be all right?"

It was as if I called him from a great distance. He turned to me again, surprised to find me there. "All right? No. I don't think so. But it isn't important, Anna. It doesn't matter at all. You mustn't worry about me." He patted my hand as he spoke.

This alarmed me even more. What could I say that would reach him, that he would care about?

"Have you found the vase you were looking for? The one that's so important?"

"Seheiah's Cup?" he asked, though he didn't seem to be speaking to me. A bitter smile transformed his face with such pain I couldn't bear to see it. "No, I haven't found it. But it doesn't matter either. I don't want to find it anymore."

"Isn't there anything I can do to help you, Logan?" I cried. It seemed that every word I spoke was making it worse.

"Poor Anna." He smiled at me, this time a sweet, gentle smile. "I don't deserve such compassion, my darling." Then he looked at me clearly, caressed my cheek with the lightest of touches. "The kindest thing you can do is to keep our friendship as a memory, a lovely memory of the past. As Beatrice has become."

Then he stood and bid me good-bye. He walked toward his rooms without a backward glance.

May 19, 1937

The strangest and most wonderful thing has happened to me. I think I have witnessed a miracle, one that fills my heart to overflowing. I can't understand why I've been so blessed.

All the guests left today. It was a subdued, somber leave-taking. I missed Logan when he left, but we'd already said our good-byes. I wonder if I'll ever see him again. I don't know if the news of what I've seen would help him or not. Perhaps he wouldn't believe me.

But I have no doubts.

This morning I woke early and went down to the Neptune Pool. I've done this many times, for I find it to be the most beautiful spot on the estate and the most peaceful, with the soothing sound of the waterfall as it flows past the statue of Venus. I needed to soak up the serenity of the wide ocean vista, the pristine white pillars. Maybe the ancient temple facade would lend the perspective of time to my troubled thoughts. Our tragedies are nothing new, after all, but only the same terrible things that have happened to people throughout history. Others have endured.

As usual, I was alone at this early hour. The only sound was the breeze ruffling the leaves nearby, the murmur of the waterfall, and the occasional call of a seagull. I felt a slight tingling sensation, a certain excitement or expectation that I couldn't identify. I heard a voice singing right beside me. A voice that I knew instantly, and loved with all my heart.

"Beatrice." I don't know if I spoke the name, I felt it so deeply.

I turned to the beloved sound, wishing to envelope myself in it. I was all feeling, all emotion, without at rational thought to dim my senses.

Then she was there by the pool, surrounded by light and energy. It was Beatrice, and not Beatrice. She was transformed, luminous, seeming to float by the edge of the pool. I was almost blinded by her radiance. Tears fell unheeded from my eyes.

She saw me then, and stopped singing. Her smile was a blessing that healed the emptiness I felt inside. Suddenly I was bathed in waves of tremulous, breathless joy.

"Anna, darling," she said clearly. "I'm so happy that you can see me like this."

She was next to me somehow, though I wasn't aware of her walking towards me.

"*Beatrice, you're alive!*" *The foolishness of that statement never occurred to me until later.*

"*Yes! More alive than I ever was on earth!*" *As she spoke I could feel her joy, and I thought I might die with it.*

We spoke together. She told me wondrous tales that I can't remember now, no matter how hard I try. I don't know if we were together for a minute or for hours. She comforted me with such peace and certainty, that I know I will never doubt my faith again. Our bond is stronger than death.

I will know forever that I was visited by an angel.

Chapter 22

Maggy sat at the desk in her bedroom, stunned by Anna's revelation. She could hardly take it in. Anna had seen Beatrice, just as Maggy had! It seemed inconceivable that Anna could have had that experience and not shared it with her.

No wonder her grandmother had been so certain of her faith. Even skeptical Maggy had recognized Beatrice instantly for what she was. As Maggy calmed down, she remembered that Anna had told her about an angel once. Just before Maggy's parents died. That explained it. Maggy had told Anna she hated angels because they wouldn't give her back her parents. And she'd never wanted to hear about angels again.

Poor Anna. She must have wanted to share that glory with her. But Maggy wouldn't have believed it, not with her stubborn materialistic view. She would have demanded proof, not hearsay, even from Anna.

At the same time, Anna's description of Logan Winter, of Harry, nearly broke her heart. She could hear his voice as Anna must have heard it, saying that nothing mattered anymore. Thank God that he had finally recovered from Beatrice's death. What must it have been like for him last week, standing beside Maggy when she described the vision she was seeing? When she described Beatrice in perfect detail?

The phone ringing on the nightstand was unnaturally loud in the silence of her room. Maggy picked it up quickly, her head still spinning.

"Hey, Maggy! Have you missed me?" Carol said. Her familiar voice brought Maggy back to earth with a thump.

"Terribly. Since it's been, what—a whole day since we've talked."

"True. I think we've talked more since you went on vacation than we usually do," Carol said. "But then, this vacation of yours hasn't been usual."

Maggy laughed. "The understatement of the year."

"I have a confession to make," Carol said in an uncharacteristically meek voice.

"Before you do, I need to talk to you about something—well, something big." Maggy didn't know how she was going to share Harry's secret with Carol. There was no question of going back, not after the things she'd already told Carol about him. "I don't know how far you'll trust me, Carol."

"Well, let's see. So far, I've been slaving over horrendous research assignments, all of which you needed immediately, by the way. For no other reason than the fact that you needed them. No questions asked. Except when I had to," she amended. "And then there's the little matter of me believing that you saw an angel. I still believe it, so I hope you aren't going to change your mind!"

"No, don't worry. I'm more convinced than ever about Beatrice. I just read in the diary that Anna saw her, too. Just like I did."

"Maggy, that's fantastic! That proves it for sure!"

"I didn't need any proof. It really doesn't prove anything, anyway. People would say we just shared the same hallucination."

"Okay, so if it isn't Beatrice, what is it?"

"Harry."

"Uh-oh. You're not going to tell me you believe his story?" Carol's voice rose to a little screech.

"Afraid so. We talked for hours yesterday. Or, rather, he did. He told me his whole history. It really was history, Carol. He was born in 1588."

Carol was silent on the other end of the wire. Maggy could hear her breathing.

"Carol?"

"I'm here. I just don't know what to say."

"I don't expect you to believe it. It's too weird, even though I know you trust me and all that. But you will believe it eventually, because it's true. Harry is Logan Winter."

"And?"

"Damn, you never give me a break, do you?" Maggy said.

"Not when there's more to the story that you're not telling me."

"I love him. Completely. Irrevocably. Forever, however long that might be. I have no idea what's going to happen, but I know that much."

"Whew. You do know how to shock a girl, you know that?"

"And?" Maggy asked.

"Okay, that's fair. Well, you're right. A four hundred year old man is a little too much for me to swallow. It just makes me worry about you more. But you're going to be home in two days, so I'll try not to go completely crazy until then. Is that still true? You're coming home on Friday?"

"Yes."

"So you're going to the big party at the castle tomorrow?"

"Yes again," Maggy said, wondering what Carol was getting at.

"That's one good thing, anyway. I said I had a confession to make. Before you told me Harry's wild story, I took it on myself to get Anna's gown and send it to you. It should arrive tomorrow."

"But that's wonderful!" Maggy couldn't believe it.

"I also sent the pearls that you wear with it. I hope you don't mind me sneaking into your jewelry drawer to get them. It was going to be a wonderful surprise, and then you dropped that bombshell about Harry. I thought you weren't going to go, and I didn't have the heart to tell you what I'd done."

"I forgive you! You're absolutely wonderful, Carol. I'd be lost without you." Maggy was thrilled at the prospect of wearing the blue gown and pearls that she loved so much. And Harry seeing them on her.

"Just so you get home in one piece, your same sweet, sane self. With or without Harry, whoever he might be. We'll talk more about that whole subject later, okay?"

"Okay," Maggy said. "And you'll eat your words, I guarantee it."

She was still elated when she hung up the phone. She looked smugly at the unfortunate teal dress that she'd borrowed from Harry. She couldn't wait to see the look on his face when he saw her in the blue gown. Then she hesitated. He had seen that gown before. Beatrice had worn it on the night sixty years ago when she sang Moonglow to an adoring crowd of partygoers.

Maggy suddenly had doubts. How could she hope to look as lovely as Beatrice had been in that gown? Would Harry really see Maggy, or the ghost of an angel? If only it was here already, she thought impatiently. She wanted to see it for herself, see if her memory of it was accurate. After all, the fabric was sixty years old. How could it still be as lovely as she remembered? Then Maggy pictured Anna wearing the gown, and she felt better. It was a gift from the heart, first from Beatrice and then from her grandmother. There was no longer any doubt. She would wear it for them, and for herself.

Maggy picked up Anna's diary again. She saw that Anna had only written a few more pages.

Anna's Diary—June 3, 1937

A pall has settled over the castle. The quiet is eerie, where we are used to hammers pounding and construction crews always at work. Unbelievable as it sounds, Mr. Hearst is in desperate financial trouble. Emma has it that Mr. Hearst's corporations are over $100 million in debt. I've tried to comprehend that amount, but I must confess it's beyond me. Father and I lived in terrible fear that we wouldn't be able to pay our mortgage of $50 per month.

But I'm sure that Mr. Hearst will keep his castle and his businesses. I don't know how he will do it, but I know he will succeed. In the meantime, the newspapers are full of his troubles (not the Hearst papers, of course). They delight in reporting that he will sell off two-thirds of his great collection of artwork. I read that Gimble's Brothers department store in New York will clear out the whole fifth floor for his art treasures. They'll go on sale to the public, and they've invited one and all to use 'Gimble's Easy Payment Plan.' All of us here at the castle are shocked beyond belief.

All construction has been stopped, leaving us in an unearthly silence. The construction crew has been let go. Mr. Hearst and Miss Davies have not had any guests since Beatrice died. We seem to rattle around in all this space.

But amidst such terrible news, I've been hard pressed to keep a properly sober expression on my face. First I was transported by the vision of Beatrice, and the reassurance I felt from her presence. Since that first day, I've seen her two times, once more at the Neptune Pool, and once sitting beside the statue of Sekhmet, as though she was communing with the ancient goddess. Each time she greeted me and asked me to sit with her for awhile. And so I sat, spellbound, basking in her presence, and filled with an indescribable joy.

Then Michael came to me at last. He told me that he had kept his job, and wouldn't be let go with the other workers. He twisted his hat in his hands as he spoke.

"I'm glad you're here, Michael," I said. The words were feeble things to describe the pleasure I felt at seeing him.

Then we both spoke at the same time, the same words. "I'm sorry," we said and stopped. And looked at each other. Then we were in each others' arms, trembling with happiness and relief.

He was so gentle with me, so sorry for doubting me. And for the tragedy I'd seen. He knew how close I had been to Beatrice.

"Anna, say you'll stay with me," he said between kisses. "These past weeks have been the loneliest in my life. Marry me, Anna."

Before I said yes, I told him that I had seen Beatrice since she died. The radiant angel that comforted my grief. I felt I had to share this with him, and prayed he would understand how important it was to me. I waited for his response, my heart hammering in my chest.

"I've never been a religious man, Anna, but I've always believed in God after my own fashion. Each of us has to find our own faith. Seeing you speak of her, I know that you have found yours, and that you will never doubt it." His brown eyes held me. "I hope I'll be able to find as much someday."

It's a start, a good one. Enough to build a life on.

June 5, 1937

I read in the newspapers today about the Duke of Windsor and Wallis Simpson. Married at last, on June 3rd. I remember back in January when I first read that he had abdicated the throne of England for his love. His wonderful voice over the radio. The romance of it had filled me with such yearning.

I'm glad they've found their happiness, but I don't envy them. So much has happened since then, I feel like a different person entirely. Poor Logan, whom I fancied myself in love with. I still worry about him, wonder if he will ever recover. I was a child then, playing at love, even though I wanted more than anything to be a woman.

Michael is the one who saw me that way from the very beginning. His passion is in his eyes with every glance he casts in my direction. A single look from him, and I come all undone.

We will be married next month, and move into my father's house now that he has married Mrs. Sully. We're lucky to keep our jobs with all Mr. Hearst's financial troubles. Mr. Soto will give us a lift to the castle each morning.

And I will be a married woman! That thought keeps me humming to myself as I go about my chores, impatient for the day to come.

Maggy leafed through the blank pages that followed the last entry. She was enchanted by Anna's account, but deeply disappointed. After all the interest in Anna's diary, all the trouble it had caused, it seemed impossible that there was nothing more there. No clue. No off-hand phrase that would explain any of the things that had happened.

The mystery of Logan Winter is solved, she thought with a tiny smile. But so much remained to be answered. Why was it just Anna and Maggy that saw Beatrice? Apparently no one else did. Not even Harry, who needed her comfort more than anyone.

And who broke into Maggy's room? She wasn't about to let that matter drop, either. But the most troubling question of all was Seheiah's Cup. Harry had convinced her it was real, but who had stolen it from him sixty years ago?

There was no solution to the mystery here. Maggy closed the diary softly. For once, she had no idea what to do next.

* * *

Harry barely glanced at the fountain as he crossed the plaza toward the Hyatt Regency Hotel in San Francisco. Market Street was clogged with traffic, horns blaring, as tourists and business people crowded the sidewalks, each wearing their identifying uniform. A bicycle delivery rider shot past him within inches. Harry looked up briefly, but was still preoccupied with his thoughts.

The 17-story atrium lobby of the hotel, with its exposed glass elevators, did little to break his concentration. He glanced at his watch, though he knew he was a few minutes early for his appointment. Just as he had planned.

Harry spotted Miles Orcutt easily in the busy lobby. Recognition brought a strange shock with it. Orcutt was the image of his father, with the same dark coloring and sharp features. Perhaps slightly taller. He looked fit, with a lined face that made him seem slightly older than his years. An ordinary-looking man, but it was not a face that Harry would ever forget.

He watched as Orcutt bought a newspaper and exchanged pleasantries with the vendor. They both laughed as the vendor gave him change. That simple interaction was surprising to Harry. Perhaps Miles Orcutt wasn't as much like his father as he appeared. In all the years Harry had known Edward Orcutt, he had never seen him smile so easily, or waste time speaking to servants, waiters, or vendors. They were all the same to Edward, and not worthy of any notice unless they failed to please him.

Harry didn't know if Miles Orcutt was the one responsible for breaking into Maggy's room. He had a terrible suspicion that the recent, apparently senseless vandalism in Maggy's room was related to the death of her grandmother. The intruder was looking for something. It could only be Seheiah's Cup. Harry's hand clenched into a fist unconsciously.

Miles Orcutt had made inquiries about obtaining certain objects dating from 300 BC or earlier. He was looking for any unusual pyxis, skyphos or amphora from that era. How much did Edward know, and what had he told his son?

If Miles Orcutt threatened Maggy's safety in any way, Harry would deal with it now.

Chapter 23

*T*he knock on her door made Maggy's heart leap. It must be Harry. She took a final look at herself in the mirror, the midnight blue gown hugging her body and flowing out to just above her ankles. The pearls glowed around her neck, their luster accentuating the creamy texture of her skin. She had felt a little rush of energy and good spirits the moment she fastened the pearls around her neck and looked at herself in the mirror. Now her cheeks were flushed with excitement.

She opened the door slowly, her eyes seeking his expectantly.

"Maggy," he said and simply stood there looking at her, his eyes widening as he took in her gown.

She couldn't contain herself any longer. "Come in, Harry." Maggy took his hand and pulled him into the room, since he seemed rooted where he stood. She turned a full circle in front of him.

"Recognize it?" she asked.

"It looks exactly like the gown Beatrice wore," he said. Curiosity was replacing the dazed look in his eyes.

"It doesn't just look like it," Maggy said. "It is the same gown. Anna gave it to me."

"But you're so much smaller than Beatrice. It fits you like it was made for you."

"Anna was an expert seamstress. She was the same size as me, but just a little shorter." Maggy paused for a moment, a worried frown shadowing her face. "Do you think it's okay? Me wearing it?"

The look in his eyes warmed her as much as the tender smile that came to his lips. "Maggy, it's perfect," he said. "I think they would want you to wear it. You are incredibly beautiful tonight, my darling."

"You're not so bad either," Maggy said with a happy grin. In fact, he looked spectacular in his old-fashioned black tuxedo, the starched white shirt immaculate. "Are you sure this isn't the same suit you wore then?"

"Who knows? I gave away all those clothes long ago, but maybe this found it's way back into the docent's wardrobe." He looked at her appreciatively for a moment, his eyes traveling down her body in a way that made her shiver.

"I see you decided against the Reeboks," he said. She was wearing a strappy black sandal with a delicate heel.

"I was going to wear them," she said. "But then I realized they hadn't been invented in the thirties, worse luck."

* * *

Maggy recognized the music that drifted on the evening air as they walked past the tennis courts to the huge North Terrace. It was still comfortably warm, with the sun low on the horizon. Tables were set up at the far end of the terrace where you could see the imposing pillars of the Neptune Pool. Harry took her hand and led her up two stairways to the

Neptune Terrace directly overlooking the pool. More tables were set up around the perimeter by the low balustrade, with a breathtaking view of the turquoise pool, and then the hillside unfolding down to the sea. Couples were dancing to the strains of "Someone to Watch Over Me."

"It seems just the same," Harry said as he looked at the crowd in their 1930's finery. The men in black tuxedoes were a perfect counterpoint to the women's colorful gowns and sparkling jewels. "I almost expect to see WR and Marion coming over to welcome us."

Instead they were welcomed by Steve Liggett, whom Maggy had spoken to on the telephone, but never met before. Several elegantly dressed couples were standing with him. There was a flurry of introductions, almost all of which Maggy promptly forgot.

"I'm happy to finally meet you, Maggy," Steve said. "Harry has been keeping you under wraps since you got here with your treasure."

At Maggy's questioning look, Harry clapped Steve on the back. "Don't worry, Steve. Maggy has definitely agreed to donate the diary to the museum. But she might want to hear about your promotion plans before she signs on the dotted line."

Maggy's head was spinning after a few moments of conversation with Steve and his ideas for publication of the diary. As soon as his attention was claimed by other guests, she turned to Harry. "Somehow, I can't imagine you'd be happy to see Anna's diary published, particularly with the kind of marketing he's talking about. Does he have any idea what's really in it?"

"Not really. Unfortunately, I told him just enough to make him curious. As long as the Cup is missing, I think it would be a mistake to publish it."

Another couple greeted Harry, and the round of introductions began again. Harry seemed to know everyone, including the governor and his wife.

"We had quite a run-in over allocation of the income from the castle," Harry said after the governor had moved on. "The legislature thought we were here to generate a profit for the state, for some strange reason."

"I'm sure you straightened them out," Maggy said.

"Eventually."

"Maggy, your dress is simply beautiful," a familiar voice said from behind her. "And Harry looks like he forgot his top hat."

"Nancy! Isn't this wonderful? I feel like we should all break out in a dance number from a Fred Astaire movie."

Nancy was wearing a full-length black dress from the 1940s with padded shoulders and long sleeves. John looked decidedly uncomfortable in his tuxedo.

They found their places at a table for eight, each place setting identified with a beautifully scripted place card. Nancy and John were sitting across the table from them. Maggy saw that mustard and ketchup bottles had been set out on the snowy linen tablecloths, next to crystal wineglasses and bone china. No doubt a nostalgic reminder of Hearst's idiosyncrasies.

The meal passed with a lively hum of conversation, as the band continued to play Gershwin, Harold Arlen and Jerome Kern tunes. Maggy felt right at home with the familiar melodies. They reminded her so much of Anna.

The sun slipped away and was replaced by blue shadows and the lovely glow of alabaster globes lighting the terrace and the pool below, as the night deepened around them. Soon the music was replaced by the keynote speaker, and Maggy found her surroundings far more interesting than the evening's program. The temple of Neptune on the opposite side of the great pool was illuminated by strategically placed spotlights that set it into stark relief and drew the eye unerringly toward it. Or maybe that was the genius of Julia Morgan, Maggy thought, as she admired the architect's sweep of columns curving toward the temple.

At that thought, Maggy wondered if she would ever see Beatrice again. Maybe the whole thing had been a mistake, just as the angel had said. Maybe she'd never know anything more than that.

A wave of applause made Maggy look around her suddenly. She saw their tables had been cleared. Steve Liggett was at the podium, making a speech. What was he saying about Harry?

"—this award is in recognition for the outstanding efforts of Harry Logan, who has continued to volunteer his time and expertise over the past three years since his tenure ended."

Maggy looked at Harry in surprise. He shrugged his shoulders, apparently just as surprised as she was. Nancy applauded enthusiastically and urged Harry to stand up. He had no choice but to walk up to the stage, though Maggy knew he didn't like to call attention to himself. The curator handed him a plaque, while the cameras flashed. And he especially didn't like to be photographed. That shouldn't matter so much now. The Cup was lost. Harry was aging, however slowly.

He took the microphone and said a few words about the castle, about Hearst and Julia Morgan and Marion Davies. Maggy smiled as she looked at the crowd, each face captivated by Harry's stories. They thought these were the reminiscences of a scholar, not a first-hand account of someone who had actually been there. Then he stepped down from the stage as the music started again. He was immediately engaged in conversation before he had a chance to return.

Couples filled the terrace once again as the band started playing a Cole Porter tune. Nancy pulled a reluctant John onto the dance floor. Maggy saw that he danced beautifully for all his protests. Harry was surrounded by a small group of people and Maggy sat alone at their table. She sipped her wine slowly, taking in the glittering scene.

"Excuse me, may I sit here for a moment?" The voice belonged to a dark-haired man in eveningwear.

"Of course," Maggy said.

"I'm Arthur Price," he said and held out his hand. "You came in with Harry, I couldn't help noticing. He's done so much for the museum. We owe him a lot."

"I'm Maggy Lane. Do you work here?"

"No, no. I'm one of the 'Friends of Hearst Castle.' We volunteer our time and money to preserve the estate. And constantly get in the way of the artisans and historians. Though I am fairly knowledgeable about the paintings and the silver collection. We sponsor these fund-raisers."

What was it about him that seemed familiar to her? She couldn't quite put her finger on it. She guessed he was about forty-five or so, and mid-height. He wasn't very striking in appearance, but did have nice dark eyes to match his hair. Maybe she had seen him on one of her tours of the castle.

Maggy looked toward the bandstand where Harry had been standing moments before. She couldn't see him now, through the crowd of people who filled the dance floor.

"Would you care to dance?" Mr. Price asked her.

Maggy hesitated for only a moment. Why not?

Mr. Price held her at a respectable distance as he chatted about the castle and some of its treasures. She was just as tall as he was with her little heels. She decided to enjoy the lovely music, even though she was dancing with the wrong man. Maggy half-listened to him as she looked for Harry. She couldn't see him anywhere. What could have happened to him?

Mr. Price was looking at her with a strange expression on his face. His next words startled her. "I wonder what happened to Harry?" he said with concern. A mind-reader!

"He must have been way-laid by someone," she answered.

"You know, Harry was working on an important piece that is going to be unveiled tonight. It's a masterful work of restoration. Perhaps there's some problem with it. Maybe that's where he went."

"Maybe," Maggy said doubtfully.

"It will be displayed in the Gothic Study this evening."

"He has been working awfully hard." Maggy remembered the morning he'd left her to get to work early. "I didn't realize his work had to be finished for this party."

"Harry is always far too modest about his contributions, don't you think?"

"That does sound like him."

"I'll take you to the Gothic Study. We can see if he's there. And if he isn't, no harm done."

They walked up the Esplanade to the main terrace in front of the massive front doors to the castle, with their spear-like iron grillwork. To Maggy's surprise, Mr. Price opened the front doors and preceded her through the vestibule. She looked down at the mosaic tile from Pompeii under her feet.

"I thought this entrance was closed to the public. They said the tile was being ruined by people walking on it."

"Yes, that's true. But we aren't the public," Mr. Price said with great authority. "Besides, the Assembly Room really must be entered from the front door, not sneaked into from a side entrance."

She thought it strange that the front door hadn't been locked. But Maggy had to agree, the huge room was even more impressive seen straight-on, all at once. It was odd to see the room empty, without a crowd of tourists straggling along the designated public walkway.

"This way, Miss Lane." He was already walking toward the next room, she didn't remember which one it was. Ah! The refectory, with its magnificent silk banners hanging high above the table. Their footsteps echoed eerily in the silence of the cavernous room. Then they passed into a hallway, and Mr. Price opened a door to reveal one of the tower staircases that wound up at a steep angle around the elevator shaft. The lights were dimmer here, and provided pools of illumination followed by spaces of darkness. Maggy felt the first stirrings of uneasiness.

"You know your way around the castle very well," Maggy commented. "These little staircases are almost hidden away from view."

"Yes, that's a unique feature that Hearst used. No grand, sweeping staircases for him. He liked to surprise people. I've become very familiar with the castle over the years."

They passed two landings and climbed up to the third, where they walked through a short hallway and then directly into the Gothic Study with it's vaulted ceiling of intricately painted wooden beams. Four crystal light fixtures hung at intervals from the ceiling, illuminating the rich tones of the dark furniture directly beneath them. Shadows filled the corners of the study, lapping at the small pools of light. Like the other rooms they had passed through, this one was completely silent.

"I must have been mistaken about Harry coming here," Mr. Price said quietly. His words fill Maggy will apprehension. But why?

She cleared her throat nervously. "Where is the piece that Harry was working on?"

"There is no piece, my dear Maggy," Mr. Price said as he moved closer to her. She backed away from him involuntarily. "Harry won't be coming. I've seen to that."

* * *

Harry took one last look at the Roman pool, his uneasiness growing. The only sound he heard was the muted strains of the orchestra floating across the terrace outside. Nothing disturbed the stillness of the cavernous room except subtle reflections of light skittering along the blue walls.

No one was coming.

He took the crumpled note out of his pocket again, though he had memorized the message. Meet me at the Roman Pool tonight at 9:00. It wasn't the terse wording that had sent him rushing her with only minutes to spare. The signature had made him snap to attention.

Logan Winter.

Whoever had written the note knew, at the very least, that Logan Winter had once owned the Cup. At worst, the faceless author knew that Harry and Logan Winter were the same person.

Harry paced beside the mirror surface of the dark water, his nerves stretched tight. He was fooling himself if he thought that was the worst that could happen. Ever since his meeting with Miles Orcutt, he'd felt a growing sense of impending disaster.

True, Miles Orcutt looked like his father, but the resemblance ended there. They had talked for several hours, over dinner and enough wine to loosen Orcutt's reserve. Harry had learned more about Mile's father than he expected. He'd learned that Miles hated his father with the hatred born of profound rejection. Edward had been indifferent to his son and to his wife, only noticing them when they failed to please him. Edward criticized his wife continually, comparing her in every way to Beatrice Page.

Miles Orcutt spoke the name with bitter laughter. He had hated the woman from his earliest memories, because she caused his mother such pain. A woman dead twenty years before he was born!

But Miles Orcutt knew very little about Seheiah's Cup. Only that his father had been obsessed with it during the last years of his life. After Edward's death, Miles had discovered some of the reports his father had received during his search for the Cup. His father craved one thing to his knowledge, and that was money. Miles figured the Cup must be worth a fortune. That didn't matter to Miles. What mattered was that he succeed where his father failed.

Harry knew then that Miles Orcutt was not the menacing presence that had been shadowing Maggy's life. It was someone else, someone far more dangerous.

He glanced at his watch in the dim light. 9:15.

No one was coming, he thought again. His disappointment was a bitter taste in his mouth. He wanted nothing more than to confront the bastard that threatened Maggy. He didn't care if his own secret was exposed to the world, or if the Cup was lost forever. All he wanted was to keep her safe.

Maggy!

With a groan he realized his error. How easily he had been lured from the safety of the party. He'd asked Steve to keep an eye on Maggy for a few minutes while he was gone, but he'd thought her perfectly safe in a crowd of several hundred people.

He ran from the chamber and across the lower terraces as though pursued by demons. He prayed to a God he had long since given up, prayed with all his will, that he wasn't too late.

Chapter 24

"What are you talking about?" Maggy choked the question past the knot of dread that swelled in her chest.

"The time for pretense is gone." Arthur Price smiled as he came closer. It was a cold smile that set alarm bells clanging in her mind. Who was this person? "Just tell me where the Cup is, and you won't be harmed."

His words shocked her into action. She whirled around and started to run away from him. But he had been prepared and was too quick for her. He grabbed her arm in a painful grip, his hand icy through the fabric of her sleeve. For such a slight man, he was incredibly strong. She felt he could snap her arm like a twig if he wanted to.

"As I said, I won't hurt you if you give me the Cup," his voice was louder now. "Quickly!"

"Who are you?" Maggy was shaking with fear, adrenaline racing through her. Why did he look so familiar? Where had she seen him before?

"You really don't know do you?" He leaned closer to her, so his face was only inches from her own. "You're just as big a fool as your grandmother was!" His voice took on a sneering, belittling tone. "And just as much trouble!"

Maggy felt her mind beginning to unravel. The voice—it was just as Anna described it! She had seen his face in a photograph, standing next to Logan and Beatrice.

"You're Edward Orcutt!" she cried out, the color draining from her face.

"But, you lived to be an old man and then—" her voice was scarcely above a whisper. "You died."

"Yes, I did," he said. "That's the whole problem, isn't it? I died an old man, withered and decayed. But Logan Winter didn't, did he?"

Finally, something snapped in Maggy as she stared at him, horrified. Without warning, she lashed out at him with all her strength, catching him completely unaware this time. In the moment before he fell, off-balance, Maggy saw his face change before her eyes, and great swathes of gray streak his dark hair.

Her scream split the silence of the room like a knife. She whirled away from him and ran wildly. Anywhere! Just away from the creature behind her. Whatever he was.

Oh God! He was coming after her! To her horror, she realized she had run in the wrong direction. She had no idea where the door was that led to the staircase. She was in a smaller room now, still with curved beams like the study. But which way now?

Maggy whirled around to see him coming in the door behind her. He didn't run, but walked deliberately, as if he had all the time in the world. He must know there was no way out of this room. In a panic she ran to the opposite side away from him.

"It's no use, Maggy. You can't get away from me. You have to tell me."

"You're crazy! I don't have it!" She saw a doorway that opened to the outside, and raced for it. She slipped out onto a small balcony twenty feet above the larger balcony of the library. Sixty feet below that was the main terrace. There was no place else for her to go.

He walked toward her across the balcony. It was Edward Orcutt. She was certain of it, though she didn't know how it could be true. Yet he was still changing as she watched incredulously. His hair was completely gray.

With a choked cry, Maggy made a desperate attempt to run past him. He caught her easily, but his grip was far from gentle. "You're trying my patience, Maggy," he said. His hand was so cold it seemed to burn her skin. He dragged her inexorably toward the edge of the balcony and pressed her against the white painted iron railing. The metal bars dug cruelly into her back.

"Tell me where it is, now! You leave me no choice. I won't be responsible for what happens to you."

Despite her blinding fear, Maggy felt something else happening. A tingling sensation in her body, an electric feeling. A change in pressure. Orcutt's face paled. He must feel it too, she thought.

Beatrice! Maggy could feel her presence.

Yes. There she was on the balcony, as luminous and perfect as she had been before. Maggy looked again at the man who was holding her. He could see Beatrice too. He continued to age before her eyes. His features softened, sagged as his body fleshed out. His hair was now completely white.

"No!" He suddenly screamed as if in pain, and tightened his grip on Maggy. His hands dug into her flesh, numbing her.

"Edward," Beatrice said with infinite sadness, "you could never face the truth about yourself. It's no use. You can't hold your youthful shape in my presence, not while you're taking a physical form. You won't be able to hide your true nature much longer." She drifted closer to them. "Why did you deceive me all this time, disguising yourself as an angel? All the lies about you and Logan. Why make a pretense of friendship?"

"I had no choice, I tell you," he shouted at her. "I had to have to Cup! Now that I've come this close, you won't take it from me!"

"Why must you have the Cup, Ambrose?" Beatrice asked. "What good can it possibly do you?"

Her calm voice seemed to infuriate him.

"You never wanted me, or the Cup. You had both, and you threw them away. Yes! I gave the Cup to you!" He laughed wildly. "This doesn't concern you anymore."

"Maggy!" Harry's shout sounded from the terrace far below. She twisted her head to look down at him. He was so far away. Too far.

"Edward, if you hurt her I'll—"

"What will you do, Logan? Kill me?" Orcutt laughed again and pushed her farther out over the railing. "A little late for that."

Harry disappeared into the castle.

"Why do you think Maggy has the Cup, Edward?" Beatrice asked him, coming closer. Her presence gave Maggy a thread of hope.

"Because I gave you the pearls and the cup, along with a note saying they were from Logan. I stole it out of Logan's room. I thought it belonged to Hearst! The maid would sound the alarm, and the stolen piece would be found in your room, Beatrice. Logan would be accused of stealing from Hearst. You would have left him and Hearst would have been a powerful enemy. But the stupid maid never said a word."

Beatrice gasped, stunned by his revelation. "I gave the pearls to Anna."

"I tried to get the Cup from her," Orcutt's voice was filled with hate. "If she hadn't cheated me by dying, I'd have it now!"

Maggy thought her heart would break at his words. He had been the burglar in Anna's house the day she died. Edward Orcutt had killed Anna! And for nothing. Anna didn't have the Cup.

"Maggy is wearing the pearls now!" Orcutt shook her as he spoke. "What did you do with the Cup?" Maggy thought her back might break as he pushed her out over the railing.

"I don't have it, damn you to Hell! I keep the pearls in a crystal jar than Anna gave me. It isn't a blue cup." Tears of pain and rage ran down Maggy's face. "I don't have it."

"Let her go, Edward." Beatrice said, closer now. "The Cup won't help you."

"It will! Stay away, Beatrice. The Cup will let me live a mortal life again." His voice took on a pleading tone. "You don't know what it's like there. The darkness. No light, no color, no warmth. The people there are vile, all of them! I'll do anything to escape it."

"The Cup won't help you," she said again.

"It will! You don't know anything. You're only an angel, doomed to forget your life, forget everything that's important. You never once remembered me. But I remember everything."

"It's too late, Edward," Beatrice said. "Let Maggy go."

"Not without the Cup," he shouted. He pushed her further out over the railing.

"Release her!" Beatrice commanded, her voice thunderous. Maggy could feel the heat coming from the angel. She closed her eyes at the brilliant light that engulfed them. Edward cringed before it, but didn't loosen his grip on her.

He changed again before Maggy's eyes. His features remained the same, but they were bathed in a horrible darkness. It was a void that drew in all light, with Edward at its center, blacker than night itself.

"Now you see me as I really am!" he shouted. "Do you like what you see?" Maggy was enveloped in a numbing cold that made her skin crawl with revulsion.

The radiance emanating from Beatrice faltered before the shadow that surrounded him. The two forces locked in silent combat.

Maggy felt the air thinning around her. She gasped for breath, but suddenly the air was sucked from her lungs. She was in a vacuum. She felt blackness closing in, a horrible pain in her lungs, then a huge roaring sound blasted her ears. She took a deep, gasping breath of air. At the same time, the hands holding her disappeared, and she was toppling over backwards. Falling helplessly, the air whistling past her.

The last sound she heard was Harry's voice calling her name.

Then, nothing.

* * *

Harry and Beatrice looked at Maggy's body lying on the tiles below, the blue gown fanned out around her.

"I was too weak to stop her fall," Beatrice said.

Harry seemed not to hear her. He climbed over the balcony and slid down the railing until he was stretched out full length, gripping the bottom of the grillwork. Then he let go.

It was a long drop. He landed on his feet and rolled with the fall, then limped to Maggy's side. Beatrice was already there, running her hands lightly over Maggy's body.

"She's alive, barely," Beatrice said. "She has several broken bones and a punctured lung. Her back is broken."

"No! Not again. Not Maggy." He looked at Beatrice like a drowning man, his face white and haggard. He shook his head, tears running down his cheeks. "The Cup could save her," he said and seemed horrified at the words he had spoken.

"The Cup will save her," Beatrice said and disappeared.

* * **

Beatrice reappeared in Maggy's room at the inn. It was in wild disarray, with clothes strewn everywhere. Edward must have been here, looking for the Cup. He didn't find it this time, or the other time he had searched her room. But Beatrice could sense its presence. It was here.

Maggy said it was a crystal jar. There was no time to look for it now. Beatrice closed her eyes and opened her senses to it, this small piece of Heaven that had been chipped off and cast adrift on earth.

She walked unhesitating to the other side of the room. She pushed aside a pile of clothing. There. It was crystalline, almost like glass, with the faintest hint of milky color. She picked it up, felt its warming glow. Then she vanished.

Beatrice appeared for a moment by the Neptune Pool. She dipped the Cup in the water, filled it to overflowing.

Harry was rocking Maggy in his arms when Beatrice returned, the Cup full and heavy in her hands.

"This belongs to you." She handed it to him carefully.

He lifted Maggy's head gently. "My darling, you must drink this." He poured the water into her mouth, but most of it ran down her cheek. Finally, she swallowed convulsively.

* * *

There was pain, terrible pain everywhere. But it was moving away now, receding. Maggy felt a wonderful contentment spreading through her body. She was asleep, but she had never felt so alive.

"Drink more." That voice again. Harry!

She opened her eyes to see his face above her, his blue eyes shadowed with worry.

And Beatrice! She hovered behind him, her light washing over them.

"Drink," he said again. She took great swallows of water until there was no more left. She felt the energy then, rippling through her body, filling her with a strange combination of vitality and peace, so that she felt she could fly to the stars or contemplate the glory of her physical body without moving at all. It was perfection.

"I know what you're feeling," Harry said. "The Cup is healing you. Not just the injuries from your fall. Everything. Your body is being returned to its perfect state."

Maggy sat up slowly and then threw her arms around Harry.

"You saved my life," she said. Then she looked at Beatrice. "You both did."

"The Cup saved you Maggy," Harry said. "Seheiah's Cup."

"But I didn't have it. How did you find it?"

"You did have it," Beatrice said. "The reason we didn't recognize it is simple. Obvious, really. The Cup changes color. More than that, its substance changes, to be in harmony with its owner."

Harry held up the Cup. It's crystalline surface sparkled in the dim light.

"The whole time I had it, it was a deep blue color, almost the color of this dress." Harry let the rich fabric fall through his fingers. "It never occurred to me that it could change."

"I gave the pearls to Anna in a brown Cup, almost like polished marble," Beatrice said. "But Ambrose thought it was green."

"Look!" said Maggy. "Doesn't it seem a little darker to you? More opaque, with blue lights in it?"

"It's Harry's Cup again." Beatrice said, as though that explained it.

"That must be what the inscription meant!" Harry said. "Behold the Color of Life. It wasn't a poetic allusion, but a literal description."

"Was there more?" Beatrice asked.

"I'll never forget it," Harry said. "I recited it every three years for centuries.

Who drinks the Cup of mortal life,
Rests unseen in Heaven's shadow,
Behold the color of life,
Behold the gift of life,
Behold the secret of immortality."

"So the Color of life refers to the color of the Cup," Maggy said. "And the gift of life—"

"That's the bond between us," Beatrice said. "That's why you were able to see me."

"But I never saw you after you died," Harry said.

"It isn't the Cup itself, it's giving the Cup freely to someone else that creates the bond." Beatrice smiled at him and touched his hand. "You didn't give the Cup away. It was stolen from you."

"If that's true, then why didn't you have a bond with Edward? He gave the Cup to you."

"It wasn't a true gift then either, not a gift from the heart." Beatrice said. "Not until I gave it to Anna."

Harry held her hand for a long moment. "I'm sorry. If I had found the Cup before your accident—"

"Don't even think that, darling. Besides, I had already given it to Anna. Neither of us had any idea what it was."

Harry looked from Beatrice to Maggy. "Are you feeling her presence as I am?"

"Yes," Maggy's smile was luminous. "I tried to describe this feeling to you. It's quite overwhelming to be near you, Beatrice."

"They call it ineffable bliss. I shouldn't stay with you long. It's too intense an emotion for mortals to withstand."

"What about Anna?" Maggy said. "I wish I could have seen her again, as I've seen you."

"There are limits to this bond of the Cup," Beatrice said. "It seems to exist between earth and the First Level of Heaven, when the souls are in physical proximity to one another."

"What's the First Level?" Maggy asked.

Beatrice laughed; a rich melodic sound. "It's the beginning of Heaven, just as I'm only a beginning angel. I bet Anna passed right by the First Level."

"What happened to Edward?" Harry asked.

She hesitated. "He's gone. He won't trouble either of you again."

Beatrice took each one of them by the hand. "These questions aren't important anymore. I must go back now. Always remember I love you both."

Before either of them could say good-bye, she disappeared. Maggy was left alone with Harry on the balcony, their hands holding empty air where Beatrice's touch had warmed them.

Their eyes met.

"I thought I'd lost you," Harry whispered. He wrapped his arms around her as though he would never let go.

* * *

They sat in the gothic study on an overstuffed couch facing the terrace. Harry had closed the curtains, giving the room a surprisingly homey feel.

Amazing how charming this room is without a monster chasing you, Maggy thought. She looked down at the Cup in her hands. It had lost its transparency altogether, and was a milky blue color now.

"Even though I'm holding it, it knows that you are the owner," she said. "It's turning back to your color."

Harry took the Cup from her and put it on the low table in front of them.

"We have to decide what to do with the Cup," he said.

"We?"

"Of course. We're in this together, Maggy. One way or another. You know what the Cup is now."

"Is this a proposal or a proposition?"

He turned her so she was facing him squarely. His hands were light on her shoulders. "I love you, Maggy. I'm asking you to marry me. Share the Cup with me."

Her heart leapt at his words, but she felt a terrible sadness as well. She didn't want to share the Cup, but how could she bear to leave him?

"Harry, I love you more than I thought it was possible to love another person. I could die from the way I love you." She looked away from him as she felt tears welling up in her eyes. "But I don't want to live forever. I can't."

"I thought that's what you'd say." He took her chin in his hand, turned her face so she had to look at him. "We're not done yet, Maggy."

"What else is there?"

"It isn't black and white. We have other alternatives."

She felt a glimmer of hope.

"I don't want to live forever without you," he said. "So that rules out living forever. We don't know how long I'm going to live. If I continue to age as I have in the last sixty years, that would give me another two hundred years or so. But we don't know for sure. I could age a lot faster than that."

"If you never drink from the Cup again."

"That's what I'm proposing. I want you to stay with me, but I don't want to watch you grow old and die without me." He pulled her close to him and brushed his lips against hers. Then he kissed her slowly. Her arms wound around his shoulders of their own volition.

"Hey, no fair!" she said finally. She pulled away from him and looked at him accusingly. "This is a rational decision, not just an emotional one. You want me to drink from the Cup every once in awhile, so I age at the same rate that you do?"

"Exactly."

"You'll give up immortality, if I add another hundred and fifty years or so?"

"Immortality is highly overrated. I'd trade it in a minute for you, darling."

Maggy had a sudden image of King Edward VIII trading his kingdom for the woman he loved. Harry was doing much better than that. She hugged that thought to her and let it comfort her. But it wasn't so simple.

"I wouldn't be able to live a normal life." She leaned back into the sofa as she considered the ramifications of living for two hundred years.

"No one knows that better than I, Maggy. I'm asking a lot of you."

"What if we get addicted to life, and can't stop using the Cup?"

"You know that won't happen. Not after what we've seen."

Maggy snapped her fingers. "I've got it! The last part of the inscription. It said Behold the secret of immortality."

"I always thought that referred to the human price that comes along with drinking from the Cup," Harry said.

"No, I don't think that's it. The Cup doesn't offer immortality, don't you see?"

She could see Harry thinking about it, and the moment when it clicked. "You said before that if you lived forever as a mortal, you'd be missing out on what came next."

She settled comfortably into his arms. "And that's the real immortality. As Beatrice said, 'ineffable bliss.' And all that comes afterward."

"But what have you decided, Maggy? Will you stay with me?" Harry's blue eyes were dark with worry.

"Yes, my darling. I think 200 years is a small price to pay, as long as I get to spend them with you."

Chapter 25

*B*eatrice stalked by the Neptune Pool, her crimson skirts whirling around as she turned and paced back the other way. She was alone in her solitary Heaven, except for Roland standing quite still near her, sunlight turning his hair a blinding gold color. His eyes followed her back and forth.

"Why didn't you tell me about Ambrose?" Beatrice could barely look at him she was so angry. "Why didn't you help me? Maggy was almost killed!"

"I've grown leery of interfering with mortals over the centuries." His voice was soothing.

"Have you really? Why?" She wasn't going to be put off by him again.

"Because they almost always surprise you." He sat down in their favorite spot and dipped his feet into the pool. "Please stop pacing, dear, and sit beside me."

She stopped and looked at him, her whole posture rigid, her arms crossed over her chest. He looked so beautiful sitting there, waiting for her. As innocent as a child. But looks could certainly be misleading. Roland had never been innocent.

"You're right about that, Beatrice."

She couldn't stay angry with him. With a defeated sigh, she plopped down next to him and bunched her skirt up around her knees. She kicked the water disconsolately a few times.

"Go ahead," she said.

"Edward was the problem, Beatrice. He had to have his chance at redemption. Jealousy and covetousness had always been his downfall, through countless mortal lifetimes. Toward the end of his life he saw Harry, quite by accident, in San Francisco. He realized that Logan Winter hadn't aged since the last time they had seen each other, over thirty years before. The day you died, my dear. Edward remembered the words Logan spoke that day, about a cup that would save your life. Once he figured out the secret of the Cup, he had a new obsession."

"Did he kill Anna? Is that possible?"

"Not intentionally. When he broke into her house she was able to see him, and the shock triggered a heart attack. He was almost as horrified as he was when you died. He never realized that he hurt himself far more than he hurt Anna. His own actions drove him further into darkness."

"Poor Edward," Beatrice whispered.

"When I learned that he had disguised himself as an angel, as Ambrose, I hoped that proximity to you might heal him."

"Instead, it just reminded him that I rejected him while he lived on earth."

"You didn't even remember what Edward looked like. That was the worst blow he could have sustained."

Beatrice couldn't help the sympathy she felt, in spite of what he had done. "What will happen to him?"

"I can't say. But you know we never give up."

She gave him a sharp look. "You still took a terrible chance. Maggy could have been killed."

"No, darling. Though I didn't know exactly how the drama would play out, I knew it wasn't her time to die. This is her lifetime to meet Harry again."

"Again?"

Roland took her hand. "Harry and Maggy have a long history together. The last time he saw her, she was a young girl named Marie. That was four hundred years ago."

A brilliant smile grew on Beatrice's face. Her dear friends! Joy coursed through her at the thought of their happiness, so long denied.

That still didn't let Roland off the hook. Beatrice glared at him but didn't say anything. A sudden thought occurred to her. "How old are you?"

He raised his eyebrows at her question. "I've never lived as a mortal. I don't have any chronological age."

"I didn't think so," she said and gave him a crafty look. "And you've been watching all this develop, even though every mortal involved was 'unseen in Heaven's shadow.' The only one in Heaven who knew of the Cup was Seheiah himself."

Roland didn't say anything when Beatrice leaned over to pat his hand. "It's all right, dear Roland. I love you madly, as always. You're secret is safe with me."

He looked at her, not really seeing the way the light glanced off her dark hair, the way it seemed to float around her. His look penetrated deeper.

"I'm more concerned with what will happen to you," he said.

"Me? What could happen to me?"

"The First Level is never a permanent destination."

"It isn't? I hadn't thought about it."

"Memories of your life are your most precious possession. Heaven doesn't strip them from you for a frivolous reason."

"I thought they just faded away after that first year of contemplation. I never thought of the reason." She frowned. "It did make me sad though. I felt I was losing myself."

"Let me see if I can explain it to you," he said. "Words are clumsy things. To evolve into the next level of Heaven, you must release all that is physical. Some souls, like Maxwell and Anna, can do that immediately. Others need the First Level, a halfway point that resembles the earth they knew. You see, dear, the rest of Heaven is nothing like the First Level. Don't be afraid that you are losing part of yourself. When you are ready to leave the First Level, you gain all that you once were.

"You experience everything you have ever known, every one of your lifetimes, at the instant that you enter the next Heaven. They will all be given back to you, to make you whole again. Not just Beatrice Page, but many lives you have lived on earth. Strength is needed to withstand the magnitude of that experience. That is why you must not be tied too closely to your most recent life."

"I'm glad. Thank you for telling me, Roland."

He stood up and helped up with a strong hand. "Are you ready?" he asked.

"Now?"

"I think it's time. If I don't bring you back now, Maxwell will drive me crazy. He's nothing if not persistent."

"I don't remember him," Beatrice said softly.

"You will, my dear. You will remember him by each of his many different names, and all of the lifetimes you shared."

The two shimmering figures joined hands and were engulfed in a brilliant light.

Epilogue

❖

One Year Later

*H*arry closed the door amid laughter and tired goodnights. Carol and David had stayed to help them with the dishes after a wonderful meal. Though Maggy's cooking had improved considerably thanks to Nancy's recipes and advice, Harry had been the chef tonight. Maggy leaned her head on his shoulder.

"They're my dearest friends in the whole world, but I'm glad to have you all to myself again," she said and yawned.

"Sleepy?" He brushed the hair back from her forehead, his hand lingering to caress her ear.

"Mmm, a little."

"I'll turn out the lights." He went into the kitchen and Maggy sat on the couch waiting for him, listening to Linda Rondstadt's album Lush Life. There was a voice made for the old torch songs, she thought.

When they were in Portland, they lived in her own modest little house. It was a nice contrast to some of Harry's more substantial homes in various far-flung cities around the world. Maggy hadn't realized she was marrying a man who was not only extremely wealthy, but who didn't seem to care about money at all. That suited her just fine. In fact, after a year of marriage, Harry suited her in every way.

She picked up the last volume of Anna's diary, the one they decided was too personal to donate to the museum.

She leafed through the pages randomly, the rounded handwriting as familiar to her now as her own. Then the last blank pages. They had found the secret of the Cup even without learning it from the diary. She pulled absentmindedly at the last page where it was glued to the back cover of the diary. To her surprise, the page came loose in her hand. She looked more closely. Several pages had been stuck together. On the last two pages, she saw a familiar, neat script.

Anna's handwriting!

With mounting excitement, she began to read. At the end of the short passage, her eyes widened with stunned recognition. She hurried to find Harry.

Anna's Diary—June 1, 1945

The war is really over. Now I can believe it. I celebrated VE day along with everyone else last month, but now I know it's true.

Michael is coming home! At last I will see my husband again, and he will see his son for the first time. I've been telling Johnny all about his father. He's just as exited as I am, though he's very dignified about it. The man of the house, at four years old! Solid, just like his dad.

It's been so long since I've written in this journal. I looked at some of the entries I wrote. It seems like another lifetime. A fairy tale in a magnificent castle, with magic and tragedy. I was the lucky one. I found Michael.

I never saw Logan again after that terrible day when he left. I stayed on at the castle for three more years, but he never returned.

Michael and I were married that June, and I moved back to Cambria with him to my old house, with father living next door. Michael and I kept our jobs at the castle, so we were able to put aside some money for the dark days ahead. We had such fun then, not dreaming that a war would separate us.

I even met the Duke and Duchess of Windsor when they came to visit Mr. Hearst. What a handsome and romantic couple they were. But they couldn't be as happy as Michael and I, despite all their riches.

Then came Pearl Harbor. Michael left within the month to join the fighting.

Soon after that, the castle was closed up for fear of Japanese attack. Mr. Hearst and Miss Davies went to live at Wyntoon, another castle far away in northern California.

I found work easily enough with all the men gone to war. Father and Mrs. Sulley—I mean, Gladys, helped me take care of Johnny. I don't know what I'd have done without them.

There have been rumors that Mr. Hearst will be returning soon, now that the war is over. That will be grand. I still think of the castle often, as you would remember a wonderful dream. I'd be happy to see it come to life again.

But I won't be going back. Michael writes that he has a wonderful opportunity in Portland, Oregon. We can't pass it up, for jobs will be scarce when all the men get back home.

This afternoon I took out the blue gown that Beatrice gave me. I can't help but think of her when I look at it, as she appeared to me in my waking visions. I touched the soft fabric lovingly. Such a lovely gown. I slipped it over my head and looked at myself in the mirror. Then I found the pearls, still in the same pretty jar. I took them out of the milky glass and put them around my neck. Perfect! I will wear it for Michael again, and see the way his eyes light up when he looks at me.

That's odd, though. I thought the jar was a chestnut brown color, like a fine piece of marble. But I must have been mistaken, because it's clearly a pale, opalescent blue. Quite lovely, really. When you look closely, you can see traces of sparkling fire where the light hits it. And a strange design carved around the base, almost like a message in an ancient language.

How fanciful I'm being! Not the practical housewife, but the swooning girl who waits for her lover to return. That's closer to the truth. I live for the day Michael will come to me.

Printed in the United States
22438LVS00003B/128

9 780595 093892